The Guilty

David Baldacci is a worldwide bestselling novelist. His books are published in over forty-five languages and in more than eighty countries, and have been adapted for both feature-film and television. Whilst researching his novels, David Baldacci has been inside the buildings of some of the world's leading intelligence agencies, meeting real-life spies and intelligence leaders. Some of his bestselling novels include *Absolute Power*, *The Camel Club*, *Memory Man* and, also featuring Will Robie, *The Innocent*, *The Hit* and *The Target*. David is also the co-founder, along with his wife, of the Wish You Well Foundation®, a non-profit organization dedicated to supporting literacy efforts across America. Still a resident of his native Virginia, he invites you to visit him at www.DavidBaldacci.com.

Also by David Baldacci

DAVID BALDACCI

The Guilty

PAN BOOKS

First published 2014 by Grand Central Publishing, USA

First published in the UK 2015 by Macmillan

This edition published in the UK in paperback 2016 by Pan Books
an imprint of Pan Macmillan
20 New Wharf Road, London N1 9RR
Associated companies throughout the world
www.panmacmillan.com

ISBN 978-1-4472-7756-9

3 5 7 9 8 6 4 2

A CIP catalogue record for this book is available from the British Library.

Typeset by Ellipsis Digital Limited, Glasgow
Printed and bound by CPI Group (UK) Ltd, Croydon, CR0 4YY

Visit **www.panmacmillan.com** to read more about all our books
and to buy them. You will also find features, author interviews and
news of any author events, and you can sign up for e-newsletters
so that you're always first to hear about our new releases.

To the memory of Donald White,
truly one of a kind.

A LETTER FROM THE AUTHOR

Dear Reader,

Will Robie and Jessica Reel are characters I've grown very close to—I feel I know them like I do good friends, if assassins can be good friends with anyone! Robie's life to date has been full of challenges, and this is why, in *The Guilty*, I wanted to take him home to face the demons he left behind in Mississippi when he was a teenager. He decided to leave not only because of his worsening relationship with his father, Dan, but also because of a broken love affair. So Robie hasn't been back for over twenty years, and now, having earlier convinced Jessica about the importance of family and not leaving issues unresolved, he knows that this is something he must do for himself. His decision to confront his past has been vastly complicated by the fact that his father, a local judge, has been arrested for murder.

Will Robie has proven to be one of my most popular characters, and so I wanted—in this fourth book in the series—to give readers more details about his background and what it is that makes up this unusual man. He may be highly trained and superbly fit and excel at what he does, but Robie is not infallible. And he has emotions just like anyone else. This novel is slightly different from others in this series in that

the bulk of the story is not focused on one of Robie's missions in hotspots around the world. Instead, this story takes Robie back to his place of birth. What confronts him there is not a terrorist or criminal organization, but something far more powerful, and potentially deadly: his own past. Yes, readers, you will finally learn from where Will Robie came. And his trip home is anything but pleasant.

Using Mississippi as a setting for *The Guilty* allowed me to provide Robie with a different backdrop, one that contains many memories—many of which he'd rather forget. It's a place I've enjoyed visiting, and I've loved using the stunning landscape in this intriguing environment as the setting for Robie's latest adventure. As many of us have learned, sometimes it's hard to go home. But for Will Robie, it may be the hardest thing he's ever done.

Thank you for reading. I hope you enjoy the story, and I'd love to know what you think about it.

D. Baldacci

The Guilty

1

Will Robie crouched shadowlike at a window in a deserted building, inside a country that was currently an ally of the United States.

Tomorrow that could change.

Robie had been alone in many vacant buildings in foreign lands over the years, tactically positioned at windows while holding a weapon. One did not normally kill from long distance with a sniper rifle chambered with brain-busting ordnance fired with the aid of world-class optics while people stood around and watched you do it.

Robie was and always would be a tactical weapon. Longer-term strategies were the professional domain of others, mostly political types. These folks made good assassins, too. Only instead of bullets, they were basically bribed to enact laws by other folks with more money than was good for them. And they harmed a lot more people than Robie ever could.

He eyed the street four stories below.

Quiet.

Well, that won't last. Not after I do what I came here to do.

A voice spoke in his ear mic. It was a slew of last-minute intelligence, and a verification of all details of the "execution plan," which was quite aptly named. Robie absorbed all of it, just as he had so many times in the past. He processed the information, asked a few pertinent questions, and received a standby command. It was all part of the professional equation, all *normal*, if such things could be in a situation where the end result was someone's dying violently.

He had not set out to kill others on the command of an elite few. Yet here he was, part of a false-flag unit loosely attached to a clandestine intelligence agency known by its three-letter acronym that people from Bangor to Bangladesh would instantly recognize.

He had come to it by degrees.

Initially came the training where the targets were first paper, then clay, and finally mannequins that bled surprisingly realistic-looking blood housed in hard paks stuffed in torsos and heads. Where precisely plastic flesh and Hollywood blood had turned to real flesh and real corpuscles he couldn't say. It might be that he had subconsciously set aside this most transformative of sequences. It was certainly true that he had never looked back and tried to sort out how he had arrived here.

He had pulled triggers and wielded blades and swung fists and fingers, legs and elbows, and even his

head in precise motions, and ended the lives of many without questioning the basis for these actions.

Official killers who questioned were not popular. In fact, for the most part, they were unemployed. Or more likely dead.

Lately, though, he had started asking questions. Which was why he wasn't as popular as he used to be with the acronym agency whose first letter was *C* and whose last letter was *A*. The letter in between stood for *intelligence*, which Robie sometimes thought was seriously lacking there.

He shook off these thoughts, because tonight he had another trigger to pull.

He gripped a pair of night-vision binoculars and took a visual sweep of the narrow building across from him. Unlike his, it was not vacant. It had lots of people inside it. People with more guns than he had. But he only needed one. There were twenty-four windows facing him, four on each of the six floors. He was concerned only about the second window over from the left on the third floor. In his mind it had a bull's-eye painted right over it.

The curtains were currently drawn over this opening, but that would have to change. As good as he was, Robie couldn't kill what he couldn't see. And right now those millimeter-thick cotton drapes might as well be two-inch-thick polycarbonate sheets with a Kevlar-threaded middle.

He looked at his watch.

Five minutes to go.

Four and a half of those minutes would seem like an eternity. The last thirty seconds would seem like drawing a breath—and a quick one at that. Normal people would experience an accompanying adrenaline rush right about now. Robie was not normal. His heartbeat would actually slow, not rise. And his features would relax, not tighten.

His left hand reached over and touched the already assembled long-range, custom-built rifle lying partially inside his duffel. It was relatively lightweight as such weapons went, and the jacketed subsonic round was already chambered. He would only have one chance to fire one round. He had never needed more than that.

His hand went out and lightly rapped the wooden windowsill.

Even state-sanctioned assassins needed a bit of luck every now and then.

He knew the background of the man he was going to kill tonight. It was like so many of the others whose lives he had terminated. The target's interests and goals were not in alignment with the United States, which had allied itself with competing—if similarly barbaric—factions that were demanding the removal of this person. Why they didn't simply do it themselves was a good question that Robie had never bothered to ask for one simple reason.

He wouldn't have gotten an answer.

Thus, he and his gun had been sent to do the deed, in the interests of national security, which seemed to be a catchall to justify any death, anywhere, any time.

The clipped voice came back in his ear.

"Target alone in the space other than the two bodyguards and the domestic. The curtains will be opened in three minutes."

"Confirmed on all counts?" Robie asked, because he wanted no surprises.

"Confirmed on all counts."

He looked over his shoulder at the window behind him. That was to be his escape route. It didn't look like much of an escape route, and the truth was, it wasn't. But he'd survived worse ones. He was simply a shadow tonight. Shadows were hard to catch. And harder still to kill.

He looked at his watch, synchronizing it in his head with the countdown point he'd just been given. Countdown to calm, he told himself. Countdown to the kill, he added.

The window he was kneeling in front of had already been raised two inches. The windowsill would be his rough fulcrum point. He lifted the rifle out of the duffel and slid the barrel through this opening until the muzzle cleared the glass by three inches and no more. He had drawn a thick bright red line on his barrel that constituted his stop point.

The night was black, and the ambient light meager. The attack was, hopefully, unexpected. Anyone spotting

the dark metal barrel would have to be exceptionally good, and the fact was the other side didn't have anyone of that caliber. That was the reason Robie had been able to gain access to a vacant building with a sight line directly into the target's home. That would never have happened with the Russians. Or the Iranians.

Right on schedule the curtains parted. It was a simple movement replicated millions of times a day all over the world. However, people usually opened the curtains when it was daytime to let in natural light. At night they usually closed them to gain privacy.

That was *always* the hitch in this plan. And Robie would know nearly immediately if that hitch turned into total disaster.

The maid stepped back from the window.

Robie thought the woman's gaze lifted just a bit to the building across the street. And she seemed to linger too long in front of the glass.

Move, Robie thought to himself, trying to will this message across the width of the street and into her head. It had taken considerable effort, money, and skill to place her right where she was, where she *had* to be for all this to work.

But if she froze now, none of that would happen. She would die and the man she worked for would not. Robie being here would all be for naught. He might die, too, since the U.S. would disavow any connection to him whatsoever. That was just how this worked.

A moment later she moved away from the opening, and his sight line once more became unobstructed.

Robie let out a long breath of relief and allowed his muscles to relax.

He rested his right cheek against the rifle stock's carbon fiber left side. The use of this material had dropped his rifle's weight from eight pounds to three. And as with an aircraft, weight was critical for Robie's task, meaning the less the better. He gazed through the optics latched down on his Picatinny rail. The inches-wide crevice in the curtains came into focus. Through his scope it looked a mile across. It would be impossible for him to miss.

There was a table in view. On the table was a phone. Not a mobile phone—an old-fashioned land-line with a spiral cord. The call would be coming through in less than two minutes. The stage was set, everything choreographed down to the last detail.

Part of Robie couldn't believe the man or his bodyguards would not notice just how carefully every-thing *had* been arranged. Through the parted curtains he could see the bodyguards doing what bodyguards did. Moving, taking in details, trying to keep their deep paranoia in check long enough to carry out their job. But never once did they look toward the window. Or, presumably, think about where the phone was positioned in front of that window.

Never once.

Which meant they were idiots. Robie's people had

long since discovered that convenient truth. Because of that they had not even attempted to buy these folks off. They weren't worth the price.

Robie started exhaling longer and longer breaths, getting his physiological markers down to levels acceptable for a shot of this kind: cold zero. In reality the actual shot would not be that difficult. The narrow street including its curbs was barely a hundred feet wide, which was the reason he was using the quieter subsonic round; it was an ordnance perfectly acceptable for a shot over such a short distance. His shot was angled down one story—again, not a problem. It was true he would be firing through glass at the other end, but at this range, glass was not a factor. There was no wind and no ancillary light sources that could possibly blind him.

In short, it should be an easy kill.

But Robie had found that there was really no such thing.

The voice in his ear spoke two words.

"Vee one."

It was the same terminology that pilots in the cockpit used. V-1 meant that the takeoff roll could no longer be safely aborted. Your butt was going up into the sky whether you wanted it to or not.

There was one small difference here, though, and Robie well knew it. So did the person on the other end of his secure line.

I can abort this mission all the way up until my finger pulls the trigger.

"Thirty seconds," said the voice.

Robie gave one more sweeping glance left, then right. Then he looked only through his optics, his gaze and aim dead on the opening between the curtains.

Place empty except for target, two bodyguards, and the maid.

Check, check, and check.

"Ten seconds."

The call on the phone would be the catalyst for all.

"Five seconds."

Robie counted off the remaining moments in his head.

"Call engaged," said the voice.

It was being done via remote computer link. There would be no living person on the other end.

A man moved into view between the curtains.

He was of medium height and build, but that was all that was average about him. Like Hitler before him, he had the extraordinary ability to whip his followers into a frenzy of such devotion that they would commit any atrocity he ordered. That skill had led him to be deemed a Category Alpha enemy of an important if fluid ally of the United States. And that category was reserved only for those who would eventually suffer violent deaths, as the United States

played the role of global wrecking ball for those willing to pony up allegiance to it, however briefly.

Robie's finger slid to the trigger guard and then to the real V-1 point for him—the trigger.

He saw motion to the right of the target but still fired, pulling the trigger with a clean, measured sweep as he had done countless times before.

As was his custom, after the muzzle recoil, he kept his gaze aimed squarely on the target through his optics. He would see this to the end of the bullet's flight path. The only way to confirm a kill was to *see* it. He had been tricked once before. He would never be tricked again.

The glass cracked and the jacketed round slammed into and then through the target. The man fell where he stood, the phone receiver still clutched in his dead hand.

There was no one alive on either end of the call now.

Right as Robie was about to look away, the target disappeared completely from sight. And revealed behind him was the child—obviously the blur of motion Robie had seen right as he fired.

The jacketed round had cleared the target's skull and still had enough velocity to hit and kill the second, far smaller target.

Through his optics Robie saw the girl, the bullet hole dead center of her small chest, crumple to the floor.

The Guilty

One shot, two dead.
One intended.
One never contemplated.
Will Robie grabbed his gear and ran for it.

2

His escape route took Robie out the fourth-floor window opposite where he had fired the shot that had killed one male adult and one female child. With his duffel over his shoulder he jumped and his booted feet landed on the gravel roof of the adjacent three-story building. He heard gunshots and then the breaking of glass.

The bodyguards had just fired their salvos at the building he'd been in.

Then he heard two more rapid-fire shots: *bang-bang*.

The maid had just dispatched the guards, or so Robie hoped.

And then she had better run like hell because Robie could already hear tires squealing on pavement.

His landing had been awkward, and he had felt the scarred skin on his arm from a past injury pull and then partially tear as it took the impact of the landing. He leapt up and ran for the roof doorway that led into the building. He took the stairs down three at a time. He cleared the building and found himself in an

alley. There were two vehicles parked there. Into one he threw his gear and his outer layer of clothes and his boots. Now he had on only skivvies. The driver sped off without even looking at him.

He climbed into the rear of the other vehicle. It was an ambulance. A man dressed in blue scrubs was in the back. Robie climbed up on the gurney, where he was covered with a sheet and a surgical cap was placed on his head. He was hooked up to several drip lines, and an oxygen mask was placed on his face. The man injected a solution into Robie's cheek that swelled his face and a few moments later turned his skin a brick red and would keep it that way for another thirty minutes.

The ambulance drove off, its singsong siren and rack lights going full bore.

They turned onto a road that ran parallel to the street that separated Robie's shooter's nest from the target's building.

Two minutes later the ambulance lurched to a stop and the back doors were thrown open. Robie closed his eyes and let his breathing run shallow.

Men with guns appeared. One climbed in and barked at the man in scrubs. He replied in his native language with just the right amount of professional indignation, and then pointed at Robie. The man with the gun drew very close to Robie's face. Then he examined the IV lines and the oxygen mask and

Robie's swollen and flaming-red face. He asked another question, which the scrubs man answered.

Then the armed man climbed out and the ambulance doors closed. The vehicle started up again.

But Robie kept his eyes shut. He didn't open them until thirty minutes later when the ambulance stopped next to a chain-link fence.

The scrubs man tapped Robie on the shoulder and then pulled the IV lines and took off the mask. Robie climbed out, his bare feet touching cold pavement. A car was waiting next to the ambulance. He climbed inside, was handed clothes and shoes, and quickly dressed.

Thirty minutes later he was wheels up in a jump seat in the back of a UPS Boeing 777 freighter that had counted him as an extra package on board. The jumbo jet banked sharply north and then west, and started its climb out on the long flight back to America.

Robie sat in his jump seat and pulled out the secure phone the scrubs man back in the ambulance had tossed him right before he'd exited the vehicle.

The message was waiting for him in the form of a text.

TARGET DOWN. OP EXIT SUCCESSFUL ON ALL COUNTS.

Well, Robie knew the first part. And now he knew the maid had carried out her role and gotten away, too. And he also knew that the folks on the other end

of this communication were trying to put a positive spin on the whole mess.

He typed in a message on the phone and fired it off.

All he could see in his mind was the face of the little girl with curly dark hair whom he'd killed tonight. Unintentional or not, she was still dead. Nothing on earth could bring her back. And he wanted to know how the hell it had happened.

The ding signaled the answer to his query.

UNCLEAR. HIS DAUGHTER. CLASSIFIED AS COLLATERAL DAMAGE.

Collateral Damage? They were really going to try to spin that one? On me?

His finger poised over the phone's keypad, Robie was set to fire back a response that matched the fury he was feeling. Then he slipped the phone into his pocket and slumped back against the plane's inner wall.

He rubbed his face and closed his eyes. Burned seemingly on the insides of his eyeballs was the little face. She had looked surprised at being dead. And who could blame her? Running to her daddy, seeing him die at the same moment she too perished?

He had come close to killing a child once, but he hadn't pulled the trigger. That had nearly cost him his career and with it his life. But this time, this time, he had done it.

He opened his eyes and bent over as the jet hit a

rough patch of air and he was jostled roughly around. He turned to the side and threw up. It had nothing to do with unsettled air, and everything to do with the small face burning a hole in his brain and his belly.

He hung his head between his knees. The unflappable man he always was, always had to be, was coming apart at important seams, like the torn scar tissue on his arm.

I just killed a little girl. I murdered a little girl. She's dead because of me.

He looked down at his trigger finger, heavily callused from all the practice rounds fired over the years. He had wondered when and if he would know it was time to walk away from all this.

He might just have found his answer.

His phone dinged again. He picked it up and looked at the screen.

BLUE MAN.

The one person other than his sometime partner Jessica Reel whom Robie could count on at an agency that would never officially recognize he even existed. Blue Man always told it to him straight, whether Robie wanted to hear it or not.

WILL BE STANDING BY WHEN YOU LAND. WE'LL TALK.

He tried to interpret the meaning behind those few words.

What was there to talk about? His trigger pull was done. The op was completed. The official response at

the senseless death of a child was "collateral damage."
Robie could imagine that explanation being input on
a form and that form being filed away wherever they
kept such records.

*On this day in a foreign land shot dead by Will Robie,
one megalomaniac and one daughter of said megalomaniac.*

He would be on to his next assignment, expected
to forget what he had just done. Like a cornerback
giving up a long touchdown pass. You shook it off,
picked yourself back up, and moved on to the next
play.

Only there, nobody died.

In Will Robie's world, somebody *always* died.

Always.

3

Robie walked down the metal steps, and his feet hit American soil for the first time in a month. He looked straight ahead and saw the man in a rumpled trench coat standing next to the rear door of the black Suburban. It was as though a Cold War-era movie was unspooling in front of him in clickety-clack black-and-white film.

The vehicles were always black, and they always seemed to be Suburbans. And the people were always wearing rumpled trench coats, as though they felt inclined to confirm the stereotype.

He walked over to the SUV and climbed inside. The door closed, the trench coat got in the driver's seat, and the Suburban pulled off.

Only then did Robie look to his right.

Blue Man gazed back at him.

His real name was Roger Walton.

But to Robie he would always be Blue Man, which had to do with his color level of leadership at the Agency. Not the highest there was, but plenty high

enough for Blue Man to know all, or at least nearly all, that was going on.

As usual he wore an off-the-rack blue suit with a red tie and a collar tab. His silver hair was neatly combed, his face freshly shaved. Blue Man was old school, professional every second of his life. Nothing rattled him. Nothing altered the ingrained habits of a long career that frequently involved killing the few to keep safe the many.

By comparison, after an eleven-hour flight in the back of an air freighter piled high with cardboard boxes filled with products made by penny labor in faraway lands, Robie looked like a corpse. He didn't feel professional. He really didn't feel anything.

Robie didn't break the silence. He had nothing to say. Yet. He wanted to hear it from Blue Man first.

The other man cleared his throat and said, "Obviously, it did not all go according to plan."

Robie still didn't speak.

Blue Man continued, "The intelligence was flawed. It often is over there, as you well know. But we have to work with what we have. The child was supposed to be with her mother. There was apparently a last-minute snafu. The mother abruptly changed her plans. The daughter was left at home. There was no time to abort without suspicion falling on our inside operative."

Everything that Blue Man had just uttered was

perfectly reasonable and, Robie knew, perfectly true. And it didn't make him feel better in the least.

They drove for a while longer in silence.

Finally, Robie said, "How old was she?"

"Robie, you had no way of—"

"How old!"

Robie had kept his gaze on the back of the driver's head and he saw the man's neck muscles tighten.

"Four," replied Blue Man. "And her name was Sasha."

Robie knew she was young. So this should have come as no surprise. But the waves of nausea, of an overwhelming sense of claustrophobia, hit him like the round he'd fired around twelve hours ago. The round that had killed four-year-old Sasha.

"Stop the car."

"What?" This came from the driver.

"Stop the car." Robie didn't say this in a raised voice. His tone was level and calm yet managed to sound more deadly than if he had screamed his guts out and pulled an MP5.

The driver's gaze hit the rearview mirror and he saw Blue Man nod.

The driver eased off the road and put the SUV in park.

Robie had opened the door before the truck had even stopped rolling. He got out on the side of the highway and started walking along the shoulder.

Blue Man reached over and closed the door. He

eyed the driver, who was still watching him in the rearview obviously waiting for an order, perhaps to speed up and run over Robie.

"Just follow on the shoulder, Bennett. Put your flashers on. We don't want any accidents."

Bennett did so and the vehicle slowly followed Robie down the shoulder as cars and trucks whizzed by.

"Let's hope a cop doesn't stop us," muttered Bennett.

"If one does I will handle it," said Blue Man impassively.

Robie walked slowly, his muscles tight, the torn skin on his arm aching like he'd been slashed with a Ka-Bar knife. He had been told sometime ago that he would need a skin graft. It looked as if that prediction had been right.

A stiff wind pummeled him as he lumbered on; his feet felt clumsy, his senses slow. But then he hadn't slept in nearly twenty-six hours. He had just crossed quite a few time zones and was also jet-lagged.

And he'd killed a kid.

He looked neither right nor left. He didn't react when eighty-thousand-pound semis blew past him at seventy miles an hour, whipping his coat around him.

The SUV followed Robie for a quarter of a mile before he walked back to it and climbed into the truck, and Bennett pulled onto the highway.

"Where's Jessica?" Robie asked.

"She's on assignment out of the country," said Blue Man.

"When will she be back?"

"Not for a while."

Robie looked out the window. He needed to talk this out with Jessica Reel. She alone would be able to understand what was going on inside his head. Not even Blue Man could get all the way there.

But there was something else. Something that needed doing as soon as possible. He could feel it in every pore of his skin, in every fired synapse of his brain.

He blurted, "I need to get out in the field again. Fast. Whatever you have, let me do it."

"I'm not sure that is advisable."

"I need to pull the trigger again," said Robie, his gaze now dead on Blue Man. "I need to. You must have something ready to go."

Blue Man cleared his throat again. "We actually have a mission that we thought would be scrubbed, but is now back on."

"I'll take it."

"You don't know what it is yet."

"It doesn't matter. I'll take it."

Blue Man let out a shallow breath and straightened his tie. "Are you sure it wouldn't be better to—"

Robie held up his hand and his trigger finger made

the pull. "This is what I do, sir. If I can't do this, then I am nothing. I need to know that I still can."

"Then you'll get the briefing papers tomorrow." Blue Man paused. "While what happened was terribly tragic, that was not the only reason I wanted to meet with you."

Robie turned to look at him. "What was the other reason?"

"It's personal." He glanced at the driver. "Bennett? The glass, please."

Bennett hit a button on the console and an inch-thick sheet of glass slid into place, sealing off the front compartment from the back.

"Personal?" said Robie. He had nothing personal if Jessica Reel was okay.

But no, that was wrong.

He stiffened. "Julie? Is it Julie?"

Julie Getty was a fifteen-year-old girl who had been catapulted into Robie's life sometime ago in the most violent way possible. They had both nearly died in a bus explosion. Julie's life had been put in danger more than once because of her connection to Robie. And also to Jessica Reel.

If anything had happened to her . . .

But Blue Man was already holding up his hand.

"Ms. Getty is perfectly fine. It has nothing to do with her."

"Then I don't understand what you mean by *personal*. Beyond them I—"

"It's your father," interjected Blue Man.

Robie tried to focus on these three words. It wasn't working. All he saw was a face transposed over Blue Man's.

His father's.

A hard, unrelenting countenance that Robie thought he would never, ever see again. In fact, Robie had not seen his father in over twenty years. He shook his head, trying to rid himself of memories he had not thought about for a long time. Yet now, with Blue Man's words, they were charging at him from all corners.

"Is he dead?"

Robie's father was at an age now where a heart attack or stroke could have claimed him.

"No."

"What then?" said Robie sharply, tired of how Blue Man was drawing this out. It was not like the man. He was normally terse and precisely to the point. And that's what Robie needed now.

"He's been arrested."

"Arrested? For what?"

"For murder." Blue Man paused, but when Robie said nothing he added, "I thought you'd like to know."

Robie looked away and replied, "Well, you thought wrong."

4

Robie swayed with the motion of the truck in which he was riding. Dust caught at his throat. The heat of the day seared through the canvas top. He felt like an egg about to be overcooked in a skillet.

He rode with one other man. His spotter. Robie didn't usually use a spotter, but Blue Man had insisted on one for this mission. And Robie had not felt up to challenging him.

In the military, snipers were almost always deployed in two-person teams. A spotter added security and firepower, set up and calculated shots, kept on top of elements like wind that could vary shots. When the shooter got tired, which often happened because waiting to kill was an exhausting exercise, the team would switch roles and spotter would become sniper.

But in Robie's line of work, spotters were rarely used. The reasons were many, but mainly it was because he was not being sent into combat zones with other soldiers, where the two-person team made tactical sense. Rather, he was acting in a clandestine manner, dropped behind enemy lines with a cover

story and localized assets. It was hard enough to do that with one person, much less two, particularly when you were going to parts of the world where no one else looked like you.

Robie looked over at his spotter. Randy Gathers was in his early thirties with sandy hair and a freckled complexion. He was lean and compact, with a wiry build. He was also former military, as almost all of them were. He had met Robie and gone over the assignment in excruciating detail beforehand. It was in some ways like a golfer and his caddy, except the hole-in-one had a vastly different meaning in Robie's world than it did on the PGA tour.

Their plan was set, their cover story intact. They had arrived here on a freighter with a Turkish provenance, had left the harbor on a rickety bus and then switched to this truck while it was still dark.

Now it was light and they would be at their next location in twenty minutes.

Robie inched up the tent flap and peered out. His gaze went to the sky where it was partially clear, but a troublesome storm front was approaching.

He looked at Gathers, who had his iPad out.

"Supposed to hit tonight," Gathers said. "Wind, rain, thunder."

"How much wind?" asked Robie.

"Enough. Do we scrap it?"

Robie shook his head. "Not our call. At least not yet."

The truck rumbled along and then deposited them at their next stop. They climbed into a car that was waiting for them. The trunk held the items they would need to perform the mission.

Robie took the wheel and drove along routes he'd memorized as part of the mission brief. If they were stopped, which was a possibility, they had the necessary papers to get them through most road-blocks, without the trunk's being searched. If that didn't work, they had one option. To kill the people who had stopped them.

Two roadblocks and no trunk searches later, they arrived at their destination.

It was now growing dark, and the wind was picking up even more.

Robie drove up to the overhead door of a large warehouse situated next to a river. Gathers jumped out, keyed in a code on a panel next to the door, and the overhead lumbered up. Robie pulled the car inside while Gathers closed the overhead door and secured it by sliding a locking arm through the roller track. They pulled out their equipment from the car's trunk, and then Robie and Gathers scrubbed the vehicle down, removing all traces of their presence.

After that Robie looked around the two-story warehouse. The place was cavernous and, except for them, empty. And most important, they were completely hidden from view.

Rain started to ping off the warehouse's metal roof.

Robie looked up and his gaze seemed to pierce the roof and venture to the outside. He glanced over at Gathers, who was checking their equipment, his manner subdued probably by the prospect of having to perform in such adverse conditions.

Robie glanced at his watch and then sent off a secure communication from his phone. The answer came back as he was halfway up a ladder that led to a catwalk on the warehouse's second story.

IT'S A GO.

He put his phone away and continued his climb, reaching the catwalk and skirting down the narrow metal path until he reached the front side of the facility.

Gathers followed him up with the gear, two duffel bags' worth. They both sat down and started to assemble the tools they would need tonight to accomplish the mission.

Spotting scope, weather and wind analyzers, and, of course, the sniper rifle.

There was one other tool required. There were no windows up here, so Robie had to make one.

He used the battery-powered saw to cut two holes of different sizes in the side of the metal. He used a suction cup to grip the metal, and when the cut was complete, he pulled the metal toward him and deposited it in his duffel.

One hole was large enough for his muzzle and his scope to fit through simultaneously. The other hole was for the spotting scope to be used by Gathers.

Each picked up their respective "weapons" and inserted them through the holes. Robie did a sweep of the street while Gathers did the same with his spotting scope. This was going to be a far longer shot than Robie's last mission, nearly twenty-two hundred meters.

A British soldier currently held the world record for the longest sniper shot. In 2009, he had killed two Afghan insurgents at a distance of nearly 2,500 meters. The shots were so far away that it had taken the .338 Lapua Magnum rounds nearly five seconds to reach and kill their targets.

Robie's shot would be almost three hundred meters less in distance. But the conditions were far from ideal, and he would be shooting in between a pair of buildings that could create a wind tunnel that might foul the shot. That was another reason that Gathers was here as the spotter. He would feed Robie all the information that he needed. All Robie had to focus on was making the kill when he pulled the trigger.

The good thing about this shot was that the target's security forces had never even considered the abandoned warehouse a potential threat. It was simply too far away from the event that would be taking place over a mile from here.

Well, Robie hoped to prove them wrong about that tonight.

Robie checked and rechecked his ammo, and then made sure his weapon was pristine and in perfect

working order. While he did that, Gathers was soaking up every bit of data that would have an impact on the shot Robie had to make.

When that was done both men sat back. They each ate a power bar, downing it with some G2.

Gathers said, "Heard about your last mission."

Robie folded up the plastic wrapper from the power bar and stuck it in his duffel along with the empty plastic bottle. Plastic wrappers held fingerprints and used beverage bottles contained DNA. Though his were on no database anywhere, the key principle was that no detail was too small to be overlooked.

"After the shot we have thirty seconds to get out of here," Robie said. "They'll be waiting for us with the RIB," he added, referring to a rigid inflatable boat. "Ten-minute ride on the water, then we load onto a chopper. That'll carry us to the harbor. We board the freighter, which leaves three minutes after we get there."

Gathers nodded. He knew all this, but it never hurt to run through it multiple times.

Over the next few minutes Robie caught Gathers glancing at him and decided to just get it over with.

"You have an issue?" he asked, staring across at the other man.

Gathers shrugged. "You know why I'm here."

"To be my spotter."

"You work alone, Robie, everybody knows that."

"Not always."

"Almost always. You accidentally killed a kid. Could have happened to any of us."

"But it didn't happen to you."

"I'm here because they have—"

"Doubts? Do you have doubts that I can make this shot?"

"Not if you're the same Will Robie, no."

"But if I'm not the same Will Robie?"

"Then I've been instructed to make the shot."

Robie sat back on his haunches. This he had not been told.

Gathers obviously read this on his face and said, "I thought you should know. In fact, we can reverse roles now, if you want. No one will know the difference."

"Have you even made a shot from over two thousand meters, Gathers?"

"Nearly so. On the practice range."

"Nearly so. On the practice range, where conditions are ideal." Robie pointed upward where rain was still pinging off the roof. "These conditions are not ideal. In fact, they're horrendous for a long-range shot. Do you still think you can make the kill here and now?"

Gathers drew a long breath. "Yes, I think I can."

"Well, let's hope we don't have to find out because 'I think I can' doesn't cut it."

5

Two hours later Robie got another communication.

"It's a *final* go," he said to Gathers.

Gathers nodded and started reading his weather instruments again and taking looks through his scope.

Robie picked up his rifle and edged the muzzle out through the hole he'd cut. The barrel was hit by rain, but his scope was still under the roof and dry. He placed his cheek against the synthetic stock and took a look through his scope. This piece of optics was the best in the world, an engineering marvel that allowed one to see great distances with superhuman accuracy.

"Feed me," said Robie.

Gathers started giving him the weather and distance information. Robie took all of this in and made corresponding and necessary adjustments to his optics. Calibrating against the weather was critical here. With the long distance that the ordnance needed to travel, the elements would have a terrific opportunity to screw the shot. And then there was gravity, which while undeniably present at every spot on earth, was

also, unlike the weather, highly predictable. He sighted through it again and the glass atrium came into view.

"It's helpful they have a flag on top of the building," said Gathers. "Makes the wind call easier, like a wind sock at an airport."

"That was why our people had it put there," replied Robie curtly.

He looked at his watch and adjusted his ear mic. The voice came on and updated Robie. He gazed through his scope again and people came into view.

The party was just getting started. The man of honor would arrive in about twenty minutes. He was incredibly wealthy in the way only a man who had plundered an entire country could become. Had he remained content with that, he would not have been targeted. But he had committed the cardinal sin of deciding to fund terrorist activities that had struck directly at America and her allies. For this, Robie had been dialed up to put a stop to his heartbeat and along with it his ambitions.

The event tonight was the man's fifty-eighth birthday. He would not celebrate another.

In an impoverished nation the limos gliding down the street might as well have been figments of a country's collective imagination—or nightmare, rather. But the country had a wealthy few and they were all coming out tonight because not to do so would probably ensure their deaths.

Since these folks had a lot more to lose than their

bedraggled fellow citizens, they came, like the obedient pets they were. What good was it to be rich, if you were dead?

"Wind call," said Robie.

Gathers checked his instruments and gave him the required data. Robie made the necessary adjustment on his optics. The biggest problem, he felt, was the gap between the buildings. The funneled wind there could do things that it wasn't doing here or at the other end where the bullet would strike. He would have to penetrate glass, and unlike his last mission, at this far greater distance, the glass would have a profound impact on a bullet that had already traveled nearly a mile and a third.

And the drop of the ordnance had to be carefully calculated. That was what the spotter, range finder, and weather conditions would determine.

If Robie had placed his crosshairs on the target's chest and fired, by the time the bullet had arrived nearly five seconds later, it would have struck the floor. The calculations involved were complex and there was no margin of error. It involved Newtonian dynamics, gravitational pull, and mathematical formulas that might well have confounded Einstein.

As the time drew closer for the shot, Gathers slid over to squat to the right and slightly behind Robie. That way, using the same opening Robie was firing through, he could follow the trace of the bullet through his scope. This was necessary if the first shot

did not accomplish the kill. In a combat zone there were usually opportunities for follow-up shots. In this scenario there probably wouldn't be. If the first shot missed, people would scatter, and the target would be surrounded and pulled to safety.

But since the bullet would take nearly five seconds to get to its target, Gathers might have the opportunity to call out adjustments to a second shot, if needed, before the first shot had even struck. If they were lucky the second shot would find its target. If they were *really* lucky they wouldn't need the second shot.

The target arrived and swept into the room. He was a big man whose appetite for food and drink neatly matched that of his desire for wealth and power. He sat down in his chair at the head of the table.

"Vee one," came over Robie's ear mic.

"Last call," said Robie immediately.

Gathers made his final calculations, focusing on the wind tunnel and the flag between the two buildings. He fed this information to Robie, who made the slight, nearly imperceptible changes to his optics.

"Dialed in and locked," said Robie. He would make no more changes. With his naked eye he looked once more at the flag. Then he settled down with his scope. From this point until the shot fired, his optics *were* his only eyes. He had to trust in them, like a pilot

did his navigation instruments while flying through fog.

His finger slid to the trigger guard.

In his mind he mouthed the term, *True Vee One*.

The target had picked up a glass of red wine. He was raising it up, as though to toast himself. He wore a tuxedo. The white shirt with the silver studs represented a huge bull's-eye for Robie, but he would not be aiming there. Because ordnance dropped over distance, he was actually aiming at a spot above the target's head. Everything was dialed in. Everything was ready to go. Gathers would tell him if the man moved from this spot.

Everything about Robie began to relax: his blood pressure dropped, his heartbeat slowed, his respiration grew even and deep as he reached cold zero.

Or rather all of those things *should* have happened.

But they didn't. Not a single one.

His blood pressure was amped, his heart raced, and his breaths were more like gasps. He was stunned when, despite the coolness of the air, a drop of sweat slid down his forehead and leached into his left eye.

He could not rub it away. Not now. He refocused. His finger moved to the trigger. Right before he touched the thinnest and most important piece of metal on his weapon—

He saw the child.

The little boy ran across the room and held his

arms up to the man. He wanted to be picked up. The man did so, cradling the little boy against his chest.

"Fire, Robie. Fire."

He thought the voice was coming from his head. But it wasn't. It was coming from his ear mic.

"Fire, now!"

This order was not coming from his head or his ear mic.

It was coming from Gathers, who squatted next to him.

But the little boy was in his daddy's arms. To kill him, Robie would have to kill the child.

"Fire, Robie, fire!"

Robie's finger was frozen, a millimeter from the trigger.

The shot rang out.

Seconds later the glass tinkled and the man fell out of his chair, mortally wounded.

Robie took his eye away from the optics and looked down at his finger. It had never touched the trigger.

"Egress, egress!" the voice in his ear mic called out.

Gathers was already pulling Robie to his feet.

"Move, Robie, move."

In a daze Robie still managed to follow Gathers down the metal steps, their duffels over their shoulders. The next moment they were running pell-mell down narrow, dark streets toward the water.

Robie remembered getting in the RIB.

It took off fast and shot through the darkened water at a furious clip.

Then came the ride in the chopper. It was brief and turbulent as hell as the storm kicked it up a notch higher.

Ten minutes later they were hustling up the gangplank of the freighter.

Three minutes after that the huge ship moved away from the pier and gathered speed as it headed across the bay and into vast and open ocean waters.

Robie looked over at Gathers, who sat opposite him on the bunk in their cramped quarters.

"The shot?"

Gathers said, "They had a backup team in place. Just in case."

"You told me you would take the shot if I didn't."

Gathers looked nervous. "I was under strict orders, Robie. I'm sorry."

Robie looked away.

"But why didn't you take the shot?" asked Gathers. "It was all lined up."

Robie looked at him incredulously. "Why didn't I take the shot? The little boy, that's why. He jumped right into the target's arms an instant before I was going to fire. If I had, he'd be dead."

Gathers stared across at him, his features full of concern. "There was no little boy there, Robie."

On hearing this Robie simply stared at Gathers. But he wasn't actually seeing the other man. He was

seeing a little boy. A little boy who looked familiar, but he just couldn't place him.

Robie lay back on his bunk and didn't move the rest of the trip.

One question kept beating into his brain.

Am I losing my mind?

6

Late at night.

Washington, DC.

A place filled with more acronym agencies than any other city on earth.

When ordinary folks were asleep, others from these acronym platforms stayed awake keeping them safe.

Or else spying on their fellow citizens.

Robie walked the familiar path to the Arlington Memorial Bridge, which took him past the Lincoln Memorial. He didn't look at the seated sixteenth president as he walked by. He had a lot to think about. And the darkness, with a bit of rain thrown in, had always been a good place for him to think.

He reached the bridge, walked halfway across it, and then stopped and gazed down at the white-capped Potomac. No jets flew overhead following the river to their final destination, because Reagan National was closed due to nighttime sound ordinances.

The wind-swept swirling waters far below neatly

matched what he was thinking. It was all a mess inside his head.

He had royally screwed up a mission. He had seen a child where there was no child. He had apparently hallucinated in the middle of a mission—a first for him. Hell, probably a first in Agency history.

And, inexplicably, cold zero had never materialized for him. He stared down at his hands. They were trembling. He touched his forehead where the sweat bead had meandered before hitting him in the eye. Unless he figured this out, he was done. He couldn't do his job. Which meant he was nothing.

Officially, he had been placed on leave. Until he got things straightened out in his head, if he ever did, Robie would not be going back into the field.

He stared down at the waters, and in their murky depths he once more saw the face. Only now he realized he had taken Sasha and, in his mind, changed her gender, moved her a thousand miles away, and given her another father, and along with it a reason for him not to take the shot.

He should have known something was wrong. How could he have seen a little boy in his father's arms if his scope was aimed at a spot above the man's head?

His mouth dried up and his hands shook with the thought of it. He couldn't imagine his mind playing a trick like that on him. Never. But now that it had, Robie could never be sure that it wouldn't do so

again. And because of that, he could never again completely rely on the one person he always thought he could:

Me.

"Have you reached any conclusions?"

Robie turned to see Blue Man standing on the other side of the bridge.

He had stepped out from the shadow of the pedestal upon which sat a large sculpture of a horse and rider. There were actually two of these *Arts of War* sculptures, one on each side of the bridge entrance on the DC side, called *Valor* and *Sacrifice*. These were fitting subjects for a bridge that led directly to the nation's most hallowed military burial grounds at Arlington National Cemetery. There was a lot of valor and ultimate sacrifice in that place.

"I didn't hear you walk up," said a clearly annoyed Robie.

"I didn't. I was here waiting for you."

"How did you know I'd come here?"

"You've come here before, after particularly difficult assignments."

"Which means you had me followed."

"Which means I like to keep on top of my charges at all times." Blue Man crossed the street and stood next to him.

Robie said, "So are you here to tell me I'm officially finished?"

"No. I'm here to see how you're doing."

"You read the briefing. I froze. I put a kid in the picture who wasn't actually there."

"I know that."

"And you must have realized that was a possibility, which is why you had a backup team in place."

"Yes."

"I can't get that little girl out of my head."

Blue Man looked at him appraisingly. "But it wasn't a little *girl*."

"What do you mean?"

"You told Gathers it was a little *boy* reaching for his father. Not a little girl."

Blue Man drew closer and looked over the side of the bridge and down at the water.

"The mind can play awful tricks on you. Particularly when you have unresolved business."

"What unresolved business?" said Robie sharply.

Blue Man turned to him. "I don't think you need me to answer that. What I would say is that you have time off. And you should use that time off to best advantage. If you can resolve your issues, Robie, you will be welcomed back. If you can't, you won't. The choice is simple and the decision is largely up to you."

"Look, this has nothing to do with my father, if that's what you're implying."

"It may not. But if it does, it needs to be addressed." He handed Robie a file. "Here are the particulars."

With that Blue Man walked away. A few minutes

later Robie heard a door open and close, an engine start up, and then a vehicle drive off.

He looked back down at the water. Then he opened the file, and by the light of his smartphone he started to read.

His father arrested for murder.

The facts of the case were sketchy.

A man named Sherman Clancy was dead. He knew Robie's father. There was evidence that pointed to his father killing the man. Because of that the elder Robie had been arrested.

Cantrell, Mississippi, was an undistinguished dot on the map on the southern border with Louisiana barely five miles from the Gulf Coast.

His father, Daniel Robie, a former jarhead disguised as a rabid pit bull from the Vietnam era, was sitting in a jail cell for murder. Part of Robie could believe it; another, perhaps deeper component, could not. There was no doubt that his father was tough and could be violent. He could kill. He *had* killed in that war. But "to kill" was different than "to murder." Then again, every mission Robie had ever successfully completed had technically been a murder, yet he did not consider himself a murderer. And why was that?

Because I was ordered by others to do it? Well, so were Mafia hit men.

Cantrell, Mississippi. It was a world and a place that Robie once knew well. For eighteen years of his life it was *all* that he knew. And then there came a time

when he had wanted no more of it. It was certainly never a place he had wanted to return to.

He had neither kith nor kin left there, except for his father. He had no brothers and no sisters. And his mother? No, no mother either.

He had known the Clancy family when he had lived there. They were farmers, well known, if not overly liked, in the small town. They mostly kept to themselves. They had their land and they worked it. They sold what they grew and they got by. They had neither money nor grand ambitions. At least back then. But it had been over twenty years now. Things might've changed.

He knew of no bad blood between his father and the Clancys. But that might no longer be the case, since his father had been arrested for murdering the man.

Dan Robie was someone who could change his opinion of you. Robie well knew that. And when the opinion was altered, the man was unlikely ever to revisit it.

His thoughts still rambling and confused, he returned to his apartment, a sparsely decorated place that contained not one personal photograph or other memento. Robie had none of those to put out. He sat in a chair and stared out the window.

He had killed a father and his daughter. Technically, the killing of the little girl wasn't his fault. In every

other respect it was his sole responsibility. He could do nothing to alter that. The dead were dead.

And then he had seen a little boy raising his arms up to his father. Not a little girl, a little boy.

He rubbed his thighs with palms that had turned sweaty. He had killed so many times with hands as dry as hands could be. And now his palms were moist. He could smell his own stink. He could smell fear in every pore. For a man who made his living by being, in many ways, fearless, it was a rude comeuppance.

Family. Everyone had one. The difference was in degrees. But those degrees could be as vast as the size of the universe. And even more complicated.

Robie had never envisioned himself making the decision he just had. It seemed that the only way he could move forward was to at least make a modest dent in cleaning up the decades-long mess that was his past. He had never had the desire to do this before. Now, it seemed like the only thing he could possibly do.

It was not easy traveling to Cantrell, Mississippi. But he would get there nonetheless.

He certainly knew the way.

And God help me when I get there.

7

Robie ended up taking a flight to Atlanta and then made a connection to Jackson, Mississippi.

From there Robie could have taken a puddle jumper to Biloxi, but decided to rent a car at the Jackson airport and drive the nearly three hours due south to Cantrell. It was a journey that would stop only a few miles before he would plunge into the Gulf of Mexico. He figured he could use the drive to get acclimated to where he was now. And it wasn't like his father was going anywhere.

He drove along State Route 49, which cut a diagonal path toward Gulfport.

The state was comprised mostly of lowlands, its highest point under a thousand feet, and nearly 70 percent of it still covered in forested lands. He passed by farmland filled not with cotton or soybeans but rather with sweet potatoes, the state's most valuable crop by acre. And then there were the chickens. There were nearly forty times more chickens in Mississippi than people. And Robie saw a few thousand of them on his drive down.

And Lord knows he smelled them, too!

Mississippi was a strange amalgam of vital statistics ranking near the bottom of all fifty states in many important categories. Yet while it was the poorest of the states, its citizens gave more per capita to charities than their wealthier sister states. And they also were the most religious of all Americans. Indeed, Mississippi's constitution prohibited anyone who denied the existence of a supreme being from holding public office. Although this article was technically rendered unenforceable by federal law, the good folks of the Magnolia State apparently did not believe in the separation of church and state, and they most assuredly did not want to be led by a nonbeliever.

But not long before Robie had left home, this same overtly God-fearing state had authorized offshore casino gambling, and the gaming industry was flourishing. Apparently, one could believe in a supreme being and yet not feel too badly about relieving folks of their hard-earned money at the craps table.

Blacks had constituted the majority of the population until the commencement of two mass migrations, first north and then west over the course of sixty years starting in 1910. This exodus was largely to get away from the oppressive effects of the Jim Crow laws passed after the Civil War. These laws effectively kept freed blacks as downtrodden as when they were slaves. Jim Crow laws went on for over a century, and

the pernicious repercussions were still clearly felt today.

Robie kept driving and looking around at a place that in many ways seemed exactly the same as when he had left. More than half the residents here still lived in rural areas. He passed many a small town that was gone before you could blink five times. His trip for the most part paralleled the course of the Pearl River, one of the major waterways in the state. The last section of the Pearl River split Mississippi from Louisiana.

As a boy Robie had become very familiar with the Pearl: swimming in it despite its sometimes dangerous and unpredictable currents, pulling fish from its depths, and gliding in an old wooden skiff over its mossy-green backwater surface.

Nice memories.

Nice but faded.

At least they used to be.

He turned off Route 49 and headed southwest. He saw a "Dummy Line" road sign. Dummy Lines were abandoned railroad tracks, not for passenger trains, but to carry lumber when the boom was going on. The boom was long gone, but the signs remained because no one had bothered to take them down. It was just how it was here.

A half hour later he hit the town limits of Cantrell at exactly one in the afternoon. Interstate 10 was to the north of him and Highway 59 to the west. He was

49

closer to the Louisiana border than he was to Gulf-port. The weather was warm and the air full of moisture as befitting a state with a subtropical climate, which accommodated short, mild winters and long, humid summers. Growing up here Robie had seen snow fall twice. The first time, not knowing what it was, four-year-old Robie had run screaming into the house to escape its effects. He had survived hurricanes, F5 tornados, and intense flooding, as had all southern Mississippians.

He had survived all sorts of things that had arisen in the small town, the population of which had been 2,367 when he had left. The population now stood at three short of 2,000, or so the town's welcome sign had proclaimed.

To Robie, it was a wonder the place was even still here. Perhaps those remaining had no way to get out.

Or lacked the will even to try.

His shiny rental stood out in a sea of dusty pickup trucks as well as old Lincolns, Furys, and wide-trunked Impalas, although there was a cherry-red late-model Beemer parked at the curb in front of a storefront advertising the best deep-sea fishing known to man.

It had been twenty-two years since he had left this place, and he swore that nothing he could see had changed much. But of course it had.

For one, his father was in jail for murder.

Unless it had been moved, Robie knew exactly

where the town's stockade was. He drove in that direction, ignoring folks staring at the newcomer. He imagined there weren't many of those. Who would travel all this way to get to a place like Cantrell?

Well, I did.

8

The town jail was in its old location, though it had been spruced up some and fortified with more bars and steel doors. Robie parked his car, got out, and stared up at the brick front with the heavy metal door and barred windows. He had on jeans, a short-sleeved shirt with the tail out, and a pair of scuffed loafers. He slipped his sunglasses into his front shirt pocket.

The sign next to the door required visitors to hit the white button. He did. A few seconds later, the voice came out of the squawk box that was bolted to the doorjamb. The words were spoken slowly and each seemed to be drawn out to the absolute limit of their pronounceable length. Growing up here Robie sometimes felt he had never heard a consonant, certainly never an *r*. And while *n*'s and *g*'s at the ends of words were clearly seen on paper they were—like children and lunatic relations—never, ever heard.

"Deputy Taggert here. Can I help y'all?"

Deputy Taggert was a woman, Robie noted. He also noted the surveillance camera above his head. Deputy Taggert could see him, too.

Robie took a breath. As soon as he said the next words it would be all over town with no possibility of ever taking it back. It was like social media, without need for an Internet.

"I'm Will Robie. I'm here to see my father, Dan Robie."

The voice said nothing for four long beats.

Then—

"Can I see me some ID?"

Robie took out his driver's license and held it up to the camera.

"Dee-Cee?" said Taggert, referring to Robie's District of Columbia license.

"Yes."

"You carryin' any weapons?"

"No."

"Well, we see 'bout that. We got us here a metal detector. You care to answer that question different now, Mr. Robie?"

"No. I'm *not* armed."

The door buzzed open. Robie gripped the handle and pulled.

He walked into a darkened space and had to blink rapidly to adjust his eyes to the low light level. A metal detector stood in front of the doorway across the space that led into the interior of the building. A uniformed man stood there, hand on the stippled butt of his nine-millimeter sidearm. He was taller than Robie, with a protruding belly but also broad

shoulders and a thick neck that made his head look shrunken.

The uniform eyed him up and down. "Y'all want'a step over here."

It wasn't a question.

Robie was searched and then passed through the metal detector that never made a sound.

The room Robie next entered looked like a waiting room because it was. He wasn't the only one in there. A young black woman, skinny and frail, was bouncing a pudgy diapered baby on her lap. In the far corner an old white man sat dozing, the back of his head propped against a wall painted the color of concrete. The place smelled of sweat and burned coffee and the passage of time, which held its own moldy stink. The confluence of smells hit Robie like a gut punch. Not because they were unfamiliar, but because they weren't.

A female deputy emerged from behind a scarred wooden desk with an ancient, fat computer resting on it. She was five-five, sturdily built, with copper-colored hair cut sharply around her narrow face, which was topped by a pair of penetrating dark brown eyes.

"Will Robie?"

He nodded. "Yes."

"Uh-huh. Let me see that ID again."

He handed it across. She studied it closely and then looked at him for comparison.

"Do I know you?" asked Robie, squinting at her.

"I was Sheila *Duvall* before I got myself married to Jimbo Taggert."

In the dim recesses of his memory emerged a skinny tomboy with a chip on her shoulder that weighed a ton and who seemingly lived to fight any boy within reach of her bony fists. Robie had given her a black eye when they were eight, and in return she had bloodied and nearly broken his nose. He also recalled a tall boy with hair the color of straw who went by Jimbo and never spoke.

"I see your eye healed up, although sometimes I still breathe funny through my nose." He tacked on a smile to this statement, which she did not return.

She gave him back his license.

"You want'a see your daddy, you say?"

"That's why I'm here."

"I like to had a heart attack when I heard your name and now you standin' right here." She cocked her head and looked up at him.

"Can I see him?" asked Robie.

She looked doubtful. "He's fixin' to eat his lunch right now."

Robie looked at an empty chair in the room. "I can wait then."

"He expectin' you?"

"Don't think so, no."

"How you know he been arrested then?" she said suspiciously.

Robie now recalled that as a child and later a teenager Sheila Duvall had been sharp and seemingly missed nothing.

"Friend of a friend."

"Uh-huh." In a more strident tone she added, "Do I look like a *dumbass* to you, Will Robie?"

He could hear the squeak of the metal detector guard's gun belt as the big man eased into the room behind him, prompted probably by the rising of Taggert's voice.

"No, you don't, Deputy Taggert. You look as sharp and professional as they come, actually."

The eyes flickered. "You go take yourself a seat, right now."

"Yes, ma'am."

Robie sat across from the black woman with the big baby. She stared over at him for a moment before dropping her gaze to the floor. But she continued to bounce her child with her stick-thin arms that were all mottled and bruised.

The old man had woken and was staring at Robie, too. His face was deeply tanned, and his hair, what was left of it, was starkly white and pitched helter-skelter over his scalp like sea spray in a storm. His jowls hung low and his lined, spotted face told of many decades under an unrelenting southern sun. He had on seersucker pants, a white shirt with sweat stains at the armpits, and scuffed white loafers on his sockless feet.

Clip-on red suspenders held up his trousers, and a battered straw hat rested on his knee.

Robie didn't know the man and wondered if he had recognized Robie's name. Everybody here must know Dan Robie, he figured. And Dan Robie's being in jail for killing a fellow Cantrell citizen must be the biggest news of the year for the tiny hamlet.

"How long do you think it'll be?" Robie asked.

Taggert looked up from her desk. "I done told you before. He's havin' his meal. Can't say how long the man'll be. I don't count *chews*."

Robie sat back in the chair. The other uniform leaned against the wall, folded his arms over his chest, and settled his gaze on Robie.

Robie gave him a quick glance and then looked away.

Thirty minutes passed, and he had counted six flies buzzing overhead in the warm, humid space, the air disturbed only slightly by an ancient ceiling fan that seemed to be on its last few whirls of mechanical life.

A minute later Robie glanced over as Taggert picked up a phone, spoke into it in a low voice, and then put the receiver back. She rose and walked over to him.

Robie stood. "Lunch over?"

"He don't want'a see you," she said matter-of-factly.

"So somebody told him I was here? You?"

"Suppose you can head on then," she said, ignoring his question.

"I've come a long way to see him."

"Yep. All the way from Dee-Cee. Don't know what to tell y'all 'cept good-bye."

This drew a snort from the other deputy.

"Well, can I at least talk to him on the phone somehow?"

"Naw. We don't do that here."

"So that's it then?"

She said nothing.

"Has he been arraigned?"

"That be in the mornin' over the courthouse."

"Can you tell me what happened at least? With Sherman Clancy?"

"I'm busy, Robie. I ain't got no time to have a conversation with the likes'a you."

"The likes of me? I'm *from* Cantrell."

"You *was* from Cantrell."

"Who's his lawyer?"

"Not my business."

"Can you suggest a place for me to stay then?"

"Why you stayin'?" she asked.

"Because my father has been arrested for murder. If you were me, would you stay?"

"I ain't you. Got 'nuff trouble bein' me."

This drew another snort from her partner.

But she walked back over to her desk, took her time writing something down on a piece of paper,

folded it over, and handed it to him. "Fair rates and clean sheets. Can't ask for mor'n that."

"Thanks."

"Uh-huh." She turned away.

Robie walked out, conscious that all eyes were on him as he did so.

He sat in his car and opened the slip of paper.

Off duty at five. Momma Lulu's on Little Choctaw.

9

Robie had a few hours to kill before meeting Taggert at Momma Lulu's on Little Choctaw, a place he knew was three streets over from the jail. He decided to spend the time exploring his old hometown.

He pointed his rental back the way he had come, conscious again of the faces peering at him from all corners. He might as well have been driving in a lunar rover for all the attention he was getting. Tourism apparently wasn't a thriving industry here, not that he had expected it to be.

Robie quickly left the tiny downtown area of Cantrell. A half hour later he turned down a narrow dirt lane that ended at the rim of a small homestead.

He had not chosen this place by chance. This had been his home growing up.

The house was old and small, about nine hundred square feet, and directly behind it was a two-story barn topped by a hayloft. It was set on twenty mostly treed acres, though the Robies had raised their own vegetables in a large kitchen garden, grew some corn

for sale, and also kept a few horses and cows. And of course chickens.

The front yard was dirt; the bushes and other minimal landscaping had gone to seed. The front porch was sagging. And if that wasn't enough evidence for Robie that his ramrod-straight father no longer called this place home, three little shirtless black boys were running in circles in the front yard, while their twenty-something mother in cutoff jean shorts and a white tank top hustled after them.

The woman stopped running when Robie pulled up and got out of the car. The three children crowded next to their mother's broad hips and warily watched his approach, their eyes big as bottle caps.

"Can I help you?" asked the woman, taking a step back and drawing her kids with her. "My husband's right inside cleanin' his gun," she added, in the form of a clear warning. "He just done him some huntin'," she added. "*Kilt* him some things."

Robie looked over her shoulder. "I used to live here a long time ago. My father Dan Robie owned the place. How long have you been here?"

She looked a bit confused and then, as he expected, realization spread over her features. "Robie? Dan Robie is your daddy?"

Robie nodded and again looked toward the house. "So did you buy this place from him?"

"Uh-uh. We moved in two years ago, but we

bought it from the Harpers. They headed on up to Chattanooga."

Robie nodded. "Okay, thanks." He turned and walked back to his car.

The woman called after him, "Your daddy done kilt a man."

He turned back around. "So I heard."

He drove off in a swirl of dust. In the rearview he saw the woman hustle inside, no doubt to tell her hunter husband all about it.

He headed back to Cantrell thinking that he should have asked the woman if she knew where his father now lived. But he hadn't, so he would have to gain that information some other way. He could ask people in town. It was small enough that someone would know. But he didn't want to do that, either. After Taggert and then the young mom, he had grown weary of seeing the looks on people's faces when he identified himself as the son of a murderer.

Alleged murderer, he mentally corrected.

He got back to the main street that cut Cantrell proper into two roughly equal halves and spied what he had earlier. An old phone booth. Through the dirty glass he could see the phone book dangling on the end of a chain.

He parked at the curb, stepped inside the booth, gripped the slender phone book, and flipped through its few pages until he got to the right section.

Dan Robie. He now lived at Willow Hall.

The Willows, as everyone in Cantrell had always called it.

Robie read through this line twice more to make sure he was seeing right.

It wasn't a street name. It was the name of the house. He knew the place well. He had once dated a girl who lived there with her family.

Laura Barksdale's father could trace his roots all the way back to when Mississippi was first settled. The Willows had once been a classic southern plantation complete with an army of slaves. The Barksdales' ancestors had commanded Confederate troops in the Civil War. They had led Citizens' Councils to keep blacks in their place when the civil rights movement came to Mississippi. They were prominent and wealthy and . . .

And now his father owned the place?

He left the phone booth to find two black men staring at him from a few feet away. One was big and bulky, wearing faded jeans, white sneakers, and a gray T-shirt.

The other man was smallish but wiry, with sculpted shoulders and thick forearms shown off because he had on a wife beater along with baggy black corduroys.

Robie nodded at them both and then started to walk past.

"Will Robie?" said the bigger man.

Robie turned to look at him. He was maybe twenty, not even born when Robie had left this place.

"Yeah?"

"You know my daddy?"

"I don't know. Who's your daddy?"

"Billy Faulconer."

The image of a huge teenager with enormous shoulders, beefy arms, and a hearty laugh, which he used often, seeped into Robie's brain.

Robie said, "We were on the football team together. He was a helluva left tackle. Protected my blind side really well."

"Y'all were state champs your senior year. Got yourselves a parade and everythin'. Daddy still talks 'bout it."

Billy Faulconer must've had kids young, Robie calculated. Pretty much right after high school. But in Cantrell that was not so unusual. There was no mad rush off to college for the high school graduates. There was only one sudden, panicked thought, really:

Now what the hell do I do?

He said, "It was a nice ride. Good for the town. No team from here had ever beaten a team from Jackson."

"He talked 'bout you, too. Said you just upped and left one night after you finished high school. Nobody heard from you no mo'."

Robie was not about to get into all that. "So how's Billy doing?"

"Not so good. He got the cancer in his lungs. Ain't long for this world."

"I'm really sorry to hear that."

The tall young man looked at him appraisingly. "You here 'bout your daddy, ain't you? What got you back here, right?"

"What's your name?"

"Named after my daddy. But folks just call me Little Bill."

"You're pretty big for that name."

"My daddy's bigger. Least he used to be before the cancer got him."

"So what do you know about Sherman Clancy dying? And my father being arrested for the murder?"

Little Bill shrugged. "Not much. Bad blood twixt the two."

"Based on what?"

The smaller man said, "Jury ain't convict old Clancy and that got your daddy all riled, I reckon."

"Convict him of what?"

"Killin' that gal," said Little Bill. "Janet Chisum. Nice gal. Till someone did what they done to her."

"I don't know anything about it. I never heard of the Chisums."

"They moved here a while back. She was a pretty white gal. One of three gals in the family. She done went out one night and never come back. Found her in the damn Pearl River the next day hooked on a tree. Shot in the head. Gator had taken a bite outta her, too."

"And Clancy was arrested for the murder? Why?"

The smaller man said, "Somebody done seen him

with the gal. That part of the Pearl is near his house. Other stuff cops know about."

"But the jury acquitted him?"

"Yes they did," said the smaller man.

"Why?"

The smaller man was about to say something but Billy broke in, "Clancy's got himself a lot of friends hereabouts." He rubbed his thumb and two fingers together. "And he got him money."

His friend gave Little Bill a funny look but said nothing.

Robie looked confused. "Money! The Clancys were dirt-poor farmers when I was here."

Little Bill shook his head. "That all changed. They done found gas or oil on his land. And then he took that money and got in early with some of the casino boys. Made himself a lotta cash. A lot. Got him a big old place down by the Pearl."

"*Had*," said his friend. "He ain't got nothin' no mo'."

Robie said, "Okay, but why would my father be so angry that he was acquitted that he would kill him?"

"'Cause he be the judge," said Little Bill.

Robie stared at him. When he'd left Cantrell his father had a small law practice that barely kept the roof over their heads. Most of his fees were paid in barter.

Little Bill seemed to read Robie's mind. "Your

daddy's been the judge here 'bout ten years now. Things change. Yes they do. Even in Cantrell."

"Yes they do," agreed Robie. "You tell your daddy I said hello."

"I sure will. Maybe you come see him while you here. We live down on Tiara Street, last house on the left." He stared dead at Robie. "He ain't got much longer, Mr. Robie. Bet it'd do him good, you know. Old times. *Good* times. Maybe only ones he ever had."

Robie nodded. "I'll sure see if I can do that."

He got back in his car and drove off.

His mind was whirling with many new facts now. His father a judge.

The Clancys, rich.

This Janet Chisum, dead.

But then his mind focused on where he was going. *The Willows.*

And with it, all those memories.

From his last night in Cantrell.

10

Willow Hall had been aptly named nearly two centuries ago, because there had been a line of willow oaks on both sides of the long drive heading up to the house. Or so Robie had been told—the trees had died away many decades before he had been born. The cause had been the drying up of an underground spring that fed the willows' thirsty roots.

In their place had been planted longleaf pines that could tolerate drier conditions and were a native species. They ran in columns eighty feet high on both sides of the pebbled drive that curved in several stretches before straightening as one approached the house.

THE WILLOWS.

Robie saw that name on the mailbox.

And then below that the name ROBIE was painted in neat white letters. He could envision his perfectionist father painting every one of them using a ruler to get the spacing exactly right.

He turned his rental down the drive bracketed by

the majestic longleaf pines that had canopies enormous enough to block out the sun.

As he turned into the straightaway he could see it.

Willow Hall was a majestic antebellum mansion built when James Monroe was president of the United States. Six columns supported the high, long front porch as well as the upper porch. That same architectural feature ran down both sides of the manor and also on the back verandah. Chimney brick stacks rose from the slate roof, and black shutters bracketed the five front windows, three up and two down with the lower ones on either side of the front door.

Parked in the circle in front of the mansion was a dark blue late-model Volvo station wagon with a booster seat in the back.

Robie stopped his car and climbed out.

A few moments later a woman about Robie's age rushed out of the house, a small boy on her right hip. She wore high heels and nearly tripped going down the plank front steps before regaining her balance. She was tall, and though probably normally lean, still carried some of the baby weight in her torso. Her swirl of blonde hair just touched her clavicle. She had sunglasses on and a large bag slung over her left shoulder. She fumbled in the bag for her car keys.

"You need some help?" he asked.

She froze and looked over at him. "Who are you? What are you doing here?"

She had found her keys and he could see that she

gripped them so that one was protruding between her fingers, as a weapon. His father had probably taught her that, because he had showed Robie how to do the very same thing.

Her speech and lack of an accent told him that she was not native to Cantrell, and probably not even Mississippi.

He looked over her shoulder at the house. "This place brings back memories."

"Why?"

"I dated a girl who lived here once. Laura Barksdale."

She used her free hand to nudge her sunglasses down a bit to get a better look at him.

Robie was not as tall as his father, but the two did resemble each other. Everyone had always said the son took after the father.

His personality more closely tracked his mother. At least he thought so.

"Who are you?" she said again, but Robie could tell in her look that she had noticed the resemblance to his father.

"Will Robie," he said. "Who are you?"

"Well, I guess technically I'm your stepmother, Victoria."

Robie took a step forward and looked at the child who hadn't said a word, but was staring at Robie with one of his fingers in his mouth. As he gazed at the boy Robie saw features that were very familiar. He saw his

father. He saw himself. And he also saw some of the woman in the little face.

"Yours?" he asked, indicating the child, though he thought the answer plain enough.

"Yes, and your father's, which means he's your step-brother."

"*Technically,*" added Robie. "How old is he?"

"Ty is two, but he'll turn three in just a couple of months."

Robie stiffened a bit. "Ty?"

"His full name is Tyler. But we call him Ty."

Robie flinched again. Tyler was *his* middle name.

She noted this apparently, because she said, "Will Tyler Robie. That's your full name."

"Did my father tell you that?"

She suddenly looked uncertain. "No . . . I saw it somewhere."

So Dad never talked about me. Robie was not surprised by this. *But he named his son Tyler.*

It wasn't a family name. His mother, he'd learned, had named him Will, after her beloved uncle. But Robie's father had selected the middle name. He told his son it was the name of a man he'd served with in Vietnam. He said he'd been the toughest sonofabitch he'd ever known. He later told his son he wanted him to be just as tough. Robie had obviously failed at that. At least in his father's eyes.

"We didn't know you were coming here," she said, interrupting Robie's thoughts.

"That's because I didn't tell anyone."

"You know about your father, then?"

"I went over to the jail and waited. Apparently, he didn't want to see me. Is that where you're going? The jail?"

"I've already been this morning. I'm taking Tyler to the doctor and I'm running late." She looked uncertain again. "You look like your father, but can I see something to prove you are who you say?"

He took out his driver's license and showed it to her.

He said, "My dad has a scar on his back. Shrapnel wound from Vietnam. It's in the shape of a backwards J. He has one gold tooth in the back, bottom row. And he'd take two fingers of Glenlivet over a beer any day."

She smiled. "He got the scar fixed with plastic surgery and the gold tooth with a synthetic implant. But he'd still take the scotch over the beer."

"Good to know."

Victoria glanced over her shoulder. "Look, you're welcome to stay here until I get back. Priscilla is our housekeeper. She can see to you if you're hungry or anything."

"That's okay. I would like to take a look around. I have someplace to be at five, but after that I'd like to meet with you if that's okay."

"Where have you been all this time, Will?" she blurted out.

He didn't answer right away. "Living my life."

She looked down at the pebbled drive. "I guess you're surprised he has a wife and young child."

"No, not really. He was obviously living his life, too."

"He never said what happened between you two."

"I would imagine not. He's a private person."

"I have to go, but I'll call Priscilla from the car and let her know you'll be around. And after your five o'clock thing, why don't you come back here for dinner?"

"You don't have to do that."

"I never do anything I don't want to do, you'll see that about me soon enough. Say seven thirty? I'm not from around here, but I can cook a damn good southern meal if I choose to."

Robie nodded. "Okay, I'll see you then." He looked at Tyler. "You said you're taking him to the doctor. Is he okay? He doesn't look sick."

"Ty has some . . . challenges," she said, gently pressing down a cowlick on the boy's head and giving the spot a kiss. Then she strapped her son in the booster, climbed into the driver's seat, and kicked up some pebbles as she sped off.

Robie watched them go for a bit and then walked the grounds of the Willows. He remembered the place as being meticulously maintained, because the Barksdales had come from money and Henry Barksdale had worked hard at maintaining his ancestral home.

Robie's father had obviously kept the grounds in excellent condition. A few features had been added, like a swimming pool, a stone pavilion, and a fenced-in kitchen garden.

Whether the Barksdales had done this after Robie left Cantrell, or his father had, or some owner in between, he didn't know. He still couldn't understand how his father had come to own such a place. Even in Cantrell, where the cost of land and living were preposterously low, this place would not come cheap to own or maintain.

He stood at a spot near a stacked rock wall at the rear of the property. He took in a lungful of air, and the briny smells from the nearby Gulf filled his nostrils. Growing up here he hadn't thought there was any other kind of air.

It had been at this spot that Laura Barksdale and he had made their plans. He had already reached his full height and his shoulders were broad and his muscles hard from year-round sports. In addition to football, Robie had played basketball and run track. You could do that back then, especially in a small town like this where there weren't enough young men to fill the various teams.

Laura was a brunette who wore her hair short. She was slender and of average height. They both had been popular in high school, he for his athletics and good looks, and she for her intelligence, kindness, and beauty, and in spite of her prestigious family,

which some at Cantrell High held against her. She had been nice to everyone, but Robie had always felt there was something she was not telling him. He caught it in a look, in something she said. Sometimes, simply in her silence. But then she would push away whatever seemed to be bothering her and come back to him. He had asked her many times to confide in him. But she would only smile, shake her head, and say that she had told him everything. And then they would kiss and the teenage Robie would forget about everything else.

Yes, they had made plans for their future. Together. Only they would never come to pass.

As he finished his exploration of the rear grounds and headed back toward the house, he caught a glimpse of a face at one of the upstairs windows before it was gone.

The face was lined and the skin the same color as Deputy Taggert's eyes.

Priscilla.

11

Robie stepped up onto the porch and knocked on the door. The heat of the day was bearing down on him; it was a humid heat, unlike the desert kind he'd recently been in. He'd take dry over wet. The humidity just sucked everything right out of you. He remembered how his mother would take a bath in the morning and then again in the afternoon for that very reason.

He heard feet coming down the set of grand stairs he remembered that flared out at the bottom, and that he also remembered were set right in the center of the substantial foyer.

The door opened and there was the face he had glimpsed a minute ago. Priscilla was in her early sixties, about five feet four inches tall, thickset, with straight graying black hair tied back in a severe bun. She had on a maid's outfit, and her feet were encased in worn, soft-soled shoes, the kind that nurses wore, only black.

"You Will Robie?" she said immediately, almost fiercely.

"I am."

"I'm Priscilla. I take care'a your daddy's home."

"Nice to meet you."

"Nice to meet you. Ms. Victoria said you was around. Liked to knock me over when she said so."

"How long have you been helping my father?"

"Four years now."

"Do you mind if I come in and look around a bit?"

She opened the door wider and moved aside, shutting the door after he entered the foyer.

She stared up at him. "You handsome, like your daddy. Though not as big. But you not too scrawny. You look like you can take care'a yourself."

Robie was gazing around at the rooms bleeding off the entrance hall. The furnishings were tasteful, solid, everything situated just so. His father's doing, most certainly. But he could see a bit of Victoria, perhaps, in the fresh-cut flowers and colorful drapes and throw pillows. And the artwork that ranged from simple to substantial carried a whimsical feel that he just didn't see his Marine father possessing.

His gaze dropped to Priscilla. "Can you tell me what happened? Why my father's in jail for killing Sherman Clancy?"

"I just made a pitcher'a tea. You want some?"

"Is it sweet tea?"

She looked at him funny. "Is there any other kind?"

She led him into the large, sunny kitchen with blackened beams across the ceiling. Priscilla poured

out two glasses of sweet tea, and they sat at a round cedar table in front of a bay window overlooking the rear grounds.

Robie took a sip of his drink and couldn't keep his face from puckering as the truckload of sugar walloped his taste buds.

Priscilla took a long drink of her tea and smacked her lips before saying slyly, "You been gone from Mississippi a long time?"

"Yes, I have," said Robie, putting the glass down.

"Sherman Clancy," said Priscilla, watching him closely.

Robie leaned in a bit and met her gaze directly. "I'd appreciate all that you can tell me."

"Sherman Clancy wasn't a good man. But truth is, I ain't see him as no killer, neither."

"Why not?"

She took another gulp of tea. "You want something to eat?"

"No, I'm good." He watched her expectantly.

"Clancy was in with those casino boys. Those junk-yard dogs drain every cent from you and laugh all the way to the bank while they givin' you another watered-down glass of whiskey cost 'em ten cents and they sell for ten dollahs."

"But he wasn't a killer?"

"What he mostly was, was fat and drunk. Doubt he'd have the energy or what you need upstairs to kill nobody and then get away with it."

"And Janet Chisum?"

"Didn't know her. Her family ain't here too long. Seem nice 'nuff. Saw 'em drivin' to church on Sundays. That's all they got to keep 'em now. God's love. He'll see those poor folks through this, yes he will. When I lost my baby, God was with me all the way."

Robie's mind went back to the tragic image of Sasha toppling dead to the floor. "How'd your child die?" he asked a moment later.

"Was livin' up near Hattiesburg back then. Big old rattler done got my Earl when he was just a little boy. Went over to the county hospital but the man there said there was nothin' they could do and I'd best take him over the clinic near where we lived. So's I took him there, but they told me the county hospital was the only place 'round got the serum for the rattler. Earl died in my arms in the car on the way back to the county hospital. I walked into that place holdin' my dead son and you know what that same man done told me?"

"What?"

"That he ain't remember me comin' in. That I must've made some mistake. That I must not be right in the head. And that I needed to take my boy's body outta there right that very second, 'cause it was upsettin' his staff." She shook her head. "Upsettin' his staff? Hear them words till I breathe my last."

"Why wouldn't they treat your son?"

She glanced up at him. "What planet you livin' on?

79

White hospital, black boy. You from Mississippi. You forget how it is down here? And this was over forty years back."

"You could've taken the hospital and the man to court. Hell, had him tried for criminal negligence or something."

"Oh, thank you for tellin' me, Mr. Will Robie," she replied in feigned astonishment. "You mean all I got to do was get me a lawyer and go to court and then they got to get to work on savin' my baby? Why ain't I think'a that? Oh, but he was already dead."

"The point is the man should have been punished for what he did."

"Oh, he was. You ain't let me get to that part. He died sudden like just a few weeks later."

"How?"

"Somebody done shot him."

"Who?"

"My husband, Carl. That why I ain't got no more husband. They executed him over at the state penitentiary. I was there watchin' him when he went. Had a smile on his face."

"I'm sorry, Priscilla. None of that should have happened."

Priscilla finished her tea and said, "Water under the bridge. Can't do nothin' 'bout it now 'cept pray to God the next life is better'n this one. So they say your daddy done killed Sherman Clancy, but I don't believe that for one little minute."

"How was Clancy killed?"

Priscilla pointed to her neck. "Slit from ear to ear. Newspaper say it was a knife like the military use."

"And my dad was in the Marines."

"Well, lots of folks down here served in the military. And lots of folks got them knives like that."

"Where was he found?"

"In his car, down by the Pearl. He got himself one'a them Bentley cars. Only one hereabouts, I can tell you that. 'Bout a half mile from his house. Lonely old swamp road. Hell, what other kind'a swamp road is there?"

"TOD?"

"What?" she said looking confused.

"Time of death," said Robie quickly, while Priscilla continued to stare at him suspiciously.

"'Bout one in the mornin', paper said."

"No other suspects? What about his family? Lots of time family members kill each other."

"Well, he ain't got no family in Cantrell 'cept for Pete. His children from his first marriage are all grown and moved off."

"First marriage?"

She nodded. "He divorced his first wife, married another lady, and they had Pete. Then Clancy divorced her too, but Pete still lived with his daddy."

"And the 'junkyard dogs' he did business with in the casinos? Could they have killed Clancy?"

She pointed a stubby finger at him. "Now that's

'xactly what I done said. What 'bout *them*? But I guess the police checked that out. And maybe they got themselves alibis. But they could'a hired somebody to do it. Maybe Clancy and them had a fallin'-out, or he was caught with his hand in the cookie jar. Or they was doing somethin' criminal-like, and he found out. Could be anythin'."

"But they arrested my father?"

"Yes they did. Mighty quick, too."

"Why? He's the judge. On the cops' side."

"Well, I hear me some stories that Judge Robie made it hard on the police to get convictions. Especially if people'a color are involved."

"You mean he was balancing the scales of justice?" said Robie.

She fingered her tea glass. "*I* would say that. Others not so much."

"Sounded like the case against Clancy for killing Janet Chisum was pretty strong. I heard he walked because he has friends and money."

"Shoot, I can tell you 'xactly why he walked."

"Why?"

Her expression changed. "Why you care 'bout all this?"

"My *father's* been arrested for murder."

"So? You been gone all this time. And now you show up out of the blue?" She shook her head and looked at him disapprovingly. "Can't say I respect you for that."

"I had my reasons."

"Not good 'nuff, Will Robie." She rose. "Now I got me work to do. Lotta house to keep clean." She pointed toward the front door. "I 'spect you can find your way out. And then why don't you go back where you done come from and forget all about your daddy? Shouldn't be too hard. You done forgot 'bout him most'a your life, way I see it." And she walked off.

As Robie watched her go, a part of him felt Priscilla was exactly right.

12

Robie walked back to his car, glancing once at the house where he, again, caught Priscilla eyeing him from an upstairs window. She didn't look pleased, and he knew she was not happy with him. But then again, she seemed loyal to his father. And though he didn't think much of the man, she apparently did.

He looked past the house to the rear grounds, where he had held Laura Barksdale in his arms on that hot, humid night in June.

They had sworn their undying love to each other in a way only the teenage heart could apparently manage. Robie had always intended to leave Cantrell, and when he shared his plan with Laura she had immediately asked Robie to take her with him. Everything seemed perfect.

Robie had his rusty Chevrolet packed with his few belongings. He had gone to the prearranged spot the next night. He had waited for Laura to come. He had waited for three hours. She never showed up.

Afraid that something had happened to her, he had driven his old clunker to this very place, parking well

out of sight. He had snuck up to the front of the house, his eyes lifting to the second floor of the well-lighted façade till they came to the third window on the left—Laura's bedroom. The light was on. Her silhouette was clear against that backdrop.

She was not coming. Her undying love had apparently lasted fewer than twenty-four hours.

Robie had gone back to his car, and—once more with the shortsightedness and accompanying stubbornness that came with being only eighteen years old—he got in his car and started driving. And he didn't stop until the next morning. Then he ate, slept in his car, and kept driving until the Atlantic Ocean came into view.

He had written her over the next couple years imploring her to join him but had never received a reply. He had called the house, but no one had ever answered. He had left messages, but she had never called him back. Despite all that, he told himself that he would come back and get her. That they would be together.

But life had gotten in the way, and the love he held for her had slowly faded. The years had zipped by. And he had never returned to Mississippi.

Until now.

He started his rental and drove down the pebbled drive.

His father had remarried, and his new wife was Robie's age.

And they have a young son named after me who doesn't talk.

The one person he had *not* thought of while he had been here was his mother. He had come to believe that he had no reason to think of her. She had abandoned him. She had made a choice that had not included him, and had left him with the near-mad Marine turned country lawyer who fervently believed that boys were meant to be tough. And whatever method you used to make them tough was just fine. And if it came close to killing the boy, well, then even better.

Laura had her own family problems, though she had never made Robie privy to exactly what they were despite his pleading with her to confide in him. Her natural positivism had been often tempered by painful bouts of melancholy. Hence the plan to leave Cantrell and start their lives over somewhere else.

Only Robie had never envisioned driving halfway across the country alone.

In many ways he had been alone ever since.

He drove back into town on roads that had heat rising off them like mist from a warm pond on a cool morning. He cranked up the air-conditioning and let the cold air pound away at the sweat beads on his face.

There was still so much he didn't know.

How Victoria had met his father and then married him. What her background was.

How his father had become the judge here.

How he could afford a place like the Willows.

He had no idea why Sherman Clancy had not been convicted. He didn't know anything about the case against his father beyond the sketchy details Blue Man had provided. But he was hoping that Sheila Taggert would fill him in when they met at five o'clock.

He kept his car pointed back toward town and was there thirty minutes later. It wasn't that far as the crow flew, but the roads here did not take the crow's route. They were in poor condition and tended to ramble rather than run straight and true back to downtown Cantrell, as though the folks around here had all the time in the world.

And maybe they did.

He parked near Momma Lulu's on Little Choctaw and started walking. He had a little time before he would meet Taggert and he needed a place to stay.

There had been a small hotel on Dubois Street when he was growing up here. He walked that way, his duffel slung over his shoulder. Dubois Street was still there, but the hotel wasn't. In its place was a large hole in the dirt with a corresponding gap like a missing tooth in the establishments that ran the length of Dubois on both sides.

Robie stood in front of this gap studying the empty space and wondering what had happened.

"Burnt to the damn ground," said a man's voice.

He turned around and saw a stooped, elderly couple

standing there. He was dressed like a farmer with coveralls, a denim shirt, and old brogans on his feet, but in an odd juxtaposition, a tweed cap was perched jauntily on his head. She wore a polka-dot dress with sandals and the thickest pair of eyeglasses Robie had ever seen. They looked to be in their eighties, or nineties. Or hundreds. Robie couldn't be sure.

The woman looked at her companion severely. "Cussing is trashy, Monroe Tussle."

Monroe looked at Robie and grinned, showing off finely sculpted veneers. "Sixty-nine years we've been married and she still calls me by both my names."

"Got to, if I want to get your attention, like most men of a certain age," she shot back. "Meanin' any man that's been married mor'n a year."

"Why, you've had my attention ever since you accepted my proposal of marriage, Eugenia."

Eugenia said, "Sweet-talkin' men, nothin' but poison!" But she patted his arm and looked pleased at his words.

Robie figured they had been making this same exchange for the last thirty years, maybe longer. They were evidently practiced at it. He pointed to the gap.

"So it burned to the ground. When?"

"Oh, 'bout, what Eugenia, say ten years ago?"

"'Bout that, yes. Lightnin', they say." She let her voice sink. "But I always said it was mor'n that."

"Insurance money," added Monroe with a knowing look.

She jabbed him in the arm with her finger. "*I* was tellin' the story."

"And they didn't rebuild it?" asked Robie.

The couple looked surprised by this. Monroe said, "Never saw the point, son. If they had mor'n two paying guests at any one time, they'd be considered full up and hang out the NO VACANCY sign."

Eugenia eyed Robie's duffel. "You lookin' for a place to stay, hon?"

"I am."

"Rooms overtop'a Danby's Tavern on Muley Road, you know where that is?"

"I do."

Monroe squinted at him. "You from 'round here, son?"

"Not anymore," said Robie. He thanked them and headed to Muley Road.

He reached it five minutes later.

Eugenia Tussle had not been entirely accurate. There weren't *rooms* above Danby's Tavern; there was just one room. It was empty until Robie rented it, paying in cash so he did not have to reveal his name. However, he was sure that by now pretty much everyone in Cantrell knew who he was. The owner of Danby's, a large man with a rough beard and thick, muscular hands, passed him the key.

"Stayin' long?" he asked.

Robie shrugged. "Not sure."

He took his duffel up to the room, unpacked his

few items into a rickety bureau, sat on the bed, and gazed out the window onto the street below.

Part of Robie, perhaps most of him, wanted to drive to Jackson and climb on a plane and fly back to DC. His father didn't want to see him. Robie didn't see any reason to be here. Yet he wasn't going to leave.

He checked his watch. Nearly five.

He washed up in the small bathroom, changed his clothes, and left his room, locking the door behind him. He hurried down the steps, and his shoes hit the planks of the first floor of Danby's Tavern.

There were three customers in the tavern now. They were all young men. And they were all looking at him from behind reddened eyes as their thick hands clasped nearly empty beer bottles. Behind the counter, a young woman glanced once at the men and then over at Robie. Her look told him all he needed to know.

She was afraid. For him.

Danby's owner was nowhere to be seen.

That figured.

When he headed to the door, the three men rose as one and blocked his way.

They were all Robie's size or bigger. Youngish, in their early twenties. He would have been gone from Cantrell probably before they were born. They wore jeans and T-shirts and were broadly muscular, smelling

of sweat and beer. And testosterone about to be unleashed.

Robie looked at the one in the middle. His arrogant features and his positioning slightly forward of his two companions told Robie he was the designated leader, like the head wolf in a pack.

"Can I help you?" he said.

The man replied, "Will Robie?"

Robie said nothing but he answered with a slight nod.

"Your daddy is a killah."

"Not until the court says he is," replied Robie.

He had already positioned himself so that his angled silhouette provided less of a target and his weight was forward on the balls of his feet but still balanced enough to ward off an attack. As his gaze took in all three of his opponents, his hands and arms relaxed but his quads and calves were tightened, like a spring about to be released. If it came to it, he knew exactly how he would do this. The plan had formed in his mind without his really having to think about it.

He could tell they were amateurs, with no time even in the military. Otherwise, they would not be lined up in front of him like tenpins.

"He killed *my* daddy!" said the leader.

"You're Sherman Clancy's son?" Robie replied in a calm, level tone. He never chose to fight, and if he could defuse the situation he would.

"Damn right I am."

"I'm truly sorry for your loss."

The man snorted. "That's right good comin' from family of the man who killed him."

"I've been gone a long time. I knew nothing about this until recently. But we need to let the court decide what happens to my father. It's just better all around. It's how it has to be."

The man pointed a finger in Robie's face. "You bein' here ain't welcome."

Robie felt his patience start to slip a bit. At this rate, he might be here all night.

"I go to lots of places I'm not welcome." This was one of the most honest statements Robie had uttered since being in the bar.

This comment seemed to befuddle all three of them. And once the brain was taken aback, that left only one alternative for punks like these: They would try to accomplish with their fists what they couldn't with their brains. And Robie had actually intended this, because he had an appointment to keep and just wanted to get this over with.

Clancy's son broke off his beer bottle against a table edge and brandished it in front of Robie.

Only Robie was no longer there.

He had moved to his right, knelt, gripped the inside leg of the man next to Clancy's son, ripped it off the floor, and then propelled him sideways into the other two. As they were all going down to the floor Robie reached over and snagged the hand holding the beer

bottle. He bent it backward until Clancy's son screamed and let go. He threw the bottle to the side, stepped back, and prepared for what was coming next.

Clancy's son pushed off the floor and came at Robie. Another mistake. They should have regrouped and attacked him together from different flanks. But they were stupid and they couldn't really fight.

Robie was now sure he would not be late for his meeting with Taggert.

One punch to the face, a shot drilled right into his nose with the base of Robie's rigid palm torqued off a V-shaped arm for max power, followed by an elbow strike delivered directly to the right kidney sent the man to the floor. He did not get back up, because the blow to the face had knocked him out. The busted face and bruised kidney would be pains he would suffer later when he came to.

The second man bull-charged Robie and managed to get his thick arms around Robie's waist. His plan, no doubt, was to lift his opponent off the floor and smash him against the wall. The flaw in his strategy was leaving Robie's arms free. Robie slammed both palms against the man's ears, which are quite sensitive appendages of the body. The man screamed, let Robie go, and dropped to all fours. Robie gripped the back of the man's neck and jerked the head down at the same time he delivered a brutal knee strike upward to the chin, which cost his opponent two teeth, and knocked him flat on his ass and out for the count.

The third man did the smart thing—he ran for it. Robie could hear his boots clattering on the plank porch before they hit pavement and were gone.

Robie looked down at the two unconscious, bleeding men and then over at the girl behind the bar. She was staring at him openmouthed, the glass-rag and beer mug clutched in her hand, but neither touching the other.

He pointed to the leader. "Is that Pete Clancy?"

"Y-yes, s-sir," she said in a trembling voice.

"If they press charges will you be able to tell the truth?"

She looked like she might faint. "I . . . Mister, I . . ."

"Don't worry about it." He turned and walked out. He would have to hurry now to make his meeting.

13

Robie walked into Momma Lulu's on Little Choctaw at one minute past five. The place was only a quarter full, and Robie recalled that most folks who ate out in Cantrell ate out late. This was usually because they labored long, and their labor was often outside in a hot, humid climate, which required at least a shower and major amounts of deodorant before heading out to a public place.

He looked around but did not see Taggert among the tables. He noticed a man at the cash register who was staring at him. With a slight movement of his head he motioned Robie over.

"Go out the way you come in, turn right. There's an alley there. Walk down it. She'll be there."

"And who are you?" asked Robie.

"A friend of hers, Mr. Robie. Just a friend."

Robie did as the man said, though part of him expected an ambush as he walked into the darkened alley. But it was a straight shot with no place for concealment. He exited the narrow path, again ready for someone to jump him, but he saw Taggert sitting in

what he assumed was her private vehicle, though she still had on her police uniform.

She pointed to the passenger door and he climbed in. As he belted up she put the rusty Ford Taurus in reverse, backed out, and sped off heading east. At the next intersection, she turned to go south.

Robie looked around the interior of the car and noted the booster seat in the back. On the floorboard were discarded fast-food containers and polystyrene coffee cups. Robie could see the pavement below through a hole in the floorboard.

The inside of the car smelled musty, layered by the stench of a fouled diaper.

"How many kids do you have?"

"Four."

He eyed the booster seat. Her gaze followed his.

"My grandson, Sammy," she said.

He said incredulously, "You're a grandmother? You're only, what, forty-one?"

"Had my first at nineteen. She had her first at eighteen. You do the math."

"Okay."

"You have any kids, Robie?"

"No."

"Married?"

"No."

"Ever been?"

"No."

She shot him a glance. "You of the homosexual persuasion?"

"Not that I'm aware."

Once they were clear of the small downtown she spoke again. "Heard you had some trouble at Danby's."

"That just happened a few minutes ago. How'd you hear already?"

"Small-town livin' is faster'n Twitter ever thought'a bein'. Got me two calls probably before the last fellow hit the planks."

"Just for the record, they attacked me."

"Not disputin' that. Pete Clancy is a royal a-hole."

"I understand he was from a second marriage?"

"Shortly after Sherm came into money, he divorced Cassandra, married some bimbo he met in Biloxi when he was probably drunk outta his mind, and wham, bam, thank you ma'am, there was Pete. Then he divorced the bimbo and she's long gone, but there's still Pete."

"So with his father gone, won't Pete be inheriting?"

"Old Sherm liked the good life and spent his money—doubt there'll be much left once the kids from his first marriage try to get their pound'a flesh. Seems Sherm didn't leave a will, so he died intestate. Which makes it all a little trickier."

"Since you wanted to meet, I guess the riot act you read me at the jail was just that, an act?"

97

"Only partly. It *did* piss me off to see you walk in that door. But you got outta Cantrell. Most of us didn't. Guess I was jealous."

"And the other part?"

"You're persona non grata here, Robie. Won't do me no good cozyin' up to you. Folks don't come into Cantrell all that often. Hell, almost never. And your daddy is an accused murderer of one of the citizens of this humble place. Not an esteemed citizen by any stretch, but still he was one of us."

Robie settled back in his seat. "So what did you want to meet for?"

"Some things you ought'a know. And I suppose you got yourself some questions."

"I have nothing but questions."

"Let me ask you one."

"Okay."

"You took on three big guys at Danby's and licked 'em. How? What you been doin' with yourself all these years?"

"Well, the last guy ran off, so it was only two really."

"You play cute with me, you can get your butt outta my car right now."

"I learned self-defense after I left here. Just a few moves, and those guys were drunk."

"Uh-huh," she said, clearly not believing him but apparently unwilling to push it.

Robie looked up ahead. "Where are we going?"

"Got a spot on the Gulf. Like to go there. Nice place to have a conversation."

"Why are you doing this, Deputy Taggert?"

"Call me Sheila, for Chrissakes, Robie. I'm not on duty."

"You can call me Will, if you want."

"No. Don't cut both ways. Can't get too personal with you."

"Okay, so, *Sheila*, why are you doing this?"

"I guess I naturally gravitate to the underdog. And you are the underdog here, Robie, make no mistake 'bout that."

"I didn't know it was a competition."

"This is small-town Mississippi. Everythin's a damn competition. We just pretend to be laid back and not give a shit 'bout nothin'. But we keep score on football games and everythin' else. Guess it makes up for most'a us not havin' two dimes to rub together our whole damn lives."

They drove along in silence until they reached the Gulf Coast. She parked her car on a narrow strip of dirt and they climbed out. He followed her down to the edge of the water. They both gazed out to where the warm Gulf waters ran to the horizon. Overhead the sun had plenty of fuel left to burn before it sank into the other side of the world.

Robie's mind drifted back to August 2005, when Katrina had slammed into this part of America. The storm had come ashore officially as a Category 3

hurricane, but its effect once on land had made it seem like a Cat 10. It crushed and drowned everything and everyone in its path, filling up New Orleans like a soup bowl once the levees failed. While the Big Easy had gotten most of the media attention, large parts of Mississippi had been devastated, too.

Sheila looked over at Robie. It was as though she could read his thoughts.

"Katrina missed Cantrell for the most part. Don't know why. Must've been God's work. Towns on either side of us weren't so lucky, though. I lost some good friends. We all did."

Robie nodded slowly. He had been in Afghanistan at the time, killing the Taliban from long range with his sniper skills. The CIA had loaned him out to the DoD to help take the fight to the enemy that had toppled the Towers and viciously struck the Pentagon, using innocent American citizens trapped inside jumbo jets as their weapons of choice. He had killed many during the day and then tried to sleep at night when the temperatures *dropped* to a hundred degrees in the proverbial shade. His tour had lasted longer than he could remember. He had gotten little news from stateside, but the whole world had known about Katrina. From nine thousand miles away he had not checked on the town of Cantrell or his father, though he might have been able to.

He had not done so because at that point in his life he didn't care.

The town and his father were no longer part of who he was. And after killing a dozen people a day himself while sniping in combat, he had grown immune to the effects of widespread death. He didn't like that about himself, but he couldn't deny that it had been how he had felt then. And maybe still did.

"Where were you, Robie?" asked Taggert quietly. "When Katrina came ashore?"

He kept his gaze on the water; the Gulf was very un–Katrina-like now—flat, smooth, like polished aquamarine glass instead of a boiling mass of fury carrying the combined destructive force of a dozen nukes. It was Mother Nature's most powerful punch, the wickedest, most indiscriminate arrow in her quiver.

"I was busy," replied Robie. "A long way away. But I'm glad that Cantrell wasn't hit." He turned to her. "My father lives at the Willows. I met his wife and son."

"Lots of surprises for you."

"How could he afford that place?"

"You really are out of the loop."

"Can you help me get back in it?"

"Why do you want to? Why are you even here—and don't feed me that crap 'bout your daddy bein' in jail accused of murder, 'cause I ain't buyin' it."

Robie started to say something but then stopped. He recalibrated his remark, moving it far closer to the truth than he had initially intended.

"I've come to a point in my life where things that didn't matter to me now do. This is one of them."

When she gazed up at him, he did not look away from her.

She said, "Now that may be the first piece of straight talk to come out your damn mouth since you been here."

He didn't respond to this. He wanted to hear what she had to say.

"Your daddy can afford the Willows 'cause he hit it rich as a lawyer."

"How? His stuff was nickel-and-dime, and he was mostly paid in chickens and vegetables."

"When you were here, yes. But then he represented four families that lost folks in a drillin' platform explosion out in the Gulf. There were safety violations, cost-cuttin', fudged paperwork, guys workin' way too many undocumented hours, the typical corporate make-as-much-money-as-you-can-and-screw-everybody-else bullshit. Facin' all that evidence, they brought in the big legal guns and tried to overwhelm your daddy. Then when that didn't work, the oil company sent in some seriously bad dudes. His office got burned out. His car got shot up. They caught up to him one night and broke his arm, but he laid two of those suckers out. And all that just made your daddy—"

"—fight harder," observed Robie. He could envision his father facing these long odds and relishing the

battle. The oil company had picked the wrong man to intimidate.

His father feared nothing, except maybe a son he had never come close to understanding.

Or perhaps loving.

She said, "Yes sir, he did. Took years, but the families got tens of millions of dollars each and your daddy got his piece. Then he ran for county judge and won."

"When did he marry Victoria?"

"Oh, a little over four years ago."

"How'd they meet? She's not from Mississippi. I knew that when she spoke."

"Well, you're from Mississippi, and you don't sound like it."

"True."

"But the fact is, she's not from here. They met, so's I heard, at a legal convention up north somewhere."

"She's a lawyer?"

"No, don't believe so. Leastways she's never hung out her shingle. But she was at the convention. Love at first sight, way I heard tell."

"From who?"

"From *everybody*, Robie. Your daddy come back with his heart all full of love. All's he could talk about was Victoria this and Victoria that. Not much later they were hitched and he brought her here. They bought the Willows. And then they had Tyler."

"Who doesn't talk?"

"That's right. They've had lots of doctors look at him, but so far nothin'. Maybe he just don't have anythin' to say right now. Maybe when he gets older, he'll never stop talkin'."

"I spoke to Priscilla."

"She's a smart lady, don't miss much."

"She said she knew why Clancy wasn't convicted, but she wouldn't tell me."

"Well, it ain't no big secret. He had an alibi."

"Who?"

"Who do you think?"

"No clue."

"You met her today."

Robie flinched. "Priscilla?"

"No. Your stepma, Victoria."

14

"You want to explain that to me?" said a stunned Robie.

"Pretty simple. She was his alibi on the night that Janet Chisum was murdered."

"If that was the case, why was Clancy even tried?"

"Well, initially there was lots of evidence against him. They were seen together earlier that day. And her body was dumped in the Pearl where it crosses Clancy's land."

"What was the alleged motive?"

"That was the other bit of evidence. Clancy liked his girls young and hot. Chisum fit both criteria. Chisum suddenly had money to buy stuff. They'd been seen together before. It was obvious that Clancy was giving her money. For what? Well, I always had my suspicions."

"You mean he was paying her for sex?"

"Hell yes he was. And he admitted it, too. Now the prosecution figured that Clancy wanted somethin' that Chisum was unwillin' to give, and he got ticked off and he killed her. Probably while he was drunk,

which he pretty much always was after three in the afternoon."

"That doesn't explain the alibi."

"Well, that came later, while the trial was goin' on. Victoria came forward and testified that she was with Clancy from eight that night till six the next mornin'."

Robie stared wide-eyed at her. "You mean she spent the night with him?"

"Well, she said she was with him durin' the night, so I guess one could read it that way."

"Doing what?"

"She said they were just talkin'. And drinkin'. And that that was all."

"Why did she wait so long to come forward?"

"Well, your daddy was a jealous man for one. And he was also the judge in the case. Pretty damn dicey. She was probably scared, but then she decided to come forward 'cause it looked like Clancy was gonna be convicted. Now he was pure scum, but if he was innocent of killin' the gal he shouldn't go to prison for it."

"But if Clancy had been with Victoria, why didn't he tell his lawyers or the police that? Then they would have brought Victoria in for questioning."

"Apparently he did. And they did ask her. And she denied all of it. Then she changed her story and admitted she was with him. They could'a got her for lyin' to the police, but they just dropped it. Figured she'd suffered enough by comin' forward like she did."

"Didn't the prosecution object?"

"Oh, they sure as hell did. Screamed till the cows come home. Thin' is, your daddy had to recuse himself the minute she said she was with Clancy. No way could he still be the judge then."

"I guess not."

"But in the end the new judge let in the testimony. And your stepmother was real good on the stand, though it was clear she didn't want to be there. I watched her. Looked like she was goin' to be sick. The jury believed her, though. And since the police said that Janet Chisum died around two o'clock in the mornin', they found Clancy not guilty." She paused. "And I think some of the jury felt good 'bout givin' it to your daddy like that. His wife? And Clancy? Holy hell!"

"Why would they want to give it to him? Didn't he help families here get compensation from the oil company for what they did?"

"Yes sir. And that very same oil company shut down their platform and upped and left the area. Two hundred men lost their jobs, over half of them from Cantrell. And they were good-payin' jobs, too. Nothin' to replace 'em. Hell, over half those boys are still on the government handout. So you see, your daddy is none too popular in Cantrell, at least with certain folks."

"And so the motivation for his killing Clancy was—"

She finished the sentence for him. "He thought his wife was sleepin' with the man, o'course."

"And was she?"

Taggert shrugged. "Who the hell knows? Sherm is a bigger a-hole than his son. Drunk, sloppy, fat, and crude. All the things your daddy ain't. Why would Victoria want to sleep with hamburger when she's got filet at home? But then again, no tellin' what's in a woman's mind when it comes to men. We women all got that stupid gene from time to time 'round the boys. Maybe that night was hers."

"How did my father react when she came forward?"

"Well, he wasn't exactly happy 'bout it, was he?"

"Did he become violent towards her?"

Taggert studied him. "You mean like he did with you when you was livin' here?"

Robie had never told anyone about the beatings. No one. He looked away.

Taggert said, "Small town, Robie. Folks see stuff. Even if a man hits where it don't show." She paused. "All I can say, and I'm not defendin' or excusin' him for what he did, but it seems to me that the man has changed."

"Good for him. So he didn't become violent? And she's still living at the Willows. And she told me she's been visiting him in jail."

"No, he didn't kick her out. And she *has* been visitin' him. I don't know how your daddy feels 'bout

all this. He don't show his emotions. Sort'a like you. But the fact is Clancy's dead and your daddy has a damn good motive for doin' it."

"Where was he when Victoria was spending the night with Clancy?"

"At a judges' seminar in Jackson."

"What did she do with Tyler?"

"Priscilla lives with 'em. She takes good care'a that boy."

"I understand that Clancy was found in his car with a slit throat? Maybe from a Ka-Bar knife?"

"You heard right. Found in his damn Bentley down near the Pearl River. Not that far from where they pulled Janet Chisum's body out."

"And my father presumably had no alibi?"

"Home alone. Victoria was in Biloxi with Priscilla and Tyler."

"Why were they there?"

"Some medical treatment for the boy."

"Any forensics tying my father to the crime?"

"I can't get into that. Ongoin' case. Shouldn't 'a told you what I did, but I figured you needed to know how things stand. Only fair."

"I appreciate that, but I still don't know why you're helping me. And it's not just because I got out of Cantrell."

"You busted up my eye and I close to broke your nose. I figure that makes us blood somethin's."

"Is that really why?"

"Works for me. So now you in the loop. What you gonna do?"

What am *I going to do?* thought Robie. "I'm going to hang around a few days, see what happens."

"Well, the boys you beat up won't let that lie. They might come back with more boys."

"So do I call the police when they do?"

"You call me." She handed him a card. "Got my personal cell on it. You call 911, I'm not sure you'll get a speedy response."

"Is that how it works here?"

"That's how it works in a lot of places, Robie. Now look, I ain't tellin' you to go out and shoot nobody, but do you know how to use a gun?"

He looked out toward the Gulf. On the horizon all he could see were storm clouds, though the sky was clear.

"I know how to use a gun," said Robie.

15

Robie turned back from the Gulf and said, "Can you show me where Clancy's and Chisum's bodies were found?"

Taggert looked at him sharply. "Why?"

"Just curious. Is that a problem?"

"Not if you don't intend on insertin' yourself into an ongoin' criminal investigation."

"Investigation? Or investigations?"

"Does it matter?"

"It might."

"I'm not talkin' 'bout a connection between the two. There might be. I'm talkin' 'bout you insertin' yourself."

"I do not intend to do that."

She looked at him skeptically. "That's about the most half-ass statement I've ever heard."

"It's the only one I've got, Sheila."

She studied him for one long moment, her gaze like his long-range optics scope, missing nothing. "C'mon then."

She drove them to the end of a gravel road, where they got out of the car.

"Clancy's place is over that way," she said, pointing to her right. "Big-ass place. Behind gates."

"Who lives there now?"

"Just Pete and whatever stupid, drunk gal he's shacking up with for the night."

"But you said the other kids might come calling over Sherm's assets."

"Yep. And I wouldn't be surprised if his second wife didn't show back up, too. They'll be lookin' to suck every last penny they can outta dead Clancy, like buzzards over roadkill."

"So he was found in his Bentley?"

She nodded and led him down a dirt road that twisted and turned deeper into the trees that lined the river.

"Watch where you step," she said. "Snakes out hot'n heavy this time of year."

Robie saw one rattler skirt away through some underbrush and then spotted a puffy moccasin gliding on the smooth, brackish surface of the Pearl as they drew close to the water.

Taggert stopped in a clearing and pointed. "Right over there. Bentley was parked next to that tree. He was inside. Front seat, driver's side. Dead."

"Do you have pictures of the wounds on his neck?"

She put her hands on her hips. "What the hell

part'a not insertin' yourself did you not understand, son?"

"What, because I want to look at crime scene photos?" he said back.

She gazed at him shrewdly. "Your daddy was in the Marines."

"I know he was."

"Purple Heart and Bronze Star in Vietnam. War hero."

"My father never talked about his time over there."

"Sayin' goes, those who did the most talk the least and vice versa. I find that holds true 'bout ninety-nine percent'a the time." She paused. "Point is, Marines teach you how to kill. They teach you how to slit necks clean."

"Is that what the police think?"

She looked away. "You want to see where they pulled out Janet Chisum? Not too far from here."

They got back in her car and drove about a quarter mile farther down a road paralleling the Pearl.

A few minutes' walk through some woods brought them to the spot. Taggert showed him where the body had snagged on the branch of a downed tree.

Robie gazed at the spot and then looked up and down the length of the river, which was fairly narrow at this point.

"The body was probably put in the water upriver, then came down here and hooked on the tree."

"Way we see it, yeah. Forensics showed she'd been

dead about twelve hours when her body was discovered. Gator had taken a nibble on her."

"Have you run a river current analysis to see where she might have gone in the water?"

"How do you know about things like that?" she snapped.

"I watch a lot of crime shows on TV."

"Uh-huh. Matter of fact, we have. With the currents, time she was in the water and so on appears she was put in close to where we found Clancy's body."

"I heard she was killed by a gunshot wound to the head."

"That's right."

"You find the gun?"

"No, but our folks said it was a forty-caliber fired from a Smith & Wesson. And Clancy had one of those, only he said he lost it when we came to collect it for ballistics."

"What was the time period between their deaths?"

"Well, Chisum's was much earlier. Had to be, o'course. Clancy was arrested and went to trial. That don't happen overnight. I'd say 'bout three months, all told."

"How long between his acquittal and his murder?"

"Only five days."

"So it was probably connected."

"One reason your daddy's sittin' in jail for the crime."

"If Clancy didn't kill Chisum, who did?"

"We're followin' that up, Robie, never you mind 'bout that."

"What has my father said to the police?"

She sighed and shook her head. "You lose all your manners when you moved from Cantrell?"

"Can't blame a guy for trying, Sheila. Who's the prosecutor on the case?"

"I guess there's no harm in tellin' you that. Aubrey Davis."

"Aubrey Davis? The one we went to high school with?"

"The same," she said resignedly.

"He was the most arrogant son of a bitch around here mainly because his parents had money and his father was a state legislator."

"I would say he ain't changed a bit. And he's got a thin' for your daddy, let me tell you. Mor'n once he got his nuts handed to him in a courtroom by Judge Robie."

"Why?"

"Let's just say the good prosecutor ain't above cuttin' corners gettin' a conviction. He's got ambition, see. He's a prosecutor now with a run for Congress in his future. All he's got to do is get the nomination and he's as good as punched his ticket to Dee-Cee. Takin' down what some folks see as a judge soft on crime would be a right good sellin' point for his campaign."

"And with that sort of personal animus against my father he's allowed to prosecute him?"

"Hell, there's only two prosecutors in Cantrell and the other one just had a stroke. Leaves Aubrey."

"And my father's lawyer?"

"He don't have one yet."

"But you said his arraignment was tomorrow?"

"At ten o'clock."

"He's been in custody awhile. Why so long before his arraignment?"

"Well, they had to find another judge to preside over it. And they don't grow 'em on trees down here. They're bringin' in a judge from Biloxi to do it. Her schedule just got freed up."

"I intend to be there."

"Along with just about everybody else in Cantrell."

"Anything else you can tell me?"

"Told you too much already. And you forget the insertin' part, Will Robie, you'll find yourself sittin' in a jail cell like your daddy. You hear me?"

"I hear you," replied Robie.

16

Pete Clancy and his buddy had woken up and were gone when Robie returned to Danby's Tavern.

The girl behind the bar wouldn't meet his eye when he walked in. The tavern area was pretty full, and all eyes turned to him when he came through the door. Robie was sure that every person in the room knew exactly what had happened here.

He reached his room and unlocked the door, bracing for what he might find. But his room had been untouched. For now. He didn't intend to give anyone a second shot.

The manager at Danby's had followed him up the stairs.

"I think you need to leave here. Don't want no trouble."

He handed Robie back the cash he had paid for the room.

Robie gave him no argument, because he had already decided to go. He carried his duffel out to the car. He would find another place to stay, preferably outside of town.

He climbed into the driver's seat and slipped his hand under the dashboard. Using Velcro he had brought with him, he had attached a pair of Glock nine-millimeters there. He patted each weapon to make sure it was secured in place and then set off.

The ride to the Willows took about a half hour as he drove along winding macadam, gravel, and sometimes dirt roads to get there.

He reached the house and turned down the pebbled drive, passing under the mingled canopies of the longleaf pines. The sun was heading down now but its glare was still intense, and the tree canopies provided welcome relief. After his fight with Pete Clancy and his walk through the woods with Taggert, his shirt was sticking to his skin. He felt like he was sitting inside a steam shower.

Good old Mississippi.

The Volvo was parked in front of the house. As Robie pulled to a stop next to it and got out, he could see that a table and chairs had been arranged on the porch. Set on the table was a pitcher full of reddish liquid and some glasses. The overhead fans that were aligned along the wraparound porch were whirling away. When Robie stepped up on the planks he could feel the breeze; it wicked away some of the sweat on his face.

The front door opened before he could knock. He expected to see Priscilla there, but it was Victoria. She was wearing a long, colorful sundress and low-heeled

sandals that showed off red toenail polish. A bandana matching her dress was around her head.

"Are you all right?" she asked, looking over his face and body apparently for injuries.

"Who told you about it?"

"Priscilla. Pete Clancy is a bully, just like his father."

"So you know Sherman Clancy?" he asked.

She didn't answer right away, but led him over to the table and poured them out two glasses from the pitcher.

"Sangria," she said. "A wonderful antidote to the heat and humidity. Actually, any alcohol will do."

He took a sip. It tasted both sweet and salty.

Victoria sat down and so did he. He glanced at the window behind them in time to see Priscilla scurry away, with Tyler in her arms.

"Everybody in Cantrell, maybe on the whole Gulf Coast, knows Sherman Clancy. *Knew* Sherman Clancy," she corrected. "He got around, made himself quite ubiquitous."

Robie had pondered on the way over how to approach this. He decided the direct way was preferable.

"And you apparently enjoyed his company at some point."

She took another sip of the sangria, set her glass down, and took a few moments to wipe her mouth with a cloth napkin on the table. She leaned back in the white wicker chair and studied him.

"So I see you've made the rounds of gossip in Cantrell. Busy day for you."

"I've made *some* rounds. But that statement didn't come from gossip. It was from your court testimony. Wasn't it?"

"I spent one drunken night with Sherman Clancy. And no, we did not sleep together. We just drank together. He fell asleep halfway through. I had to keep waking him up."

"Why drink with him at all? You apparently don't think much of him. And while I haven't known you very long, you don't strike me as being, well, that sort."

"If you must know, I had a little problem, and I needed Clancy's help in order to solve it."

"What was that little problem?"

"That is none of your business," she said sharply.

"Did you testify about it in court?"

"No. That was also none of *their* business. They just needed to know that I was with Clancy when Janet Chisum was killed. They didn't need to know why."

"You took a long time to come forward, I understand?"

"Of course I did. It was eating me up inside. My husband was the judge. I would have to testify that I was with another man that night. A man that Dan didn't get along with in the first place. And though I know I didn't sleep with him I was well aware that everyone in Cantrell, and that probably includes my

husband, would assume that Sherman Clancy had screwed my brains out."

"But you *did* come forward?"

"Yes, I did. They were seeking the death penalty against Clancy. I didn't care for the man, but I couldn't let the state of Mississippi execute him for a crime I know he couldn't have committed. I admit that I lied to the police when they initially questioned me about it. But later I knew I had to tell the truth. And the real killer was still out there. If they convicted Clancy, they'd never catch the person who really did it."

Obviously agitated, she drank down her glass of sangria and poured another. "Maybe I should have just kept quiet," she said. "Then Clancy would be in prison and my husband wouldn't be."

"How did my father take the news about you and Clancy?"

"Not well," she said tersely. "He . . . sometimes he doesn't know his own strength."

"So he beat you?"

"I wasn't talking about his physical strength, though he has plenty of that. No, I was talking up here." She tapped her forehead. "He can be quite cruel with words."

Don't I know that, thought Robie. "Do you think he killed Clancy?"

Her look told him that she had expected this question. "I don't want to believe it."

"What does he say?"

"He doesn't say. When I visit him he asks me how Ty is doing. He asks me how I feel. He wants to know what is going on at the Willows. He does not talk about the case against him."

"I need to get in to see him."

"He has to allow it, Will. Otherwise they won't let you in."

"Can you ask him? Tell him I want to see him?"

She hesitated. "Why? What good would it do?"

"I don't know if it will do any good at all. But it's something I have to do."

"I don't know anything about the falling-out you two had. Or why you went away. Dan never talked about it."

"I wouldn't expect that he would."

"And your mother? He never talks about her, either."

"She was as unlike my father as it was possible to be."

"Well, they do say opposites attract."

"But can opposites exist together for the long term?"

"Have you ever been married?"

"No."

"Ever wanted to be?"

Robie didn't answer right away. He was thinking back to a woman he thought he had loved. Right up until the moment he had put a bullet in her head.

"Maybe."

"Well, I wanted to be married to your father from the very first moment I saw him."

"You met at some sort of legal convention?"

She nodded. "I'm not a lawyer. Don't have the mind for it. I was a pharmaceutical rep for years and a very successful one, if I do say so myself. Frankly, I'd flirt with the male doctors and they bought whatever I was selling. I attended some of our national conventions and learned how they were set up and run. Then I started doing event organizing, and my business really took off. Well, when your father walked into that room, my God, he was tall, robust, beautiful white hair, tanned skin. He just commanded the place. All the other judges flocked to Dan Robie. He just had that sort of presence about him." She paused. "I'm sure they all hate me for what's happened. My jealous husband kills my alleged lover."

"Is that how you see it?"

"Doesn't matter what I think. It's what everyone else thinks. That's reality."

"Will you tell him I need to talk to him?"

She lifted her gaze to his. "If you really want me to, I will."

"Thank you."

"Don't thank me yet. He might refuse. And if he does agree to see you, it might be even worse."

"How do you figure?"

"Because you'll be stuck smack in the middle of this mess. Shall we go in to supper?"

17

The dinner was finely cooked and graciously served by both Priscilla and Victoria. Chicken-fried steak, green beans with salted pork, fat roasted tomatoes, seasoned squash, soft-as-butter bread, and banana pudding with a cinnamon crust for dessert.

Robie finally put his fork down and said, "One of the best meals I've ever had. Thank you."

Victoria looked pleased by his compliment. "It was a joint effort between Priscilla and me. She does all the foundation work and I add a bit here and there as the finish. The woman *can* cook. All I have to do is try to keep the fat and sodium levels down. The state of Mississippi is not exactly known for healthy eating."

"But you get to die happy then," interjected Priscilla as she walked in and started clearing the table. "I put Ty in bed, Ms. Victoria, if you want to go up and say good night. Boy won't go to sleep till you kiss 'im on the head."

Robie followed her up the stairs. He expected that his father had fallen for Victoria quite as fast as she had for him. Robie's mother had been petite and

124

pretty, and in her son's eyes, nothing less than perfect, right up until the moment she had abandoned him. But Victoria's beauty was exceptional. He wondered, and not for the first time, whether she had allowed herself to be bedded by Sherman Clancy. And if so, why? Was all not right in her marriage?

Tyler was sitting up in bed waiting for his mother. When he saw Robie, his expression changed slightly. It was not a fearful one, just curious. While still staring at Robie he reached out his arms for his mother. She sat down on the bed and swallowed the little boy up in her arms.

She put Tyler on her lap and pointed at Robie. "Ty, this is Will. He's family. Your brother. Your big brother."

Robie could see the little boy mouth the word *brother*, but no sound came out. But then he touched his chest and pointed at Robie. Robie didn't understand, and looked at Victoria.

"It's his way of saying he loves you," said Victoria. She placed her hand on her son's chest. "He knows his heart is right there."

Robie nodded and slowly put his hand on his chest and pointed at Tyler.

The boy immediately broke out into an enormous smile that managed to cut right through Robie's normally hardened shell. Robie felt his mouth edge upward into a reciprocating grin.

He had never had a brother or any siblings at all. It had been just him for so long now. It was a bit

overwhelming to realize that he had another "family" he never knew existed until he'd come back to Cantrell.

Victoria laid Tyler back in the bed and covered him with a sheet before kissing him on the forehead. "You have yourself a fine sleep, Ty Robie, okay?"

He nodded, ran his small fingers up and down her cheek, and then turned on his side and closed his eyes.

When Victoria rose from the bed Robie could see a tear sliding down her face. She brushed it away and said, "I'm going to have a glass of port to finish off the meal. Care to join me?"

She didn't wait for an answer. Robie followed her downstairs, where she snatched two glasses and a bottle of tawny port off a sideboard before heading out to the back verandah.

They sat in hanging wicker chairs, drank their port, and looked out onto the rear grounds. The water from the pool shimmered under the moonlight. The briny smell of the Gulf, mixed with the chlorine from the pool, filled Robie's nostrils. His eyes came to rest on the spot where he had last held Laura Barksdale.

He turned to Victoria. "Who did you buy the Willows from? Was it the Barksdales?"

"No, at least I don't believe so. Dan handled all that. I remember he brought me here one day before our wedding and wanted to know if I cared to live here." She smiled. "I mean, what woman wouldn't? It's beautiful. We put in the pool and spruced up the grounds

and did some interior remodeling, especially with the kitchen, but the place had the most wonderful bones."

"I knew the Barksdales. Are they still around?"

"Not that I know of. Dan never mentioned them. But if they were a prominent family I'm sure somebody here knows. Were they a nice family?"

"Yes," said Robie. He took a sip of his port. "There was a daughter, Laura, who was very special."

He turned to see Victoria's gaze on him. "Special to you?"

"Back then, yes."

"What happened?"

"People make different choices. Go different ways."

Victoria sighed, kicked off her sandals, and drew her legs up under her. "Yes they do."

"How did the doctor's appointment go?"

"Not all that well. No breakthroughs or anything like that."

"Are they sure it's not a physical thing?"

"Yes. He has all the anatomical equipment necessary to speak."

"Could he be autistic?"

"It's possible. We've had him checked for that, of course, but there are so many different forms on the spectrum I don't think the doctors can keep them all straight. And they're making new discoveries every day in the field. Right now, they're just puzzled."

"He seems intelligent and aware of things."

"He is. He's perfectly normal except he doesn't

talk." She paused, took a sip of port and said, "Our having Ty wasn't exactly planned. Frankly, I'm a little old to be having kids, but it just happened. I think your father wasn't too keen when we found out we were going to have a baby. But let me tell you, when Ty was born that man scooped him up in his arms and I don't think he ever wanted to let him go. There's something special about watching a big, strong man be so gentle with a baby, like they're afraid they'll break it if they're not careful. Your father loves that little boy." She added wistfully, "Sometimes I think he loves Ty more than he loves me. Maybe that's a good thing, I don't know."

Robie searched around for something to say to change the direction of the conversation. "I guess it's good that Ty is so young. He can't really understand what's going on with his father."

"He understands more than people think. He may not be able to communicate in a conventional way, but that boy sees everything. And he *feels* things, too. Senses if folks are sad."

"Like you are now?"

"Like I am now, yes."

"His arraignment is tomorrow morning at ten. I assume you're going?"

She looked unsure.

"Victoria?"

"I haven't decided. I know it'll look bad if I'm not there. But because I provided Clancy his alibi and the

rumor mill is going strong that I slept with the man, folks might think it's all disingenuous."

"I still think you should be there."

"Even if your father doesn't want me to be?"

"Did he say that?"

"Sometimes it's what people *don't* say that's the most important."

"Well, I plan to be there."

"I'm sure you do."

"And I'm not leaving here until I get to talk to him."

"Then I hope you're prepared to be here a long time, because he is one stubborn son of a bitch."

"In that regard I am my father's son."

"Where are you staying?"

"I was at Danby's Tavern, but after my little run-in with Pete Clancy and his buddies, I was asked to leave."

She put her bare feet on the planks. "Then you're going to stay here."

"Victoria, you don't have—"

"Don't give me any back talk, Will Robie. This is your father's home, which means it's your home, too. I'll have Priscilla get one of the guest rooms ready. It's not like we don't have the space. And what's southern hospitality if I can't offer my stepson a roof over his head?"

She went inside to talk to Priscilla.

Robie continued to sit in his swing seat, staring out

at a darkness that he was coming to understand might hold more uncertainty for him than any of his missions around the world ever had.

So much for coming home.

18

It was the darkest point of the night immediately before the growing lightness in the eastern sky.

Robie rose from his bed in his comfortable guest room on the second floor of the Willows, slipped on his jeans, and padded out onto the rear upper-story verandah. There was a breeze that carried the salt air of the Gulf to the south and mixed it with that of the freshwater Pearl from the west. The comingled smells had been natural ones for Robie growing up. Indeed, he could hardly remember a morning here when he had not been greeted by that confluence of sea and river air.

Robie was a man well used to seeing everything around him, even if some things (and people) did their best to remain unseen. The slight movement to the left of the rear of the house immediately caught his attention. There was wildlife here, to be sure. But wildlife never walked upright on two feet.

It was a man.

Robie's gun was under his pillow. He retrieved it, placed it in the back of his waistband, and clambered

down the verandah column, alighting softly on the ground.

He squatted down, his eyes roaming from the point where he had last seen the movement and then to the left and right. He didn't pick up on it again. And he heard no noise after that, neither feet running nor a car starting up.

He stood and tried to reconstruct what he had seen in his head.

Male. Six feet tall or maybe taller. Dark hair, dark clothing. Face partially obscured. About two hundred pounds.

It could have been Pete Clancy, who was around that size. He might have figured that Robie would be staying here after getting kicked out of Danby's. It was a small town. Everyone knew everyone else's business.

But had he come here on foot? Doubtful. It was a long walk from anywhere. But he'd heard no car start up. A bike? In the silence of the night he would have heard the wheels on the pebbled drive.

He hustled to the front of the house. His rental and the Volvo were parked there. He checked the Volvo. The doors were unlocked. He opened it and peered inside.

It had been searched. Things were strewn all over the place. He tidied up the mess and closed the door.

He looked at his car. It was still locked. It also had an alarm. He would have known if someone had tried to break in.

He turned to look back at the house. There was a light on in an upper window. He watched as she passed back and forth in front of it.

His stepmother was up early. Perhaps to check on Ty? Or was it something else? Did it have something to do with the guy in the bushes?

He reversed his path, clambered up the column to the second floor, and reentered his room. He checked his watch. Nearly five a.m. It would be an hour later in DC. He picked up his phone and made the call.

Blue Man said, "I was surprised you hadn't communicated yet."

Robie told him what he had learned thus far. "Is there any way you can get me more information on what the police know? Autopsy report on Clancy? Anything on Janet Chisum? Stuff they have on my father? Anything else at all?"

"That would of course breach all professional decorum. On top of that we do not operate domestically."

"And I have two heads. Can you?"

"I'll see what we can find out. In the meantime, keep your *only* head down and watch your back. The last thing I need is for you to get killed down there."

"I recall you being the one who suggested that I come here."

"Still, watch your six."

"Jessica?" he asked.

"Still out."

Robie put his phone down and listened as feet padded down the hall. He rose and opened his door in time to see Victoria open her bedroom door. Her room was next to his. She had on a bathrobe that ended mid-thigh. Her long legs were pale and her feet bare.

"Everything okay?" Robie asked.

"Ty was restless. Are you okay? It's still pretty early."

"Just adjusting to the time zone." He thought of telling Victoria about the man in the bushes and that her car had been searched, but then decided against it. He needed to think that through a little more. And he didn't want to alarm her unnecessarily.

She said, "Okay, I'm going to catch a little more sleep. I'll see you later."

He went back to his room and sat on the bed.

Victoria was right about one thing. It was still early. And he had time before the arraignment. He dressed, left the house, got in his car, and drove off.

19

The dust from the roads kicked up and swirled around the windows of Robie's car as he drove along. The sun was starting to rise and burn off the fog that had lifted from the warmer ground. He passed the spot where Clancy and his slit neck had been found in his Bentley and continued on.

Using the general directions Taggert had given him earlier, he reached Clancy's place about three minutes later. It was unmistakably the man's residence because, as Taggert had said, it was big-ass and behind gates. He figured this was the only big-ass place behind gates in all of Cantrell.

Only the gates were open. Robie parked his car across the road and behind some bushes before slipping through the entrance and heading up the drive to the house.

The mansion was a jumble of stone and siding with slanted bricks thrown in apparently for good, architectural measure. He eyeballed it at about twelve thousand square feet, rising up three full stories to the sky.

The house looked dark from here. There was one car parked in front. A Porsche with plates that read: PETE.

Well, Sherman Clancy's son certainly wasn't subtle, which wasn't surprising. Robie had seen this very same car parked in front of Danby's when Pete and his boys had tried to jump him.

As he passed the Porsche he felt the rear hood where the engine was located.

It was cold to the touch. If Pete had been the one lurking in the bushes at the Willows, it was doubtful he had driven there and back here in his sports car.

He took a minute to walk the perimeter of the property and came away with the conclusion that the estate, while obviously initially costing a ton of money, was in seriously bad shape. The grass was high and struck liberally through with weeds. The pool and numerous fountains on the property were in poor shape and dirty. The wood siding was chipped and peeling, and the stone steps and pavers were uneven and in numerous places crumbling. The air of neglect was evident in the outbuildings as well, including the five-car garage. One of the rollup doors was off its tracks, and three of the five inside bays were filled with garbage and piles of junk resting next to the Bentley and a dark blue Range Rover.

Robie stepped inside the garage and walked over to the Bentley. The engine was cool to the touch. He checked the Range Rover with the same result.

He went back to the Bentley. It was unlocked. He opened the driver's-side door and looked around the interior. There was nothing much there, although faded red splotches on the front seatback were probably blood. The jugular and carotid arteries were superhighways of blood circulation. The entire front interior of the Bentley had probably been doused until the heart stopped pumping after Clancy had rapidly bled out and died.

A sound from nearby made him crouch down and then scuttle over to the open garage bay door. He peered out, well aware that he was trespassing and that Pete Clancy would well be within his rights to shoot him. Robie did not intend to give the punk the opportunity.

Clancy stumbled out of the back door, a beer bottle in one hand and a cigarette in the other. With a bit of satisfaction, Robie could see that the man's nose was bandaged, and that he moved with a limp from the kidney punch. Clancy looked around, took a deep breath, turned to the side, and threw up on the back steps.

He plopped down, finished his beer, flicked away his cigarette, and then lay back. A minute later Robie could hear the man snoring.

Robie retraced his steps and was soon back at his car. He drove off as the dawn broke cleanly. He doubted Pete was the man in the bushes. He'd obviously been drunk and here all this time.

He had one more place to visit.

A few minutes later he had wended his way down the dirt road and pulled to a stop. He first eyed the place where the Bentley had been parked near the Pearl River. Then, when he continued to gaze around, he saw it, leaning against a tree.

An old bike. He got out of his car, walked over to it, and looked around. And listened.

He thought he could hear footsteps moving through the trees.

He followed the sounds into the woods. A few minutes later he cleared the trees and reached another open space. A moment later, and for the second time this morning, he glimpsed movement. But this time he didn't lose track of it.

It was a young woman, very young. She could barely be eighteen.

When she looked over and saw him, she gave a little cry of panic.

He held up his hand. "I didn't mean to startle you. I'm sorry." He made no move toward her.

"Who are you?" she gasped. "What are you doing here?"

"My name is Will Robie. And I might be here for the same reason you are. To see where Sherman Clancy was killed."

She was petite with strawberry blonde hair and an upturned nose sprinkled with freckles. She had on loose-fitting jeans, sneakers, and a tight pink T-shirt

that emphasized her large breasts. There was a leather bag slung over her shoulder.

"I'm not here because of that jerk!" she exclaimed.

"Why then?"

"Wait a minute. Robie? Are you related to—"

"He's my father."

"Well, he did us all a good service by killin' that bastard."

"*If* he killed him. But why do you say that?"

"I'm Sara Chisum. Janet was my older sister."

"I'm sorry," said Robie. "But then I don't understand why you're here. Back there on the dirt road is where they found Clancy's body in his car."

She looked around, her face twisted in confusion. "I . . . I didn't know that. This spot was where Janet and me would come."

Robie leaned against a tree and folded his arms over his chest. "Why would you come here?"

Sara Chisum looked uncertain for a moment. The next second she stared defiantly at him and said, "What the hell business is it of yours?"

Robie said, "I was young once. And I had spots along the Pearl where I came to drink beer. And do other . . . *things*."

This assessment seemed to take all the fight out of the young woman. She plunked down on a fallen tree. "We'd smoke some weed, too. Not something our parents would understand. But there's just nothin' to do around here. I hate it."

"Why'd your family move here?"

"Work. For my dad."

"What's he do?"

She looked nervously at her shoes. "He's the preacher over at the Jerusalem Baptist Church. We came from Mobile. He ... he doesn't know about what we do here. Or *did* here," she added hastily, her lips quivering.

"Your secret is safe with me."

She looked at him curiously. "You're not from around here?"

"No, but I was." He paused, choosing his next words carefully. "They say your sister spent time with Clancy?"

He thought she might get angry again, but she didn't. She just kept looking down at her shoes, even as her hand slipped into her bag and pulled out a can of Coors Light. She popped the top and took a swig.

"He gave her money." She looked up. "He gave me money, too."

"So he liked giving people money?"

She nodded. "But not for nothin'," she said slowly. "No, not for nothin'. We had to do stuff for him." She said in a small voice. "*To* him."

"Did your parents know about any of that?"

"They didn't till that stuff about Janet came out in the trial. I had to testify. Like to kill my daddy. Then they didn't even convict the bastard."

"Because he had an alibi."

She took another sip of beer and held it up. "You want some?"

"No thanks."

"Right, he had an alibi." She looked at him accusingly. "Your daddy's wife gave it to him. She was with him the night Janet was killed. That's what she said."

"And if she was, that means someone else killed your sister. Any idea who that might have been?"

"I . . . I couldn't say nothin' 'bout that."

"I didn't ask you if you *could*. I asked if you had any ideas." She didn't answer him, and Robie waited a few moments before adding, "I know you want your sister's killer to pay for what he did."

"Of course I do!" she snapped.

"Have the police talked to you about it?"

"Not yet. But I guess they will. I guess they're sort'a focusin' on your daddy for killin' Clancy. Police department ain't that big, I reckon."

"You have another sister, don't you?"

"Emma. But she's only thirteen. She don't know nothin'."

"Have you talked to her about it?"

"She don't know nothin', okay!"

He put up his hands in mock surrender. "Okay."

Robie made a mental note to check out what Emma Chisum might actually know.

"I gotta go," said Sara.

"Do you live close by? I guess that's your bike back there, but I can give you a ride."

"No thanks. It's not that far." She eyed him suspiciously. "And I don't know you from Adam."

"Well, I'll let you get on." He turned to leave but then said, "If you think of anything, you should tell Deputy Taggert. She'll be able to help you."

"I already done told you, I don't know nothin' 'bout nothin'."

"Memories are a funny thing. Sometimes you know more than you think you do."

He pulled out a piece of paper and a pen and wrote his phone number down on it. He passed it over to her. "Just in case."

She took the paper and stuffed it in her pocket.

He walked back through the woods to his car and then waited until she passed by him on her bike before driving off.

20

Robie headed back to the Willows, showered, and changed his clothes. As he was heading downstairs Victoria came out of Tyler's room, carrying the little boy. She was still wearing her robe.

"Are you heading out already?" she said in surprise. "It's early yet."

"I thought I'd get into town, have some coffee, and get over to the courthouse. I doubt there'll be many seats left." He studied her. "You decided whether to go or not?"

"Not yet," she admitted, averting her gaze and taking the opportunity to rub a smudge of dirt off Tyler's cheek. "Priscilla can make you some breakfast."

"That's okay. I'm good."

He headed out to his car, got in, and started it up. He glanced at the house and saw Victoria and Tyler staring at him from an upstairs window and Priscilla doing the same from a lower one.

He drove into town, found a diner, sat at the counter where he had two cups of coffee and a bowl of buttery grits and a fat biscuit, and checked his

messages. Nothing from Blue Man, but Robie had asked him to look into things only a few hours ago. And even Blue Man needed a little bit of time to work his magic.

He gazed around at the others in the diner. Every eye had ventured to him when he walked in, and most were still casting him furtive, curious glances. The folks were more diverse than Robie would have thought— whites, blacks, and a sprinkling of Latinos. Most were men. All but a handful of them were dressed in work clothes. Those in suits, Robie assumed, might have something to do over at the courthouse, or maybe labored in a bank or a medical practice.

He didn't see Pete Clancy and his buddies, which was a good thing. They might bring a gun to the next fight and Robie had left his in the car, since he was going to the courthouse later.

One of the gents in a suit rose from a table in the back. Robie watched him in the mirror hung on the rear wall of the diner as he made his way slowly toward the counter. He was about five-ten and flabby, with his short, grayish-brown hair precisely parted and cemented down with hair spray. His suit was a three-piece seersucker with a bright red tie over his starched collared white shirt, which made it look like his chest had been slashed open. He stopped along the way to pat backs, shake hands, and chitchat with the other folks there. Not many looked happy to be pressing the flesh with the man.

When he came to a stop next to Robie and put a hand on his shoulder, Robie knew who it was. In fact he had known who it was from the man's swaggering walk. It hadn't changed since high school.

"Hello, Aubrey," he said.

"Damn, Will, sight for sore eyes, man, sight for sooorrre eyes," replied Aubrey Davis, his twangy speech so exaggerated that Robie felt sure the man was doing it in front of the locals simply to increase his potential vote count when he ran for Congress.

He sat on the stool next to Robie and unbuttoned his jacket. He flicked a finger at the waitress, and a few moments later a cup of black coffee was set in front of him.

"Thank you, darlin'," said Davis before turning sideways on his stool and eyeing Robie.

"What the hell you been doin' with yourself, Will?"

"This and that."

"You got outta here right after high school, didn't you?"

"Something like that."

"Guess you know what I do for a livin'," Davis said, not really trying to sound modest.

"I heard."

"And I guess it's no secret why you're back here. Sad day for the Robie family. Sad day. I'll be the first to say it."

Robie sipped his coffee and stared straight ahead. "I guess that depends on how it turns out."

"O'course, o'course. Justice will have its day and say, yes sir it will. Leastways while I'm the prosecutor for Cantrell, Mississippi."

"Must be difficult for you to do this, I mean with a judge you've appeared in front of so many times. Hope you don't feel *conflicted*."

Davis smiled though it didn't reach his eyes. He took a moment to light up an unfiltered Marlboro he pulled from a pack in his side pocket along with a metal lighter with the initials AD engraved on it. He blew smoke out of his nostrils and dropped his ash in the cup saucer. "Well, damn good thing I've always been able to see the big picture. Petty shit don't influence me one bit. Now I take no pleasure in prosecutin' your daddy, I'm sure you know that. But it is my job and I'll carry my duty out faithfully." He waved his hand at the other folks in the diner. "Hell, it's what all these voters here who placed me in this honored position would expect." He rapped his knuckles against the countertop. "And nothin' less."

"You going to let him out on bail?"

"Can't get into that with you, o'course. But I'm a fair man, always have been." He blew more smoke and tapped more ash. "You seen your daddy yet?"

Something in Davis's voice told Robie that he knew his father had refused to see him at the jail.

"I'll see him today."

Davis's shrill voice dropped an octave as though to evidence confidentiality. And sincere concern. "How's

your stepmomma holdin' up? Heard you were stayin' out there with her, and ain't that fine. I'm sure your support is . . . appreciated."

The network here is faster than the Internet, thought Robie.

"She's holding up."

"Uh-huh. She's a damn good-lookin' woman. Everybody knows that. I been married 'bout fifteen happy years but I got me two good eyes, don't I?" He laughed and then grew serious. "My point is, if things go against your daddy, and I'm not sayin' they will, but if they do, she'll be okay. Still young and all. Find somebody else." He dropped his voice lower and leaned in closer to Robie. "But let me just voice a concern I got me." He paused and cleared his throat. "Now she's just got to be better at who she spends time with." He scrunched up his face like he'd swallowed something foul. "Sherm Clancy? Now, I got to prosecute his killer to the fullest extent of the law o'course and I will. But that don't mean I had to like him, 'cause I didn't. Poor choice for Victoria. Poor choice. You might want to talk to her 'bout that. Know it drove your daddy—" He paused and sighed heavily. "Well, we seen what it did to him. So sad. So damn sad, and I don't normally cuss. Hell, I'm a deacon at the Baptist church." He tapped Robie on the shoulder and said in a conspiratorial tone, "Now speakin'a Clancy, I heard tell you had you a run-in with Pete and some'a his boys. Now don't you worry

'bout that. I know Pete. He can be a little hotheaded. But he comes to me 'bout prosecutin' you for assault, you just leave it to me. I'll handle it."

Robie noted that the lawyer didn't say *how* he would handle it.

Davis straightened on his stool and smoked down his cigarette, looking pleased with his soliloquy.

Robie just drank his coffee, figuring any response he made would simply prolong this encounter. Lawyers were really good at taking your words, twisting them around, and firing them back at you. Robie used bullets to kill. This man used nouns, verbs, and the occasional adjective to do the same.

"So how long you stayin' in our fair town, Will?"

"Long as I need to."

"Well, we do things right fast down here. Could'a done that O. J. Simpson case in two days, so help me God. So's you won't have to wait too long, I reckon."

"That's good to know, so long as you don't leave justice out of the equation."

More smoke was exhaled and more ash tapped. Davis grinned. "Remember that state championship?"

"Not until I came back here."

"We did the town proud, didn't we?"

Davis had been a third-stringer on the team and saw action only in the final few minutes of the championship game. Cantrell had been so far ahead that the coach had seen fit to give everyone who hadn't played a chance to share in the glory. And Robie

hadn't minded. Despite the lopsided score, the game had been hard fought, and his body had been a mass of bruises and contusions. And he later learned he'd played the second half with a concussion and a broken thumb.

"Yes we did."

"Old Billy Faulconer ain't doin' too good. You 'member him?"

"Best left tackle in the state. I plan on seeing him while I'm here."

"Fine, fine!" Davis stubbed out his cigarette and rose. "You have a good day, Will. Let's have a drink sometime, okay? Got me a homegrown whiskey put hair on your eyeballs, man."

He laughed and slapped Robie on the back far harder than he had to and walked out of the diner, waving and smiling at all he passed.

Robie set his cup down, paid his bill, and walked out behind him.

He didn't give a crap about Davis's taunts.

He was focused on one thing only.

In a very short while he was going to see his father for the first time in twenty-two years.

And that suddenly scared him more than possibly anything ever had.

And for Will Robie, that was definitely saying something.

21

The courtroom was small, plainly furnished, warm as an oven but still buzzing with suppressed excitement. Robie's intuition that seats would be hard to come by had proven correct. The place was almost full by the time he stepped inside, nearly a half hour before the arraignment was scheduled to take place.

He wedged himself into a seat on the aisle near the middle of the courtroom. After he sat his gaze swept the space. Pete Clancy was here minus his entourage. He had cleaned up his face and his bandages were gone. But the beating Robie had given him was still quite evident.

Sheila Taggert, in her uniform, stood near a door leading into what Robie assumed must be the holding cell for prisoners waiting their turn before the judge.

Little Bill Faulconer was sitting across the aisle from Robie. He motioned for him to join him.

Faulconer made room and Robie settled down next to him.

Robie said, "I plan to visit your dad today if he's up to it."

"He'll be real glad to hear that, Mr. Robie. I'll be sure to let him know."

Robie looked around at some of the people. "Is any of the other Clancy family here?"

Faulconer pointed at a group near the front. "His three boys and one daughter from his marriage before. And damn if his two exes ain't sitting right next to each other."

Robie took in the four grown children, who all looked miserable. Then his gaze fell on the two women. One was Sherman Clancy's age. She must be Cassandra Clancy, deduced Robie. The other was about twenty years younger.

The bimbo.

"I'm surprised they're sitting together," said Robie.

"Well with Sherm gone it's all about the money, ain't it? They probably figger it's better to work together than fight it out and let the lawyers get it all."

"You're probably right."

Little Bill grinned. "But if it does get ugly over the dollars, we might have another murder trial on our hands, too."

Robie spotted Sara Chisum sitting with another group of people, a man and woman who were probably her parents. The younger girl next to Sara was no doubt her remaining sister, Emma.

Little Bill confirmed that this was indeed correct when Robie asked him.

"I've listened to Chisum's sermons," said Little Bill. "And I walked out feelin' like I'm on a straight line to Hell no matter what I do while I'm still drawin' breath."

Mr. Chisum was dressed in black with a white shirt. He did have a stern, pious look to him, thought Robie. His wife was small and mousey, and while her husband simply looked angry, her flickering gazes showed a woman utterly defeated in body and spirit. Sara looked at the back of the person in front of her. Her sister Emma kept her gaze on her lap.

Twenty minutes later Aubrey Davis made his appearance. He walked in with the same swagger he had shown in the diner. He carried a bulky briefcase and set it down next to the counsel table. He turned and put his hands on the railing separating the audience from this section of the courtroom and surveyed the crowd. As they all stared back at him, Robie could easily tell, from the man's satisfied look, that Davis was enjoying every second of this spotlight.

Davis sat down at the table, opened his briefcase, took out some papers, and started riffling through them, looking both focused and important.

Robie glanced over to see Pete Clancy shooting daggers at him. The young man lifted his hand, pointed his index finger at Robie, and, using his thumb as an imaginary gun hammer, shot Robie in the head.

Unconcerned, Robie looked away. From what he had seen of the man, he doubted Clancy could hit anything farther than a foot away, with either gun or fist.

He next saw Sara Chisum staring at him. Her look was worried and somewhat pleading. Robie guessed that she was fearful that what she had told him would end up as public knowledge. He inclined his head slightly at her, trying to be reassuring. As he lifted it back up her father was staring dead at him. He looked from Sara to Robie and then at his daughter once more. He said something to her. She went pale and immediately looked down.

Mr. Chisum turned back to Robie and gave him an expression that was, politely put, uncharitable, particularly given he was a man of the cloth.

Robie looked away when Taggert opened the door she was standing guard by, and there he was.

Dan Robie was dressed in an orange prison jumpsuit, the same outfit he had no doubt seen other prisoners wear many times in his courtroom. His white hair was neatly combed, his chin shaved, his physique still formidable, and his posture bolt upright, even as he shuffled along in the shiny shackles binding his waist, hands, and feet.

Taggert and another uniform escorted Robie to the counsel table, unshackled him, and he sat there alone. He had on a pair of wire-rimmed glasses. His

hands were tanned, big, veiny, and balled into fists as he rested them on the worn wood of the table.

Robie watched as Davis cocked his head and glanced at the man he would shortly be prosecuting across the width of the space between the tables.

Robie could not see Davis's expression but supposed it was one of barely contained glee.

Taggert looked at her watch, took a step back, and announced, "All rise for the Honorable Judith Benson."

They all did as the back door to the courtroom opened and out stepped a woman, tall and big shouldered, with short, graying hair. She had on thick glasses and carried herself with assuredness as she climbed the steps to the raised bench and sank down in her chair.

"Be seated," said Taggert as soon as the woman's butt had hit the leather.

"Call the case, please," said Benson, her tone no-nonsense.

Taggert picked up a clipboard and called out, "State of Mississippi versus Daniel Robie. Charged with murder in the first degree for the willful killing of Sherman Clancy. This here is the arraignment hearing."

She put the clipboard down and stepped back.

Judge Benson ran her gaze first over the courtroom and then she eyed Davis and then Dan Robie. She came away puzzled.

"Does the defendant not have counsel?" she asked.

Davis rose. "Your Honor, over the state's heated objections, defendant has waived the right to counsel and desires to represent himself."

Benson did not look pleased by this. Her gaze swiveled to Dan Robie.

"Mr. Robie, you understand that the charges leveled against you could result in your imprisonment for the remainder of your life or even bein' put to death?"

Robie stood. "I do."

"And with that in mind you still do not desire counsel?"

"I believe that I am my own best counsel, Your Honor."

"I have no doubts as to your legal abilities, but I want you to understand that I strongly recommend that you seek independent legal counsel. As you well know if you cannot afford one, counsel will be appointed for you."

"I understand that, but I stand by my decision."

"We will revisit this question, Mr. Robie, at a later date. How do you plead, sir?"

"Not guilty," Robie said immediately.

She turned to Davis.

"Counsel?"

Davis strode out in front of the table to let everyone get a better look at him. Hands in his pockets he said, "Your Honor, everybody hereabouts knows Dan

Robie. He's been a member of the Mississippi bar for a long time. And as you well know, for many a year he sat in the very seat you are now currently occupyin'."

Benson looked annoyed. "We can forgo the history lesson, Mr. Davis. We are only here for an arraignment. Defendant has pleaded not guilty. Let me hear your position on bail."

"We request that no bail be set, Your Honor. Instead we ask that the defendant be remanded into the custody of the Cantrell jail until his trial."

She looked askance at him. "I realize that the charge is a serious one, but do I understand that you're not proposin' any bail whatsoever?"

"No, Your Honor, we are not."

She looked at Dan Robie.

"Mr. Robie, you care to respond?"

Robie cleared his throat and said, "I've lived in Cantrell for the better part of my life, Your Honor. I have substantial ties here. My wife and young child are here. I own a home here, and I have a job here. I have no criminal history whatsoever. I've never even been cited for speedin'. I do not represent a flight risk and thus I argue that reasonable bail is appropriate and should be set, regardless of the seriousness of the charges, to which I have, this day, emphatically pleaded not guilty."

"Mr. Davis?" said Benson. "Care to rebut that?"

"I agree on all points with the defendant, Your Honor. Perhaps I did not explain myself adequately."

"Apparently you did not," said Benson in a chiding tone.

"I do not necessarily consider the defendant a flight risk. But it has come to our attention that it would be safer for the defendant to remain in jail pendin' his trial."

Benson hiked her eyebrows. "Safer? Can you explain that?"

"To come to the point, Your Honor, we have received threats against the defendant's life." He pulled some pieces of paper from his briefcase and asked permission to approach the bench. It was granted and he showed her the pages.

She read over them slowly and then handed them back.

"You consider these credible?"

"We do."

"You understand that simply because the defendant has been threatened does not necessarily mean he should be kept locked up? The state does have a duty to protect him from such illegal threats regardless of the charges against him."

"Of course we do, Your Honor, but we must be practical, too. We're not a big city with lots of deputies available to watch over the defendant twenty-four hours a day. I sincerely want him to remain safe so that he may be tried for the crimes he's charged with. And I don't want his bein' free on bail to serve as an incitement for others to commit the very same act

with which he's charged. I hope you can understand my dilemma."

Benson looked uncertain for the first time. She glanced at Dan Robie.

"Mr. Robie, do you have anything else to say?"

"Only that I can take care of myself, Your Honor. And anyone seekin' to harm me or those connected to me would do well to rethink such action because it *will* end in a way other than what they intend."

As he said this Dan Robie turned and looked over the entire courtroom.

When his gaze hit upon his son he stopped, but only for an instant. Then he kept going and turned back around.

Benson nodded. "I will take the arguments under consideration. Until such time as I render a decision the defendant will be remanded into the custody of the State of Mississippi."

She smacked her gavel, rose, and left the way she came in, not even giving Taggert a chance to say "All rise."

Dan Robie was being removed from the courtroom right at the moment that the main door opened and Victoria appeared there. She was dressed all in black, with a skirt that hit right at her knees. Her high-heeled shoes matched the color of her clothes.

All heads turned to her, including Dan Robie's.

Husband and wife locked gazes for a moment and

then he turned and was led away. The door closed behind him.

Davis stuffed his papers back in his briefcase, then turned and glanced at Victoria, who still stood framed in the doorway, looking surprised that the hearing was already concluded.

Davis flicked a gaze at Robie and smiled.

Right before folks got up and started heading out, Victoria fled.

As everyone quickly filed out, Davis came up to Robie.

"Well, that was interestin'," said Cantrell's sole remaining prosecutor.

"What credible threats?" asked Robie.

"Can't really say. We're investigatin' them, o'course. But I think your daddy will be a lot safer in jail than out."

"He should have a lawyer," said Robie. His mind, though, was on the expression in his father's eyes when he had seen his son. It had not been what Robie had expected.

Indifference.

It was more painful to him than anger would have been. And here he had convinced himself that he didn't care what his father felt toward him.

Davis said, "I'm not disagreein' with you. He sure as hell needs a lawyer. Right now he's got a fool for one, if you believe the old adage. Which I happen to. You got any influence, you should talk him into hirin' one.

Sure as hell got the money for it. Now I'll be seein' you. And let's not forget 'bout that drink sometime, man."

Davis walked off, leaving Robie alone in the court-room.

22

Based on the man's threatening gesture in the court-room, Robie had thought that Pete Clancy and a group of his cronies would be waiting for him outside.

He wasn't.

But someone else was.

Sara Chisum's father was leaning against the hand-rail on the courthouse front steps.

He pushed off when Robie appeared at the door-way.

"I'm Lester Chisum," he said, holding out his hand. The men shook. "I understand that you're Will Robie, Judge Robie's son."

"I am."

"As a man of God I can't condone what he did."

"Allegedly did," said Robie.

"Allegedly did. But as a father I can't say I'm un-happy."

"But it's clear now that Sherman Clancy didn't murder your daughter," countered Robie.

"Is it?"

Robie looked at him curiously. "He has an alibi."

"And people lie all the time, Mr. Robie. I see it in my work. Humans are frail. They seek the easy way out too often. Lyin' as opposed to tellin' the truth. Tellin' the truth is hard."

"And why would Victoria lie? It had to have been embarrassing for her. She had every reason *not* to come forward. She could have just let Clancy be convicted. Telling the truth *was* hard for her."

"Unless there was somethin' compellin' her to do so. That was stronger than her natural inclination not to come forward, as you say."

"And what might that be?"

"I have no idea. I'm just pointin' it out as a possibility."

"I understand that your daughter knew Clancy."

"My daughter was a sinner. A slut, if you will. As is her younger sister. That is all clear to me now. I don't blame them. I blame myself. I have obviously failed them as a father. Sometimes I spend too much time on my congregation. Perhaps I have been too restrictive with them. So while they fell down, I also fell down. I have prayed over it ever since Janet was killed. I prayed over it even harder when certain facts came to light showin' that my daughter was . . . complicit in certain things of a depraved nature. If your father or someone else hadn't killed Clancy, I might have."

"Don't let Aubrey Davis hear you say that."

"I know that it's unbecomin' of a man of the cloth

to say such things. But I'm only human, too. And losin' your child goes against nature. Children are supposed to bury their parents, not the other way around."

Robie's thoughts turned for a moment to the dead Sasha, whose mother would have had to bury her. "No argument there."

Chisum looked at him closely. "I suppose you came back because of your father's situation?"

"Yes."

"We only came here three years ago. From Mobile, though I was born and raised in Mississippi."

Robie was about to say that he knew some of this from Sara, but caught himself.

"Mobile is a nice town," he said.

"Well, it's certainly bigger than Cantrell. With far more to do. But I was offered my own church here. In Mobile I would have been an associate pastor my whole career."

"So you made the choice to come here for your career?"

"I did. When I should have been thinkin' of my family."

"Life is complicated," said Robie.

"Life shouldn't be so complicated if you listen to the Lord."

"Well, maybe sometimes he wants us to make mistakes so we learn for the future."

Chisum took a moment to respond to this. "Maybe that's what he did for me."

"Will you stay in Cantrell?" asked Robie.

"Highly doubtful. We'll wait to find out what happened to Janet, of course. After that, I think we'll move on. To a bigger city. Even if I have to be an associate pastor. I've got two daughters left. I do not intend to bury another."

"Big cities have big temptations," cautioned Robie.

"And associate pastors have more time to spend with their families."

He nodded at Robie, turned, and left.

Robie reached the street and saw it.

The prison van was coming around the corner. The sole passenger was Dan Robie.

He was shackled to the last seat. He looked out the window as the van slowed to make the turn.

Father and son were eye to eye, at least physically if not in any other way.

This time Robie looked away while his father still stared at him, his look inscrutable.

Then the van and his father were gone.

Robie stood there on the street gazing at the place where his father's face had been moments before. A part of him felt he was living someone else's life. This couldn't possibly be him back here in Mississippi. He had been gone for twenty-two years. It might seem to some that no family rift could be so bad that the son would have made no contact with the father.

After Robie had arrived on the East Coast, his life had changed drastically. He had hoped to start a new life with Laura Barksdale. That had not happened. He had arrived at his new life alone, and both confused and angry.

His life and future had been saved by a confluence of events that had propelled him into the beginnings of the career he now had. He had thought of his father several times over the years. But his work involved a level of secrecy that had prohibited him from contacting his father or thinking of going back to his old home.

But things had changed. His father's being charged with murder had been the catalyst for him to deal with a past that he probably should have confronted long ago. And he had been unable to complete his last assignment. His finger couldn't pull the trigger. And it hadn't been the face of the little girl that had held him back.

So now, to go forward, it looks like I have to go back.

And so here I am.

I've executed many missions over the years. But I always went in with a plan.

Now, I have no idea how the hell I'm going to do this.

23

Tiara Street.

It was full of tiny, ramshackle houses with dirt patches for yards and not a trace of hope in sight.

Robie had always thought the name of the road had to have been somebody's idea of a very bad joke.

Billy Faulconer's house was just as small and run-down as all the others. Robie didn't know what his former teammate had done after high school, but it apparently didn't pay much money.

And then the cancer hitting him probably meant he could no longer work. He might be drowning in medical debt. It was a sad situation for anyone, but even more so for a man in his early forties.

Robie knocked on the front screen door. There was movement inside, and a black woman appeared in the doorway. She was tall, thin, and worn. Her long hands were veined, her nails short, and her forearms wiry. Her dark, curly hair was rapidly spreading to gray. The lines in her face spoke of a hardscrabble existence on this little patch of Mississippi soil.

"What can I do for you?" she asked, wiping her hands on a not-overly-clean cloth.

"I'm here to see Billy Faulconer."

"He's not seein' nobody right now. He's not well."

"I know. His son told me. I'm Will Robie."

She clapped a hand to her mouth and dropped the towel. Tears sprang to her eyes and she gripped Robie by the hand.

"Oh my God, Little Bill told me you were in town and might come by, but I never thought you would."

"I'd really like to talk to Billy."

"Come on in, Mr. Robie, please."

"Just call me Will."

"I'm Angie."

"Did we go to school together?"

"No. I'm not from Cantrell. Billy and me met up in Oxford. He was a trucker and was passin' through and had some lunch at the diner where I worked. Then he came by again and again. Pretty soon we was married. And then I come to live here."

"You had kids early."

"Well, we just got the one. I was twenty when Little Bill was born. We wanted more, but God had other plans for us."

While they chatted, she led him through the tiny house and out the back.

"When did Billy get sick?"

"A year ago. Lung cancer. Too many cigarettes, I guess."

"He's been seen by doctors?"

"The one here, yes. He said there was nothin' to be done for Billy."

"Did you get a second opinion?"

Angie stopped and looked at him. "No. I mean, the doctor here said the cancer had spread and that was that."

"Did he go through an operation? Is he on chemo or did he undergo radiation?"

"None of that stuff. Billy said he'll die like a man. He won't hang on and suffer, and give us pain by watchin' him suffer. And all that costs a lot of money. Money we don't have."

"Do you have insurance?"

"No. When Billy lost his job the insurance went too."

"You could get a policy. They can't refuse him now for a preexisting condition."

Her face tightened and she said stiffly, "I think we're okay on that score, Will. But thanks for your concern."

They had by now passed through the backyard and turned a corner.

There stood a battered, old Airstream trailer.

When Robie looked at her, Angie averted her gaze and said quietly, "Billy likes bein' out here. He got that old trailer from a friend of a friend. Fixed it up and now he lives out there. Says he'll die there. We can just

close it up and leave him there when he does. Least that's what he says."

Her words were said lightly, but Robie could see the undeniable pain in the woman's face at this terrible thought.

She led him up to the Airstream and rapped her knuckles on the door. "Billy, I got a surprise for you." She turned and smiled at Robie. "Got me somebody you used to know real good."

Then she opened the door and motioned Robie to pass by her. "Thank you for comin', Will, know it'll mean the world to him." She turned and hurried back to the house.

Robie stepped up into the Airstream and looked first right then left.

Right was a small table with dirty plates and cups on it.

Left was in shadows, but as he moved toward the darkness, it lifted a bit.

"Son of a bitch, Will Robie," came the weak voice.

Robie moved closer and the man came into full view.

Billy Faulconer had been one of the biggest human beings Robie had ever known growing up. Now he looked like someone had deflated him to barely a third of his former size. His skin was far darker than his son's or wife's. Back when they were teenagers, folks in Cantrell would come to cheer the team on, every game. They treated all the players the same,

black or white. But when football season was over, things went back to the old ways, meaning that Billy became simply black and thus shunned by white society.

He was lying on an old, raggedy couch, his head propped up by a trash bag that was filled with something. Robie hoped it was soft.

He had on an old, tattered robe and his bare calves and long feet stuck out from below the hem. His short hair was filled with gray. His face was gaunt, his sunken chest drawing in and out in slow, elongated movements. There was sweat on his skin and not much life in the eyes. An oxygen tank on a little rusted roller sat next to him, its attached lines running up to his nostrils. He seemed to suck greedily on the air.

Robie looked around. He found a little stool covered in junk. He set the items on the floor, pulled it up next to Billy, and sat down.

Wheezing, Billy said, "Shit, man, you look like you could still suit up for Cantrell High."

"We both did our bit there."

"You 'member that goal line play in the second quarter of the state championship?"

Robie thought for a moment. "Read option right, faked the handoff to Kenny Miller on the A-gap, faked the pitch to Junior Deacon on the end-around. I ran left, you crashed down on the end and then had

enough gas left to pancake the OLB, and I scored standing up. Just like Coach drew it up on the board."

Billy smiled big and wide. "That was so sweet. And then in the third quarter? 'Member that play?" he said. "'Member? Tell me you do, man."

Robie cracked a smile, thinking back, way back. "Your moment of glory. On the sidelines you told me they were overcommitting to stopping the run, and the O-backer and the strong safety kept cheating up to the box. So when we went back on the field you checked in receiver eligible. I ran a fake sweep to Donny Jenkins on the weak side, pulled the ball back outta his gut, turned and lofted you the prettiest pass in the end zone on the other side. And you caught it in those big mitts of yours. And then you fell on your ass!"

A crooked grin spread over Billy's features. "Ain't a defender within five miles'a me. All I could think was 'Don't drop the damn ball.'"

"I met Little Bill. Nice young man. You obviously raised him right."

Billy shifted his withered body a bit so he could look more directly at his old teammate. His glee fell away and his features turned somber.

"He done okay. But what he needs to do is get outta this here place."

"Think he can?"

Billy nodded. "Got me a life insurance policy. Premium's all paid so's they can't screw me now. Get him

some money. Angie too. They be good." Billy touched his forehead. "Little Bill's smart. Good with computer shit. Ain't nothin' he don't know 'bout computers. Don't know where he got that from. I don't even know how to turn one on."

"Same with me."

Billy looked him over. "You look like you done good for yourself. Where you livin'?"

"East Coast. Job's okay. Nothing special. I go to an office, push paper around. Pays the bills."

"You lit outta here right fast after high school."

"Just wanted something different."

Billy looked around the Airstream. "Ain't we all?" He picked up a plastic bucket and spit mucus into it. He wiped his mouth with the sleeve of his robe and looked back at Robie.

"Know why you come back. Your daddy." He pointed to a pile of newspapers on the floor. "Been keepin' track of it. Ain't got much else to do."

"I guess not. Angie seems very nice."

Billy nodded and looked away. "She wants me to come live in the house."

"Why don't you?"

"So she can look at my big beautiful face every day?" He swiped a hand through his hair and said, "Man, you think I want her to 'member me like I am now?" He started to cough so hard that Robie helped him sit up some more and poured out a glass of water from a pitcher on the small kitchen sink.

After Billy drank the water and had settled back down Robie said, "I think if you don't have long to live you should spend it with people who love you."

Billy shook his head. "I'm a drain on 'em, Will. Soon as I kick off they can get on with their lives." Before Robie could respond he added, "How's your daddy doin'?"

"Well since he's in jail for murder, not too good."

"You 'member Sherm Clancy?"

"Yeah, when he was a dirt-poor farmer."

"He got him a good ride, all right."

"Gas on his property?"

"Oil, gas. Somethin' like that. But then he really hit it big with the casinos when they come in."

"How did he get in with people like that?"

Billy shrugged. "Don't know nothin' 'bout that. But he done it. Then he was rollin' in money. Built that house. Bought himself that car. One he died in."

"With a neck slit maybe by a Ka–Bar blade."

"Like your daddy had. I 'member seeing it when we was kids."

"Good memory."

"But I got me one of them knives, too."

Robie studied him. "How?"

"My uncle was in the Marines over in Nam. He left it to me when he died."

Robie nodded. "They find the actual knife that killed Clancy?"

"Not so's anybody done said. And I been readin' 'bout it every day. Like I said, all I got to do now."

"What about Janet Chisum?"

Billy struggled to sit up more. Robie rose and helped him, adjusting the trash bag pillow to support him.

"What 'bout her?"

"If Clancy didn't kill her, who did?"

"He was screwin' her. Paid her to do it. What the papers say. That come out at his trial. Disgustin'. He was old enough to be her damn granddaddy."

"And my stepmother provided the alibi."

Billy nodded. "And your daddy maybe killed him 'cause of that."

"You know Victoria?"

"Naw. Seen her around and all. But after you left I never spoke to your daddy no mo'. He just sort of curled up on life, so to speak. Didn't see nobody. Just worked. He won that big case. Then he come back with Victoria and they bought the Willows. Like to knock everybody in town over with a stick when they done that."

"And they have a little boy."

"He ain't talk none, so's folks say."

"I know. He doesn't."

"So you talked to your daddy yet?"

"Don't think he wants to see me."

"You left a long time ago. You ever talked to him over the years?"

"No."

Billy fell silent and looked at his old friend. "Hell, Will, my daddy done beat me, too. Lots of daddies do that shit. I swatted Little Bill on the ass couple times is all when he was small. But I never hit him with my fist. Never took a switch or a tree branch to him. Never busted no beer bottle over his head. My daddy did that to me. And mo'. Lot mo'. Told myself I ain't never doin' that to my kids."

"That's good to hear, Billy. Kids have enough shit to deal with without somebody who is supposed to love them beating the crap out of them."

"So was there somethin' else then, Will? What made you leave?"

Robie ran his eye over the oxygen tank.

"Who's the doctor that diagnosed your cancer?"

"Doc Holloway."

"Is he an oncologist?"

Billy made a face. "A what?"

"A cancer specialist."

"Oh, naw, he ain't that. But he a good doctor. Took care'a all of us over the years. Everythin' from a broken arm to some of Angie's female problems. Kind'a jack'a all trades."

And master of none, thought Robie.

"Do you need anything, Billy? Money?"

Billy waved this off. "I'm good, Will. But thanks."

Robie rose. "I've got to get going. It was good to

see you. If you think of anything you might need, will you let me know? I'm staying at the Willows."

Billy nodded, looking pensive. "Hey, Will, you think maybe you might come back and we have a beer or two, talk some more 'bout the old days?"

"Sounds good, Billy. And I'll bring the beer."

24

It wasn't hard to spot them. In fact, Robie was sure they had *wanted* him to see that they were back there. It was three men inside the car. It wasn't Pete Clancy and his buddies. It looked to be a far more formidable force.

They were all about his age and wearing suits and carrying hardened expressions. And if Robie had to guess, they had guns under their jackets.

Robie kept his speed steady and also kept gazing in the rearview. The road he was on was macadam sprinkled over dirt and wound in and out of tree lines. It was also empty except for the two cars.

The sedan sped up and passed him, then pulled over and slowed to a stop.

Robie could have whipped around it and kept going, but he decided not to. He pulled over, too, right behind the other car.

The three men climbed out of the sedan and walked back to him. One on the driver's side, the others on the passenger.

Robie rolled down his window when the man on his side reached into his jacket pocket.

Robie said, "Isn't the FBI field office in Jackson? You guys are a long way from home."

The man took his hand away from his jacket but Robie climbed out of the car and said, "No, go ahead and show me your credentials. It'll make me feel better."

The man did so.

"Special Agent Jon Wurtzburger," read off Robie.

"How'd you ID us?" asked Wurtzburger while the other two men warily watched Robie.

Robie pointed to the car. "If you really want to go clandestine, take off the government plates." He next pointed to Wurtzburger's suit and tie. "Standard Bureau dress down to the tie pin. And if you were bad guys you would have rammed me when you passed. But you get a ding on your car, you have a month's worth of paperwork to fill out."

Wurtzburger put his ID pack away. "And how do you know so much about the FBI?"

"I have some buddies in the Bureau back in DC. We go out for beers together, shoot the shit."

"We ran your background, Mr. Robie. There's not a lot there."

"Well, I haven't done a lot, so I guess that makes sense. What can I do for you?"

"Your father is accused of murdering Sherman Clancy."

"I know he is."

"We're interested in Clancy."

"Why?"

"He has ties to some casinos."

"And why is that a problem? Gambling is legal here."

"You're an outsider, Mr. Robie. We checked. You haven't been back here for over two decades. Which is one of the reasons we're contacting you like this."

Robie leaned against the fender of his rental and studied them. "And why is that important?"

"Do you believe that your father killed Mr. Clancy?"

"I don't know. Like you said, I just got here."

"Well, if he didn't, there might be another explanation."

"Clancy's casino partners, you mean?"

Wurtzburger looked intrigued. "Why do you say that?"

"Well, you brought up the ties to the casinos. And they've been described to me as junkyard dogs who may have had a reason to kill him."

"Who told you that?"

"Can't remember exactly. But I think pretty much everyone in Cantrell will tell you the same thing if you ask."

"So local scuttlebutt?"

"Which often turns out to be spot-on."

Wurtzburger looked at him curiously. "And you're here because of your father?"

"I am."

"But you think he *could* have killed Clancy?"

"I've found that given the right circumstances, people are capable of pretty much anything."

"Based on your experience in a life where, to quote you, you haven't done a lot?"

"I like to observe people, Agent Wurtzburger. You can learn a lot by keeping your mouth shut and your eyes and ears open."

Wurtzburger nodded and then handed Robie a card. "Well, if you see or hear anything, will you give me a call?"

Robie took the card. "You haven't really told me why the FBI's interested in this case."

"You're right, I haven't. Have a good day."

Wurtzburger and his men returned to their car and drove off in a swirl of fine Mississippi dust.

Robie got back in his car and headed on.

He pulled to a stop later in front of the Willows. Victoria's Volvo was parked in front. He went inside.

Priscilla met him at the door.

"Where's Victoria?"

"Upstairs with Ty. How'd it go at the courthouse? She didn't say."

"Not much happened. He pled not guilty, and the

judge wants him to get a lawyer." Robie didn't mention the threats against his father.

He headed up the steps and got to the top landing in time to see Victoria come out of Tyler's room.

"I see you made up your mind about the hearing today," he noted.

She stood there, seemingly frozen in the doorway. "I almost didn't go. That's why I was late. I sat out in my car." She came forward. "What happened?"

"He acted as his own lawyer, pled not guilty, and asked for reasonable bail to be set."

"And was it?"

"It might have been except that Aubrey Davis said there have been credible threats against him and he would be safer in jail. The judge has taken it all under advisement. So for now he stays in jail."

Victoria placed a hand against her throat. "What credible threats?"

"I was hoping you could tell me."

"Dan never mentioned that anyone was threatening him."

"Well, he made some enemies with the oil platform lawsuit he won."

"That was years ago."

"Some people have long memories."

And don't I know that, thought Robie.

Victoria said stubbornly, "I can't believe that. They would have had ample opportunities to hurt him. Or us. And they haven't. And what would the threats be

for? We'll kill you if you what? Do something? Don't do something?"

Robie had to concede that these were all good points. He also knew that if he wanted to answer any of these things he would have to do what he had come here to do in the first place.

See his father.

He hustled back down the stairs.

"Where are you going?"Victoria called after him.

Robie didn't answer her.

25

"It's time, Deputy Taggert," said Robie.

He was standing in front of her desk at the jail.

"Robie, I don't know what to tell you. Your daddy—"

"He's in trouble, people have made threats against him, and he's not going to be leaving here until his trial is over. And I think I can help him. But I can't do that until I talk to him."

"But he said—"

"I know what he said. But if it were your father what would you do? Give up and go home with your tail tucked between your legs?"

Robie figured this jab would get to the chip-on-her-shoulder deputy.

She drummed her fingers on her desk, then stood, took a set of keys off her gun belt, and said, "If this goes bad, I'm goin' to say you overpowered me and you're goin' to go along with that, damn the consequences. Understood?"

"Understood."

She unlocked a steel door and led him down a

narrow passage. At the end was another door that she unlocked using a different key. They entered a cell block area. The doors were solid so one couldn't see inside. She led him to the last one on the left. She rapped on the door.

"Judge Robie, you got you a visitor."

She looked at Robie, hiked her eyebrows, pointed a finger at him, and said in a low voice, "Ten minutes. That's it."

She opened the door and Robie walked through. A second later the door was shut and locked. He heard her booted feet going back down the hall.

The next instant Robie was slammed up against the wall. His cheek hit the brick and he felt it start to swell.

"What the hell are you doin' here?" barked Dan Robie right in his son's ear.

Robie broke his father's grip, with some difficulty, circled him, bent Dan's arm back and then behind the older man, and wrenched it upward, but not enough to do any permanent damage.

"You going to calm down?" asked Robie quietly. "Or do I have to break it?"

"I told them I didn't want to see you."

"But here I am. Can we talk this out?"

"You're assaultin' me."

"I'm acting in self-defense. You jumped me first. Now we can just stand here looking stupid or we can do something productive."

"Well, you can start by lettin' go of my damn arm!"

Robie released his father and stepped back.

Dan Robie rubbed his limb and turned to look over at his son.

"Why are you here?" he barked.

"I got word that you were in trouble."

"I've been in a lot of trouble over the last twenty-two years. I didn't see you show up then."

Dan Robie sat down on his bunk, which gave Robie a chance to observe his father more closely. The man was sixty-four now. He was still taller than his son, still lean with broad shoulders and ropy muscles. His hair was all white and starting to thin a bit, and his face was weathered in the way that only living near the ocean can inspire.

"No, you didn't," replied Robie.

"So why now?"

"Maybe it has more to do with me at my stage of life than you."

"Okay, you've seen me. We've talked. Now leave."

His father turned away from him.

"Did you kill Sherman Clancy?"

His father said nothing.

"If you didn't, and I don't think you did, then the person who *did* kill him is out there. Maybe it's the same person who killed Janet Chisum."

His father didn't break his silence.

"I thought a Marine and a judge would not want to see a killer or killers walk free."

"I don't. But that's not my job, is it? And I'm hardly in a position to find out who it might be."

"That's why I'm here."

His father turned to him. "You?" he scoffed. "What makes you think you can do anythin' about it? Where have you been? What have you been doin' with your life?"

"Things. I've been doing things with my life."

"You think you can just waltz back in here and—"

"I left you a phone number where you could reach me," broke in Robie. "As soon as I got to where I was going. Twenty-two years ago." He paused. "You never called."

"Why the hell should I? *You* left home. Snuck off in the middle of the night like the damn coward you were. Could never face nothin' head-on, boy. Nothin'."

"If I remember right you left home when you were seventeen, lied about your age, and joined the Marines. Did you ever go back home? Because I don't recall you ever mentioning that you did."

"That's none of your damn business."

Robie ignored this and said, "I wondered why I never met my grandfather. Why you never even mentioned him. Did he beat the shit out of you? Did he insult you every day of your life? Because if he did, we have a lot of things in common."

Dan Robie looked across the narrow width of the cell at his son.

"So you're here to what? Vent? Stand up to me? Kick my ass to show you're a man in your own eyes?"

"I know I'm a man. I don't have to vent or kick your ass to prove anything."

"Then why are you here?" snapped Dan.

"Because you're in trouble. And I help people who are in trouble. Even if they don't deserve it."

"Oh, so you're some kind of Good Samaritan?" his father said sarcastically.

"I don't think anyone who knows me would describe me that way."

A long moment of silence passed between the two men.

"Did you kill Sherman Clancy?"

"Well, if I did, it's doubtful I would confess it to you."

"Did you think Victoria had slept with him?"

"You stay the hell out of my life."

"I'm *staying* at the Willows."

Dan Robie looked like he might attack his son again.

"The hell you are! I forbid you to stay in my house. You have no right to be there."

"I don't think you have any say in it, what with your ass being locked up in here."

"I won't be locked up in here forever."

"No. If you're convicted they'll send you to the state pen. Doubt it's as nice as this place. By the way, you need a lawyer."

"I'm actin' pro se. Do you even know what that means?"

"Yeah, it's Latin for 'dumbass.' I'll ask around and find you somebody."

"You will do nothin' of the kind, boy."

"And I'll protect your family from harm."

Dan started to say something but then stopped. He looked at his son warily. "What do you mean by that?"

"Credible threats? I've already met some folks down here that could constitute that. And I've also met some other folks who think the credible threat could be coming from a pretty dangerous source. If so, I doubt they'll give a shit who they kill. So who do you want to rely on to protect them, the police force of Cantrell, Mississippi?"

"And you think you're any better?" his father said dismissively.

"I don't think. I *know* I'm better. That's what I've been spending my life doing, *Dad*." He rolled up his sleeve to expose the burn. "Sometimes it gets a little hairy. But you just keep soldiering on. And now that I know Ty is my little brother, it will take an army of them to get past me."

His father ran an eye up and down his son's lean, muscled physique, but he came away looking unsatisfied.

"Hell, you even know how to use a gun? Because everybody around here does."

Robie said, "You're the second person in Cantrell to ask me that. And yes. I know how to use a gun. Better than anyone you'll ever know."

26

"Think of three lawyers and then tell me the one you'd want to hire if your butt was on the line."

Robie was staring at Sheila Taggert as she sat behind her desk.

She looked back at him, her gaze resigned.

"Toni Moses is who you want."

Robie gazed skeptically at her. "Toni Moses? Is that a real name?"

"Couldn't tell you. But if you need a kickass lawyer, she is it."

"A woman, then?"

"A black woman, *then*," amended Taggert. "And the other good thing is she and Aubrey Davis can't stand the sight of each other. I bet she'd do anythin' to get this case."

"She's that good?"

"Thirteen capital cases in the last dozen years. Here and over to Biloxi and up on to Hattiesburg and even one in Jackson. She won 'em all. I'd say that was pretty damn good, considerin' none of her clients were exactly upstandin' citizens. And almost all of 'em

were the same color she was. Which in Mississippi ain't just good. It's a damn miracle. So I'd say she's aptly named. Least the Moses part. Leadin' people to the promised land."

"Where can I find her?"

"Right next door. She says she likes being next to the jail 'cause she can just walk over and pick up clients. Only exercise she gets, so she claims, anyhow."

"You know her well?"

"Well as anybody 'round here can."

"Thanks."

"Guess it went all right with your daddy, seein' how you're still alive and all."

"It was a close call for a while."

"You want somethin' for that swollen cheek where he belted you?"

"I'm good."

Outside Robie gazed up and down the street until his eyes settled on the black metal shingle dangling from a small, tidy, brick building painted a stark white.

He walked over and read off the sign. "Toni Moses, J.D. Counselor at Law."

He knocked on the door and could immediately hear a buzzer go off somewhere. He pushed open the door and walked in.

A young woman sat at a desk in the small foyer. The desk held a sleek computer along with neat stacks of files. The woman was in her late twenties,

Robie estimated, and had long red hair, a face covered with freckles, and beautiful green eyes. She rose and came forward.

"Can I help you?"

"I was looking for Toni Moses?"

"Can I say who's askin'?"

"Will Robie. I'm here to see about her representing my father."

Her look told Robie that she knew exactly who his father was.

"Just give me a minute, Mr. Robie."

She disappeared into an internal office. About ten seconds had passed when the door opened and Robie saw her.

Toni Moses was barely five feet tall, but as wide as she was tall with a massive bosom. Her kinky dark hair fell over her shoulders. She wore glasses tethered to a cord. Her pantsuit was a bit small for her stout frame, and her thick feet were wedged into open-toed heels.

Her brow was full and furrowed, and her eyes enormous and darker than her hair. Her mouth was wide, the lips painted a muted red. The nails were long and manicured.

But when she spoke Robie forgot all about what she looked like.

"Where have you been?" she demanded in a quiet voice that nonetheless seemed to have the impact of a clap of thunder.

"Excuse me?" said Robie. He stepped back as she charged forward.

"Where have you been? Simple question."

"I just came from the jail."

"Uh-huh. Your butt hadn't eased across the county line for ten seconds when I knew all there was to know. Come on in. We have things to talk about."

She turned and walked back into her office. Over her shoulder she called out, "Your daddy could be a dead man walkin'. So time is definitely of the essence."

The young woman had eased out of Moses's office and was looking sympathetically at Robie. "Would you like some coffee?" she asked.

"No. And don't get her any. Or any more."

"Robie!" cried out Moses. "Get your butt in here."

Robie hurried into her office, and the young woman quickly closed the door behind him.

He looked around the small space that was dominated by, in addition to Moses, a huge desk piled high with paper.

"Sit," said Moses, indicating a chair piled high with paper files. "Just move those, honey. No, over there to the right on the floor," she said, when Robie attempted to put them on another chair. "Have to keep organized."

He sat and looked at her. She stared back at him.

"Well?" she said. "Are you here to retain me on behalf of your daddy?"

"He doesn't know I'm here. But we talked."

She pointed to the fresh bruise on his cheek. "I can see you *talked* all right. How many shots on him did you get?"

"He needs a lawyer."

"Damn right he does. Representin' himself? Damn fool. And he's told that to quite a few folks in his own courtroom. I can say his spiel word for word: 'Tryin' to be your own lawyer is like playin' Russian roulette with a full chamber of bullets. You got no chance 'cept to die.'"

"You come highly recommended."

She inclined her head. "I was wonderin' when you were goin' to get around to askin' Sheila Taggert 'bout hirin' a lawyer."

"She speaks highly of you."

Moses nodded. "My terms are nonnegotiable. You pay my hourly fee, which isn't cheap, but compared to New York or DC I'm basically free. I work my butt off on the case, leavin' no stone unturned. If I win I get nothin' extra."

"And if you lose?"

"I get my fees paid in full. No hard feelin's."

"I hear you have a lot of experience with capital cases."

"In Mississippi they have lots of laws where they can kill you if you break 'em. Now, they don't execute folks on the level of say a Texas or Florida, but not for lack of tryin'. The main reason they don't put more folks to death is because poor counties, of which

there is an abundance here, can't afford to provide defense counsel to indigent defendants, of which there is also an abundance here. And without that you're not goin' to survive an appellate challenge. So courts just give the defendant life in prison instead. And *everybody's* happy," she tacked on in a sarcastic tone.

"Sorry state of affairs," said Robie.

"Just the way it is. Now one big thing your daddy's got goin' for him is he's white. Mississippi doesn't execute many white folks, particularly those with money or a position of respect, both of which he's got. Mississippi has executed about eight hundred people over the last two centuries, and eighty percent of them were black men, so you can see the odds favor your daddy."

"Okay," said Robie slowly.

"Now, capital cases involve two parts. First, the trial to determine guilt or innocence. If guilt is found you enter the second part, which is the sentencin' phase. That's when both aggravatin' and mitigatin' circumstances are raised. The only aggravatin' circumstance I see with your daddy is the catchall in the statute, namely, that the crime was especially heinous, atrocious, or cruel. Slittin' a man's throat? Maybe it is or maybe it isn't. But they also may hold your daddy, since he's a judge, to a higher standard, I don't know. But on the plus side, he has lots of mitigatin' circumstances to his credit. So odds are he won't get the needle. But they can still lock him up for a long damn

time, and he's no spring chicken. So twenty years is like a death sentence."

"And if he's guilty?"

"That question doesn't interest me not even one little bit."

"Why?"

"It's Aubrey Davis's job to prove guilt beyond a reasonable doubt, so says the Constitution and the United States Supreme Court. He's got the full resources of Cantrell and the mighty State of Mississippi behind him. All your daddy will have is me, but let me just say that I am a damn handful in any court in which I set foot. My job is to make sure Aubrey doesn't get to where he wants to go, which is a conviction. He gets that, he's the next congressman or maybe even senator from our great state, and I might have to slash my wrists and bleed out right here at my desk if that ever happens."

"I take it you two don't get along?"

"I hate his guts, as he does mine. If that fits your definition of not gettin' along, then, no, we do not get along."

"You're not from Mississippi, are you?"

"No. But I am here now, which is fortunate for your daddy."

"Where are you from?"

"The three *H*'s."

"Excuse me?"

"My life can be defined as Howard, Harvard, and Hard Knocks, and not necessarily in that order."

"You went to Harvard?"

"For law school. Howard University for undergrad, and Hard Knocks for everythin' else."

"How'd you end up here?"

"I like to think I go where I'm needed. My case-load tells me I was right."

"So you'll represent my father?"

"I've been waitin' all mornin' for you to get your butt here. Been callin' Sheila Taggert every twenty minutes."

"So you two are tight?"

"We're both in law enforcement, so to speak. She carries out the laws and I make sure the laws are carried out fairly and impartially, and not based in any way, shape, or form on personal prejudices of a litany of persuasions, the dominant one havin' to do with skin pigment the same as mine. And let me tell you I have seen most of these prejudices here in Cantrell as well as other places in this fine country, north, south, east, and west. And they can be uh-uh-ugly."

"What do you need from me?"

"Five thousand dollars and a retainer agreement signed by you and your daddy, so if one doesn't pay me the other one's got to."

"Can I put it on my credit card?"

"You can put it on your ass so long as it clears the Second National Bank of Cantrell."

"And my father has to sign the retainer agreement too?"

"Way attorney–client privilege attaches. He knows that. Why? Is that a problem?"

"I hope not."

She smiled big. "I can tell you and me are goin' to get on real good, Will."

27

"Where the hell have you been? You just shot outta here without a word."

Victoria was standing on the porch at the Willows, her hands on her soft hips, staring at Robie as he climbed out of his car.

"Getting some things done."

"What things?"

Robie walked up to her and leaned back against the railing.

"For starters, I saw my father."

She gaped. "You did? How did it go?"

Robie pointed to his swollen cheek. "He can still pack a wallop."

She stared at the spot. "Oh my God, do you want some ice for that?"

"No, it'll be fine. I also got him a lawyer."

"Who?"

"Toni Moses."

"I hear she's really good."

"I think he needs really good."

"Dan agreed to this?"

Robie shrugged. "He will, when I tell him what I've done."

"You hired a lawyer for him without telling him?" She shook her head. "Well, if I were you I'd tell him from the other side of the cell door."

"Why, does he get physical with you?"

The two stared at each other.

"Why do you ask that?" she said.

"You don't really seem surprised that I did, Victoria."

"That's none of your business."

"Sort of like why you spent the night drinking with Sherm Clancy. Again, none of my business, right?"

She sat down in a rocking chair. "I would say right, only it would be none of your *damn* business."

"But it makes a perfect motive for my father to kill the man."

She closed her eyes and rubbed her temples. "I have regretted that night ever since it happened."

"Well, if it costs your husband his life I guess you *should* regret it forever."

"It's not like I told Dan to kill the bastard," she barked.

Robie said firmly, "*If* he killed the bastard. So you think he did it?"

"I don't want to believe he had anything to do with it."

"He has no alibi. You were in Biloxi with Ty and

Priscilla. So he had the opportunity. The weapon was like one that he possessed at some point and could have used to kill Clancy."

"I *know* all of that, Will. Do *you* think he did it?"

Robie shrugged. "I have no idea. I don't know enough. I don't think anyone does. That's why they're having a trial."

Victoria opened a bag on a table next to the rocker and pulled out a pack of cigarettes. She lit one and offered the pack to Robie.

He shook his head. "How's Ty?"

"He's fine. He's with Priscilla. Why?"

"Credible threats."

"We've been over this. What threats? Dan doesn't have any enemies."

"You can't know that for sure. And if you're wrong?"

"So what do you suggest we do? Hire an armed guard?"

"I'll stay here with you. I can look after you. But I can't be with you all the time."

"Are you really taking this seriously?"

"I saw a man in the bushes on the rear grounds early this morning. I tried to follow him but he was already gone by the time I got outside. And your car had been searched."

For the first time Victoria looked scared. "Someone was outside the Willows early this morning?"

"A tall man. White guy probably. Any idea who it might've been?"

"How should I know?" she said defensively.

"I'm just asking questions, trying to assemble some useful information. And what might he have been looking for in your car?"

"What, are you playing at detective now?" She paused, studying him. "You're not a cop, are you?"

"Right now, I wish I were. I feel a little out of my depth."

"Even so, I don't understand what you're doing. Are you saying you're going to investigate the case and try to get to the truth?"

"Pretty much."

"Why? And don't tell me it's because of your father. You've been gone longer than you were here. And you've never contacted him. Dan would have told me."

"I don't like questions without answers."

"Well, like them or not, I think that's what you're faced with here."

Robie's phone buzzed. He checked the screen.

It was Blue Man.

"I have to take this," said Robie.

He headed for the back of the property as he answered the phone.

"How is Mississippi?" asked Blue Man.

"Not as friendly as the tour guides say, at least for me."

"Have you seen your father?"

"I have."

"And did it go well?"

"No."

"You still want to follow through with this?"

Do I want to follow through? thought Robie.

"Like it or not, I think I have to."

"I expected you to say that. And I think you're right."

"What have you found out?"

"Not as much as I would have liked. It was damn tricky, Robie. You head down and all of a sudden the federal government gets interested in a murder in Mississippi. We had to tread carefully."

"I understand that, but you must've found out something."

"Sherman Clancy was intoxicated when he was killed. His blood alcohol was twice the legal limit."

"Meaning he was pretty much incapacitated, incapable of defending himself?"

"Yes. The murder weapon was a serrated-edge knife. The police believe they have enough evidence there to say it was a Ka-Bar knife, though I'm not sure that would hold up in court. But it was definitely a serrated blade."

"And evidence tying my father to the crime?"

"Well, the motive was obvious."

"His wife was with Clancy and he found out."

"Right. Have you talked to his wife, well, I guess also your stepmother?"

"I have. In fact, I'm staying at their house. She says she was just drinking with Clancy, nothing more."

"And you believe her?"

"I don't believe anyone. What else is there tying him to the crime?"

"Dan Robie was seen driving his car near the spot where the murder took place."

"Who saw him?"

"A local fisherman and his son."

"Their names?"

"Tuck Carson and his son Ash. They told the police they saw your father in his Range Rover driving from the direction where the body was found about one in the morning. That would be about the time the death occurred."

"What were they doing out at that time of night?"

"They said they were out to get bait for the next morning."

"What else?"

"At the crime scene forensics found a boot print matching one of your father's by the driver's-side door. The ground was damp and muddy and the impression was clear. There were also several hairs that they said matched his found in the Bentley's interior."

"He could have ridden in the car before. Or they could have been planted. So could the boot prints."

"Yes, they could have. But the witnesses apparently did see him in the area at the time."

"Anything else?"

"Your father publicly threatened Clancy outside a restaurant in Cantrell two days before Clancy was killed. Several people heard it. Your father said he knew what Clancy had done and he was going to make him pay." Blue Man paused. "So even if your father isn't the murderer, you can understand why the police arrested him."

"I can," conceded Robie. "Anything on Janet Chisum?"

"Not much more than you probably know. Gunshot to the head killed her. Body thrown in the river. Fished out downriver the next day. Clancy was tried for the crime because of their, well, their relationship, but he was acquitted."

"Principally because my stepmother provided him with an ironclad alibi."

"The same alibi that may have provided the motive for your father to kill him. And the cause and effect didn't take long. Five days after he was acquitted and released from jail, Sherman Clancy was dead."

"So if Clancy didn't kill Janet Chisum, who did?"

"Why are you concerned about that? It has nothing to do with your father."

"We don't know that. There might be a connection."

"And there might actually be a Loch Ness monster, but I wouldn't bet the farm on it. Anything else?"

"Jessica?"

"Still out. Listen, Robie, I understand why you're down there doing what you're doing. And I know that I was the one who suggested that you resolve past issues. But you are a highly valuable asset of your government. We have spent a lot of time and money training you. The last thing any of us want is you getting killed down there over a matter best left to others."

"I think you should know by now that I can take care of myself."

"And life is highly unpredictable. And small rural towns hold dangers sometimes that the worst hot spots in the world couldn't match. You remember that."

Blue Man clicked off.

Robie put his phone away and concluded that Blue Man was a very wise person indeed.

He stood there lost in thought for a few moments. He was putting together a to-do list and there were now many items piling up on it.

He assembled them in some order, then climbed into his car and left in pursuit of the first one.

The eyewitnesses.

28

Tuck Carson's house was on the Pearl River, befitting a man who made his living from pulling fish out of its depths and taking those who wanted to do the same on guided tours. It was more a shack than a house. There was a pressure-treated wood pier out back at which two boats were docked. One was a sleek bass boat, low to the water with a Yamaha engine on the stern and a bow trickle thruster when it came time to fish. The other boat was a twenty-two-foot, center-console hardtop with twin engines on the back and fishing poles resting in holders up and down the sides of the watercraft.

The smell of fish guts was strong as Robie got out of his car and walked up the gravel path to the house.

Before he got to the porch the door opened and out stepped a short, stocky man around forty with thick forearms and greasy hair that sprawled out from under an oil-stained Briggs & Stratton ball cap. He had on a dirty work shirt that revealed his top-most chest hair. He wore cutoff shorts that showed bandy legs that were deeply tanned and muscled.

In his right hand he held a gutting knife. In his other was an unopened can of Michelob.

"What can I do you for?" said the man. "We go out at five in the mornin', back at ten. Full up for the next two days. Talk to the wife 'bout schedulin' somethin'."

"I'm not here to fish," said Robie.

The man gripped his knife more tightly. "What then?"

"I'm Will Robie."

The man's eyes widened, as Robie knew they would.

"Are you Tuck Carson?"

Carson stuck the point of his knife into the porch railing, popped his can of beer, and took a long swig. "I done said all I had to say to the police."

"I'm sure. But you'll have to testify when the time comes, that you saw my father where and when you did."

"Don't think you should be here, bein' his son and all."

"I just want you to tell me what you saw."

The screen door opened and a boy about thirteen came out. He was dressed in jeans, sneakers, and a white T-shirt badly in need of laundering. His hair was a tumble of brown and blond strands. He wore round glasses, and in his fist was clutched a can of Pepsi.

"What's up, Pop?"

"Are you Ash?" asked Robie.

The boy continued to look at his father. "What's he want?"

Carson took another drink from the can and wiped his mouth with the back of his hand. "Man wants to know what we saw that night."

"Why's he care?"

"He's the judge's son. That's why."

Ash took a step back from Robie and took a swig of his Pepsi. "Saw him clear as day. He was drivin' that Range Rover'a his. Ain't nobody got one'a them here but him."

"No, Sherman Clancy has one, too," countered Robie.

The boy shot his father another glance.

"It was the judge's truck," said Carson. "'Sides, Clancy was in his old Bentley at the time. Dead!"

"Okay, you saw the truck. But did you see my father driving it?"

"'Course we did," growled Carson. "Like the boy done said."

"Can you tell me where exactly? Please?" added Robie.

"You know where they found Clancy's body?" said Carson.

"Yes."

"You hang a left outta there onto the road and go a quarter mile north. That's where we saw him. We was comin' back from catchin' bait for the mornin'

run. We go to four or five spots and that's always one of 'em. Good bait there."

"Wait a minute. If you were catching bait, why were you in a car? Why not your boat?"

"One of the places is in a little cove. Can't really get to it by boat. So's we drive over and park near the bank. Catch 'em real good from there with our nets."

"Okay, what happened next?"

"Well, he comes tearin' up that road, like to hit us. Dust swirlin' all over. I banged my horn but he just kept'a goin'. Could'a give a shit he near killed us."

"But it was dark out, and headlights were coming at you. And it happened fast, presumably. How did you get a look at him?"

"I was as close to him as my boy is to me right now. Couldn't miss that, could I?"

Robie looked at him curiously and then glanced at Ash. "And did you see him too?"

"Boy was in the passenger seat of the truck."

"But I seen him too," said Ash. "Clear as day."

"But it wasn't day, it was night," pointed out Robie. "And were you wearing your glasses?"

Ash suddenly looked uncertain and again glanced at his father.

Robie looked at Carson, and next his beer. "And I take it you hadn't been drinking?"

Carson finished off his beer, his Adam's apple sliding up and down with each swallow. Then he crushed the can against the porch railing and tossed it into a

plastic bin at his feet that was filled with flattened beer cans. Carson pulled his knife from the railing, took a step toward Robie, and said, "You best be movin' on. And don't come back here 'less you want trouble or you got fish you wanna catch."

"Thanks for talking to me," said Robie.

He drove off thinking that these two *eyewitnesses* were anything but.

Later, he pulled up in front of the Cantrell jail armed with the retainer agreement that his father needed to sign. He should have gone right from Moses's office to his father next door, but his courage had failed.

Taggert was at her desk.

"Wonderin' when you were goin' to show up," she said.

"What are you talking about?"

"They've been meetin' for a while."

"Who?" said a bewildered Robie.

"Your father and his lawyer."

"Toni Moses is in with my father?"

"She doesn't let the grass grow under her pumps."

Taggert led him back into the cellblock area, but past the actual cells.

"Where are we going?" asked Robie.

"Visitor's room."

"Didn't know you had one."

"Where else would visitors meet with prisoners?"

"I met with my father in his cell."

211

"Well, I was afraid he'd get violent with you."

"He *did* get violent with me, Sheila," barked Robie.

"See, it was good I kept you two in the cell then."

She opened a door at the end of the hall and ushered Robie in before leaving him and closing the door.

Toni Moses was seated at the small table in the center of the room. His father sat opposite, his shackles locked into a steel ring mounted on the floor.

Moses looked up and did not seem unduly surprised by Robie's appearance. "Glad you're here. Have a seat."

Next to her was a stack of files. She had a legal pad in front of her and was busily jotting down notes.

Robie eyed his father, who had not yet looked at him.

"I thought you said he had to sign the retainer agreement."

With her free hand Moses held up a document. "He already signed it."

"Then why did you tell me I had to get him to sign it?" said Robie, trying to keep the anger out of his voice.

"I guess I wanted to give you a goal to shoot for, Robie. Never thought you'd actually get it done, so I did it myself."

Robie eyed his father. "So you agree you need a lawyer?"

Dan Robie looked at Moses. "Why is he here?"

"He's a client."

"Not with me he's not. And his being here breaks attorney–client privilege."

Robie sat down. "I signed the agreement, too."

"Then take off your signature or I represent myself."

Robie looked at Moses. "What if I'm working for the defense?"

"How do you mean?" said an interested-looking Moses.

"As your private investigator."

"Bullshit," said Dan.

"I have one of those already," said Moses.

"I've been out to see Tuck Carson and his son. I'm not sure how they could have seen my father late at night, in a swirl of dust and headlights zooming past them. The kid wears glasses and he probably didn't have them on that night. And the father likes his beer. He drank down a whole one while I was talking to him. So I don't think their eyewitness testimony stands up."

He looked at his father. "Unless you tell us you were driving at that spot at that time in your Range Rover and almost hit the Carsons."

"I don't have to tell you anythin'," said the older Robie, looking pointedly at his son.

Robie turned back to Moses. "I can work on the case. I can dig stuff up. I can check things out."

"I guess you're expectin' to get paid?" said Moses.

"No, I'm not."

"Well, then that works for me. If you know what you're doin', that is. No margin of error here."

"I don't want him workin' on my case," yelled Dan.

Moses put up a hand. "Judge Robie, with all due respect, you're not the one makin' the decisions on things like that. I am."

"And I'm payin' for your services."

"She put the five grand retainer on my credit card," pointed out Robie.

"And I had her cancel that and put it on mine," countered his father.

"What the hell is your problem? I'm trying to help you."

"And I don't remember askin' for your help, boy."

Moses stood. "Look, you two knuckleheads, I'm tryin' a case for murder in the first degree." She turned to Dan Robie. "Your butt is lookin' at goin' away for the rest'a your life. So pardon me if I avail myself of help in defendin' you." She turned to Robie. "I have no idea why you dragged your butt back here 'cept you got some daddy issues need sortin' out. But if you're workin' this case for me, you don't do nothin' that'll jeopardize my defense, you hear me?"

"I hear you." He studied her. "Now you really sound like you're from Mississippi, not Harvard."

"Hell, baby, when I go in that there courtroom you won't hear nothin' *but* Mississippi come out my damn mouth."

She sat. "Now what you said about the Carsons is interestin' and helpful. And it would be more helpful if your daddy would tell us whether he was out that night or not drivin' in his Range Rover."

Robie looked at his father. "Were you?"

Dan Robie simply looked away.

Robie turned back to Moses. "Can I get a copy of the file on this case? I assume the prosecution has to turn over its stuff to you."

"Aubrey Davis had been duly informed of my appearance and he promised that his office will forthwith be sending me their evidence. I will not hold my breath while I wait. But when I get it so will you."

Robie nodded. "Do you think you can get him out on bail?"

Moses shrugged. "Well, I need to see these credible threats Aubrey is going on about. Maybe we don't want him out on bail."

"Do you want to be out on bail?" Robie asked his father.

His father said nothing.

Robie rose. "Well, good luck with your client. When you get the files let me know."

"Where are you goin' now?" asked Moses.

"To check out some things."

"Well, then report back to me with whatever you find."

Right before Robie hit the door his father said, "If

215

you're doin' this to make amends, don't bother. It's too damn late for that."

Robie took a cue from his father and said nothing. He just left.

Moses turned to Dan Robie. "Whether you beat this or not, Dan Robie, let me tell you somethin'."

"What?" snapped the man.

"You're a damn fool."

29

It was one o'clock in the morning and Will Robie was on the move. He preferred to do his work at night.

He had returned to the Willows and had dinner with Victoria and Tyler. The little boy had stared at his far older stepbrother the entire meal. Robie had once caught Tyler smiling at him.

Afterward, Victoria had shown Robie a picture that Tyler had drawn. It was stick figures, one big and one small, and a large heart was drawn between them.

"I guess you are officially loved," said Victoria.

Robie had taken the picture, carefully folded it, and slipped it into his pocket.

When he'd told her about Moses meeting with them, she had asked, "Do you think he'll seek bail?"

"Too early to tell. We need to evaluate the credible threats first."

Now he stared up at the house. Clancy's mansion. Dark and hopefully empty. He had seen Pete Clancy head out in his Porsche a half hour before. Probably to go drinking with his buds.

Robie made his approach from the rear. He had seen signs stuck in the ground announcing that there was a security system in place here. He doubted Pete would make use of such a thing, but he would need to check.

He reached the rear porch. The same one Pete had thrown up on. Robie noted with disgust that the vomit, hardened and dried out, was still there.

What a catch he would make for some young woman.

He peered through the glass and noted the alarm pad on the inner wall. It glowed green and thus off. He tried the door. Locked.

He pulled out his pick tools, and a minute later the door swung open.

His Glock was in a waistband holster. He hoped he had no cause to draw it.

He was here for a number of reasons, but principally because if his father had not killed Sherman Clancy, then his son Pete had a great motive to do so.

Money, or whatever was left of it.

There might be something here that would prove this, starting, hopefully, with a Ka-Bar knife with Sherm Clancy's dried blood on it along with his son's prints.

The place was garishly decorated. Every room was overstuffed with furniture, every window overwhelmed with huge drapes, every table bursting with expensive

and ugly knickknacks, and every wall covered with oil paintings of questionable taste.

And since Pete was now the master of the house, it was also trashed. Empty beer, wine, and liquor bottles were everywhere. Crusted dishes were piled high in the sink. Bugs scampered over them. The fridge was pretty much empty.

Yet Sherman Clancy had not been dead that long. And the pool and grounds had clearly been left to fall into disrepair for a much longer time. Robie thus assumed a lot of this had been going on while the old man was alive.

Was the pot of gold running out? If so, why? Taggert had said Clancy had been a big spender. Was that the reason? Or was there something else?

The house was large and there were many places to look, and Robie was one to be methodical. After an hour or so he finished with the first floor and headed up the winding staircase. The second floor was all bedrooms and bathrooms. He searched each one and found nothing useful.

There was one more floor to go.

There were five rooms up here. One was a club room with a full bar, pool table, steam and sauna room, and a hot tub that looked like it was actually clean and operating normally. Robie thought Pete might bring some of the ladies up here for a quick steam, sauna, and dip in the hot tub. And probably more than that.

He hoped the chlorine level in the water was set on high.

One room was set up as an office. Robie took his time going through this one. There was a desk lamp with a frayed power cord. Robie turned it on and drew it closer to some paper files he had found, moving a half-full can of Budweiser out of the way.

He took pictures of these files. There was also a computer. It was password protected, but Robie finally hit the jackpot when he typed in "Redneck."

Pete had evidently been using this computer, because he saw e-mails coming in and out from Pete's account.

It appeared that since Sherm's death, his son had been contacting various folks at one of the casinos in Biloxi named the Rebel Yell Grand Palace. As he read through these e-mails, it became clear to him that Pete was angling to replace his father as a business partner with these folks.

That could be a terrific motive to kill the old man.

Robie copied these e-mails to a flash drive he had brought. He also copied other e-mails that he didn't have time to read but that looked interesting. He would read them later.

The next room was apparently Pete's sleeping quarters.

It was like one would have expected from a young man living alone.

Disgusting.

Robie wondered whether his tetanus shot was up-to-date as he surveyed the interior of the room. He couldn't see the floor for all the crap everywhere: dirty clothes, two guitars, magazines, a rifle and two handguns, video game packs, dishes, empty beer cans and liquor bottles, a chin-up bar, some dumbbells. The walls were covered with posters with three basic themes: music, sports, and porn. Over the doorway hung a string of women's colorful thongs.

Notches in the bedpost, twenty-first century style.

If there was a desk in here anywhere, Robie couldn't see it under the junk. There was a pair of head-phones lying on the bed that Robie had seen before in a store. They cost about a thousand bucks.

Then he saw it. He slipped across the cluttered floor and picked up the laptop with his gloved hand. The same password worked here.

He started going through files and downloaded to his flash drive anything that seemed relevant. He had just finished when he heard a door slam from down-stairs.

He hadn't heard a car drive up. But apparently Pete was home again.

Robie checked his watch. It was nearly four in the morning. Time had moved fast.

Robie stepped to the door and peered out. Pete would probably come up to his room and crash. Or he might not be alone. Then he might hit the hot tub with whomever he had with him.

Either way, Robie had to clear out of this room.

He slipped into the hallway, thinking that he would hide in another room up here and wait for Pete and whoever else might be with him to pass by. Then Robie would make his escape.

He had just stepped into another bedroom on the top floor and eased the door almost shut when he heard the footsteps coming up.

And then he heard the voices.

And with that, everything Robie had planned to do changed completely.

30

Pete Clancy indeed was not alone tonight. But on his arm he didn't have a half-stoned, half-naked girl waiting to get bedded.

There were three others with Pete. And all were men.

They wore slacks and jackets, but no ties. They were large, looked tough and probably were. Two of them were on either side of Pete, who was struggling to no avail.

"Let me go, please, I don't know nothin'. I swear to God."

"You'll be seein' God you don't give us what we need."

This came from the third man who was walking ahead of the other two.

He was a bit smaller than his two companions, and his suit looked more expensive. He also had a colorful pocket square. His face was lined and his hair had a touch of gray, while the other two were in their early thirties. They were obviously the muscle.

"Please, what do you want from me? I don't know nothin'," wailed Pete.

The third man turned around and threw a haymaker directly into Pete's jaw.

Pete slumped, held up only by the men on either side of him.

As Pete began to cry and spit blood from his mouth, the man who had struck him said, "Well, you sure act like you know somethin', dickhead. You send shit out and act like the big man, which makes it seem like you're in the loop. So if you're not, too bad for you, asshole. Lose, lose."

They dragged him into the office but didn't close the door behind them.

Robie checked to make sure there was no one else coming up the stairs, and then he slipped out, crossed noiselessly to the office doorway, and peered in.

They had forced Pete to sit down at the desk. The leader of the pack had his hand clamped around the back of Pete's neck.

"Okay, little Petey, all you got to do is show us what you got. Or what your old man had. And then we'll leave."

"You . . . you mean you won't hurt me?"

"Nah, why would we? You give us what we want, we're outta here. No hard feelings. You go your way, we go ours."

From the young man's expression Robie realized

that even Pete Clancy was not stupid enough to believe that.

Pete blurted out, "You're gonna kill me, don't matter what I do."

"Gee, Petey, you got me there. But there are degrees of killin', principally fast and painless, or the opposite. Which do you want? 'Cause your old man's got a copper soaking tub in his 'master suite' that's perfect for slow death by sulfuric acid bubble bath. There won't be a drop of you left, boy, but you'll feel all of it until you just can't stand it anymore. I know ways to keep you conscious till your skin's almost all gone." The man slammed Pete's face down on the desk. "You want that, huh, you little pissant?"

"Please, so help me, God, I don't know nothin'," pleaded Pete.

"Have it your way."

The man drew a gun.

And that was when Robie stepped into the room, his gun pointed at the man's head.

"Gun down. Step back, all three of you. Hands interlocked behind your heads."

They didn't do any of that.

The man lifted his gun. Or he tried to before Robie shot it out of his hand.

"Fuckit," screamed the man, who hunched over, holding his injured hand.

The other two men now stepped back from Pete Clancy.

Robie eased farther into the room.

The injured man slowly straightened and looked over at Robie. "Okay, slick, I can tell that you know what you're doing. So good for you. But why are you stickin' your nose into our damn business?"

"I don't know what your business is. Why don't you tell me?"

"Why don't you put down the gun and we can talk about it?"

"Pete, get over here, now," said Robie, his gaze on the trio of men.

The injured man said, "Way I see it, there's three of us and one of you. You might get two of us, but the last one will get you."

"Well, why don't I equal out the odds a bit then?" said Robie. With his left hand he pulled his spare Glock from his rear waistband and pointed both guns at the men.

"You got one dominant hand," pointed out the man.

"I'm ambidextrous, just so you know. And at twelve feet or so, not so good for you." He glanced at Pete. "Get over here, Pete."

The man put his uninjured hand on Pete's shoulder. "I think he should stay right here."

"You act like you're the one holding the guns."

"Maybe I am."

The man's elbow hit the half-full can of beer that was on the desk. It spilled out and over the base of the

desk lamp and its frayed power cord. There was a spark and the lights went out.

"Shoot him!" screamed the man.

Both his men drew their weapons and emptied their mags at the doorway. But Robie was no longer there.

The man on the right doubled over when Robie kneed him in the nuts. Then his right arm was wrenched up his back and Robie torqued it at an angle perpendicular to the man's back, blowing out both the radius and ulna bones in his forearm, leaving it limp and useless.

And very painful.

The man screamed as Robie shoved him over the desk. The other man was reloading his weapon when Robie struck. He slammed the point of his elbow into the base of the man's back. He cried out, jerked back, and managed to swing a fist at Robie. Robie took the hand, torqued the wrist back, and then wrenched it sideways, snapping the bone and then forcing it through the surface of the skin. He swung the arm around and jammed the exposed jagged wrist bone into the man's gut.

The man dropped behind the desk.

The third man had knelt to the floor. When he rose he had a gun in his good hand.

Robie disarmed him with a two-stroke maneuver, a grip on the muzzle forcing the weapon down, followed by a forearm lock immobilizing the limb,

coupled with a knee strike on the elbow, jamming it in a direction the bones normally didn't go. The weapon once more fell to the floor as the man howled in pain.

Robie placed the muzzle of his Glock in the center of the man's forehead.

"On the floor. Now."

The man dropped to his knees.

"For Chrissakes," exclaimed the man. "Who the fuck are you?"

Robie slammed the butt of his gun against the man's temple, knocking him out. Then he gripped Pete by the hair and pulled him up.

"Let's go!"

"But—"

"Move your ass. Now!"

He dragged Pete out of the room.

"I think my jaw is broken," screamed Pete.

"I don't really give a shit," said Robie.

"Where are we goin'?" yelled Pete.

"Away from the guys with guns and sulfuric acid."

They reached the back door and Robie kicked it open.

They stepped outside.

"I'm outta here," cried out Pete.

"No, you're coming with me."

"Why!"

"What did those men want with you? Who were they?"

"Leave me the hell alone!"

Pete pushed Robie away, but Robie regained his balance, stuck out his foot, and tripped the other man. Pete tumbled down the steps and landed in a crumpled heap at the bottom.

He stared up at Robie. "I'll kill you."

"Right."

Pete jumped up and sprinted off into the darkness. A few moments later Robie heard the Porsche start up, and it came careening around the side of the house. Pete slammed it into second; the wide wheels gripped the asphalt, and smoke streamed out from behind them as he accelerated to third and was past Robie, who had hurtled down to the bottom of the steps and aimed his weapon.

But he wasn't going to fire. For all he knew Pete would lose control of his ride and end up slamming into a tree. Hell, he might do that anyway.

Robie holstered his weapon, checked to make sure his other Glock was secure in his waistband, and hustled to his car. He drove off, certain that he had made multiple new enemies tonight. He just didn't know who they were.

But maybe one of them had killed Sherm Clancy. Which meant his father hadn't committed the crime and would go free.

He accelerated and zoomed down the road, his wake whipping low-hanging Spanish moss on trees.

Only Robie wasn't really sure where he was going.

31

By the time he had decided to return to the Willows it was after five in the morning, and the dark sky was just beginning to lighten a bit.

He sat in his car in front of the house, closed his eyes, and did his best to think things through.

The guys at Pete's house might very well be these casino junkyard dogs he had heard about. They thought Pete knew what his father had known, whatever that was. Pete apparently had sent them some communications that had pissed them off, resulting in the "meeting" tonight.

But Robie had intervened and saved Pete's life, risking his own by doing so. As a way of thanks, the "pissant" Pete had run off. He might well be in Louisiana by now. Maybe he'd never stop running.

Only the guys Robie had taken out weren't going to be leaving. If they didn't know who Robie was, they would soon find out. And he was sure other junkyard dogs would be sent out to finish the job the other three could not.

Which meant Robie was a target now. He stared

up at the house. He had promised to protect Victoria and Tyler, yet now he might be simply driving trouble their way.

Robie slipped the flash drive out of his pocket and palmed it, staring down at the little slip of plastic and metal that he hoped contained answers to many of his questions.

He looked back up at the house. But what to do about that?

Did he stay or did he go?

And even if I left here they could find out the connection and come here and hurt or threaten them to get to me.

He pocketed the flash, got out of the car, and slipped inside the house from the rear, scurrying up the column to the second-floor verandah and from there into his room.

He grabbed a quick hour's worth of sleep and then showered, letting the cold water fully wake him up. He had blood on his clothes from his fight. None of it was his, only the other guys'.

He washed off the blood as best he could and stuck the dirty clothes in the bottom of his duffel.

It was nearly seven a.m. now.

He called Blue Man and told him what had happened. Understandably, Blue Man was not happy.

"Things seem to be spiraling out of control, Robie. I want you to come back. Now."

"I can't do that."

"I am ordering you to return to DC."

"I'm on leave. I don't think you can order me to do anything."

"This is far more complicated than you think, Robie. If the Director gets any inkling about this . . ."

"Evan Tucker already hates my guts. I don't think this could make matters that much worse."

"You would be very wrong about that."

"I appreciate the advice. But if you want me back in the field one day with the ability to actually pull the trigger, then I have to see this through."

He clicked off and threw the phone down. He hadn't asked about Jessica Reel's status, because he figured the answer would be the same.

Still out. And now, he didn't want her around him. After last night things had gone to a whole new level, and Robie had no idea how things would turn out. But if the world fell on his head on this little strip of the Gulf Coast, he wanted it to be his head only. Not hers, too. She didn't deserve to be buried under his personal troubles.

He ate breakfast with Victoria and Tyler. The little boy snatched glances at Robie while he was eating.

Victoria seemed subdued, her mind far away.

As they were finishing up she said, "Did I hear you come in early this morning?"

"Not me. I slept like a baby."

She nodded. "Maybe it was the man you saw coming back."

"Maybe it was," said Robie. "I'll have a look around before I leave."

"Where are you going?"

"To see my father. Are you going to see him today?"

"I see him every day. And I'm going to take Ty with me this time."

Robie glanced over at the little boy. "I think that would do them both some good."

She lowered her voice. "You think so? Seeing his father locked in a cage?"

"He doesn't have to know that's what it is. It could be just a visit."

Victoria looked away, clearly frustrated.

"Keep your phone nearby. Anything comes up, call me."

She glanced up at him as he rose. "Why would something come up?"

"You just never know."

Priscilla followed him out of the house.

"Where were you last night? 'Cause I saw you climbin' up to the second floor of this here house at five this mornin'."

"Just getting some air."

"What, ain't no air in this house?"

"Different kind of air."

"And the stairs don't work for you?"

"Just my way of exercising."

"Uh-huh. You gettin' yourself in some trouble, Will Robie?"

"Not if I can help it."

He got in his car and drove off.

And that was when he heard the sirens.

As he neared the main road into town a fire truck flashed past him. Then another. Behind that was a police car and behind that an ambulance.

Robie was going to turn right to head to town. Instead he turned left and followed this posse of emergency vehicles.

Twenty minutes later he saw thick, black smoke billowing up from behind a forest of trees. Ten minutes after that the squad of emergency vehicles roared through the gates of the Clancy estate. The smoke was so thick that Robie, as he pulled his car to a stop on the other side of the road, couldn't see much past the gates.

A few minutes later he heard the rush of water as the firefighters combated the blaze. The police car had blocked the entrance to the house, moving only when another fire truck pulled in to join the effort.

Robie got out of his car and leaned against the front fender.

A minute later another cop car pulled up and Sheila Taggert climbed out. First she looked at Robie and snapped, "You keep your butt right there, Will Robie."

Then she hustled across the street to the other

police unit. The cop there rolled down his window and they spoke for a bit. Then she walked back over to Robie.

"What in the Sam Hill are you doin' here?" she said, getting right in his face.

"I was driving past and saw what was going on. Whose house is it?"

"Why do I think you already know whose house it is?"

"Because you have an overly suspicious mind, maybe?"

"It's the Clancy estate. What's left of it."

"Anybody hurt?"

"Don't know yet. And when I find out I won't be tellin' you. You can hear it through the gossip lines like everybody else 'round here."

"Know the cause yet?"

"Same answer to your last damn question."

"Well, I guess I'll be heading on."

She gripped his arm. "Robie, anything you need to be tellin' me?"

"If I think of something, you'll be the first to know, Deputy Taggert."

He drove off, checked his rearview once, and saw her staring after him.

He knew one person he had to talk to. And hoped that she would keep it confidential.

If there was such a thing as confidential in a place like Cantrell, Mississippi.

32

"Are you a damn fool or what?"

Toni Moses was staring up incredulously at Robie from her desk.

He had just finished telling her what had happened.

The lawyer's reaction had been reasonably predictable.

"I'm not sure what else I could have done," he countered.

"How about callin' 911? How's that for a damn plan?"

"Didn't seem like the best idea at the time, for a lot of reasons."

Her mouth curled to a frown. "You have put me in a precarious position. And I do not like to be put in precarious positions. I put others in them. Others do not do that to me. Particularly someone workin' for me. I specifically told you to do nothin' to jeopardize my case!"

"Well, since you're not paying me I'm not sure technically that I *am* working for you."

She rose, barely coming up to his chest. "Are you tryin' to split legal hairs with *me*? Seriously? 'Cuz I will whip your ass in a New York minute."

"Look, the point is, there are other people out there with a great motive to kill Sherman Clancy."

"But you don't know who they are?"

"We can find out."

"And you let Pete get away. He could tell us all about it."

"We can find him."

She sat back down. "I need to think about this, Robie. I need to really think this through."

"But you don't have to tell Aubrey Davis, do you?"

"I might very well. Crimes were committed. Folks tried to kill Pete and you."

"And someone set fire to the house."

"I heard about that a little bit ago. You think it's the same folks?"

"I didn't kill any of them. They had to get out at some point. And if they wanted to cover their tracks or destroy anything incriminating, that would be one way to do it."

She eyed him suspiciously. "So you overcame three armed men all by yourself?"

"I got the drop on them. No telling how far a little luck will carry you."

"Well, when your luck runs out they might just be carryin' you to a grave."

"Not the first time I've heard that." He held up the

flash drive. "I downloaded everything that looked material and relevant."

"And got that by breakin' and enterin', a crime in Mississippi and everywhere else in the civilized world. Doubt it'll be admissible. Tainted fruit, as they say."

"But even so, maybe we can use it to reach the truth."

"Are you dead set on gittin' on my last nerve?"

"Not my intent."

"Who do you think these men were with?" she asked.

"They seemed to be business partners of Sherman Clancy."

"So the Rebel Yell casino then?"

Robie shrugged. "Unless he had other businesses. And partners."

"I've heard stories."

"Like what exactly?"

"That this particular casino makes a lot more money than other casinos do."

"And how do they do that?"

"Your guess is as good as mine. Drugs, guns, human traffickin'? We got all those things down here."

"And the police don't know about this?"

"If they do, they're not doin' much to stop it."

"Why?"

"Mostly because of jobs. The Rebel Yell Entertainment Company has three casinos, two resorts, a theme park, and other business interests includin' film and

TV projects. It employs over three thousand hard-workin' Mississippians. One of the top employers in the state, in fact."

"And it doesn't matter if part of what they're doing is illegal?"

"Provin' it would be difficult. Havin' the desire to prove it appears to be impossible. You shut them down, you got a lot of folks without work. And the state already has enough of those."

"But I can tell you've done your homework on them."

"I know lawyers who work for them. Folks I respect."

"And what do they tell you?"

"Exactly what I would expect. Nothin'. They make good money, they do their work, they go home to their families, and they keep their mouths shut."

"And that doesn't bother you?"

"I didn't say it didn't bother me. But I can understand it. Lots of companies do bad things. Tobacco manufacturers pollutin' our lungs, coal and oil companies pollutin' our land and air, food manufacturers pollutin' the stuff we eat. Assholes on Wall Street stealin' us blind and buyin' five yachts and four jets with the proceeds and laughin' all the way to the proverbial bank as the anointed one-tenth of one percenters. Most of what they do is legal because they paid off the lawmakers to make it legal. But some of it's not. But they got money and jobs and lawyers and lobbyists

and politicians in their pockets, and so nobody touches them. Same with the good folks at the Rebel Yell. Welcome to America, Mr. Robie, where the only thing that's really *fair* is the color of most of these folks' skin."

"Okay. I think I get the picture."

"Do they know who you are?"

"They will by now. And they'll be coming for me."

"What are you goin' to do about that?"

"Be ready for when they do," he said.

She sat and steepled her hands. "Can I ask what it is exactly that you do for a livin'?"

"You can ask," replied Robie.

"But you can't say?"

"Look at the files on the flash drive and tell me what you think. I'm going to see my father."

"What are you goin' to tell him?"

"The truth. And in return I hope he does the same."

Taggert wasn't at the jail, so Robie was escorted back by the same deputy who had run him through the metal detector previously.

His father was sitting on his bunk. And this time he did not attack his son.

Robie leaned against the wall and in calm, succinct sentences explained to the man what had happened last night. When he was done, Dan Robie didn't say anything for several minutes. To his son it seemed his

father was thinking through every possible scenario, like he had first as a Marine, and then as a lawyer.

Finally, he cleared his throat and said, "They're goin' to want to kill you for what you did."

"I assume so."

"There's no assumption about it," said Dan Robie sharply.

"Do you know these people?"

"The Rebel Yell? Not really."

"Toni Moses thinks they're into illegal stuff."

"Could be," said his father. "Lots of that goin' around."

"Which means that they have a great motive for killing Sherman Clancy. After what I heard last night it seems to me that they're the prime suspect."

"Good luck provin' that."

Robie cocked his head. "We don't have to prove it. We just have to use it to cast reasonable doubt. Then you don't get convicted. Isn't that legally the way it works?"

"Legally, yes. Practically, no."

"Explain that to me."

"I get off on what folks round here will conclude was a technicality. They'll still assume I killed the man because my wife slept with him."

"Since when do you care what people think?"

"I *do* care what people in Cantrell think, because it is my home. They are my neighbors. They are my friends."

"Your real friends wouldn't believe you could kill anyone."

"Would your 'real friends' believe that you couldn't kill anyone?" his father shot back.

"No," admitted Robie. *They would know better*, he thought.

"So you're saying that you want conclusive proof of your innocence to come out of all this. Which means you did not kill Sherman Clancy."

"I never said I did kill him."

"But you never said you didn't. And while we're on the subject, was it you driving the Range Rover that night?"

"How is Ty doin'?" his father asked.

Robie took a deep breath and held it before letting it go. He had to remind himself that he could not get it all done today or tomorrow or the next day. Small steps, like executing a mission. You check off one box and then the next. And then the next.

"Seems to be holding up. Victoria said she was bringing him to see you."

For the first time Robie saw distress in his father's eyes.

"I'm not sure that's a good idea."

"Why not?"

His father barked, "I don't have to explain anythin' to you. I don't even know why the hell you're here."

Robie pushed off the wall. "I've got things to do. Anything you need?"

His father started to say something but then shook his head and looked away.

"I didn't hurt your arm, did I?" asked Robie.

"About as much as I hurt your face, so not much."

Robie turned to go.

"Watch out for those casino boys," said Dan Robie.

He turned back around, but his father still wasn't looking at him.

"I will," said Robie.

33

When Robie left the jail they were waiting for him.

"Agent Wurtzburger," he said, nodding at the FBI agent and two of his men, who were sitting in the vehicle parked next to Robie's.

"We need to talk," said Wurtzburger.

"Do we?" said Robie. "I said I'd call if I had anything to tell you. And I don't."

"We received a call about you from DC. Would you rather talk about it in the privacy of our car or do it right here in the open?"

Robie gave the three men a searching look and then climbed into the backseat of the sedan.

"What call?" asked Robie.

"From a sister agency that does not officially operate domestically."

Robie did not react to this externally, but the term *son of a bitch* floated across his thoughts.

"To do with me?"

"To do with you specifically. They didn't go into detail, but it was clear that you are a valuable asset that they do not want to see damaged or worse. I told my

244

superiors that I would do my best, but that I could hardly guarantee your safety unless I got you to leave town or locked you up somewhere."

Wurtzburger looked back at Robie from the front seat. "And I gather you would not be amenable to either of those options."

"No, I wouldn't."

"My superiors were also told that if we tried to force you to do so we had better bring in several teams of special agents loaded for bear, or it would ultimately be a losing proposition for us."

To this Robie said nothing.

Wurtzburger continued, "I tend to believe my superiors, so this will be a voluntary association, Robie, and nothing more than that. The last thing we need is for Feds to be duking it out with each other."

"Agreed."

"We understand that Sherman Clancy's house was set on fire either last night or early this morning."

"I heard that, too."

"Did you hear any more than that?"

"I might have."

"Can you enlighten us?"

"Pete Clancy is trying to follow in his father's footsteps with his casino partners. This apparently did not sit too well with some of them. They paid Pete a visit at his house. I happened to coincidentally stop by at the same time. They were giving Pete a hard time and I politely asked them to back off."

"And did they?"

"Surprisingly, they did."

Wurtzburger's expression was one of healthy skepticism. "Right. Did you kill any of them?"

"No. If I had that would have required me to report it to the police."

"Did you injure any of them?"

"Not permanently," said Robie. "Except maybe for two. It was hard to tell. It was dark and things happened a bit fast. I didn't wait around to triage them."

"I can understand that. Where is Pete Clancy now?"

"He was not as grateful as one would have expected, so he drove off in his Porsche. He might be a long way away by now. If he's smart, that is. But he might not be smart."

"And these folks burned down the house?" asked Wurtzburger.

"I wasn't there when that happened. But if I had to guess, they would have burned it down after they finished looking for what they wanted."

"Which was what exactly?"

"They said Pete had sent some e-mails to them that evidenced he knew things about them that his father had known. They weren't pleased about that. And they voiced that displeasure. They wanted him to show them what he had in the way of documentation backing up his position of knowledge. They threatened him with an acid bath unless he complied."

"And a quick bullet if he did?" said Wurtzburger.

"Yes."

"Could you ID these men?"

"Probably. But I doubt they'll be available for a lineup."

"Can you give us descriptions?"

"I can."

Robie took a minute to do so while one of the agents wrote it down.

"What sorts of things do you think they were looking for?" asked Wurtzburger when Robie was finished.

"Probably anything that had to do with their businesses. The Rebel Yell makes a lot of money. Apparently a lot more than the other casinos. So maybe they have more product lines in addition to the cards and chips."

"Local scuttlebutt again?"

"It's amazing what you hear if you just listen around this place. Folks love to talk."

"Have you told anyone else about this?"

"No," lied Robie.

"What you found out could be a great motive for killing Sherman Clancy. Which might mean your old man gets off the hook."

"That had occurred to me," said Robie.

"But keep in mind that if you screwed with the casino boys they're going to want retribution. And they probably already know who you are."

"I agree, on both points."

"You want some protection? I can spare an agent."

"I think you have your hands full. I'm good. But thanks."

"Change your mind, give me a call."

"I'll do that."

As Robie was getting out of the car Wurtzburger said, "I can understand that you're probably very good at what you do, but nobody's invulnerable."

"I've never thought otherwise," replied Robie.

34

"Hello?"

Wurtzburger and his men had just driven off. Robie turned to see the girl standing there next to his car. She was staring up at Robie with the expression of a child lost in a storm.

Emma Chisum. He remembered her from the arraignment. She'd been sitting next to her sister, Sara.

"You need something?" asked Robie, drawing closer to her. Then something struck him. "Shouldn't you be in school?"

"Mom homeschools me. She had some stuff to do this mornin'."

"Okay, everything all right?"

"You talked to my sister. She told me."

"I did. Yeah." Robie paused. "I'm very sorry about Janet."

"She made her choices. That's what Dad says. And then she paid the price for those choices. *Bad* choices."

Robie was taken aback by the bluntness of the statement. And then he noted that the girl actually didn't look lost in a storm. She just looked indifferent.

"What can I do for you?"

"Sara said you wanted to know things. Stuff that she might know about."

"That's right. I do. You know about my father?"

"Of course I do. Everybody in Cantrell knows about that."

"Do you know anything about it?" asked Robie.

"Yes. And I can tell you. But it won't be free. It'll cost you."

Robie nodded slowly, repulsed by the Chisum girls' obsession with money. But maybe they had never had any. He doubted Baptist preachers in backwater towns made much.

"How much?"

"A hundred," she said promptly, as though she had planned this all out.

"That's a lot of money. How do I know what you have to tell me is worth it?"

"That's the catch. You don't. And I want the money up front. Then I tell you. Then I leave. Those are my terms. Take 'em or not."

She swished her long hair out of her face and stared up at him with a coldness that was unsettling.

Robie gazed around. "It might look funny to folks if I gave you a hundred bucks out in the open."

"Do you really wanna do this in *private*? You and a young teenage girl exchanging money?"

Well, thought Robie, she had a point there.

"How about at the café over there. You thirsty? I can slip you the money while we're sitting."

"Let's go," she said. "I have to be back home in an hour."

They got their drinks, Robie a Coke and Emma a cup of coffee.

Robie said, "Coffee stunts your growth."

"That's bullshit," she said taking a sip. "And what did you expect me to get, a glass of good, wholesome *milk*?"

They were sitting at a corner table in the rear of the place that was pretty much empty at this time of day.

Robie had taken out five twenties from his wallet and under cover of passing her a napkin slipped them to her.

She counted them unobtrusively and placed them in her pocket.

"I could just leave now and not tell you anythin'. And if you tried to stop me I'd say you were tryin' to pay me to give you a blowjob or somethin'."

"I guess you could," said Robie evenly. "And I could tell your father all about it. He already told me Janet and Sara were sluts. Why not just make it all three? You're thirteen, right? I'm sure he'd be great to live with for the next five years."

Emma stared at him with emotionless eyes, took a sip of coffee, then leaned forward. "Janet told me she was goin' to meet someone that night."

251

"Who?"

"She didn't say who, just someone. But she thought it could mean a lot of money. Enough, in fact, to go back to Mobile."

"That was her plan?"

"That's all of our plans, except for Dad. We loved Mobile. We hate this place. Janet would be alive if we hadn't moved here."

"I think your father realizes that."

"He realizes shit."

"I don't think that's fair."

"Do you want to hear what I have to say or do you want to analyze how dysfunctional my family is? Because I'm not goin' to do both."

"Go on."

"Janet knew somethin'. I don't know what. But it was a big secret. She said it had to do with some important people in town."

"And that was where the money, the payoff, would come?"

"That's right."

"Did Sara know about this, too?"

"I don't know. Maybe."

"Maybe it was Sara who told you, not Janet."

"Why do you say that?"

"They were closer in age. I bet they spent more time together. You were just the kid sister to keep in the dark."

"So what!" she snapped. "I can still hear things."

"Yes, you can. What else?"

"Janet went out that night to make a big score. She was happy, really lookin' forward to it. And then she ended up dead."

Robie sipped his Coke and thought about what she had told him.

"What was Janet wearing that night?"

"What?"

"What was she wearing that night?"

"What does that have to do with anything?"

"Just indulge me. Sexy stuff, like for a date?"

"No. Jeans and a long-sleeved shirt. And sandals."

"Good memory."

"I watched her get dressed. Those were her favorite casual clothes."

So she wasn't going to hook up with a guy. This was money for something else.

"Okay. Did she say where she was going for this meeting?"

"The same spot, she said. I guess Sara knew what that meant. I didn't."

"You know what they were doing with Sherman Clancy?"

"What, you expect me to be all upset and stressed out? Yeah, I'm pissed that Janet is dead although she just thought of me as her dorky kid sister. But they needed money, and if Clancy was willin' to pay them, so what?"

"So you don't see anything wrong with that?"

"Consensual sex? No, not really. We're livin' in the twenty-first century, in case you hadn't noticed."

"Sex for money is illegal."

"Lots of things are illegal, that doesn't make them wrong."

Robie rubbed his eyes. He had little experience with teenagers, but he still couldn't believe he was having this conversation with a thirteen-year-old. Had the world really changed that much while he wasn't looking?

She said, "I was also pissed that I couldn't get any of that money. I bet Clancy would have paid me, too. Sara said he liked them young. And I wouldn't have done anythin' that would get me pregnant. I'm not stupid."

Okay, enough was enough. Robie stood. "Right, thanks for talking to me."

She took another slow sip of her coffee and rose, too.

"God, I never would've taken you to be such an uptight jerk."

"Yeah, me neither."

They walked out together. And right into Sara Chisum.

She looked at Robie and then at her sister.

"What are you two doin'?" she demanded.

"Just talkin'," said Emma sweetly. "He had some questions and I had some answers. And now I can get those shoes I wanted," she added gleefully.

Sara scowled at Robie. "I told you she knew nothin'. You stay away from her." She grabbed her sister's arm and jerked her away. "You stay away from us both!"

Emma looked back and called out, "Nice doin' business with you."

Robie looked over his shoulder and saw Victoria staring at him from across the street. She had Ty on her hip. She was in front of the jail. She was apparently going to see her husband.

Robie hustled across to her.

"What was all that about?" asked Victoria.

"What? The Chisums?"

"Yes, of course the Chisums."

"Just paying my respects and conveying my condolences."

She looked at him with great skepticism. "Right. That's exactly what it looked like, all right. Come on, tell me the truth."

"Emma had a little bit of information about the night Janet died. That she was going to meet someone and that she expected a nice payoff for it."

"Really? And who might that be?"

"She didn't know. Or didn't want to tell me. She's quite grown up for thirteen."

"Hell, Robie, girls down here get married at *fifteen* with their parents' consent. What'd you expect?"

"You going to see Dad?" Robie said quickly.

"Yes."

"With Ty?"

"Yes. I told you I was. Why?"

"I was in to see him a while ago. I told him you were bringing Ty. He didn't think it was a good idea."

"Well, like it or not, we're going in."

She turned and walked to the jail.

Robie watched her go and then turned in time to see the sedan pull out.

There were four men inside it. One of them Robie recognized. It was the guy from Clancy's house, the one he'd shot in the hand. His face was bandaged from where Robie had clubbed him with his gun.

And they had seen him with Victoria and Tyler.

Well, damn.

35

Robie called Blue Man and told him of this latest development.

"Wurtzburger touched base. He said he'd gotten a call. I have to say I was surprised that the Agency was so open with information about me."

"If you were indeed surprised, then you managed to miss the meaning of everything I said during our last call. Now it seems that you have been made by the people from the casino and they will undoubtedly seek payback."

"I'm prepared for that."

"And if they go after Victoria? Or her son?"

"I said I was prepared for that."

"Saying it and it actually being so is not the same thing."

"Why is Wurtzburger down here? I'd assumed it was for the folks at the Rebel Yell and whatever it is they're involved in that makes more money than gambling."

"I don't know and didn't ask. I was only focused on

the Agency's side of the equation, meaning you. What are you going to do now?"

"I'm not sure."

"Well, if I were you, I would achieve some clarity on that point. And do it sooner rather than later, Robie. That is my best, and *last*, advice to you on the subject."

This time Blue Man was the one who clicked off, leaving Robie to stare down at his phone and wonder if he was making a colossal mistake. That was as close to showing anger as Blue Man was likely ever to come. And it had shaken Robie more than a dozen people screaming at him.

He contemplated his next move and then made up his mind.

He bought a six-pack of beer and headed to Billy Faulconer's house.

"Damn, that tastes good."

Billy had just finished chugging one of the beers and then crushed it against his forehead.

Or tried to. The big man didn't have the strength to finish the job. He let the partially crumpled can fall to the floor.

Robie sat across from him sipping on his beer. He looked around the Airstream. It seemed that Angie had come and cleaned up quite a bit. The dirty dishes were gone, the floor and counters were free of litter, and the place smelled of bleach and air freshener.

Billy popped another can.

"Shouldn't you go slow on that?" asked Robie. "It might mess up your meds."

Billy looked at him in surprise. "Ain't on no meds, less you count the oxygen."

"Isn't the pain bad?"

Billy held up the beer and smiled weakly. "That's what this here is for."

He took a long drink and then rested the can against his chest. "How're things goin' with you?"

"Okay. Did you hear the Clancys' house burned down?"

"Little Bill done told me. Ain't had a fire like that for years and years. Lotta house to burn. Pete okay?"

Robie shrugged. "I don't know. Haven't seen him. By the way, my father pled not guilty. And he has a lawyer now. Toni Moses."

"Hear she's real good. And damn expensive."

"Well, when you're fighting for your life, what's money?" As soon as Robie said it, he regretted his choice of words.

"Guess you right 'bout that." Billy sank back on the couch and his breathing got a little heavier. "Fightin' for your life," he said in a low voice. "Only I'm past fightin', right? Hell, done is done." He tried to laugh but it died in his throat.

"What's the name of your doctor again?"

"Huh, oh, Doc Holloway."

"Where's his office?"

Billy stared at him. "Why, you sick?"

"Got a thing on my arm I want him to look at."

"Oh yeah, he's real good. He's on Wright Street. Near the Gulf Coast Diner. You 'member that place? Dollar pitchers and all the shrimp you could eat."

"I remember. How many times did we get thrown out of there for eating too much?"

"At least five times. But they kept lettin' us back in."

"Because we kept winning ball games. The ass-holes."

Billy laughed so hard he started choking. Robie rose quickly and got him breathing properly and settled again.

"So you got a problem with your arm?" wheezed Billy.

Robie nodded. "Nothing major. Just getting old."

"Sounds like a good deal, gettin' old," muttered Billy. Then he finished the second beer in one gulp.

Robie left Billy's an hour later and headed to see Doc Holloway.

He was in his fifties, slightly built, with a crown of graying hair and a bushy mustache. His blue eyes were capped by a pair of wild eyebrows.

Holloway had not been in Cantrell when Robie lived here, but he knew Robie's father, he told him.

Robie had him examine his arm. Holloway looked over the burn and scar tissue and said, "You're going to need surgery on this."

"Know a good one?"

"Not in Cantrell. You'll need to go over to Biloxi. I can give you a referral. How'd you come by that anyway? That's a right bad burn."

"Got too close to a fire."

Holloway gave him a condescending look. "Well, I figured something like that."

"I've been to see Billy Faulconer. Pretty sad to see him like that."

Holloway took off his glasses and cleaned them with a paper towel.

"Well, people's choices do have an impact on their health."

"So lung cancer then? From smoking?"

"I can't talk to you about that. Patient privacy."

"Right, only Billy told me it was lung cancer."

"Well, if he did I can't dispute it, but I also can't talk about it."

"I guess if he had come in earlier, gotten an X-ray, PET and bone scan, CT scan, and had a biopsy done, you might have caught it. But I suppose it showed up on all those tests confirmed as lung cancer?"

Holloway wrote something down on a piece of paper. "Here are the referrals for surgeons in Biloxi. For now keep it clean and don't exert yourself. Looks like you partially tore some of the scar tissue already."

Robie took the paper. "Right, thanks."

He walked out thinking Holloway was either just following the rules in not discussing Billy's case, or he

hadn't done the tests he was supposed to have done to confirm the man actually had terminal lung cancer.

Only Robie wasn't sure what he could do about it.

He drove back to the Willows.

Victoria's Volvo was there. She must have finished her visit at the jail. He walked inside and looked around. Priscilla came out from the kitchen rubbing her hands on a towel.

"You should keep the front door locked," said Robie.

"Since when? Ain't nobody in Cantrell lock their doors. 'Specially durin' the day. What if you got company comin'?"

"Then they can knock and you can come and *unlock* the door."

"I'll have to ask Ms. Victoria 'bout that."

"Don't worry about it. I'll talk to her about it. Where is she?"

"In her room."

He climbed the stairs and knocked on Victoria's bedroom door.

"Who is it? Priscilla?"

"It's Will."

"Oh, come on in."

He opened the door and stepped inside.

Victoria was lying on the bed, her shoes on the floor next to her. She sat up a bit on a pillow. Her face was puffy with sleep.

"I must have dozed off."

Robie stood next to the bed.

"How did it go at the jail?"

She propped herself up more and rubbed at her face, then pushed loose strands of hair back into place. "I must look a mess."

"You look fine. How was Dad?"

"Not too bad. He was mad at me for bringing Ty, but once Ty went over and hugged him all was right with the world."

"Good."

"He told me about Pete Clancy and those boys from the casino. My God, Will, you could'a been killed." She reached out a shaky hand and gripped his arm.

"Which is why I came up to see you." He sat on the edge of the bed. "You need to start taking some security precautions. For starters, locking the doors so no one can just walk right in."

"You really think these folks will try something?"

"They saw me in town talking to you. They saw Ty."

Victoria now sat up straight. "Oh, shit!"

"Yeah. It was bad luck, but we can't do anything to change that now. It is what it is."

"If they try to harm one hair on—"

Robie clutched her shoulder. "That won't happen, Victoria."

"You don't know that!"

"Do you own a gun?"

"Everybody in Mississippi owns a gun."

"Then I would start carrying it with you and keeping it handy around here. But don't leave it around for Ty to stumble across."

"As if I would, Will. I'm not stupid or careless."

"I know. I'm just being overly cautious."

She took several deep breaths. "I think I'll go check on Ty."

"I'm sorry for bringing this down on your head."

"I'm sorry too, Will," she said, and her tone was not friendly.

"I can move out of here," he said, interpreting her unspoken thoughts.

"Well, it's too late for that now. They saw you with us. They'll put it all together. Hell, they probably already have. Are they also the source of these credible threats?"

"I don't know, since I haven't seen these credible threats. Davis hasn't shared them with Toni Moses yet."

She rose, slipped on her shoes, and headed out to check on Ty.

Robie went to his room and sat on the edge of the bed, lost in thought. It hadn't occurred to him before, but as he looked around he realized that this had been Laura Barksdale's bedroom.

He should have noted it before. Late at night he had shimmied up to the second-floor verandah and into her bedroom enough times.

Her bed had been set here as well, and with the way the room was configured, it was the most logical place. Her desk had been against the wall facing the front of the house. She'd been an A student, unlike Robie. But he figured his grades were good enough, considering he played sports year-round and had far from a perfect home life.

He rose and went to the window overlooking the front of the house. This had been the same window where he had seen her silhouette.

His mind went back to that night over twenty-two years ago. It had been the biggest shock he had ever received: that she had chosen to stay here instead of go with him. If he had ever bothered to psychoanalyze himself, he might have concluded that his problem getting close to people might stem from that.

But he had never bothered, and thus never concluded.

His phone buzzed. The number was one he didn't recognize.

"Hello?"

"Mr. Robie?"

"Yes, who is this?"

"Sara Chisum."

He froze, but only for a moment. She was the last person he ever expected to be calling him, especially after what had happened with her younger sister earlier.

"Sara, what is it?"

"Uh, you said if I remembered anythin' that I should give you a call."

"And did you remember something?"

"Well, to tell the truth, I never forgot it."

"What is it?"

"It has to do with Janet. Who she was meetin' with the night she was killed."

"Who?"

"I don't want to tell you over the phone."

"Why not?"

"Look, Mr. Robie, Emma told me what you did."

"You mean what I *paid* her?"

"Right."

Now Robie understood the call. Little sister got paid, now big sister wanted her cut. Damn, thought Robie, these Chisum girls were nothing if not enterprising.

"All right, where and when?"

"Where we saw each other before. Tonight. Around eleven."

"Why so late?"

"Because I can't get away until my parents are asleep. My dad's been watchin' me like a hawk."

"Okay, how much?"

"Triple what you paid Emma."

"And if what you remembered isn't worth that?"

"Trust me, it will be."

36

Robie got there at ten, because he didn't like other people picking the spots for meetings. He had left his car about a quarter mile away and approached on foot.

He was currently motionless behind a tree taking stock of the land in front of him. He didn't like walking around out here late at night. Snakes were plentiful, and most of them were venomous. But even worse than that were the gators. The Pearl had its share of the deadly creatures. And though gators were mostly afraid of humans and avoided them whenever possible, sometimes the two species butted heads. And the gators won their fair share of those encounters.

The gator population had almost been wiped out in Mississippi by the 1970s. To replenish it the state had handed out baby gators at the state fair and asked folks to go drop them in the rivers. It had worked. Now there were nearly forty thousand of them in the state's waters. They were territorial creatures, and they did most of their hunting at night.

Robie had almost lost a leg to one while swimming at dusk in the Pearl as a teenager.

The one thing he had never forgotten from the encounter was how big the suckers were. And fast.

He had both pistols with him, and he would use them, if necessary, on snakes, gators, or anything threatening him that moved on two legs.

He continued to look around, listening for both human footsteps and the rattles of snakes.

At two minutes past eleven he heard them.

Footsteps. Light, uncertain, hesitant.

Then Sara Chisum appeared in the same clearing where she had encountered Robie earlier. Near where Clancy had died. Probably where her sister had gone into the Pearl with a hole in her head.

She had on cutoff jean shorts, tennis shoes, and a long-sleeved shirt that hung past her waist.

"Mr. Robie?" she called out.

Robie did not step out into the clearing.

"Are you alone?" he said.

"Yes," she replied.

A bit too quickly.

Robie's hand went to his waistband and out came one of the Glocks. A round was already chambered. He had three spare mags on him as well as his other Glock.

"Come all the way out in the clearing," he said.

She did so.

And then so did the other man. Right behind Sara.

It was the same guy from the other night: bandaged face in the car.

He held up his gun hand, which was also heavily bandaged. He had his gun in his left hand.

"Hello again," said the man. "Remember me, Mr. Robie?"

The guy was murderous intent all dolled up in gauze and attitude.

Robie looked around for the others. No way this guy came alone. They were probably starting to out-flank him now, coming from all corners.

Bang-bang you're dead.

Stupid for him to have come here alone at night. He fished for his phone. But who would he call?

Taggert?

Who knew how long it would take for her to get here?

And if she did manage it she'd be outgunned and end up dead like him.

911?

He remembered what she'd said about that.

They'd get here tomorrow to take pictures of the body. What was left of it.

He put the phone away.

"You better come out, Robie," said Sara, a touch of nervous triumph now in her voice. "They got you sur-rounded," she added, her voice quavering. "Should've offered to pay me more than three hundred!"

"Shut up, bitch!" yelled the man. He slugged Sara

with the butt of his gun. She screamed and fell to the ground, holding her head where he'd struck her.

The man pointed his gun at her.

"Robie, you got till the count of five and then she's dead."

"How about you being dead too, then?" replied Robie. He lined up his iron sights on the man's face. There was just enough moonlight to make this an easy kill.

"I've got lots of guns aimed at her, Robie. Even if you kill me, she's dead. And when you fire you reveal your position. And then you're dead."

"Looks like I'm dead either way, so why not take you and as many of your boys with me as I can?"

"Because if you come out with your weapon down I'll let her go."

"Bullshit."

"Please, Robie," sobbed Sara. "Please do it. They're goin' to kill me!"

"You were dead the minute you did the deal with them."

She shrieked, "Robie! I don't want to die!"

Robie was on the move. If the head guy was in the middle of the clearing he figured he had deployed his troops in a circle around that area, which would include where Robie was right now. If they had come in from the direction Sara had stepped from, that meant the guns assigned to get in behind Robie were

the farthest away and probably still getting into position.

He did not intend to allow that to happen.

He encountered the first sentry thirty seconds later. The man had a gun and a knife.

Robie stripped him of the gun and used the knife to slit the man's throat. He laid him quietly on the dirt and turned to his left.

"Robie, I'm going to shoot her in three seconds unless you walk out here."

"Kill her. Then you have no more leverage. Then I'll kill all of you. Guaranteed."

The man gripped the gun more tightly and looked around the dark woods. His confident look slowly fell away as though he had just realized his costly miscalculation. "One . . ."

Robie slipped to his left, passed by a tree in a low squat, found the second sentry anxiously peering around in suit and polished shoes, and snapped his neck cleanly. He laid this man down, too.

"Two . . ."

"Robie, please!" screamed Sara.

"Okay," said Robie. "I'm coming out."

He stepped toward the clearing, aware that as soon as he stepped into it a number of weapons would be pointed his way.

He had one gun in hand, his backup in the small of his back. And a knife palmed on the inside of his left hand.

He stepped into the clearing and looked over at the man and then down at Sara. The girl was trembling all over. When she saw Robie, she said, "Thank God."

She started to get up.

The man kicked her. "Stay down."

She sank back to the dirt, sniffling.

The man stared over at Robie from a distance of ten feet.

"Drop the gun."

Robie did so.

"I think you got other weapons."

"Maybe I do."

The man pointed his weapon at Robie. "You don't look so tough now."

"Neither do the two guys I already dealt with. You'll need to hire more."

"Not a problem. The position pays well. So should I kill her first or you?"

"What?" wailed Sara. "You said you'd let me go if he gave himself up."

"I was lying, you stupid piece of shit. You think I'm gonna kill him and leave you to tell everyone? Jesus, get a freakin' brain, willya? I'll be doing the gene pool a favor getting rid of you."

"Omigod, omigod," whimpered Sara.

Robie could see she was just about to go into hysterics, which meant he would kill her first. He slid the knife into place. Ten feet, not a problem. Aim for the neck, move to his left, pull his backup.

"Bye-bye, Sara, baby," said the man. He aimed his pistol at her head.

She shrieked and covered her head with her hands, as if that would matter.

Robie pulled his knife, took aim . . .

The sound of the shot shattered the night.

The man holding the gun on Sara stood there for a moment, not quite realizing what had just happened.

Which was that he had just died.

He dropped first to his knees, then to his hands, and finally onto his face, what was left of it.

Sara screamed and rolled away.

Robie slid to the side and pulled his backup Glock.

Shots erupted from all over.

Bullets whizzed and zinged overhead and more than occasionally smacked into trees. Bark flew off in jagged chunks, birds scattered from trees, small animals scurried away in the darkness as man, the world's most dangerous predator, got down to battle.

They were pistol shots, Robie could tell.

Mostly pistol shots.

But some weren't.

Some were high-powered rifle shots. The one that had killed the guy certainly was. And every time he heard it fire a moment later he heard a man grunt. And then he heard a body hit the dirt.

Robie raced over to Sara, grabbed her by the arm, and flung her behind a stand of trees.

He took up position behind an oak and peered

around the trunk, trying to take in the details of the battlefield.

A shot hit close to his head. He slid to the other side of the trunk and fired back at the spot from where the shot had come.

The firefight went on for another five minutes. Robie had used up both pistols' original ammo and eaten into one of his backups. He had killed one more guy for a total of three, and the rifle, he thought, had equaled that.

Then there were no more shots.

Only running feet. Bad guys were in retreat, leaving the dead behind.

Once they had disappeared, Robie surveyed what had become a battlefield complete with the requisite corpses.

"Omigod, omigod," whimpered Sara. She was still on the ground, curled into a little ball. "I could have died."

Robie looked at her in disgust. "You had no problem helping those guys come here to kill me!"

She didn't answer. She just kept on whimpering.

He whirled when he heard the sound. Two feet smacking dirt, as though someone had leapt from a tree.

"Don't shoot, I give up," said the voice.

A voice Robie instantly recognized.

He holstered his gun and peered around the tree.

The Guilty

Jessica Reel was standing there, her rifle over her shoulder.

She said, "I leave the country for five minutes, and you get yourself in so much trouble I have to come here and save your ass?"

37

Reel strode forward.

"Jessica, what the hell are you doing here?" Robie exclaimed.

"Blue Man called me back from assignment. Sent a jet to bring me directly here. Said you needed some backup over a family matter. Since I could easily relate to that, here I am."

"When did you get here?"

"Early this morning. I picked up your trail at the house where you're staying. Been following you ever since."

"I didn't see you."

She cracked a smile. "Would you expect to?"

"But why didn't you tell me you were here?"

"Blue Man told me to cover your six. Showing myself might have made that difficult. But with what happened tonight, I had no choice."

"Well, it would've gotten a little hairy without you here."

"Hey! Could you guys catch up later?"

They looked down at Sara, who was still crouched

on the ground. There was a small pool of sick next to her where she'd thrown up.

"I'm bleedin', okay?" she snapped. "I need medical attention. Now!"

Reel said, "I don't know, Robie. She was going to let these guys kill you for some quick cash. What say we just pop her right now and leave her for the gators? I saw one on the riverbank over there. Big sucker. Probably swallow her whole."

Sara stood and backed up against the tree. "You . . . you can't do that."

"Why not?" said Reel. "You were going to help murder my friend here. Why should you get to live?" She looked over at the body of the man who had held the gun on Sara. "He didn't."

"But I'm just a kid," whined Sara.

"No, you're an adult. You made choices. Really shitty ones." She looked at Robie. "What do you say? One right between the eyes, like her buddy over there."

Sara dropped to her knees again. "Omigod, omigod."

"As much as I like the idea, I think we just need to call it in," said Robie, hiding his smile.

Sara looked up. "So you're not going to kill me?"

Reel said, "He's not. I haven't made up my mind yet."

Sara collapsed flat to the ground. "Omigod, omigod!"

In a low voice Reel said, "Shit, I'd like to shoot her just to shut her up."

Taggert showed up a half hour later. She was not in uniform and her hair was full of cowlicks, but she had her gun out. When she reached the clearing and saw them, she said, "What in the hell is goin' on, Robie?"

Before he could answer she saw the dead body. "Holy shit! Who's he?"

"He's the dead guy," replied Reel. "At least one of them."

Taggert scowled and said, "And who are you?"

Robie answered. "She's a friend of mine who came to my aid. Without her Sara and I would be dead."

Sara pointed at Reel and cried out, "That bitch said she was goin' to kill me."

Taggert looked from Reel to Sara and then back at Reel.

Reel said, "She lured Robie here so these guys could kill him."

"Did not!" screamed Sara. "He . . . he arranged to meet me here for *sex*. He was payin' me for it! The sick bastard."

"Then exactly how do you explain the dead guy?" said Reel.

"He . . . he was here to rob us," said Sara lamely. "While we were doin' it. Scared me to death. I was all naked and all."

"So if we examine you, we'll find traces of . . . Robie here on your body?" asked Taggert.

Sara looked doubtful. "Um, well we hadn't gotten to that part yet. We were just kissin'."

"But you just said you were doin' it and you were all naked when this guy came to rob you in his suit and tie in the middle of the woods," Taggert pointed out.

"Oh, right, well, I mean—"

Taggert had obviously had enough. "Just sit your butt on the dirt and shut the hell up," she barked. "Before I arrest you for obstruction of justice and wastin' police time. But mostly for bein' a dumb shit."

Sara sank to the ground, her face in a childish pout.

Taggert turned to Robie. "Okay, talk to me."

He took five minutes to explain it all. They walked around the area and found six more bodies. All men, all in suits, all with guns.

Robie said, "I killed three of them. Reel here got the other four, including the guy over there who was going to shoot Sara. Whoever was left beat a fast retreat."

"And you think they're with the Rebel Yell?"

"I don't know, but they were the same guys that were at Pete Clancy's that night."

Taggert gave him a triumphant look. "So you *were* in the middle of that."

"Yeah, I was. I saved Pete's butt. They were going to kill him."

"You should have told me," she said crossly.

"I did tell the FBI."

"FBI!"

"In the form of Special Agent Wurtzburger from Jackson. They're in town. Didn't you know?"

"No, I didn't know. Why are they here?"

"I imagine they're here investigating the Rebel Yell for various and sundry infractions of federal law."

Taggert scratched her head and placed her hand on the butt of her service weapon, which hung in its holster. She looked over at Sara. "And I see you're head over heels involved in this crap."

"Please don't tell my dad. Please!"

"If you think that's all you have to worry about, missy, you're even dumber than I think you are," snapped Taggert.

She gazed at Reel and the rifle she still held. "And where did you come in from?"

"I can't say."

"Why not?"

"It's a secret."

"You shot all them men, in the dark?"

"I was up a tree. Gave me a nice line of sight. Like picking off tenpins all lined up in a row."

Taggert looked at Robie. "And you slit one guy's throat and broke another one's neck? And they were both armed?"

"Well, yeah."

"Who the hell are you people!" exclaimed a clearly exasperated Taggert.

"Just concerned citizens standing our ground," said Reel. "You folks have that law down here, right?"

"I'm going to have to call the sheriff, get some deputies down here to secure this scene then process it, and then y'all are goin' to have to make statements 'bout all this." She gazed at Sara. "Includin' you."

"But my daddy!"

"I don't give a damn 'bout your *daddy*, okay? This here is a crime scene and things are gonna be done in a professional manner. You understand me?"

Sara finally nodded, though she looked like she wanted to grab a gun and shoot herself.

Taggert stared at Robie and Reel. "Now if you two have a problem with that, I'm just gonna have to arrest you and take you in."

Reel looked at Taggert like she might just shoot her instead. The deputy seemed to realize this, because she turned to Robie and said quickly, "It's my job, okay?"

Robie nodded. "I know it is. And we'll cooperate."

"To the extent we can," interjected Reel.

Taggert started to say something but then just shook her head and pulled out her phone.

As she walked away to talk in private, Reel said in a voice only Robie could hear, "Blue Man filled me in some, but there's still a lot I don't know."

"You'll know it all, Jess, before the night is out." He paused. "It sure is good to see you. I have some things I want to talk to you about."

"Blue Man mentioned that, too."

"Did he tell you everything about . . . that?"

"I think he preferred that you told me, in your own way."

Robie looked relieved.

"So how has it been, coming home?" asked Reel.

"You remember how it was for you?" he replied.

"That bad, huh?"

"That bad," said Robie.

He put out a hand and gripped her rock-hard shoulder. "Thanks, Jess. You saved my butt tonight."

"This doesn't come close to making us even," she said. "Not that anything will."

"I just know that I'm really glad you're here."

"Where else would I be, Robie?"

"Are you two like, datin'?"

They looked down to see Sara staring at them in mild disgust.

"What if we are?" said Reel.

"Well, aren't you two kind'a old to be doin' that?"

Reel raised her rifle. "Keep it up, Sara, and you won't get close to our *advanced* age."

Sara hugged herself tight and started whimpering, "Omigod, omigod."

38

Robie and Reel sat across from Sheriff Keith Monda in the latter's office on the main thoroughfare of Cantrell, which was barely two car lengths wide. They had been up all night. It was past eleven in the morning now.

Monda was a heavyset man in his fifties, with iron-gray hair gelled straight back. He was in uniform, and an unlit cigarillo rolled around in his mouth, while a deep scowl was set in his features.

His office was small and cramped, with cinderblock walls and an old-fashioned calendar hanging on one wall. There wasn't a computer on his desk or any other evidence that the man had entered the latter part of the twentieth century much less the twenty-first.

When he settled back in his old roller chair, it squeaked and so did his gun belt.

Taggert stood next to him. She was in uniform now and had a nervous expression on her face.

Monda took the cigarillo out of his mouth and said, "I've been briefed on all of it by Taggert here. And I got a call into the FBI but I haven't heard back

yet. Now I'd like to hear things from you two, 'cause I don't much cotton to people havin' shootouts 'round here."

Robie explained everything that had happened thus far.

Monda looked at Reel. "So where do you come in exactly?"

"I come in exactly as Robie's professional colleague."

"Which neither one'a you have elaborated on. What is it that you both do?"

"I have a phone number that you can call," replied Robie.

The man's scowl deepened. "I'm not interested in callin' anybody. I want to hear it from you. Right now."

Reel said imperturbably, "The number is in Washington. It's a federal government phone number. They can tell you certain things at their discretion."

"And you can't?"

"We're not allowed to," said Reel. "You can lock us up if you want, but that won't change things."

Monda placed the cigarillo back into his mouth and eyed her. "Taggert here said you shot down four armed men with a rifle in the dark."

"Well, they were shooting at me. And I don't much *cotton* to that."

"I don't doubt that. What are you two, like special forces or somethin'?"

"Or something," said Robie. "The phone call will explain things."

"To a degree," amended Reel.

Monda nodded and asked for the phone number. He wrote it down as Robie recited it for him.

Monda said, "Okay, just so we're straight on all this, we are not releasin' any information about what happened. I don't want any panic. I've told Sara Chisum to keep her mouth shut or she'll get in trouble. And you two keep this to yourselves."

"You know Cantrell," said Robie. "Small town where everybody knows everybody's business. Hard to keep something like this quiet."

"Well, we're sure gonna try."

"You might want to put Chisum in protective custody."

"Well, if I did that it would let the cat out of the bag."

"But if those guys come back?" pointed out Robie. "How about giving her protection at home?"

"I don't have the manpower for that. But I will have my deputies check on her periodically. And discreetly."

Robie wasn't satisfied by this answer, but it wasn't like he had much leverage.

Monda leaned farther back in his chair and said, "You're Judge Robie's son, I understand. You left before I came to Cantrell. I was up in Hattiesburg till about ten years ago."

"I've been gone over twenty years now."

"And back here because of your daddy?"

"Yes."

"He was a good judge. Hard on us cops, but he was fair. If he didn't kill Sherm Clancy I hope things turn out all right for him."

"Me too."

"So these dead men were interested in Pete Clancy?"

"They were. As I told Deputy Taggert, his father had dealings with these people. Pete was apparently trying to replace his father in that relationship, I'm assuming, with the Rebel Yell people. They didn't particularly care for that. They wanted Pete to give them whatever his father had in the way of information, I guess, on those dealings. Then they were going to kill him."

"So you think they might have killed Sherman Clancy?"

"It's possible, certainly. Seems like they might have had a strong motive."

"None of 'em were carryin' ID. We're runnin' prints and such, but they haven't come back yet. Point is, we don't know who they are. May never know. And if we don't we can't connect 'em to the Rebel Yell."

"What exactly do you know about the Rebel Yell?" asked Robie. "I've just heard local gossip."

Monda's expression became guarded as he tapped

his fingers on the desk. "They're a big company. They got some locals on their board and runnin' some of their operations. But the real ownership is sort of a mystery. Could be Chinese or Saudis runnin' the place for all I know."

"And they seem to be incredibly profitable. Able to build all this stuff out of their cash flow," said Robie.

"That's the word hereabouts, yes. But they're a big employer. Pay a lot in taxes. They got politicians in Jackson lined up to support 'em. You're talkin' tens of millions of dollars and thousands of jobs and for a place like Mississippi, it's hard to mess with that."

"But if they're doing something illegal?" said Robie.

"Well, we got to prove that. And I don't see anythin' here that would do that."

"It'll involve some digging," said Robie.

"I don't have the manpower or resources to dig unless I got some probable cause to do so," countered Monda.

"Do you mind if we do some digging?" asked Robie.

"I don't want nobody gettin' hurt, includin' you two."

"If the Rebel Yell had an incentive to kill Sherm Clancy, then that's a defense for my father in his murder trial."

"I'm aware of that," replied Monda. "But what I'm tellin' you is that you go stickin' your nose in places

like the Rebel Yell, don't think that the Cantrell Police Department can protect you if things go sideways."

"We would never think that," said Reel in mild disgust. She rose. "Can we go now? I could use some shut-eye. It's been a long night."

Monda stared up at her. "Didn't think they let women in special forces stuff. More of a man's world, right?"

"Well, you know the old saying: 'If you want it done, send a man. If you want it done *right*, send a woman.'"

Reel turned and walked out.

Taggert had to look away so Monda would not see the smile on her face.

Monda eyed Robie. "She always that—?"

"—decisive? Yeah."

Robie stood. "If you need us for anything else, Taggert can get hold of us."

"Robie, I meant what I said. My job is to uphold the law. But takin' on the folks at the Rebel Yell? Well, let's just say we're not equipped for that."

"I hear you," said Robie. "But it's my father's life on the line. So whatever road will get him off, I'm going down it. Rebel Yell included."

After he left, Monda eyed Taggert.

"So what do you think 'bout all this, Sheila?"

She considered this for a moment.

"Well, sir, if I were the folks they're goin' after, I think I'd be shittin' my pants."

39

"I don't have to stay here," said Reel.

She and Robie were standing in front of the Willows.

"And this looks a little too fancy for my tastes," she added. "I'm more into bunk beds and potbellied stoves. Antebellum structures and mint juleps on the verandah just aren't my thing."

"Victoria is nice. And there's really no other place to stay around here."

"Are you sure she'll be okay with it?"

"Okay with what?"

Victoria had come around the side of the house with Tyler in tow. He had on shorts and a T-shirt. She had on white Capri pants and a sleeveless, pale blue blouse against the heat.

"With my friend Jessica staying here at the Willows."

Victoria walked over to them and each woman ran her gaze up and down the other, completing a quick but in-depth appraisal.

Victoria said, "So you're Will's friend?"

"Yes."

"Just got into town?"

"Just."

"How long will you be staying?"

"Long as Robie needs me."

Victoria eyed Robie. "Need her for what?"

"For what's going on with my father."

"But what can she do? Is she a lawyer?"

"No, just someone I've worked with in the past."

She slowly nodded. "You weren't here when I came down this morning. Did you go out early again, Will?"

"Something like that."

"You know if you're staying in my house I do expect some common courtesy. You're a grown man and you don't have to account for your whereabouts, but I was worried about you. What with all that's going on. I don't want to have to go tell your daddy that something has happened to you."

"I'm sorry, Victoria. I should have called."

Reel looked down at Tyler, who was staring up at her with his finger in his mouth.

"And who's this little guy?" she asked.

"This is Tyler, Will's stepbrother."

Reel shot Robie a glance. "Meaning that you're his—?"

"—stepmother? Yes, I am. But I'm not wicked. At least to my friends."

Robie avoided Reel's piercing look. "So it's okay

that she stays here? She can actually help with what we talked about."

"You mean security?" said Victoria, looking skeptically at the slender Reel. "How about I just hire some big, burly guys?"

"If you want the JV team, go ahead," said Reel matter-of-factly.

"Jessica can help us," said Robie. "I mean really help us."

"If you say so," replied Victoria, shrugging. She picked up Tyler. "I need to get this boy some lunch. You two want to settle in and then join us? We're eating in the pavilion. Get some breezes down there that will feel really good on a day like today."

She walked off.

Reel looked at Robie. "Stepmother? Did you know before you came?"

"No."

"Must've been a shock."

"It was."

"Cute kid."

"He doesn't talk. Has some issue."

Reel stared after Victoria and Tyler as they reached the house and went inside. "That's too bad."

Robie leaned against the front fender of his rental. "We need to find Pete Clancy."

"He might be dead."

"Don't think so. He's on the run."

Reel said, "Well, then he might be far, far away."

"You think Blue Man could help us there?"

"I think you need to stop stomping on the good graces of Blue Man."

"He said that?" he asked.

"No, but I interpreted that. You've got me. I think that's going to be it. He doesn't even want you down here."

Robie sighed and stared up at the Willows.

Reel followed his look. "What's up?"

"I have memories of this place. A . . . girl."

"Do tell."

Robie filled her in on Laura Barksdale and the night he had left Cantrell for good. Or so he thought.

"So Romeo lost his Juliet?"

"Something like that."

"Whatever happened to the Barksdales?"

"I don't know," replied Robie.

"Well, maybe you should find out."

He shot her a glance. "Why, what does it matter?"

"I can tell that it does, to you. And if you come back to your hometown, you might as well address everything while you have the chance. You might not get another."

Robie glanced over at her, surprise on his features. "You speaking from experience?"

"What else?"

"I wouldn't really know where to start."

"How about with your father?"

"My father? I'm not sure I can talk to him about that."

"Robie, my father was someone you couldn't talk to about anything. But unless your dad is a racist murderer like mine, then I think you can probably have a conversation with him."

40

At the luncheon outside, Tyler kept his gaze swiveling between Robie and Reel.

Victoria picked up on this and said, "He's wondering why you're here."

Reel put a hand on Robie's shoulder. "I'm Will's friend."

Robie nodded.

Tyler immediately touched his heart and then pointed at Reel.

She looked taken aback by this and glanced over at Victoria.

"Congratulations, you've been officially inducted into Tyler Robie's Hall of Love."

Reel stared quickly down at her plate while Victoria studied her closely.

"Do you have children, Jessica?"

Robie glanced sharply at Reel but said nothing.

Reel lifted her gaze to meet Victoria's. "No."

"Well, it's not too late for you. Look at me. We're probably the same age."

"Yeah," said Reel tersely. "About."

After lunch, Priscilla cleared the dishes. Victoria had gone into the house with Tyler, leaving Robie and Reel at the table.

"So you be stayin' with us?" asked Priscilla, eyeing Reel.

"For a while, yes."

"I'll set up a bedroom for you."

"Please don't go to any trouble. I don't need much."

"No trouble."

She swept some crumbs off into the grass and said, "Heard tell there was some trouble last night."

"Who did you hear that from?" asked Robie.

"I forget. Might be some folks that were in the woods last night on the north side of town doing some gator baggin'."

Robie and Reel exchanged a glance.

Priscilla continued. "But I'm sure you two don't know nothin' 'bout that."

"We don't hunt gators," said Reel.

"How 'bout people? You hunt them?"

"Well, that would be illegal," pointed out Reel.

"Uh-huh," said an unconvinced Priscilla as she gathered dishes in her arms.

Robie rose. "Let me help with those."

"No, no, just sit yourself down and enjoy this fine Mississippi heat and humidity."

She sped off to the house.

"I think we've been made," said Reel.

"Small town," said Robie. "But 'made' by gator hunters is a first for me."

"So instead of taking in this fine Mississippi weather, why don't we go see your dad?"

"Let's go see his lawyer first. I want to find out if she learned anything from the files I found at Pete Clancy's."

As they walked toward the front of the house, Reel said, "So what is this lawyer like?"

"Toni Moses? Well, let's just say that the phrase 'force of nature' doesn't do the lady justice."

"Gotta meet her," said Reel. "If just for the novelty."

Moses met them in her office. Robie had introduced the two women and then Moses had immediately launched into discussion.

"These files you brought me?"

"Anything helpful?" asked Robie.

"The money part was easy. Sherm Clancy made a lot. And he spent a lot. And he recorded every dime of it."

"What else? Anything about the Rebel Yell?"

"I'm sure there would be, if I could read it."

"What do you mean?" asked Robie.

"Take a look for yourself."

She spun her computer screen around so they could both see it.

They read down the screen.

Reel said, "It looks to be in code."

"That was my conclusion," said Moses.

Robie sat back. "I wonder if we can find someone to break it."

"Like who?" asked Moses.

"The FBI, maybe? They're down here investigating."

"I wouldn't advise that," said Moses.

"Why?"

"You stole this from the Clancys' residence. Which means it's tainted. So, technically, the FBI can't use it. I doubt they'd even look at it. Could get them folks in trouble. Condonin' a felony."

Robie looked at Reel. "How about our folks?"

"Remember what I said? I wouldn't go there. Know any nerds down here that could do it?"

Robie thought about this. "I might." He turned back to Moses. "But we do have something to fill you in on."

He took a few minutes to tell Moses about what had happened the previous night.

Her jaw dropped lower and lower as he spoke. When he was done she shot a glance at Reel. "Who the hell are you people?"

"You're actually not the first one to ask that," said Reel.

"And the answer would be?" persisted Moses.

"We can't tell you," said Robie.

"You're gonna give me a heart attack, you know that!"

"Not our intent. Have you seen my father today?"

"Went over this mornin'. You plannin' on seeing him?"

"Going over there next. How's his mood?"

"I can say truthfully that it hasn't changed." She paused. "Well, maybe it has."

"How so?" asked Robie.

She peered up at him. "He seems, well, resigned."

"To what, his fate?"

"To somethin'."

"I don't understand."

"Look, Robie, I've seen it happen before. Sometimes people just shut off and let the process do what it will do. And sometimes they do that because ..."

"They do that why?"

"Maybe from guilt."

"So you're saying he killed Clancy? I thought that didn't matter to you."

"It doesn't. To me. But maybe it matters to him."

41

They left Moses's office.

Robie had a copy of the files from Clancy's computer on a flash drive.

"What are you going to do with that?"

"I have a guy who's good with computers. He might be able to figure it out."

"What about your dad?"

"I need to see him, too. And then I have to talk to a doctor. His office is a couple blocks from here."

"A doctor? Are you sick?"

"No, but a friend of mine is."

"Look, why don't we split up then? You need to see your dad and this doctor. Why don't I run down your computer guy? We can meet up back here."

"You sure?"

"There're two of us. Why not make the most of it?"

"You armed?"

"Hell, do you really have to ask?"

He gave her the name and address, and she drove off.

Robie went to the jail where Taggert appeared to be waiting for him.

"There's already talk goin' round 'bout what happened," she said in a low whisper, so the other visitors in the waiting room couldn't hear.

"Did you really expect to keep that quiet? Priscilla already knew about it."

"Shit! I guess you want to see your dad?" she said.

"I guess so. I understand that Toni already saw him?"

Taggert nodded. "Yeah, she didn't look too happy when she left."

He and his father met in the visitor's room. Taggert did not chain the prisoner to the hook in the floor. Robie flashed her a grateful look for this.

The two men sat across from each other. The senior Robie looked thinner and haggard, with gray stubble on his chin.

"You okay?" asked Robie.

His father shrugged. "Under the circumstances, fine."

"Some things have happened that you need to know about."

This got his father's attention. Robie recounted for him the events of the previous night.

"So this Jessica Reel saved your neck?"

"Not the first time."

"You two in uniform?"

"Not exactly."

"Then what exactly?"

"We serve our country in a different capacity."

Dan Robie looked taken aback by this. He looked at his son's arm. "You got wounded servin' your country?"

"Yeah, I did."

The man nodded slowly. "Why don't you and your friend just get on back to doin' what you do then? No reason to stay here."

"No reason? Other than you're on trial for murder?"

"Why is that your concern?"

"I've made it my concern."

"Let's not pretend there's any love lost between us, okay? That's just a waste of both our time."

Robie scowled. "Why do you have to make this so hard? I'm here. I came all this way."

"That was your choice, not mine." Before Robie could respond his father held up a hand and said, "I'm glad you're not dead. I'm glad your friend Jessica was there to help you. But considerin' all the facts, I think it best for you and her to leave."

"And what about Victoria and Tyler?"

"I'm goin' to tell them to leave, too."

Robie looked shocked. "What!"

"I've thought it through. Just until the trial is over and things get back to normal. Although if I'm convicted there'd be no reason for them to come back. She can sell the house and move somewhere else. Get on with her life."

"Have you talked to Victoria about this?"

"Not yet."

"There is no way in hell she's going to leave you, I hope you know that."

"I'll make her see reason." He stared grimly at his son. "I've never had trouble makin' myself clear, have I?"

"She's still not going to go."

"Well, that's my problem, not yours."

"You're making no sense."

"And you're not listenin'. Just like when you were a punk kid. You don't listen, Will, to a damn thing!"

Robie sat back and crossed his arms over his chest. "It's a two-way street, isn't it? The not-listening part?"

"I was the parent. You were the child. It was my job to tell you what to do and it was your job to do it."

"No, I was your son, not some Marine recruit you were trying to turn into a killing machine. And how could I grow up as your son and not learn to question everything? Just like you did?"

Dan Robie started to say something but then stopped. He snorted and looked away, shaking his head.

"I'm not leaving," Robie said quietly. "I did remember one lesson you taught me. Never leave a job unfinished."

His father glanced at him. "You really servin' your country?"

"Yes."

"You good at it?"

"Yes. Some might say one of the best. So is Jessica."

"That's interestin'. A girl doin' what is traditionally a man's job."

"She might be even better than me. And I recently ran into a woman from another country about half my size who could take on five veteran jarheads and kill them all before they even knew what had hit them."

"Seriously?"

"Very seriously."

His father fell silent and Robie watched him closely.

He said, "Why the change in attitude? Where's the fighter inside you?"

"Need somethin' worth fightin' for."

"And your life isn't?"

His father shrugged.

Feeling he was going in circles over this, Robie decided to change the subject. "Whatever happened to the Barksdales?"

Dan Robie glanced up. "The Barksdales?"

"Yeah."

"Why?"

"Just wondering. I'm staying at their old home."

His father nodded, his look wary.

"What is it?" asked Robie.

"You and Laura. That was a mistake, you know."

"What the hell do you mean by that?"

His father said, "You came from different walks of life. Never would have worked out."

"You don't know that!"

"I do know that. And it didn't work out, did it?"

"I'm not going to waste time discussing this with you," snapped Robie.

"You just won't listen, will you?" said his father in disgust.

Robie barked, "What happened to the Barksdales? I know you didn't buy the Willows from them."

"I didn't. They were long gone by then."

"Gone where?"

Dan Robie shrugged. "Don't know. They just up and moved out one night. They were just gone." He added, "Like you."

"When?"

"I don't remember exactly. It was a long time ago."

"How long after I left?"

His father thought about this for a few moments. "Not that long, actually."

"So you didn't see them before they left?"

"I wasn't that close to them. They were the aristocracy of Cantrell. I was just a lowly lawyer. I was surprised that they let you date their precious daughter. Henry Barksdale was so damn proud of his ancestral roots. He thought his family walked on water. That his shit didn't stink. I thought he was a pompous idiot."

"They had a lot of money," pointed out Robie.

"Goes to show that money doesn't buy class."

"So you didn't do their legal work?"

"Hell no. I wasn't established enough. They used Parnell and Longstreet. Been here forever. The founding partners have long since died. Stuart Longstreet is still here, though. He handled their affairs when they were livin' in Cantrell." His father studied him. "Why all the questions about the Barksdales? What's going on?"

"It's pretty simple. Regardless of what you thought, I loved Laura. And I just would like to know what happened to her."

"Well, good luck with that. Not that she'd care. You just up and left all of us, didn't you? Her included."

Robie rose. "Hey, Dad, keep your spirits up. You never know, you might just beat this rap."

42

"Is Little Bill here?" Reel asked Angie Faulconer, as the two women stood on the front porch of the Faulconers' home. "I'm a friend of Will Robie's. He wanted me to give him something."

"He's at work right now."

"Can you tell me where?"

"What is this about?" the woman asked suspiciously.

"Robie said that your son is really good with computers. He has a job for him to do. A *paying* job," Reel added, eyeing the poor state of the woman's house.

"Oh, okay. I can do that. He works over at the mall. At a video game store."

"Didn't know you had a mall here."

"It's just a strip mall. Half the stores are closed, but kids like their video games, I guess."

She gave Reel directions and also told her she would call her son so he would be expecting her. Reel drove there in about twenty-five minutes, mostly on winding back roads that weaved in and out of forested land interspersed with swamps.

As Angie had said, the strip mall was half boarded up. The sidewalks were cracked, with grass growing in the crevices. The parking lot's asphalt was lumpy and she could count the number of cars at the mall on two hands. But they were all parked in front of the video game shop, which seemed to have a lot of activity.

When she walked in a bell on the door tinkled. Reel looked around approvingly. The shop was clean, the displays sharp and eye-catching, and the games neatly racked. There were about twenty customers in the shop, mostly teenagers but some adults, too.

A tall, burly young man came up to her. "Are you Jessica?"

"Yes, you must be Bill."

"Mom called. She said you had a computer problem?"

"Will Robie does. Which means it's my problem, too." She looked around. "But you look pretty busy. Is this a good time?"

"Oh, yeah. They all know what they want. They're just wastin' time, playin' games. And the longer they stay the more they tend to buy. And there're two other people on duty. Come on back."

He led her into the rear of the shop where there were some desks and shelves and stacks of boxes. On each desk was a shiny Apple computer.

"So what's the problem?" asked Little Bill.

Reel pulled out the flash drive. "There's information on here that we need, but it seems to be in code. I know that's not exactly a computer problem, but we thought we'd ask."

"Can I see it?"

She handed it across. Little Bill sat down and popped the drive into the desktop's USB slot. With a few clicks he brought the file page up.

"Uh, Mom said you were goin' to pay me?"

"How about two hundred bucks?"

"Damn, sounds good to me!"

"You know about codes?" asked Reel, who was staring over his shoulder.

"I know how *to* code. Which isn't the same thing, I realize. But a lot of the games we sell here have codes you have to break, so I know some things about that."

He studied the files and keyed up one.

"Looks like gibberish to me," said Reel.

"Where'd this come from?" asked Little Bill.

"I'd prefer not to say."

He stared up at her. "Why?"

"I'd also prefer not to answer that."

"Is this somethin' illegal?"

"It's something that could lead to the truth coming out," she replied diplomatically.

"Is this somethin' about Will Robie's daddy?"

"Could be."

"It would help if you told me where you got it."

"Why?"

"It just would."

Reel debated and then said, "Pete Clancy."

Little Bill smiled. "Well, then I think I can get it to make sense."

"Why?"

"Because Pete is one of my best customers. And this 'gibberish' looks like a tactic code from one of the games I sold him."

"Tactic code?"

"Yep. Pete's lazy. He wouldn't have taken the time to create his own code. He'd just piggyback on somethin' else."

"Whatever happened to just playing Pac-Man?"

"We've got Pac-Man. It's in the classics session. Has a whole new interface and some really sick turboed graphics."

"Thanks, but it was a rhetorical question."

Little Bill turned back to the screen.

"How long do you think it will take you to crack it?"

"About an hour should do it. You want to leave and come back?"

"No, I'm going to sit here while you do it. And Bill?"

"Yeah?"

"Don't remember anything you might see on these files."

"Why?"

"It would not be good for your health if this whole thing blows up in our faces."

"I appreciate your seeing me, Mr. Longstreet."

Robie sat across from the lawyer in the latter's large, paneled office. Stuart Longstreet was in his sixties, with creamy white hair, a clean-shaven chin, a pair of listless blue eyes, and a large belly that protruded between the flaps of his suit coat, which looked like it had been tailored to his flabby proportions. His expression was one of privileged contentment.

"It's certainly a tragedy with what happened to your father," he said in a tone that made Robie believe the lawyer was actually enjoying the development.

"Well, I'm hoping that justice will be served."

"Yes, yes, of course," the man said hastily and without a trace of sincerity. His manner suggested he wanted to hasten this interview to an end. "Now, you have some legal issue?"

"Well, I guess it's more of an information issue."

"Oh, yes?" said Longstreet, looking curiously at him.

"The Barksdale family?"

The expression of privileged content withdrew and was replaced by one of heightened suspicion. The listless blue eyes transformed into a pair of flickering propane gas jets. Robie could just see the wheels turning in the legal brain.

"The Barksdales, you say?"

"I knew the family when I was growing up here. I dated Laura Barksdale. I just wondered what had happened to them. As you know, my father bought their old home."

"The Willows, yes," said Longstreet absently. "Still a lovely place. Even with the *changes* they've made." He sniffed, his expression one of disapproval. "I was stunned along with many others of my . . . circle when he purchased it."

"I'm sure."

"The oil platform case."

"Yes."

Longstreet's features hardened. "Cost Cantrell a lot of jobs. Some say it ruined the town."

"And the men who lost their lives would no doubt say differently. As would their survivors."

"Yes, of course. No, I have to admire his, um, professional tenacity."

And you would have caved a minute after the company's hardasses came to your office and said Boo, thought Robie.

He said, "But the Barksdales? I understand you handled their legal work?"

"Who told you that?"

"Was that information wrong?"

Robie noted the lawyer's hand had made a fist so tightly that his index finger was turning pink as the circulation constricted.

"No, no. Our firm has proudly handled the Barksdales' legal matters for well over a century. My grandfather worked on it as did his father before him."

"But not anymore?"

"Well, no. They're no longer here."

"Which is why *I'm* here to see you. Do you know what happened to them?"

"No, I don't," said the man.

He rubbed at his nose.

Lying caused a physiological reaction that cut the flow of blood to the capillaries located at the end of the nose. It caused a tingling feeling that usually made the liar rub at the spot.

Robie knew this.

Longstreet obviously did not.

"I heard they just up and left one night. And no one has seen them since."

"Indeed?" said Longstreet.

"Is that what you understand happened?"

"I really couldn't say."

"Did you hear from any of them before they left?"

"If I did, and I'm not sayin' that I did, that would be privileged and I would be barred from revealin' it."

"I thought attorney-client privilege protected *communications*, not the fact that you simply saw or talked to someone."

He smiled patronizingly. "Well, I could argue the law with you, but since presumably you are yourself not a member of the bar, I will refrain from doin' so,

as the debate would be unfair to *you*. Now, is there anything else?"

Robie rose. "No, I think you've told me all I needed to know. Thanks."

The lawyer's blue eyes sparked at this comment and then faded.

As Robie walked out of the building he wondered if Longstreet had picked up his phone yet to call someone.

There seemed to be a lot going on in this small, sleepy southern town.

His phone buzzed.

It was Reel.

"Well, Little Bill was as good as advertised," she said.

"What's in the files?"

"Something you're not going to believe."

"Tell me."

"No, you really need to *see* it, Robie."

43

Robie sat next to Reel in the car and stared at the laptop.

"I'm not getting this," he said.

"You're not the only one. I thought we were looking at drug or arms dealers or maybe human trafficking. But not this."

"This" was a series of photos showing a man in his forties with very young children in grossly perverse sexual situations.

"Who is this prick?" asked Robie.

"Don't know. But I'd love to put a round in the sucker's head."

"All the kids are either black or Latino."

Reel nodded. "I wonder why."

"But why would these photos be on Sherm Clancy's computer? Blackmail?"

Reel nodded. "Well, the guy's not Clancy, right?"

"No, not even close."

"Then blackmail it could well be. Probably what these guys were looking for when they came after Pete. But you beat them to it."

"But they may not know that. They might think they got the laptop and all the files."

"Then why come after you using the girl as bait?"

"Because I jacked them and they wanted to put a bullet in my head as payback," said Robie. But he knew that probably wasn't right. They risked a lot coming after him, and taking Sara Chisum to do so. There had to be a more compelling reason than simple payback. These guys weren't street punks like Pete. He had a sudden thought.

"Is there a way to tell if a file has been copied from a computer, like I did with these?"

"I asked Little Bill that very question and he says there is. A few keystrokes and you'll know if files were downloaded to another storage device."

"So that's the answer. They know I made copies."

"Well, they know *someone* made copies. They couldn't know for sure it was you. But they needed to cover that end. They might think Pete has other copies, too."

"Which is why he ran for it," added Robie.

"Which is why he ran for it," agreed Reel.

"So Sherm Clancy was blackmailing this person presumably for money."

"Do you think the guy in the photo is connected to the Rebel Yell casino people?"

"I wouldn't bet against it."

"When did Clancy hook up with the casino?"

"I don't know exactly. I was told he made money

selling the mineral rights to his farmland. Then he used that stake to buy into the Rebel Yell."

"Who told you that?"

"More than one person, actually. So it seems to be an accepted fact."

Robie leaned back in his seat, his brow furrowed.

"I know that look," said Reel. "What's going through that head of yours?"

"Mineral rights," said Robie.

"What?"

"We need to go check something out."

"What is this place, Robie?"

They had driven a long way through dusty back roads to arrive at a place that, even for Cantrell, was in the middle of nowhere. They were now standing in the middle of that nowhere.

"This is, or rather was, Sherman Clancy's farm."

"Looks like the wilderness has reclaimed it."

"Looks like it."

They spent thirty minutes walking the property before Robie sat down on the trunk of a fallen tree.

Reel came to stand in front of him.

"So?" she said.

"This property hasn't had anything done to it in a long time. The fields are all overgrown. The farm-house and barns have pretty much fallen in. The only thing left intact really is that shack at the very rear of the property."

"Okay, what did you expect to see?"

"I expected to see some evidence of drilling for any oil and gas under the property. That process leaves signs, even after all these years. I don't even see traces of an access road for the big equipment they would have hauled in here."

"Well, maybe they didn't find anything here."

"There would still be evidence of them looking. And I was told that Clancy got a pretty penny for his property. No energy company is going to shell out big dollars unless they're pretty damn sure whatever it is they're looking for is here. They typically will do an exploratory contract to check. Or get permission to drill in from an adjacent property. But there really isn't an adjacent property here. The rest of it is forest. There was one road in and out when I was growing up here and knew the Clancys. There's still only one road. The one we walked up, because we couldn't drive up it anymore. And it wasn't nearly wide enough or sturdy enough for the sort of equipment they'd be bringing in to extract either the oil or gas."

Reel sat down next to him. "So you think the sale of the mineral rights story was just a cover for how he really came by the money? A payoff for the photos?"

"I don't see any other way it makes sense. Then Clancy could have used that money to buy into the Rebel Yell business."

"So we need to find out who the guy in the photo is. He might have a motive to kill Clancy. Which

might very well let your dad off the hook. By the way, when do I get to meet him?"

"You want to meet my father?"

"You got to meet mine."

"He was in prison," began Robie. Then he paused as Reel hiked her eyebrows at him.

"I just love ironic symmetry," she said.

44

Robie had called Toni Moses on the way over and she was waiting for them with Dan Robie, in the visitor's room at the jail.

Dan Robie eyed Reel curiously. "You saved Will's butt?"

"One could interpret it that way," said Reel matter-of-factly.

Dan looked at the wall. "Good you were there to clean up his mess."

"Well, since he was there trying to save *your* butt maybe I cleaned up *both* your messes."

Dan shot her a look while Moses studied both of them. She interjected, "Before we get too far down that road, did you find out what the files said?"

"We found out what they *showed*," amended Robie.

He slid open his laptop and brought the images up on the screen.

"Damn," said Moses. "Who the hell is that?"

Robie looked at his father. "Recognize the guy?"

He shook his head and looked like he wanted to

punch the screen. "I don't know any pedophiles," he snapped.

"We think Clancy was blackmailing this guy. That's where his seed money came from. Not from selling his land to an energy company."

Now Dan Robie looked interested. "How do you figure that?"

"Everybody told me that Clancy had hit a home run because his farmland had oil or gas under it. Only no one could tell me if it was oil *or* gas. Or who the energy company was, for that matter. Jessica and I walked the property today. There is no sign that anyone ever tried to get any oil or gas out of that land."

Dan Robie sat back in his chair. "And the photos were used to blackmail the guy who's abusin' the kids. And that was Clancy's jackpot?"

"Yes," said Robie.

"Damn good incentive to kill him," said Moses. "Aubrey Davis will shit a brick when I bring this up."

Reel said, "But if Clancy had these photos all this time and the guy never tried to kill him, why would he kill Clancy now? What changed?"

Robie said, "Maybe Clancy kept squeezing the guy and he got tired of it. Maybe he was afraid that Clancy would screw up and inadvertently show someone. From what I've heard around town, he'd been going downhill for years now. Drunk most of the time."

"Well, it seems that it has to be this guy, or at least

his goons," said Moses. "They were goin' to kill Pete, because they assumed he knew about the pictures. They wanted them back. So maybe the guy *was* sick of payin' off Sherm. And he sure as hell wasn't goin' to start payin' off his son."

"Which brings us back to the guy," said Robie. "Who is he? He must be rich, because he could afford to pay Clancy a lot of bucks."

"Maybe the FBI can help us there," said Reel. "They could run it through their databases for facial recognition."

"And then we go ask this person some questions," said Moses. "Like did he kill or have Sherman Clancy killed."

"It's too bad we shot down all those guys," said Reel. "I should've just wounded one of them so he could answer our questions."

Moses looked at her wide-eyed. "Remind me not to get on your bad side, girl."

"Do you think Sara Chisum might be able to tell us something about them?" asked Robie. "They took her. She thought they were going to do a deal with her. She might have seen or heard something."

"Worth a shot," said Reel. "How do you want to do it?"

"Delicately." He looked at his father. "You want to answer my question now?"

"Which one?"

"*Were* you driving your Range Rover the night Clancy was killed?"

"You do what you need to do," said his father grimly. "And I'll do what I need to do."

"He's not how I pictured him to be," said Reel.

They were in Reel's car outside the jail.

"How did you picture him to be?" asked Robie.

"I don't know. Just not like that."

"He doesn't want me down here. He told me to go back to where I came from."

"Well, what did you expect, Robie? For him to welcome you with open arms after twenty years? Hell, you never talked about your family. I didn't even know your old man was still alive."

"Well, I did come back. And I am trying to help him. That should be worth something in his eyes."

"Do you really care about that?"

Robie shot her a glance. "What do you mean?"

"I mean is this about your dad or your inability to pull the trigger on a target because you inadvertently shot a little girl and then imagined you saw a little boy in the way of another shot?"

"I see that Blue Man *did* fill you in."

"Would you expect him not to?"

"Why are you really here?"

"My mission, which I chose to accept, was to come down here and help you."

"But you didn't expect to drop into a firefight."

"No, that was just gravy on top of the mashed potatoes."

He smiled weakly at her comment and then leaned back against the car seat.

"I'm sort of screwed in the head right now, Jess."

"I've been there. And there is a road back."

"That's why I kept asking Blue Man when you were getting back. I . . . thought we could talk about things. That you would understand."

"Every situation is different. And I'm not a qualified shrink. But I can give you the benefit of my experience, Robie."

"It's complicated."

"Of course it is. It's in your head. How can it not be complicated?"

"You're right. I came back here more for me than my dad."

"Okay."

"I felt like I had unfinished business."

"I can relate to that. You helped me clean up my past."

Robie rubbed at his temples. "And after seeing the little boy in the middle of my last shot, I began to think I had to go back to move forward, if that makes sense."

"It does."

"Right before I was to take the shot on my last mission . . . everything was off. I thought I, I don't know, that I might be having a heart attack."

"Or more likely a panic attack."

"I couldn't make the shot, Jess. Even if I had fired, I would have missed."

"So to get back to where you *can* do your job, you need to work through Mississippi?"

"Unfortunately, this isn't a peaceful walk down memory lane while I get my head straight. My dad's on trial for murder. And people are shooting at us."

"You take life as it comes at you, and it's rarely perfect."

"But things aren't going to get any better between my father and me."

"You sure about that?"

"You saw him today."

"I saw a man mightily confused and unsure what to do. And I'm not just talking about you."

"You saw that?" Robie said skeptically. "In both of us?"

"Yes, I did. Now tell me what happened between you two to start this whole thing."

Robie took a long breath. "It wasn't one incident. It was years of incidents. He was a jarhead back from Vietnam. He was one of the toughest men you'll ever meet. Never asked for any quarter and never gave any. He would beat the shit out of me for the slightest thing. But it wasn't the fist or the belt that hurt the most."

"It was the words," said Reel.

"Yes. He made me feel worthless. Like I would

never amount to anything. No matter what I did to please him, it was never good enough. Would never be good enough. I finally stopped caring. I didn't feel anything toward him. He wasn't my father. He was some guy I had to live with until I got old enough to where I didn't. I couldn't wait to get the hell out of Cantrell."

"And your mother?"

Now Robie took a shallow breath. "That was the other thing. He drove her away. She loved me, but she hated him more. She was the only thing that made my life here tolerable. After she left . . ."

"Did you ever see her again?"

"No," Robie said curtly.

"She never tried to contact you?"

"No."

"So do you feel she abandoned you?"

"Of course not," snapped Robie. "It was my father's doing."

"But she *did* leave you."

"Because my father made her."

"You know that for a fact?"

Robie sat up straight. "Look, we need to get going on other things. We need to talk to Sara Chisum. We have to find Pete. We have to ID the guy in the photo. So let's hit Sara first."

"If you say so," replied Reel, looking troubled by his response.

Robie slid on his seat belt. "I do."

45

"So where is she?" Robie asked.

They were standing in front of the Chisums' residence about two miles out of downtown Cantrell. Lester Chisum, Sara's father, was facing them looking pale and nervous.

"I don't know. We haven't seen her since we went to bed last night. She must have snuck out after that."

"She snuck out all right," said Robie. "But then she came back. And obviously left again."

"How do you know that?" demanded Chisum.

"So you didn't see her when she got home late last night?" asked Robie, ignoring the man's question.

"No, but I spoke with Emma this mornin'. She said Sara looked really wiped out. Scared, even."

"Did she say anything to Emma?"

"I don't know."

"Where is she?"

"Inside."

"We need to talk to her," said Robie.

"Why? And why are you even here?" demanded Chisum. "What do you have to do with any of this?"

"Sara has gotten herself into something bad, Mr. Chisum. There *was* an incident last night. Folks ended up dead. I was there. I saved your daughter's life."

Robie felt no need to mention that Sara had set him up and then gotten double-crossed. Her father looked stunned enough by what he'd said.

"I . . . I can't believe this."

"You can call Deputy Taggert if you want. Or Sheriff Monda. They'll tell you. And you should call them anyway and tell them that Sara is missing. Because this is not good, not after last night. I know for a fact that the police drove Sara home last night after she got medical attention for an injury. She was not supposed to leave here."

"Omigod," said Chisum. He grabbed the porch rail. "She didn't wake us up. She didn't say anythin'."

"She was told not to. *Now* can we talk to Emma?" asked Robie.

Chisum slowly nodded and led them inside.

A couple minutes later Robie and Reel followed Emma out the back door and into the small yard that was remarkable for nothing other than a massive Spanish moss-draped oak that held court in the center of the dying grass.

They sat at an old, rotting wooden picnic table.

Emma faced them calmly, her hands clasped primly in front of her.

Robie looked at her closely. "What can you tell us about Sara?"

"What do you want to know?"

"Everything you can tell us. Did you see or hear her leave?"

"No. But she came in late last night lookin' all scared and beat up. She had a bandage on her head."

"Did she say anything to you?"

"Only to shut the hell up when I asked what she'd been up to."

"Why were you up when she got home?" asked Reel.

Emma swiveled her gaze to Reel. "You know, information is not free."

"Your sister could be in serious trouble," Robie pointed out.

"Okay. But it's still not free."

"So the money I gave you before?" said Robie.

"Was in payment for what I told you *before*."

"Don't you care about your *remaining* sister?" asked Robie.

"Sure. As much as she's cared about me. Which is jackshit. Same for Janet. They couldn't've given a crap if I died. Why should I care? They hated me! Treated me like I was nothin'."

Robie pulled out five twenties. "Then tell us what you know."

Emma reached out and tried to snatch the money, but Robie held on to it. "This time," he said, "I'll decide if the information is worth the cash." He eyed

Reel. "And she's my witness that nothing untoward is going on."

Reel raised an eyebrow at this statement but didn't comment.

Emma sneered, "Well, maybe she wants a threesome. Do you classify that as *untoward*?"

"No," said Reel calmly. "And you're wasting our time."

"Okay, do you want to know what I know or not?" snapped Emma.

"We do," said Robie.

Emma looked triumphant until Reel spoke.

"Come on, we don't really need her, Robie."

"What?" said Robie, looking surprised.

"Let's look at this logically. They killed Janet. They've taken Sara because they think she knew something that Janet knew. When they find out Sara doesn't know anything they'll come back for the kid sister. We keep watch over her, and when they come and take her we'll be able to follow. And when they slit her throat or put a bullet in her head, we can nail them, right then and there. And it saves you paying this piece of crap a hundred bucks."

"You really think so?" said Robie.

"These are guys. All guys think girls talk to each other. They'll come back for the kid for sure."

"You're just tryin' to scare me," said Emma smugly.

Reel shrugged. "We don't need to. They killed one

sister. They've probably got Sara now. They'll kill her too, like they tried to do last night."

"What?" said Emma, looking startled.

"Robie, I'm telling you, let's just ride this out. We can use her as bait to get to them. Just like they used Sara last night to get to you. They tried to kill you. I say we return the favor. You only killed three last night. I shot another four. But there were quite a few of them left."

"You . . . killed . . . people," Emma said slowly.

Robie shot a glance at Emma and then said sharply to Reel, "Just shut up about them. You know what the cops said."

"Look, I'm just trying to do you a favor and save you some bucks at the same time. She's not worth risking your life for, that's for sure. She's just bait. She'll die, but then we kill *them*."

"I don't know," said Robie doubtfully.

Emma said in a shocked tone, "You're talkin' about killing people and then lettin' me die like . . . like . . ."

"—like you don't matter," finished Reel. "Yeah, that's right. Because you don't."

She rose. "I'll take the first watch, Robie. I doubt they'll try anything during the day, but you never know."

Robie slipped the bills back into his pocket. "Okay, I guess you're right."

He started to rise, too.

"Wait, wait!" exclaimed Emma.

They both looked at her.

Reel said, "What!"

"You can't just let them come and take me."

"Why not?"

"I'm just a kid."

"I could not give a crap," said Reel casually. "When I was your age no one cared about me. Why should you be any different?"

Emma's hard exterior completely collapsed. "Please, I can tell you about Sara."

Reel held up her hand. "Just don't even go there. I've listened to enough of your bullshit. You know zip about anything other than how to con somebody. And we're not buying."

She turned to leave but Emma gripped her arm.

"I do know things. I know what Sara was up to. I heard her."

Reel peeled the girl's fingers off her arm, then sat across from her.

"Okay, listen up. This is your last chance. You try to juke us now, we are out of here and you are dead. Do we understand each other?"

Emma's lips trembled but she nodded her head.

Reel looked at Robie.

He said quietly, "What did you hear, Emma?"

"She was talkin' to somebody on her phone. In her bedroom."

"So how could you hear?" asked Reel sharply.

"Because I was hidin' in her closet."

"Do you do that often?" asked Robie.

"I went in there to steal some of her pot, but then I heard her comin'. So I jumped in the closet to hide."

"Go on," said Robie. "What did you hear?"

"She was talkin' to somebody."

"Do you know who?"

Emma shook her head. "She never said a name. But I did hear what she said. They were talkin' about meetin' somewhere. Tonight."

"Where and when exactly?" asked Reel.

"Where they used to go. I mean her and Janet."

"Near where Sherman Clancy's body was discovered?" asked Robie.

She nodded. "Yes."

"What time?"

"Midnight."

"What was the meeting about?" asked Reel.

"Sara wanted money, in exchange for somethin' she had. Somethin' I guess the person wanted."

"Do you know what that was?" asked Robie.

"No."

Robie and Reel exchanged glances.

Robie said to Emma, "How much money?"

"Enough money to go somewhere else."

"Smart girl," said Robie.

46

"Well, at least our 'good cop, bad cop' routine worked," said Reel as she drove herself and Robie away from the Chisums. "But what a piece of work. I just wanted to slap her face."

"She's screwed up," said Robie. "But then lots of people are screwed up."

"Present company definitely included?" said Reel, eyeing him.

"Definitely included."

"If Sara took a call from this person, the cops may be able to trace the call," said Reel.

Robie pulled out his phone, called Taggert, and relayed this information without telling her about what Emma had told them of the meeting planned for that night.

"She's checking it," said Robie.

"We have a lot of time between now and midnight. Where to now?"

Robie pulled out a card. "I need to call them first."
"Who?"
"The FBI."

★

333

They met about ten miles east of Cantrell.

Special Agent Wurtzburger was there with two of his men.

Robie introduced Reel to the agents.

Wurtzburger eyed her. "So you work with Robie here?"

"I have the privilege, yes."

Wurtzburger nodded. "Same agency?"

She shrugged.

"Good enough," said Wurtzburger with a tight smile.

Robie held up the photo of the man and the kids he had printed out from the flash drive and explained to Wurtzburger how he had come by it.

Wurtzburger studied the image. "We can run this through our facial recognition databases, see what pops. So a pedophile, then?"

"Looks to be," said Robie. "It might tie into the Rebel Yell."

Wurtzburger put the photo away in his pocket. "I appreciate this, Robie. And in return let me be more frank with you than I have been."

Robie studied him appraisingly. "Frankness is good," he said.

"When I told you we were down here investigating casinos, that was not exactly true."

"What exactly would be true?" said Reel sharply.

"I'm assigned to ViCAP."

"Violent Criminal Apprehension Program," said Robie.

"Yes."

Reel added, "But that really deals with serial killers."

"Among other things, yes."

"So are you saying that you're down here hunting a serial killer?" asked Robie.

"You could say that, yes."

"Can you fill us in? Why here?"

"Sherman Clancy and Janet Chisum."

"But what's the connection?" asked Reel.

"There have been eight other killings in four different states in the last nine years."

"Okay, but what connects those to the murders in Cantrell?"

"They were killed roughly in pairs with the same backstory. Older man, younger girl. The older man paid for the sex. Then the older man gets his throat slit in his car. The girl gets a bullet to the head and is tossed in a body of water."

"Where were the other killings?" asked Reel.

"One was in New York. One in Pennsylvania. One in Tennessee. One in Arkansas. And now possibly the fifth set of murders here."

Robie said, "So the killer presumably is going east to west. Nine years of operation? Is that usual?"

"I can't say it's unusual. I've worked serial killer cases covering decades of activity."

"When were the murders in Arkansas?"

"Four years ago."

Reel did a quick calculation in her head. She said, "So the other murders were spaced roughly eighteen months apart?"

"That's right," replied Wurtzburger.

"So the four-year gap might be significant," she said.

"It might be, yes. There could have been an intervening event. The person might have been in prison, that actually happens quite a bit."

"If so, he got out and is now killing again?" said Robie.

"Presumably, yes."

"I haven't heard about these killings," said Robie.

"We made the decision not to publicize it. We didn't want the killer to know that we believe them to be connected. The person might go deep underground if that information got out."

"And you're sure the murders here are part of the pattern?" said Reel.

"We can't be certain, you understand. But I've worked a lot of these cases and the similarities are pretty solid."

"But even so, my father did have a motive to kill Sherm Clancy," said Robie.

"But not Janet Chisum," countered Wurtzburger.

"In the other cases was there a longtime gap

between the murder of the girl and the killing of the older man?" Reel wanted to know.

"Not as long as in this case."

"But in the other cases the girl and the older guy were connected? They were having sex. For payment?"

"Yes. The murders in New York took place at the same time. The bodies were found together. In the other cases, the two murders were separate, one by as much as three weeks."

"So, similar but different," said Robie.

"You think that's important?" said Reel curiously.

Wurtzburger said, "In my experience, when serial killers take pains to create a pattern, they must have a really strong reason to deviate from that pattern."

Robie said, "Okay, we just have to find out what that really strong reason is. And if we do that, then maybe we find our serial killer."

47

Robie sat across from Reel in his room at the Willows.

It was a bit before dinner, and they could hear Priscilla clanging pans in the kitchen downstairs.

They had not seen Victoria or Tyler.

The chirp of cicadas reached them from outside. The air was warm and humid, the sun settling down into the west but not wicking away even a bit of the moisture with its descent.

Reel watched Robie's gaze flick around the room.

"What?" she asked.

He turned to find her staring at him.

"I know that look, Robie. Something's in your head."

"This was her bedroom."

"Laura's?"

"Yes."

"You could have tried to talk to her before you drove off into the sunset, you know."

"What was the point? She'd obviously made up her mind."

"I'll forgive your naïveté, since you were only eighteen."

"What the hell does that mean?"

"I could explain but it's over twenty years too late, so I'm not sure what the point would be."

Clearly frustrated by her response Robie changed the subject. "How do you want to do the Chisum thing tonight?"

"Pretty basic. We get there early and nail whatever and whoever comes along."

"And if it's a serial killer?"

Reel shrugged. "I don't discriminate. I'll nail him, too."

"Do you really think this is a serial killer's work?"

"I don't know. Wurtzburger presented a pretty compelling case. Although, as you pointed out, there are differences this time."

"Something is still bugging me."

"What?"

"My father won't say whether he was driving the Range Rover that night."

"Does that really matter? Do you think he killed Clancy?"

"If he didn't, why wouldn't he say whether he was driving that night or not?"

"He's a complicated man. Like father like son. We still need to find Pete."

His phone buzzed. It was Taggert.

The phone call in question had been untraceable. She wanted to know the significance of it.

Robie said, "I don't know if it is significant. But now it's a dead end."

He clicked off and looked at Reel.

"Maybe we should bring the cops in on this," she said.

"Taggert is good. But I don't know about the rest of them. And I don't want this to get screwed up. It might be our only shot."

"Okay," said Reel.

There was a knock on the door.

Robie answered it, revealing Victoria standing there in jeans, a white short-sleeved blouse, and heels.

"You two have time for a drink before dinner?" she asked. "Or do you have to keep on staying behind closed doors conspiring?"

They followed her downstairs, where there was a pitcher of vodka martinis on the rear verandah.

Victoria drank hers down. Robie sipped on his. Reel just held hers.

"We saw my dad today," said Robie.

Victoria looked at Reel. "And what did you think of him?"

"Wasn't like I had time to psychoanalyze him."

"Your gut reaction."

"Good guy, tough, proud, unbending. Doesn't suffer fools gladly or any other way."

Victoria looked impressed. "You have a perceptive gut."

"I've had a lot of practice."

"So, do you think you can find out what really happened to Sherman Clancy?"

"I hope we can."

"Making progress?"

"Little by little."

Victoria finished off another vodka martini.

"Where's Tyler?" asked Reel.

"In his room. He was tired today. Think it's the heat. Even if you're used to it, it can wear you down. I guess that might be why life is slower down here. If people move too fast, they'll just melt."

After dinner Reel went back to her room and Robie joined Victoria on a walk of the rear grounds. They ended up next to the pool where they sat in low-slung lounge chairs.

"Jessica seems like someone you can depend on," said Victoria.

"She is. And I have."

"You two are tight?"

"As tight as anyone I know."

"Good, Will, we all need somebody like that."

"Did Dad talk to you about his idea?"

"You mean the one where Tyler and I get the hell out of Dodge?"

"Yes."

"Not going to happen. I told him that. I'm here for the long haul, come what may."

"I told him that would be your answer."

She smiled. "Oh, so you think you can read me like a book, Will Robie?"

"Not saying that. But you didn't strike me as the type to abandon someone."

Her face fell for an instant before she regained her composure.

"I'm not," she said firmly. "I wish others I've known had thought the same way. Had the same backbone."

"So you've been abandoned?" asked Robie.

"In a way, Will, we've all been abandoned, haven't we? Some of us just don't know it, is all."

48

Robie and Reel were on the move two hours before the set time.

The sky was cloudy with low rumbles of thunder, the breeze hot and the air so thick with moisture that a storm unleashing a tropical downpour appeared imminent.

They parked their car about a quarter mile away and hoofed it the rest of the way. When they reached the spot they split up and started their vigil.

They were armed with both weapons and night optics, which Reel had brought with her. They were also commed together.

Robie was hunkered down behind a stand of bushes. In front of him was the spot where he and Sara had first met. In his ear he heard Reel's voice.

"I've got the high ground," she said. "As soon as I see anything, I'll ping you."

"Roger that."

He settled farther down behind his cover and let his sector sweeps go into automatic. He saw everything in wispy green thanks to his optics. He didn't

know what they would be encountering tonight. They had struck quite a staggering blow to what might be forces from the Rebel Yell casino. These men had planned on killing Sara Chisum after using her as bait to get to Robie. He did not believe the young woman would be stupid enough to try her luck with them again.

But then again, you could never underestimate the stupidity of some people.

He checked his watch. Two minutes to go.

He let out a long breath. He wasn't going to achieve complete cold zero now, but he also knew something else:

I'm in my element. This is what I do.

Robie heard the sound of the vehicle approaching in the distance. It would be pulling down the dirt road. It would go as far as it could go. And then the person would have to get out and walk the rest of the way, as Robie had when he'd first come here and stumbled upon Sara.

But where was Sara?

He assumed she would be arriving either by foot or by bike.

He spoke into his mic.

"You hear that?"

"Roger."

"See anything?"

"I don't have a sight line to the road from here. You want me to get one?"

"No, stand by. They're supposed to meet in this clearing. The driver will have to get out of the car and walk to reach this spot."

"You think Sara is coming by car?"

"Doubtful."

Though he still couldn't see it, Robie heard the vehicle come to a stop.

He knew he would next hear the engine being killed, the door opening, and feet smacking dirt.

But he didn't hear any of those things.

The gunshot seared the silence of the night like a branding iron on skin.

Robie immediately spoke into his headset.

"Got a sight line of that shot?"

"Muzzle flash from the west."

That was directly ahead of them. The direction from which the car had been coming.

Robie swept out from behind his hiding place, keeping low and with his target silhouette shrunken to a sliver. He aimed his pistol in front of him.

A few moments later Reel spoke into his ear.

"I'm on your left flank. Eight on the dial."

Robie instantly started to move toward the sound of the shot. He wasn't going to rush this and knew Reel wasn't, either. It was all about urgency under control.

But when he heard the car's engine roar he started to sprint forward.

He cleared the last of the trees and looked to his left.

Reel was emerging just at that instant, but on his left, about thirty yards away.

Her sniper rifle was in hand. She peered toward him, a set of NV goggles over her eyes.

He gave the hand sign, which he knew she could see with the aid of the goggles. He didn't wait for her to confirm. He shot forward, turned to his left, and came out onto a section of the dirt road.

He saw two things.

First was Sara Chisum lying on the left shoulder of the road. She was on her back, her body in the short grass.

The second thing Robie saw was the set of tail-lights. They were nearly out of sight.

He raised his gun and fired six times at the fleeing vehicle.

His odds of hitting it at this distance, and in these conditions, were low. But he thought he might have struck it once. At least it sounded like metal hitting metal.

Reel burst out onto the road a second later. She lifted her rifle. She would have a far better chance to hit the vehicle, but before she could fire, it turned and was completely out of sight.

And as good a shot as Jessica Reel was, she could not force a bullet to defy the laws of gravity and bend

its flight path at a forty-five-degree angle in order to hit a target.

"Damn!" exclaimed Reel.

Robie was already next to Sara Chisum. He pressed his finger against her carotid, searching for a pulse.

He didn't find one.

He slipped a flashlight from his jacket and shone it over her.

He saw the patch of blood on the left side of her head, right near the ear.

He knelt closer, careful not to disturb the body, and examined the wound under the light.

Reel raced over and squatted down next to him. "Dead?"

He nodded. "GSW to the right temple. Would've killed her instantly. No exit. Round's still in her." He smacked the flashlight against the palm of his hand. "I can't believe this! This wasn't the meeting spot."

"Nothing we could do, Robie. Maybe it was changed somehow. Or the driver and Sara arrived at the same time. Point is, she made her choice and it cost her her life."

He looked at her. "Did you get a plate on the vehicle?"

"No."

"I might have hit it with one of my shots."

"That would leave a telltale sign. You get the make?"

Robie shook his head. "Just saw the red taillights.

Too far away and too dark to make out the shape, but I think it might've been an SUV."

"What do we do now?"

Robie used his hand to close Sara Chisum's eyes. Then he pulled out his phone.

"Now we call in the cops and hope they don't arrest us."

"Well, if they do, you and your dad might end up with some quality time together."

"I'm not sure that will ever be possible."

49

Sheriff Monda stared down at Sara Chisum's body, which was in the exact position where she had fallen. They were waiting for the coroner to come and examine it. And since the town coroner was also the owner of the local funeral home and not an employee of the state, he had been away at a convention in Louisiana when the call came in. They were told his arrival might still be a couple of hours away.

Chisum's bike was parked next to a tree. She had arrived silently, as silently as she had died.

Monda walked over to where Robie and Reel were standing with Sheila Taggert.

He said, "Okay, let me get this straight, so you came out here hopin' to get a line on the person Sara was tryin' to get money from?"

"That's right," said Robie.

"And it didn't occur to you to call us?" said Monda irritably.

"Frankly, no it didn't," replied Robie. "We had no idea if Emma Chisum was really telling the truth. I

didn't want to involve the police and waste your time and resources for what might turn out to be nothing."

Monda looked back over at the body. "Well, it didn't turn out to be nothin', did it?"

"I can't disagree with you there, Sheriff."

"So you think it was an SUV?" said Taggert.

Robie nodded. "And I'm pretty sure I hit it. So there's something you can track down."

"You have any idea what Sara was goin' to tell this person? I'm assumin' the person just killed her instead of talkin' to her?"

"We didn't hear anyone speak," said Reel. "We heard a car approach and then the shot was fired. We didn't hear Sara coming in on her bike. We were waiting around the perimeter of the clearing. That's where we thought the meeting would take place. Either the killer changed the location to the spot next to the road or it was unlucky timing on Sara's part, I don't know."

Robie said, "You might want to put the rest of the Chisum family in protective custody."

Monda nodded. "I think, under the circumstances, that's a good idea. Do you think Emma has any inklin' what this is about?"

"She swears she doesn't," said Reel. "But I don't believe her."

"Anythin' else?" asked Monda.

"Have you been in contact with the FBI?"

Monda nodded. "They let us know they were in the area."

"Did they tell you why they were in the area?" asked Reel.

"No. Do you know why?"

"If they didn't tell you, it's certainly not my place to."

"Listen, Robie, I want to know what the hell is goin' on in Cantrell," barked Monda.

"Then I suggest you call Agent Wurtzburger back and demand that he tell you. I would if I were you."

He looked over at Sara's body.

Monda followed his gaze and said, "Guess you couldn't save her this time."

"Guess not," replied Robie.

Robie and Reel drove back mostly in silence to the Willows. They had failed in their mission and someone had died. This fact was not going down well with either of them.

Reel finally stirred. "Sara was our best chance to get some traction on this and we screwed it up. Okay, she wasn't the nicest person in the world, but that doesn't entitle someone to just blow her away."

"We have one more option. Pete Clancy."

"Only he's gone and we don't know where he is."

"I didn't say it would be easy."

"Why didn't you tell Monda about the serial killer angle?"

"Because he needs to get that information from

Wurtzburger, not us. I'm not poaching on the FBI's turf."

"You think our serial killer was driving that SUV tonight?"

"I don't know. Maybe."

"If you hit the truck with a pistol round there'll be evidence of that."

"Granted. But where do we start looking? In every garage and swamp in Cantrell?"

"If Sara was there to cut a deal with her killer, what was the quid pro quo?" asked Reel.

"They searched her clothing," said Robie. "And found nothing helpful. Her phone was in there. Maybe they can check to see if she had another recent phone call. Although they couldn't trace the other one."

"But it could be something she had in her head. Or she was smart enough not to bring whatever she had with her. She gets paid off and then tells the person where it is."

"I'm not sure the killer would have been that understanding."

"What else then?"

"I don't know," admitted Robie. "Things are more muddied than when I got here. And that's saying something, because they were as muddied as the Mississippi Delta when I pulled into Cantrell."

"Clancy dead. Janet dead. Now Sara dead."

Robie shook his head. "I know what Wurtzburger

said, but what would Sara have to bargain over with a serial killer?"

"Well, either Wurtzburger is totally barking up the wrong tree and another killer is doing this, or his serial killer *is* involved, which means Sara did have something on him, we just don't know what."

"Well, I'm not buying it."

"I'm not saying I do, either. But we don't have an abundance of leads to track down. And the ones we do have get killed or turn up missing."

Robie looked down at his phone, on which he had brought up the photo of the man with the little kids. He had snapped a picture of the original before giving it to Wurtzburger for his facial recognition search.

"What?" said Reel, looking in disgust at the image.

"Just thought of something."

"Well, don't leave me in suspense."

Robie held up the image.

"Who the hell took the picture?"

50

It was nearly eleven in the morning when they got back to the Willows.

As they drove up, Robie and Reel heard peals of laughter coming from the rear of the house.

They headed that way and when they turned the corner they saw the detached garage where Victoria's Volvo and Dan Robie's Range Rover stood side by side. Next to the car was a big bucket with soapy water in it and a sponge next to the bucket.

In front of the vehicles stood Victoria. She held a hose in one hand and was spraying Tyler, who was running in circles with a big smile on his face, while his mother laughed.

Victoria saw Robie and Reel and shut off the hose.

"Well, I see you two were out before the sun came up," she said, clearly annoyed.

"We had some things to look into," said Robie, deciding not to tell her they had actually been out all night. He looked at the bucket and the drenched Tyler. "He's having fun."

"We were just doing some chores when I decided this little guy needed a cooling down."

"I can see that," said Robie, who was watching Tyler with amusement. He was pointing at the hose and then at himself.

Reel said, "I think he wants another blast."

Victoria sprayed Tyler again, while he once more ran in a circle. If he could speak Robie could imagine the boy screaming with delight. The day was already very hot and the water was no doubt very cold.

Robie eyed his father's Range Rover, his gaze flitting over the New Orleans Saints sticker on the back hatch. He still didn't know if his father had been driving the SUV on the night of Clancy's murder. The fact that his father had refused to say whether he had or not made Robie suspect that his father *had* been driving the Range Rover. If so, where had he been going to or coming from at that time of night?

"So what have you two early birds been up to?" asked Victoria.

Robie glanced at Reel, who shrugged.

"We've actually been out all night," he admitted.

"What?"

Robie explained to her what had happened, keeping his voice low so that Tyler couldn't hear.

She dropped the hose, went over to Tyler, and lifted him, soaking wet, and pressed him to her chest.

"I . . . I don't understand. What is going on?" she said, her voice cracking.

"We don't understand it, either," said Robie. "It seems like whenever we start to make some headway, we lose that advantage. First Pete disappears and now this."

Victoria stroked Tyler's head. "What are you going to do now?"

Robie shook his head. "Not sure."

"Do you think Dan should be kept in jail?" she asked. "At least there no one can"—she glanced down at Tyler—"do anything to him."

"That might be best, actually," said Robie.

Victoria carried Tyler over to a little red wagon and put him in it. "We'll head back to the house in a minute, sweetie, and get you all dry." She turned back to Robie and Reel.

"So if Dan didn't kill Sherm Clancy, then the person who killed the Chisum girls might have killed him, too?"

"It's certainly possible. We know that my father couldn't have killed Sara Chisum. He was locked up. So if the murders are connected, then that lets him out."

Victoria nodded thoughtfully, the look of fear still evident in her eyes.

"Well, that's certainly something to be thankful for. But—"

"But that means a killer is still on the loose," said Reel.

Victoria nodded. Then she took the wagon handle and slowly pulled Tyler back to the house.

"That woman is scared," said Reel.

"That woman *should* be scared," replied Robie.

51

Late that night Robie opened his eyes when he heard it. He blinked a couple of times then sat up, his body tensed, his mind alert and ready.

There it came again.

Outside.

No, inside.

No, it was both outside and inside.

His mind clouded over for a bit but then snapped back.

Two sounds, in and out.

Two sources for those sounds.

He rose, slipped on his pants, and gunned up.

He chose to work from in to out.

The hallway upstairs was clear. Robie stood next to his door in a crouch, his gun pointed in front of him, directed in a swiveling arc at the darkness.

He waited, listened. His head jerked to the left when he heard the sound again.

Crying.

Someone was crying.

It wasn't Reel, he knew that. The woman didn't cry.

It wasn't Tyler, because it was clearly a woman and Tyler didn't make any noise at all.

It might be Priscilla, but her room was downstairs and on the other end of the house.

That left Victoria.

He slipped over to her door and knocked.

"Victoria?"

The weeping instantly stopped.

"What?" said a hoarse voice.

"Are you okay?"

"I'm fi—no, I'm not okay."

Robie placed his gun in the waistband at the small of his back. "Can I come in?"

He heard footsteps crossing the floor and a few moments later the door was opened.

Victoria stood there wearing a T-shirt and silk pajama shorts.

Her eyes were puffy and her hair was in disarray.

"You were crying?" he began.

She didn't answer, but turned around, walked over, and perched on the edge of the bed.

Robie closed the door, pulled up a chair from a small vanity, and sat across from her.

"You want to talk about it?" he said.

"What's there to talk about?" she snapped. "My life is for shit. End of story. I'll probably be crying the rest of my life."

"You can't know that, Victoria."

She reached over, snagged a tissue from a box off the nightstand, and blew her nose.

"I can know that. I *do* know that. Even if Dan gets off, so what? People around here will always have doubts. That will kill him as much as being found guilty and sent to prison."

Robie slowly took this in. That was what his father had told him, too. Perhaps he had told his wife the same thing.

"You need to take this one day at a time. Don't jump ahead. Don't think too much about it. It'll overwhelm you." He paused. "And you have Tyler."

She nodded, tears still leaking from her eyes. "If I didn't have him, I think I'd already be in the loony bin."

"Well, you do have him. And you have me, too."

She looked up at him. "Your being here has really helped, Will. I mean that. With all my heart."

She leaned over, gave him a hug, and kissed him on the cheek.

Then she dried her eyes with the tissue and said, "Well, thanks for letting me vent. I'm sure things will look better in the morning."

"We're going to find the truth, Victoria. I promise you that."

She looked at him, her eyes raw. "And what if you don't like the truth, what then?"

"I'll deal with that when it comes."

She blew her nose once more. "I guess we all will."

"Good night, Victoria."

"Good night, Will. You should get some sleep. Sorry I woke you."

He left the room and closed the door behind him. His father, he felt, had married a good person. A strong woman. He would need that. He would need all of that.

And that was when he remembered.

The sound from outside.

And then he heard something moving in the hall.

He turned in an instant, his weapon out and pointed at the new noise.

Jessica Reel was staring back at him, her gun in hand.

She said, "What's up, besides you?"

"I heard a noise."

"I did too. From outside."

"Let's go check it out."

"I also thought I heard somebody crying. Did you?"

"It was Victoria. She just needed to talk to someone. This all has to be overwhelming."

"What'd you tell her?"

"That we were going to find the truth. So let's see if we can start with whoever's outside."

52

The sound was not repeated.

At least not right away.

But Robie and Reel were patient. They could sit for hours or days or weeks waiting for what needed to come along and be killed.

And finally their patience was rewarded.

The crack of a twig.

The flutter of leaves on a bush.

A breath released too quickly for concealment.

They converged in an instant, guns pointed at their prey.

"Don't shoot. Sweet Jesus, please don't shoot me."

Pete Clancy put up his hands and dropped to his knees. He sat on his haunches, cowering.

Robie and Reel glanced at each other before lowering their weapons.

"What are you doing here, Pete?" asked Robie. "And where the hell have you been?"

Pete let his hands drop and stared up at them.

Composing himself, he said, "On the run, man. You know why."

"Get up," said Reel.

When he stood she patted him down and pulled out a short-bladed knife from his front pants pocket.

"What, no guns?" she said.

"I don't actually like guns all that much," said Pete in an embarrassed tone. "I just own 'em 'cause you're supposed to down here."

She put the knife in her jacket pocket and stepped back.

Robie said, "Who were the guys at your house?"

"Heard you killed 'em later on. In the woods."

"Who'd you hear that from?"

Pete shrugged. "Somebody," he mumbled. "Does it matter?"

"It may," replied Robie. "But we'll leave that for now. Who were the guys? Rebel Yell thugs?"

Pete looked confused by this. "Rebel Yell? The casino?"

Reel and Robie exchanged another glance.

"Yeah," said Robie.

"Nope, it wasn't them."

Robie said, "Okay, if not them, who? And we know about the pictures on your computer. The man and the little kids?"

Pete looked startled at first but then nodded slowly. "How my old man made his money. Then he took that and made a lot more at the Rebel Yell."

"So no oil and gas dollars for his land, then?" said Robie.

"He told me that was just a cover story."

"Okay, one more time. The guys. Who are they?"

"I don't know exactly. But you saw the pictures, right?"

"I told you we did," said Robie irritably. "Who's the guy in them?"

He said furtively, "Don't know that either. Dad never said."

"Where did the kids come from?"

"I don't know."

"Is there a reason that all of the kids are either black or Latino?" asked Reel.

Pete exclaimed, "I don't know! Okay? I came to all this late in the game."

"Why would he tell you about any of this?" wondered Robie.

Pete snorted. "Why else? He was drunk off his ass."

"But the guys obviously knew you had something. Why else would they have come around?"

Pete said nothing.

Robie said, "You showed up at your house with them. How did that happen?"

"They grabbed me when I was comin' out of a bar."

"And they brought you back to your house to get what you had on the computer," said Reel. "How did they even know about that?"

Pete shrugged again.

Robie slammed him up against a tree.

"Shrugs don't cut it, Pete," snarled Robie. "And roundabout bullshit nonanswers don't, either. They knew about it because you put the squeeze on them. In order to do that you had to have information. So, last time, who was the guy in the photo?"

When Pete didn't say anything Robie put his gun against the man's forehead.

"Last chance," said Robie.

Pete snorted. "You ain't shootin' me. That'd be murder. Lock your ass up forever in a Mississippi prison."

Reel said, "Robie, if that's what you want to do, use this." She pulled a suppressor from her pocket and tossed it to him. He caught it and spun it onto the barrel of his pistol.

Reel added, "We can cut him up and drop him in that swamp we passed earlier. No lungs to inflate, the body stays down. Then the gators can have him. What's left of him. So go ahead and kill him. It'll be light soon and we need time to dump the body."

"You two are killers!" Pete exclaimed.

"Damn, you are a genius," said Reel.

Robie put the suppressed muzzle against Pete's forehead and his finger slipped to the trigger guard.

"Nelson Wendell," a panicked Pete blurted out.

"And who exactly is Nelson Wendell?" asked Robie.

"Dude in the photo with the kids."

"And?"

"And he was chairman of Coastal Energy. Coal, gas, oil, you name it. One of the richest men in Mississippi, hell, the whole south. You must've heard'a him."

"No. But he likes kids?" said Reel.

"Guess so."

"And how did your dad come by those pictures?"

Now Pete looked very nervous. "I don't want'a say."

"Well, you're going to have to overcome that," said Robie, pressing the muzzle tighter against the young man's head.

"Okay, okay. He had a shack at the back of his property."

"I know. I've seen it. It's still there."

"Right. And it was secluded. He . . . he let this guy bring the kids there."

"And he was paid for it?"

"Yeah."

"Why would a rich guy put himself in your dad's power like that?"

"He told Dad he was bringing his girlfriends over. That wasn't so bad, I guess. Men back then screwed around as a matter of course. I mean this was a long time ago."

"They still screw around, as a matter of course," noted Reel.

"But your dad found out it wasn't grown women having consensual sex?"

"He started watchin' the place. He saw the kids. He

got hold of some pictures. Then he started black-mailin' the dude."

"Enough to set him up in business with the Rebel Yell casino?"

"Pretty much how it was," admitted Pete.

"And his first wife. The one that was in court?" asked Robie. "Did she know?"

"I don't know. Dad never said. Swear to God."

"But she must have known his money didn't come from oil and gas rights on their land. Since no one did even any exploratory work there."

"I guess that's right."

"And your mother, did she know about this?"

"We never talked about it. But I don't think she did. My mom wouldn't have liked that at all. She's a good Christian. Goes to church every Sunday."

"Well, maybe she did know and that's why they divorced," pointed out Robie.

"Could be," conceded Pete.

"Which brings us back to the photos. How did your dad meet someone like Wendell?" asked Robie. "He's rich and your dad was poor back then."

"Well, back then Wendell wasn't as rich. He and my dad run into each other some way. My old man didn't want to be a farmer his whole life. He was always anglin' for a way to get rich. And Wendell had money. Family money." He looked up at the Willows. "Like the folks who owned this place did."

Robie followed his gaze. "The Barksdales?"

"Yeah."

"You know what happened to them?"

"Not really. I remember my dad talkin' about them a few times. He said they just upped and left. Nobody knew they were even gone till the house come on the market for sale." He looked around. "Pretty out of the way. Folks don't come 'round here 'less they're visitin', and apparently folks didn't visit much with the Barksdales."

"Did you know them? Laura and her brother, Emmitt," said Robie. "You ever see them in town?"

"No, I think they were gone before I was even born."

"Did your dad know Henry Barksdale, the father?"

"If he did he never said so to me."

"How'd your dad get the pictures?"

Pete looked away.

Robie raised his gun again but Pete put up his hands. "Okay, okay. Dad told me he had a deal with the man who took the pictures."

"What sort of deal?"

"He'd give my dad the pictures if he never told about him being involved in all . . . that stuff."

"So this other guy was into kiddies, too?" said Reel.

"Yeah. I guess."

"And he gave Sherman Clancy pictures of Nelson Wendell with the kids so Clancy wouldn't rat him out for what he was doing?"

"That's right."

Robie absorbed all of this and said, "Do you know who the other guy was?"

"Dad never said."

"I'll ask you one more time. Do you know who the other guy was?"

"No, I swear. I don't. I wish I did, but I don't. I just knew about Wendell."

"And you communicated with Wendell's people because you wanted to keep the cash coming in?" said Robie.

"Well, you seen the house and everythin'. It's all goin' to hell. Dad's bank accounts are cleaned out. Son of a bitch spent every last dime he had. I can't even afford gas for my Porsche. What was I supposed to do?"

"Oh, I don't know, how about get a job?" said Reel disgustedly.

He said angrily, "Hey, I grew up kind'a rich. Didn't prepare me for workin' for a livin'. Not my fault."

Reel looked at Robie. "Can I just shoot him anyway?"

Robie said, "Where can we find Nelson Wendell?"

"At a cemetery over in Tupelo."

Robie looked stunned. "You're saying he's dead?"

"Yep. He died 'bout a month before my daddy did."

"So it wasn't Wendell you were communicating with? And it wasn't Wendell who sent the goons after you. So who was it?"

"Coastal is looking to go on the New York Stock Exchange."

"How do you know that?" asked Robie.

"Looked it up." Pete added defiantly, "I took a semester of business classes at the community college. I'm no dumbass."

"Okay, Mr. Business, how does that tie into all this?"

"Well, Nelson Wendell ran Coastal right up to his death. So's I bet the company don't want all this crap comin' out about Wendell. It might mess up the deal. Could cost the family billions. And a public shamin' on top of it."

"So it's the family that's coming after you?" said Reel.

"Guess they didn't like my proposal. Thought they'd get the pictures and send me on into the here-after without payin' me one dime, the pathetic jerks."

Reel said incredulously, "And this possibility hadn't occurred to you?"

"Look, this blackmail crap is new to me, okay? My old man made it look easy."

Reel sighed and looked at Robie. "What the hell do we do with him?"

Robie said, "Why did you come here, Pete?"

"Heard you were here. I need protection."

"And why is that our problem?"

He started speaking fast. "I'm a material witness. I can talk about stuff that'll get your dad off. Lots of

folks had reason to kill my old man. But if I get killed, all that goes away."

Now Robie sighed. "Okay, we'll take you down to the police station where you can make a full statement and they can protect you."

"But I won't get in no trouble, right?"

"That's not up to me, but I suppose if you cooperate they'll overlook certain things."

"Look, man, I ain't goin' to jail. I can't be in no box."

"You're lucky you're not in a coffin," said Reel. "Because you are that *stupid*."

"Sticks and stones," said Pete smugly.

Reel pressed the muzzle of her gun against his forehead and the smug look vanished.

She said, "Let me make this as clear as possible. I don't care if you get killed. I might end up being the one to pull the trigger, actually. But you are in way over your head. So you better drop the smartass routine and start treating this situation like it's life and death. And in your case my money's on death."

She stepped back, holstered her weapon, turned, and walked off, leaving Pete Clancy looking like he might be sick to his stomach.

53

"You mean you're not even going to talk to them?"

Robie was staring at Sheriff Monda.

Pete had given his statement and signed it. He was now in protective custody, which in Cantrell meant he was sitting in a spare jail cell.

The man had not been happy about it, but it was better than being dead, Robie had told him.

Taggert was hovering next to her boss, looking extremely nervous.

Reel was watching all of this while leaning against the wall with her arms folded over her chest.

"Do you know who Nelson Wendell is, or was?" asked Monda.

"Yeah, some über-rich asshole who likes to play with children in a very inappropriate and illegal way."

"Solely based on Pete Clancy's word and the admission that he was trying to blackmail those folks."

"We have pictures."

"Of a younger man who may or may not be Nelson Wendell."

"If Wendell was that well-known I think we'll be

able to find folks who can ID him in those pictures," Reel pointed out. "Are you sure you don't recognize him, Sheriff?"

Monda glared at her. "No, I don't. I never met the man. And another thing is the statute of limitations has long since run out on this. Which means he couldn't be prosecuted for this, even if he wasn't dead."

Reel said, "You're forgetting about those guys who kidnapped Pete and Sara, and nearly killed me and Robie. And they might have killed Sara, too. Those are all *new* crimes."

"And we don't have one shred of proof that those fellows are connected to the Wendell family," countered Monda.

"But if you investigate you may find that evidence," pointed out Robie.

"Do you know how influential the Wendell family is in Mississippi, hell, all the way over to Atlanta, for that matter? They're worth billions. And they give a lot of it away. And all told they account for over a hundred thousand good-paying jobs."

"Which is all wonderful but not an excuse to commit crimes," replied Robie curtly.

Monda hitched up his pants. "Well, I don't have probable cause to investigate them for anythin'. Probably get my ass sued if I tried."

"Then turn it over to the state police."

"Same problem. They're not lookin' to take a black

eye over this, either, based on some old pictures. Hell, they might've been doctored for all I know."

"What about Pete?"

"Pete Clancy is a liar. I'm not riskin' my career on anythin' he says! And the Wendell lawyers would rip him a new one on the stand."

"How about the FBI?" asked Reel. "I doubt they care how rich the Wendells are."

"You can go there if you want. I'm not."

"Is there something you're not telling us?" asked Robie.

Monda looked away but Taggert said, "His wife and his brother and his son are employed by Coastal."

"That has nothin' to do with it, Sheila," barked Monda, giving Taggert a scathing look.

"Are you sure about that?" asked Robie.

"Damn sure. Now if you can bring me some usable evidence, maybe my mind can be changed." He pointed a finger at Robie. "It's all well and good for you to want to go after those folks, but you don't live here. You just flit in and out. But I can't do that. This is my home."

Robie looked at Taggert, then returned his gaze to Monda. "Well, we'll see if we can get enough to change your mind, Sheriff."

"Okay, but keep in mind if the Wendells come after you, don't look for any help from me. Not 'less you got some strong evidence they're connected to all this."

"Message received loud and clear," said Robie as Taggert gave him a sympathetic look.

Robie and Reel left the office.

Outside Taggert caught up to them.

"Monda is a good guy, Robie. But he's caught between a rock and a hard place here."

"I get that, Sheila. But it's apparently up to us to do his job."

"What *are* you going to do?"

"Check out the Wendells. Any help you can give us on that?"

"Their main house is up in Jackson. But they keep a place down on the Gulf over near Biloxi. Makes the Willows look like a shanty."

She gave them the address. "They're there this time of year."

"Do you know anything about the family?"

"Norma Jean is the mother, the widow of Nelson. There're a bunch of grown kids and then grandkids. I hear tell that Bobby Wendell, the oldest boy, is runnin' things now. He's the only son. The others are daughters. They get their share of the money and they all live wonderful lives, but they have nothin' to do with the business."

"So Bobby's the one taking the company public?"

"That's right."

"How do you know so much about them?" asked Reel.

"Everybody down here knows about the Wendells.

Sort of like royalty to us. And the sheriff is right, they do a lot of good. Names on hospitals and museums and colleges all across the south. Good, charitable folks. And they provide a lot of jobs."

"So why are you helping us then?" Reel wanted to know, her tone suspicious.

"I don't have anybody worth carin' about that works for Coastal. And I don't like folks gettin' away with shit, no matter the size of their bank account. Especially when it involves kids."

"Works for me," said Reel.

They left Taggert and walked back to their car.

"So how do you want to approach this?" Reel asked.

Robie leaned against the fender of the car.

"They have to know that their guys were killed. And the ones who got away are probably long since gone. If they were outside contractors we may not be able to trace a connection unless we get ahold of financial records showing transfers of money to the muscle."

"And even if we had access, Coastal probably has lots of slush funds to ferry money like that around and make it untraceable."

"Agreed. And despite what I said to Monda, I doubt the FBI will be interested in pursuing this with the little we can tell them."

Reel said, "And Wurtzburger is after a serial killer, not a corporate titan run amok."

"If the cops can't tie the dead guys to Coastal that is a complete dead end. Even with Pete's testimony. Monda is right. Pete is not going to be seen as a reliable witness. Blackmailer, yes. Honest citizen telling the truth, no."

"Which gets me back to my question: How do we do this?"

"Sometimes the direct approach is the best."

"So go to Bobby Wendell?" said Reel.

"Yeah."

"With what?"

"With the only leverage we have."

"Which is?" she asked.

"Pictures of his dear old dad playing with kids."

54

Bobby Wendell looked up at the pair.

"I don't usually encourage visitors without an appointment."

Robie and Reel were in the palatial Gulf Coast retreat of the Wendell family that looked more like a Ritz-Carlton resort than an individual home.

The rich weren't just unlike other people—they apparently lived on an entirely different planet.

"And yet here we are," said Robie.

"Well, your communication was . . . provocative."

Bobby Wendell was taller than Robie, lean with longish graying hair and a slab of rock for a chin. His dark green, penetrating eyes held on the pair as he sat on a couch with sweeping views of the water.

Robie and Reel had been escorted in by beefy security when they had sent in a four-word message at the front gate of the estate.

Your father in pictures.

"Yes, it was. Intentionally so."

Without waiting for an invitation Robie sat across from Wendell.

Reel remained standing. They had left their weapons in the car, because they figured they would be confiscated. But the security guards weren't that good on the pat-down at the gate.

They had missed things.

A blade inside Robie's belt.

And a garrote wire hidden in Reel's sleeve.

"And why was that?"

"Dead guys back at a swamp in Cantrell."

Wendell shrugged. "So? What does that have to do with me?"

"If they were working for you it has everything to do with you."

"I have lots of people who work for me. But no one who's dead."

Robie said, "I figured you'd say that. So let's get to the pictures. Unless you want us to leave now?"

"I'm listening."

"We talked to Pete."

"Pete who?"

"Nice one," said Reel.

Wendell glanced up at her. "You look very serious. Very professional."

"Then looks *aren't* deceiving."

Wendell glanced back at Robie.

"Pictures?"

"Your father. And his *young* friends."

Wendell winced, looked away, and rubbed his mouth with his index finger.

"I hope you're better at blackmailing than that little shit was."

"Is that a confession?" said Reel.

"What do you want?"

"A man is in prison right now, on trial for killing Sherman Clancy."

"Okay. What does that have to do with my situation?"

"It has a lot to do with it if you had Sherm killed. That would mean the other guy is innocent."

Wendell leaned forward and said, "Until my father died I didn't even know who Sherman Clancy was. In fact, I didn't know who Pete Clancy was until he tried to blackmail me."

"So you admit you know who Pete is?" said Robie.

"Trust me, I wish I didn't."

"But you knew about your father's . . . problem?"

"That he liked to diddle little kids? No, I had no clue about that until Pete sent me the pictures."

"So you're saying you didn't have Sherman killed?"

"If I did, why in the hell would I admit it to you? But the fact is, no, I had no idea my father was being blackmailed for anything. When I saw the pictures . . ." His voice trailed off and he rose, walked over to the window, and looked out at the view.

"We have a hundred and forty-seven oil and gas platforms out in the Gulf," he said. "We're not as big as ExxonMobil, but we do really well. My father was a brilliant businessman; none better in my mind. I

couldn't hold a candle to him when it came to doing deals and making money. I think it's because I'm not a psychopath. He evidently was. But then again, some of the best capitalists are."

He turned back around to face them. "But when I saw those pictures I wanted to vomit. I wanted to kill my old man."

"And how exactly did he die?" asked Robie.

"On the operating table. He'd had an aortic aneurysm. No question how his life ended. They didn't even bother with an autopsy. And I didn't see the pictures until *after* he died."

"And you hired people to get the pictures back from Pete?"

Wendell shrugged. "I may not be as smart as my father but I'm not stupid. So, again, I have no idea what you're talking about."

"People have been kidnapped and people have died," Robie said.

"Don't know what to tell you."

"You're planning to go public with your company?"

"We are."

"So you have a lot to lose if this comes out," said Robie.

"In the grand scheme of things, no. My old man had withdrawn from the business over the last five years. Our underwriters are banking on me, not him. He's dead. I'm not. Even if he was a pedophile, the

boys on Wall Street won't give a damn. All they care about is the bottom line, and we make a shitload of money. We invested well, got our fingers in all the best places. We weathered the recession and had the capital to buy at bargain-rate prices when everybody was bailing. All we have is upside. The story is great. The IPO is going full steam ahead, bad news about Dad or not."

"So why do you care about the pictures, then?" asked Reel.

When Wendell said nothing Robie answered. "Because his mother Norma Jean is still alive."

Wendell looked away again. "My old man was an asshole. Treated me and my sisters like shit. I'm running the company now largely because my father was too busy living his life of decadence."

"*Diddling* little boys?"

"I always thought he was off with other women. I wish he had been. Now, I guess I know better."

"And your mother?"

"Heart of gold. Innocent as they come. Maybe as naïve as they come. If she saw those photos it would kill her." He turned to look at them. "*Kill* her. And that's just not something I can live with."

"So you wanted the pictures back?"

"Wouldn't you?"

"And you're sticking with your story that you didn't have Sherman Clancy killed?"

"Like I said, I had no idea who Sherman Clancy

was until his son showed up. Then I went back over the company's financials. I found a rogue account that had been set up a long time ago. Money was funneled in and money was funneled out over decades. Millions of bucks. Maybe tens of millions. I tried to track where the dollars went but it was like a black hole. Even had my CPAs on the job, but they couldn't do it either. Like I said, my old man was smart. Then Pete shows up on my doorstep and starts talking about pictures and money. That's when I put two and two together."

"But that was after Sherman died?"

"And after my father died, too. I had no reason to look at that part of his life until that punk showed up trying to blackmail my family. I guess he figured with my father dead and his old man dead, too, he needed to keep the gravy train going. Least that's what he intimated."

"So you met with him face-to-face?"

"Yeah, right here in fact."

"Based on the pictures?"

"I recognized my father. Enough said."

"And did you know the kids in the photo?"

Wendell shook his head. "No. They looked like . . . just kids." He glanced down, his face turning pale.

"None of them were white, Mr. Wendell," pointed out Robie. "They were either black or Latino. I'm wondering if that's significant."

"What do you mean?"

"I mean it might tell us where they came from."

"Yeah, well, I don't know anything about that."

Robie said, "I was at Pete's house when he showed up with those men. They were there to get the pictures and kill Pete. They said they were going to give him an acid bath."

"Maybe they did and maybe they didn't. I can't tell you. Maybe they were just trying to scare him so he'd give up the pictures and go away for good."

"And you of course won't admit to siccing them on Pete?"

"No, I won't. That's why I have a room full of lawyers. And I know you two don't have recording devices on you. They would have set off the sensor built into the door frame you walked through."

Robie glanced at the door. "Your doing?"

"No, my old man's. Like I said, smart. And paranoid."

Robie studied him. "You and your sisters? Did he ever . . . ?"

"Never," snapped Wendell. "I mean not with me. And I don't believe with my sisters, either." He paused. "But it's not like I ever came out and asked them after I saw those photos. But . . . but wouldn't they be screwed up or something if that had happened to them? If their own father had done that to them?"

He looked up at them in a pleading fashion.

"And they're not screwed up?" asked Reel.

"Not so they admit," replied Wendell.

"Well, maybe it's a hard thing to admit," said Robie.

"I didn't kill Sherman Clancy. And I didn't have anybody else do it. I just didn't want my mother to ever see . . . to ever see those pictures. And if these men threatened Pete or went over the line, that wasn't my doing. I didn't want it to go down like that. I just wanted the pictures."

"And if the FBI were to go through your accounts, would they find money paid to certain contractors that would seem mysterious? Like the men who were killed?"

"I'm a careful man. Interpret that how you want."

"The pictures we saw," said Robie. "Someone had to take them. Did Pete ever tell you who was the cameraman?"

Wendell looked genuinely puzzled by this question.

"Hell, I was fixated on seeing my dad like that, I never even thought about the person taking them. You mean another adult was involved in this?"

"That's exactly what I mean."

"But who? Who is the sick son of a bitch? Was it this Sherm Clancy?"

"I wish I knew," said Robie.

"And the photos?"

"I won't use them unless I have to. But be prepared, Mr. Wendell, that this all might very well come out."

55

Robie and Reel were sitting in their car outside of the Wendells' Gulf Coast home. He had left his phone number with Wendell in case the man wanted to talk to them again.

Robie was now on his phone doing a search. He pulled up a screen and read down it. "News feed. 'Billionaire oil man and noted philanthropist Nelson Wendell died on the operating table after emergency surgery to repair an aneurysm in his aorta.' Like Bobby said, he died before Sherm Clancy did."

"So you believe the son's story?" said Reel.

"Yeah, I do. While he wouldn't incriminate himself, what he did tell us about his father seemed sincere."

"Yeah, I thought so, too."

"Which means we have to find out who took the photos."

"Why? Do you think that's connected to the recent murders?"

"You don't think they are?"

"Well, those photos were taken a long time ago. The murders of Clancy and the two Chisum sisters

are very recent. There may not be a connection, especially if we believe Bobby Wendell that he didn't kill Clancy."

Robie shook his head. "I think all three murders are linked, Clancy and the Chisums."

"And your father is being framed? Why?"

"I think he *is* being framed, but I don't know why."

"I'm not convinced of any of this, Robie."

"Okay, but do you have another lead I'm not aware of?" said Robie curtly.

"No. I'm just trying to see the big picture on this."

"The big picture, I think, includes somebody being involved in this who we don't have a clue to as yet. An unknown factor that is driving all this."

"Okay, Clancy dead. I get that. He was blackmailing Wendell. But if Wendell's son didn't kill him, then who?"

"How about the guy who was taking the pictures?"

"Now *that* makes sense. Pete Clancy said his dad made a deal with this person, but he could have gone back on that deal. And that could have cost Clancy his life. But what about the two Chisum sisters? How did they know about any of this?"

"I've been thinking about that. And my best guess is pillow talk."

"What?"

"Pillow talk. They both had sex with Clancy. He was probably drunk at the time. According to Pete his dad was mostly drunk all of the time. He has sex with

the girls and he talks, says stuff he ordinarily wouldn't. You've seen something of the Chisum girls. They are opportunistic to a fault. They knew that information might get them money. Money they needed to get the hell out of Cantrell. They took the risk and it cost them their lives."

Reel nodded thoughtfully. "That seems to hold together. Janet Chisum goes to meet the person for a payoff and ends up shot and thrown in the river."

"Wait a minute," said Robie. "Emma Chisum told us that Janet had something on an important person or persons. That was where she was going to make a lot of money."

"So the Wendells then? Maybe Bobby just fed us a load of crap."

"Maybe. I guess if Janet Chisum had those pictures too."

Reel nodded. "And when she gets popped Sara takes up her sister's opportunity and dies, too. Although it was pretty stupid of her to meet the person out in the middle of nowhere after what happened to her sister, don't you think?"

"And Sara wasn't stupid. Which means something is off there. I just don't know what."

"We could be missing a few pieces of this puzzle," pointed out Reel.

"Granted. But how do we find out what they are?"

"By playing detective. But that's all we'd be doing—playing—since that's not what we do, Robie."

"I'm not leaving this damn place until I figure this out."

"What if you can't figure out all of it?"

"What do you mean?"

"You might piece together who killed whom. But that's not your endgame, is it?"

"Then what exactly is my endgame?"

She touched his trigger finger. "Getting this to work again. Isn't that what you want?" When he didn't say anything she said, "Isn't it?"

"What if I can't answer that question?"

"Then I'd say that's an answer in itself."

"Why are you doing this?"

"Doing what?"

"Asking all these questions about me?"

"I thought that was obvious. I'm trying to get to the bottom of what's going on inside your head. It's not easy, Robie. It wasn't easy for me when I had to do it. But you do have to do it. You were right. To go forward, you have to go back. You get this square, your foundation is set. You can move on. But until then, you're going to be damaged goods."

"This all started with a screwed-up mission. Me killing a little girl."

"I think this would have happened regardless. The moment you learned your father was in jail for murder."

"You can't know that for sure."

"Why not? Seems obvious to me."

"Look, you can stop interfering in my personal life. I don't need that. Not now. Not from you."

"Okay, so do you want me to leave?"

Robie said nothing. For a very long time.

Reel waited him out, her gaze held steady on him.

"No, I don't want you to leave. I need you."

"Are you sure, Robie? It won't hurt my feelings if you tell me to go to Hell. I'm a big girl. I can take it."

"I don't want you to leave, Jessica," he said slowly.

"Okay, then I'll stay. So where to now?"

"We need to find the guy who took the pictures."

"Okay, how?" asked Reel.

He let out a long breath. "If I knew that I would have already found him."

56

Victoria was not at home when they returned.

Priscilla was taking care of Tyler.

"Don't know where she went, don't know when she'll be back" was all the normally loquacious Priscilla would say on the subject.

Robie's phone buzzed.

It was Toni Moses. She wanted to see them.

"Is my dad okay?"

"He's fine. But I've met with Aubrey Davis. And we need to do a pow-wow with the fine, upstandin' prosecutor. Can you be here in thirty minutes?"

"Yes."

With Reel driving they made it in twenty-eight minutes, although their car was caked with road dirt by the time they got to town. Reel parked in front of Moses's office and they climbed out.

"Hey, Mr. Robie."

Robie looked over to see Little Bill holding a plastic bag from the local supermarket.

They walked over to him.

Robie said, "Thanks for the help on the computer. My partner here says you're really good."

Little Bill said, "Hell, gave me somethin' to do besides add to my scores on *Kill or Be Killed*."

"You ever think about a career in cybersecurity?" asked Reel.

Grinning, he said, "I'm from Cantrell. I ain't thought about a career in nothin', really."

She studied him so closely that his grin disappeared.

She said, "You clearly have the technical skill. But do you have the drive?"

Little Bill looked at Robie and then at Reel. "My daddy is real sick."

"But we're not talking about your daddy. We're talking about *you*."

She handed him a card. "Think about it and then, if you want to pursue it, give me a call."

Little Bill took the card. "Are you folks with the government?" he said.

Reel replied, "Does it matter who we're with, so long as it's not the bad guys?"

"I guess not."

"Think about it," said Reel.

Robie said, "How's your dad doing?"

"The same."

"I'll be by to see him again."

"Okay, thanks."

And they left him there staring down at the card Reel had given him.

Robie said to her, "You have to be careful with making offers like that."

"We still want the best and the brightest, right?"

Robie shrugged, and a minute later they were in Toni Moses's small conference room. Aubrey Davis sat across from her.

The man looked like someone had stolen all of his toys, but the Mississippi prosecutor was evidently trying to put on a game face.

"Hey, there, Will. How you doin'? We still got to have us that drink."

Robie and Reel sat next to Moses, who had papers and files spread out in front of her.

Robie looked at Moses. "So what's happening?"

"What's happenin' is that with all of the stuff I've shared with my colleague over there, I believe it's time he strongly reconsiders his case. And I wanted you two here to help convince him."

Davis began to protest. "Look here, Ms. Moses, the defendant has been charged and it is my duty to—"

"To what?" broke in Moses. "Screw up your chance to be the next congressman from the fine state'a Mississippi? Because if you try this case and lose it, that's exactly what you'll be doin'. You couldn't win an election for town drunk after that."

Davis swelled with indignation. "I take umbrage at the accusation that I am puttin' any political ambitions I may have over—"

"Aubrey," she said, interrupting him again. "Do you or do you not want to find the real killer in this case?"

"Of course I do. How dare you suggest otherwise?"

"Then let's get down to it. First things first. What do we do with my client?"

"He is still charged with murder," said Davis promptly. "And he's the only credible suspect we have."

Moses looked at Robie. "What do you say to that?"

Robie kept his gaze on Davis. "Quite a few people have been killed," he began. "And that nearly included my partner and me. I'm convinced that Sherman Clancy's murder and the murders of the two Chisum girls were done by the same person."

"Which lets Dan Robie out because he was in prison when Sara Chisum was killed," said Moses promptly.

"*If* they were committed by the same person," said Davis. "And from where I'm sittin' that's a mighty big if."

Robie told him about the suspected serial killer that Special Agent Wurtzburger had informed them about.

"Why the hell didn't he come and tell me that!" barked an obviously irritated Davis.

"No idea," said Robie. "And on top of that, Clancy was blackmailing someone, which gives a prime motive for murder."

"Who was he blackmailin'?"

"I take it you haven't talked to Sheriff Monda," replied Robie.

"Meanin' what exactly?"

"Meaning that we already told him the person being blackmailed was Nelson Wendell."

Davis sucked in a breath. "Bullshit! Nelson Wendell! He died just recently."

"I know he did. We've just come from talking to his son, Bobby Wendell."

"But they are one of the finest families in Mississippi. Hell, in all the south."

Moses eyed Davis severely. "Don't tell me that the Wendells are going to be backin' your congressional run?"

"I haven't even decided whether I'm goin' to run or not," snapped Davis. He turned to Robie. "And what did Bobby Wendell tell you? What was his daddy bein' blackmailed for?"

Robie took out the photo and passed it over to Davis.

The man looked down at it and then flinched. "What the hell is this?"

"Sherman Clancy's blackmail tool."

Davis looked up. "Pedophilia?"

Robie nodded.

"Are you tellin' me this is Nelson Wendell?"

"Yes. Bobby Wendell confirmed it was his father. The picture's from many years ago, of course."

Davis studied the photo and then his features

395

became resigned. "My God. I guess money and bein' from a fine family don't matter a'tall."

Reel said, "For the record, you can find scum in the rich, the middle class, and the poor."

Robie added, "And while of course he wouldn't admit to it, it's nearly certain that Bobby sent a bunch of goons after Pete Clancy when he decided he wanted a piece of the blackmail action after his father died. I saved his butt from them. Then they kidnapped Sara Chisum to use her as bait to try to kill me and my partner here."

Davis nodded slowly, his penetrating gaze on Robie. The "aw shucks" demeanor of the man had completely disappeared. And in that look Robie seemed to realize that the insufferable man might actually be a cagy prosecutor.

"Did Bobby Wendell have Sara Chisum killed?" asked Davis.

"I don't think so but I can't be sure. Same answer on whether he killed Clancy and Janet Chisum."

"So who then? This serial killer just happens on the scene and starts killin' folks that are blackmailin' rich folks? And Clancy I get, but how did the Chisum sisters get involved?"

"Clancy probably told them while he was drunk and having sex with them," replied Robie.

Davis shook his head. "The Devil gets inside'a you, no tellin' what trouble you'll get into. So the girls were after money too? They bit off mor'n they could

chew. But your gut says you don't think the Wendells killed them?"

"No, I don't think so. Bobby tried to get these photos back. And the men we killed were part of that effort. And after she was nearly murdered by those guys, I seriously doubt that Sara would have arranged to meet with them alone late at night in the woods."

"But that just leaves this serial killer person," said Davis.

"No," said Reel, tapping the photo. "That leaves whoever took this picture."

"And how do we find this person?" asked Davis.

"Working on it," said Robie.

"You said you talked to Sheriff Monda?"

"We did. And with only Pete the blackmailer's word to go by he's not touching the Wendells with a ten-foot pole."

"But you said that Bobby Wendell said this was his father."

"Yes. But that only gets us so far. And he'll have lawyered up by now, so no one will be talking to him."

Davis sat back. "Shit," he muttered. "You think somethin's nice and straightforward and then before you know it it's all twisty-turny like the damn Missis-sippi River."

"Huh, who would'a thought life wasn't black-and-white," said Moses.

Davis shifted his gaze to her. "Okay, Toni, okay, I get

your meanin' loud and clear." He looked at Robie. "So what do we do now?"

"The killer is still out there and we have no idea who it is."

"But what do we do with your daddy?" said Moses.

Davis said, "I'd leave him in jail. He'd be safer there. But—"

"But what?" asked Robie sharply.

Moses answered. "That was the other reason I wanted you to come in. The judge has set bail for your father. And he's paid it. Which mean he gets out in about twenty minutes."

57

"Here he comes," said Robie.

He and Reel were sitting in their car across the street from the jail.

The door to the jail opened and Taggert appeared there. Right behind her was Dan Robie, presumably wearing the clothes he had been arrested in: chino pants, white shirt, and loafers.

As Robie started to get out of his car, a Volvo roared down the street and screeched to a stop in front of the jail. Victoria jumped out of the car, hurried over to her husband, and wrapped her arms around him.

Observing this, Reel said, "Apparently, you're not the only one feeling guilty."

"Apparently," said Robie as he climbed back into the car and closed the door.

Victoria led her husband over to the Volvo. They got in and she drove off. Taggert went back inside the jail and closed the reinforced door behind her.

Reel said, "So what now? I assume they're heading back to the Willows."

"Then so are we," replied Robie.

"Well, this could get interesting," remarked Reel.

By the time they reached the Willows the empty Volvo was parked in front.

Robie and Reel walked up the steps and through the front door.

Priscilla met them in the foyer with Tyler in tow.

"They gone upstairs," she said.

"I guess they haven't been able to . . ." asked Robie.

"Well, man's been absent from his wife a long while," said Priscilla primly.

Robie looked up the stairs. When he glanced back he found Reel staring at him. Priscilla had taken Tyler outside.

Robie hurried up the stairs with Reel on his heels.

"Robie, you're not going to—"

"No, of course I'm not."

He turned to the left and went to his room, shutting the door behind him. He heard Reel outside the door for a few moments, but then she walked to her room and closed her door.

Robie sat on his bed, his face pointed downward. Then he jumped up and started pacing the room. And then his pacing slowed and then stopped as he arrived at the window. He peered out and once more his mind went back to that night. The last night he would see Laura Barksdale. He had been looking up at this window and had seen her silhouette pass across

it. After that, crushed beyond all reckoning, he had climbed back into his car and set off for his new life, alone.

In the ensuing months, he had written to her several times. He had also phoned and left messages.

He had asked why she had not shown up that night. What had kept her from her promises. Then his letters and phone messages had grown angrier. Finally, he had simply stopped writing. Or calling.

He left his room and walked outside, sat in front of a pond, and watched a couple of ducks paddling their way across its surface.

A shadow fell over him about a half hour later.

It was Victoria.

Her hair was damp and she carried the fresh scent of a recent shower. She had on shorts and a tank top. Her feet were bare, her shoulders freckled.

"How's he doing?" he asked.

"Better now," she said, a satisfied smile playing over her lips.

"Toni told me he was getting out on bail," he said, ignoring her look.

"He never should have been locked up in the first place."

"Well, the case against him was pretty compelling." She sat on the ground next to him. "'Was'? So there are developments?"

"There is reason to hope he'll get off, yes."

She searched his face and then looked away.

"He didn't kill anybody."

"I know that. We just have to convince everybody of that. Beyond all doubt," he added, recalling their earlier conversation. "So he can stay in Cantrell with his head held high."

"You make that sentiment sound silly. It's not. At least for him."

"If it came out that way, I apologize."

"I love your father."

"I'm sure you do."

"And I'm not a slut. I never cheated on him. I know what people said about me and Clancy, but I never slept with that man."

"But you also never explained why you were with him that night. You said you had business with him. You never said what."

She stared over at the water, her brow creasing.

"He was blackmailing me."

Robie flinched. "Blackmailing you? How?"

"Before I met your father I had some issues."

"What kind of issues?"

"Specifically, I had a drug problem. I was hooked on painkillers from an accident I was in. Then I got hooked on stronger stuff. Then I had to steal to support my habit. I sought help, went into rehab, kicked my problem, and started my life over."

"But Clancy found out about that? How?"

"He never said. Apparently, he makes a business out of doing stuff like that."

"What makes you say that?"

"Things he let slip." She looked at him. "You believe me, don't you?"

"Yes. We've actually uncovered other instances where Clancy was blackmailing people. So what did you do at the meeting?"

"Paid him off. He insisted I do it in person."

"But you stayed with him a long time. If it was just a payoff, why drink with the guy for hours? Why not just drop off the payment and go?"

"Because that was another condition of his, Will. He wanted me to stay and drink with him. And he also wanted me to sleep with him. I refused and told him to go to Hell. After that he stopped asking. But I had to stay and drink with him. He wanted it that way, because I think he was planning on blabbing about it to everyone to rub Dan's nose in it. Let them think we had slept together. But at that point I didn't care. I didn't want Dan to find out about what I had done. That was more critical to my thinking. The stuff with Clancy far less so. I knew Dan would never really believe I had slept with that jerk."

"But maybe he did believe it," said Robie. "He threatened Clancy about it in public."

"That was just him being a man, protecting his territory. I told him I didn't sleep with Clancy, and I really think he believed me. I didn't tell him about the blackmail stuff. I just said we'd run into each other and had a few drinks. No harm, no foul. On the

other hand, Clancy had details about my past that would prove far more compelling. And he threatened to show them to Dan. I couldn't let that happen. Your father wouldn't have understood."

"How much was the payoff?"

"Fifty thousand dollars."

"In cash?"

"That's how he wanted it. And that's really how I wanted it. I didn't want any trail of money going to him from me."

"Where'd you get fifty thousand in cash?"

"I had a life before Dan," she said in a defensive tone. "My convention-planning business did very well. I had saved most of it, since I worked too hard to enjoy any time off. I dipped into that."

"You could have gone to the police."

"I could have, yes, but I didn't."

They sat in silence for a few minutes.

"This is all so screwed up," she said in a hushed voice.

"Yeah, probably in more ways than you know."

She looked back at the house. "This Laura Barksdale?"

"What about her?"

"You never saw her again?"

"Never."

"But you thought about her?"

"Yeah, I did."

"She must have been important to you."

"She was."

"Like your father is important to me."

"I guess. But you have him. I don't have Laura."

"If he goes to prison I won't have him." She shot him a glance. "And neither will you."

58

Dinner was tense, awkward, and uncomfortable for everyone.

Only little Tyler seemed to be able to rise above the somber mood. Every few minutes he would reach out and touch his father's cheek.

Robie could never remember his father smiling like that when he'd been a kid. But he couldn't begrudge Tyler his positive effect on his old man. He felt his own mouth tugging upward in a smile when Dan Robie reached over and tousled Tyler's hair.

He caught Victoria looking at him once, but when he caught her eye she busily passed more food around the table.

Reel sat there taking it all in, registering every move, every word, and she seemed profoundly unsatisfied with the results.

Dan Robie took a drink of tea, set his glass down, wiped his mouth, and said, "Toni filled me in on everythin' before I left jail." He glanced first at Reel and then at his older son.

"I appreciate all the work, and the risks you two

have undertaken. I probably would've been set bail regardless. But I don't think my case would look as good as it does right now without your efforts. Actually, I know it wouldn't."

"Reasonable doubt," remarked Reel.

Dan pointed a finger at her. "Exactly. Alternative explanations and motives."

"I thought you wanted a slam dunk to wipe away all doubt, not just from the jurors but from everyone in Cantrell," interjected Robie.

"I do want that. But right now I'll take what I can get." He glanced at Tyler and then Victoria.

"For two reasons."

Tyler reached out both arms and his father gently lifted him up and set the boy on his lap. He kissed Tyler on top of the head and looked at Victoria.

"You seem tired. You been sleepin' badly?"

Victoria coughed. "Not too good, actually. For obvious reasons."

"I hope you'll sleep better tonight."

"I'm sure I will. With you back next to me."

"You want to take Ty on out and see if Priscilla has some ice cream for him in the kitchen, hon?" Dan said to his wife. "I need a few minutes with Will and Jessica." In a lower voice he added, "Not for Ty's ears."

Victoria swept Tyler up in her arms and carried him into the kitchen.

As soon as the door had closed behind them Dan

pulled his chair in closer. "Bobby Wendell is in a lot of trouble."

Robie said, "If he hired those people to do what they did, he is. But it still has to be proven."

"But you don't think he had anyone killed? Clancy? The Chisums?"

"No, we don't," said Robie.

"Aubrey Davis is still goin' to try the case against me, unless we can deliver him definitive proof that someone else was responsible."

"I would have expected nothing less from him."

"Talk to me more about this serial killer."

Robie and Reel took turns filling him in on what Wurtzburger had told them.

Dan rubbed his jaw. "You know it seems a little convenient that a serial killer would just happen along and kill three people who had, by their actions, given other people motivation to murder them."

"Sort of what we'd been thinking, too," said Reel.

"How do you explain away the forensic evidence against you at the crime scene?" asked Robie.

"Planted."

"Then I doubt it was our roaming serial killer who's responsible. Why would he want to frame you?"

"He wouldn't," said Dan. "No reason to. Which is why I think your FBI buddy is barkin' up the wrong tree here."

"Which gets us back to question one. Who killed them?"

"If it's just one person," said Reel. "Clancy and Janet Chisum, maybe the same person. But it might be that a second party killed Sara Chisum."

"It could be," agreed Dan slowly. "But then it gets really complicated. Maybe too complicated. In my legal experience most murders are pretty straightforward and the person responsible readily apparent."

"Why didn't you stay in jail?" asked Robie. "Safer in there for you."

"Yeah, that's what someone would say who hasn't been in a jail cell. It's not a lot of fun. Besides, I would rather be out here protectin' my family in case there is some nutjob out there gunnin' for me."

"That's why we're here."

"Even so. They're my responsibility." He paused. "I know all of this has been a surprise for you. My bein' married. And havin' a young son. I hope you and Victoria have been gettin' along okay. I could understand if there's some friction there."

"It's been fine," said Robie. "She's very nice. And I know she loves you very much. And she's a great mother to Tyler."

"Yes she is. I'm a very lucky man. Never thought I'd have a second shot like this at happiness." He grinned like a schoolkid.

Reel said, "Dan, you still haven't answered one big question for us."

Dan settled his gaze on her. "Let me guess. Was I or was I not drivin' the Range Rover that night?"

"You get an A plus. Now an answer would be even better."

"The fact is, I don't remember," said Dan.

Robie and Reel exchanged a glance.

"And you don't believe me?" said Dan.

Robie answered. "Doesn't matter if we don't. And by the way, we don't. It'll only matter to the jury. And no one sitting on it will believe that you can't remember whether you were in the Range Rover that night or not."

"Are you protecting someone?" asked Reel.

Dan looked at her sharply. "Like who?"

"I don't know. That's why I'm asking. We know that Victoria, Tyler, and Priscilla were out of town. So who else might be deserving of you falling on your sword?"

"Nobody, because I'm not protectin' anyone. Maybe I was out that night. Or maybe the two witnesses didn't see what they thought they saw. I'm not the only one who drives a Range Rover in Cantrell. Clancy had one, too."

"Damn," muttered Robie. He stood abruptly.

So did Reel.

They headed out together.

Dan called after them. "Where the hell are y'all goin'?"

Neither one answered him.

59

The stench of the burned house was still thick in the night air.

They approached Clancy's destroyed mansion from the front, after having left their car on the other side of the road.

Robie and Reel slipped through the partially opened gates and headed up the walk.

He said, "I don't know why I didn't put two and two together before."

"Range Rovers. How close is this one to your dad's?"

"Pretty close, if I'm remembering correctly. I only saw it once when I was here the first time."

They had eaten dinner late, and the time it had taken to drive here meant that it was nearly dark. The low hum of insects, the slithery movements of creatures in the nearby woods, the occasional bark of a fox, and the sounds of something large plopping in the not-too-distant water were their companions as they made their way to the garage.

When they reached it and went inside, Reel said, "So that's the Bentley where he died?"

Robie nodded. "And there's the Range Rover."

They both headed to the rear of the SUV.

Robie had illuminated their path with a flashlight he had brought. The lights in the garage, they had found, were not working.

"There it is," Reel said, pointing to the hole.

Robie knelt down and examined it more closely.

"Looks like a pistol round all right. And it's not that old. No rust."

"So *this* is the vehicle that was fleeing the scene where Sara Chisum died."

Using his jacket so as not to mess up any latent prints Robie opened the rear hatch of the Rover and noted the exit hole on the inside of the door.

"My round went through. Let's see if we can find it."

They searched for half an hour, being as careful as possible not to disturb any forensics.

But there was no slug.

"That means whoever was driving this knew I'd hit the Rover and when he got back here he searched the back and found the round."

"But didn't bother to hide the site of the entry," noted Reel.

Robie closed the rear hatch door and nodded. "Well, you'd have to take it in to a body shop. And then they might alert the police."

"So stick it in here and hope nobody notices?"

"Probably," said Robie.

"Next question. Who was driving it? Because that person murdered Sara Chisum."

"Pete?" Robie looked around, as though the youngest Clancy would somehow walk into the garage.

"If so, why?"

Robie said, "He found out she knew about the folks his father was blackmailing. Maybe she was blackmailing him. Or wanted a piece of the action. He gets pissed, drives out in the Rover, and kills her."

"That's one theory," said Reel, not sounding convinced. "Although he said he didn't like guns."

"And you believed that?"

"Not necessarily, no."

"What then?"

"We still don't know who your father is protecting. And I doubt it's Pete Clancy."

Robie said, "We'll have to let Sheriff Monda know about the bullet hole. It's material evidence in a murder investigation."

"Right. We'll see if the guy can manage to investigate this without getting his panties in a wad. But Pete doesn't have any money, so maybe the good sheriff won't get scared off like he did with the Wendells."

Robie walked over to the Bentley and peered inside.

Reel joined him, looking over his shoulder. "Your

dad's prints, hair, and a boot mark in the mud next to the vehicle?"

"Yes."

"Prints are problematic. It's not nearly as easy to plant them as TV and the movies make it out to be."

"He could have been in Clancy's car before."

"But they weren't friends."

"But I don't think they were enemies either, up until what happened with Victoria."

"Did Victoria ever tell you what all that was about? Her and Clancy?"

Robie took a minute to fill her in on what Victoria had told him earlier.

"Well, I guess I can understand that. The lesser of two evils. She didn't want your father to know about her past. So she caved in to Clancy's demand. Damn, what a piece of work that guy was."

"Yeah, well it cost him in the end."

Reel tapped the top of the Bentley. "Do you really think Pete killed Sara?"

"Anyone could have taken the Range Rover. The garage door is off its roller. Keys were probably hanging on a hook in the kitchen or maybe kept in the garage somewhere. But no, Pete doesn't strike me as smart or methodical enough to have done this. Slit his father's throat? Gunned down two young women? Framed my father? Sold us a bill of goods? Hell, he couldn't even blackmail Wendell without nearly getting killed. Then he runs like a scared kid only to

come back with his tail between his legs begging for protection. If he is behind it, the guy is one lucky SOB."

"And he might be."

"Or he might be innocent and clueless," commented Robie.

"Well, he's sitting in a jail cell right now. Why don't we go ask him?"

"And you think he'll tell us the truth?" Robie said skeptically.

"Depends on how we ask him."

They left the garage and walked toward the main house, which was now merely a jumble of caved-in walls and a partially collapsed roof.

"The bigger they are the harder they fall," noted Reel. "It's why I never wanted to be rich. Too much shit to take care of. Eventually, what does it matter anyway, right?"

"Meaning you can't take it with you?"

"No, meaning you get old and someone, usually your family, is trying to take it away from you while you're still breathing. Not how I want to spend my golden years."

"There you go again, talking about retirement."

Reel shot him a glance. "Why not? You think we're going to be doing this forever?"

"I can say definitively no, at least I'm not."

"And you never know, we might be replaced by drones."

"Not even assassins can stand in the way of technology," said Robie sardonically.

"So retirement then?"

"Or an early grave."

"You need to think more positively, Robie."

"Ask me that again when I'm out of Mississippi."

His phone buzzed.

He pulled it out and looked at the screen.

"Don't recognize the number."

"Better answer it."

Robie did so.

Bobby Wendell sounded frantic. "Mr. Robie, we have a problem."

"What sort of problem?" said Robie warily.

"Well, it's more your problem right now than mine."

"What are you talking about?"

"The men that I may or may not have hired to resolve that issue?"

"What about them?"

"They are pissed about what you and your colleague did. And they have called in reinforcements, more badass than they are, apparently. And they are on their way to do something about it."

"Who are they?"

"I don't know."

"Then how do you know they're coming for us?"

"I got a call from someone, a friend. He's in the loop. He told me. This group thought the job would

be easy. Put the screws to Pete. But then you showed up and wreaked havoc. They want their pound of flesh, Mr. Robie. And you and your friend are it. And then they might come after me. Which is why I'm flying my family out of the country right now."

"Where are they now, do you know?"

Reel tapped Robie's shoulder and pointed ahead.

"They're here," she said quietly.

60

Reel had spotted the headlights of two vehicles driving in through the gates.

The SUVs were moving fast, and their drivers obviously didn't care who heard them approach. They stopped next to the house.

Both Robie and Reel drew their weapons and slipped back inside the garage.

He had his nine-mill plus his blade.

She had her pistol and an ankle backup. And her garrote wire up her sleeve.

Robie tapped the number on his phone.

Taggert answered on the second ring.

He explained the situation to her.

"I'll get there fast as I can with as much firepower as I can," she said tersely. Then the line went dead.

"They're coming," said Reel.

Robie put the phone away as car doors started opening.

Reel looked around the garage and then her gaze fixed on the open door.

"Huge hole in our defense. If they swarm that and

then hit us from the rear, we're in a pincer we can't get out of." She lightly tapped one of the wooden walls. "Or they can just open fire right through this until they hit us."

He nodded, agreeing with her assessment. "Then let's extract ourselves," he said.

Robie looked at the Bentley and then the Range Rover. The Rover was only a couple years old, he estimated. Much harder to hot-wire. All electronic. The Bentley, on the other hand, was vintage.

He climbed into the driver's seat as footsteps marched toward the garage. They obviously knew exactly where the pair was.

"Cover us," Robie said, as he ducked under the steering column and started fiddling with the wires.

Reel stepped to the edge of the open garage door. Her breath relaxed, her weapon was held in the same way she had always held it. It was more an extension of her hand than a mere gun. She listened intently, trying to discern what the opposition was doing.

She looked over at Robie. As soon as the car started up, the forces outside would charge. That was a given. She stopped when she heard the voice.

"We know you're in there. The place is surrounded. You can't get away. Give up now, you get it fast. If you don't, you get it slow."

Robie continued to work away.

Meanwhile, Reel thought about a possible opportunity.

She slipped over to Robie, told him what she was thinking.

He nodded, handed her his gun, and said, "Do it."

She left him and went to the spot, a narrow sliver behind some junk that provided a clear view of the outside through the open door.

Reel evaluated the probable forces aligned against them. There had been two large SUVs coming down the drive. Max capacity was eight each. Perhaps sixteen men then. Maybe more if some of them had crammed into the cargo area in the very back. But they would have guns. That took space. So maybe *just* sixteen.

Robie called out softly to her. "Ready." He held two wires in his hand and was about to cross them.

Reel took her optics from her small backpack, slipped them on, and fired them up. She rested her pistols on top of a metal trash can.

The same voice said, "You have ten seconds to decide, then the option is no longer available."

"Three . . . two . . . one," said Robie.

He crossed the wires and the big Bentley roared to life.

Robie was glad whoever had last parked it had backed the Bentley in. It would be dicey enough without having to cut a J-turn under these conditions.

The men outside charged toward the garage, firing their weapons.

And revealing their positions.

Reel fired, methodically, unhurried but with pin-point accuracy.

Four men who had exposed themselves with their muzzle flashes fell dead, while the others took cover.

"Move, Jess," cried out Robie.

She sprinted across the garage floor as bullets ripped through the space. Reel tumbled into the front seat of the Bentley and then immediately slipped over into the backseat. She rolled down both windows, a pistol in each hand.

"Hit it!" she said.

Robie put the Bentley in gear and slammed down the gas. The big car lurched forward and smashed through the garage door, sending big chunks of it flying away.

They heard a scream and a thunk and then another body fell, presumably by collision with a part of the garage door or the car.

The Bentley careened down the driveway. They were taking fire from all sides now. Robie sat low in the seat, his head barely above the dash. He was glad that the old Bentley was built like a tank with heavy metal sides. He jerked the wheel to the right and clipped a guy reloading his weapon, sending him sailing away where he slammed into a pile of burned objects that had probably been carried out of the house earlier by the fire department.

Reel was firing out of each of the open rear windows. She wasn't firing wildly but she wasn't necessarily firing at targets, either. She just needed to get them through this gauntlet.

Glass exploded as a round wiped out the Bentley's rear window. Bullets hit a front tire and a rear tire, shredding them. Still, Robie kept the accelerator flat to the floor and the Bentley kept moving, though not as smoothly.

The windshield exploded as multiple rounds hit it. Robie ducked in time but he heard Reel grunt from the backseat.

"You okay?" he called out.

"Just keep going," she yelled back.

Robie swerved to avoid one of the SUVs, which caused the Bentley to crash into the other one. It moved the other vehicle enough to get by and the front right wheel of the SUV was pushed in, making the truck inoperable.

Seconds later they were through the gate. Robie hung a left when the car hit the asphalt, and the wounded Bentley rumbled down the road.

Robie glanced in the backseat. He saw the blood on Reel's face.

"How bad?"

"Not bad." She paused and added, "But it's getting in my eyes. This car have a first aid kit?"

Robie popped open the glove box, and fumbled through it as he drove.

He pulled things out, tossing them on the passenger seat.

His fingers finally closed around the small, plastic box.

"Here," he said, tossing the tiny first aid kit to her.

Robie glanced back and then down at the passenger seat.

His gaze fixed for a moment on what he was seeing.

A photo. It was bent and creased.

He picked it up.

The recognition was immediate.

Laura Barksdale.

He put it in his pocket.

Then he heard Reel hiss.

"Robie, they're coming."

61

Robie had made a mistake. He had disabled one SUV using the Bentley as a battering ram, but he had left the other intact.

That error could end up killing them. He could understand making mistakes playing detective, but this sort of thing was what he did for a living. He had definitely lost his mojo. He might never have a chance to get it back now.

The SUV was right behind them and gaining, as the shot-up Bentley on its shredded tires continued to slow.

"We're running on nearly metal," said Robie. "And I smell fuel."

"I know," said Reel, who was being pitched and tossed across the backseat.

The next volley of bullets shredded the rear of the Bentley.

Reel dove to the floorboard just in time as glass and metal and leather blew around the car's interior.

Robie felt blood rush down his face as something struck him.

He wiped the blood away and looked back. The SUV was right on them. He could see men leaning out the windows.

"They've got MP5s," called out Reel, who was watching this, too.

They heard the sirens wailing and engines roaring.

"Cavalry's on its way," said Reel.

Robie nodded. Only the cavalry would be seriously outgunned.

Robie kept the gas pedal pressed to the floor, but he knew that wouldn't be enough.

"Hang on," he told Reel as he slid on his seat belt. "And toss me a pistol."

She gave him his Glock, buckled her belt, and then braced her feet against the back of the passenger seat.

Robie screeched the Bentley into a one-eighty, losing hubcaps, more rubber, and other bits and pieces of the once stately car.

He slammed down on the gas and they were flying right at the SUV.

This was a clear game of chicken, with a twist.

Robie aimed his gun where the windshield had been and fired his entire mag at the windshield of the SUV. It shattered and blood spurted against the glass as the SUV swerved to Robie's right.

Robie cut his wheel, sending the lumbering Bentley to the left.

The vehicles still passed so close to each other that the side mirrors collided and snapped off.

Robie could see the SUV driver was slumped over the wheel, the man next to him as well.

Two men appeared at the rear windows and prepared to strafe Robie with fire from their MP5s.

First one man and then the next stiffened as the rounds fired by Reel from the Bentley's backseat slammed into them.

Then the Bentley was past the driverless SUV, which slid onto the shoulder, flipped, hit a tree, and exploded.

"Robie, we're on fire!"

Robie looked in the rearview and saw flames flickering from the rear of the car.

He slammed on the brakes, slipped off his belt, and kicked open the door.

Reel called out, "My seat belt's jammed."

Robie reached back over the seat.

"Go, Robie, go!"

He ignored her and tried not to look at the flames creeping up the back of the trunk. When the vapor in the gas tank ignited, they were dead.

Robie slid the knife out of his belt compartment, placed its cutting edge under Reel's belt, and jerked. The belt was cut, but not all the way.

"Will you get the hell out of here?" cried out Reel. "It's going to blow."

"Shut up!" snapped Robie.

He made one more cut and the belt broke clean.

He pulled Reel over into the front seat, then they both fled out the driver's-side door.

They were twenty feet from the Bentley when the vapor ignited.

The concussive force knocked them off their feet, sending them tumbling head over heels across the uneven ground. They landed hard near the tree line.

And neither moved after that.

"Robie? Robie!"

Something slapped his face. Robie slowly opened his eyes.

Taggert stared back down at him.

"Are you dead or what?" she said flatly.

Robie slowly sat up then flinched in pain and grabbed at his arm.

"You shot?" asked Taggert.

He shook his head, unbuttoned his shirt, and slid it off.

His scar tissue had completely torn along with maybe some other things.

"Damn," said Taggert. "That looks like it hurts."

He pulled his shirt back on. "Must've happened when the car exploded."

He looked over as Reel came to and sat up.

"You okay?" he asked.

"Okay?" exclaimed Taggert. "Damn, you two definitely do not look okay."

Beside her were two state troopers in full riot gear.

Robie said, "The other guys look worse. Pretty sure they're all dead."

"They are, least the ones in that truck over there. Burnt to a crisp."

"Well, we shot most of them before that happened," said Reel.

One of the state troopers looked at her. "You mean while you were driving?"

Reel looked at him. "Well, they weren't polite enough to stop so I could shoot them standing still."

Robie said, "This started at Clancy's house. There are other guys back there."

Taggert looked at the troopers. "Better go check that out. I'll stay with them. And call in some reinforcements. This ain't a crime scene, it's a damn war zone."

The troopers hurried off and Taggert looked back at the pair. "I can call an ambulance."

"Who needs an ambulance?" asked Reel.

"Hell, if only you could see yourselves. Blood everywhere."

"All superficial."

"Yeah, we'll let the docs confirm that if you don't mind."

"Later, Taggert," said Robie.

"Okay, so why don't you tell me what you were doing at Clancy's?"

"It's a long story," said Robie.

Taggert squatted next to him. "Well, I got nothin' but time."

62

Any men left alive back at Clancy's had apparently escaped on foot, because the damaged SUV was still there.

Robie and Reel spent hours going over what had happened.

When Monda arrived, Robie showed the sheriff and Taggert the bullet hole in the Range Rover in the garage.

"So this was the vehicle you shot at?" said Monda, running his hand over the damaged metal.

"Yes. Which also means that Sara Chisum's killer was driving it."

"I'll get the forensics team out here to go over this thing," said Monda. "What else?"

"Bobby Wendell gave us the heads-up about these guys gunning for us."

Monda looked surprised by this. "So he's more or less admittin' that he was involved?"

"Maybe less than more. But he's out of the country by now with his family."

"What!" exclaimed Monda.

"He was concerned about his family's safety," explained Robie. "Don't know if he's coming back, but I don't think he murdered anybody. So he can keep."

"Damn it to hell, Robie," said Monda. "I got people to answer to."

"Well, you weren't interested in going after him before."

"Well, the situation has changed. I got me dead bodies all over the damn place. I don't like it, not one bit."

Robie rubbed his injured arm. "Well, I can't say I care for it either."

Taggert noted this and said, "Okay, you and Reel ought to go get checked out."

Monda said, "I'll drive you. We can talk some more."

"No thanks, Sheriff. We have a car here. We can drive ourselves."

"I'll call Doc Holloway," said Monda. "He's an early riser. You know where his office is?"

Robie nodded.

He and Reel climbed into their car and drove off.

Reel drove because Robie was having trouble with his arm.

"Bad?" she said.

"Old wound just got worse."

"That one was my fault. But you should have had it fixed before now."

"Famous last words."

He reached into his pocket and pulled out the photo.

Reel glanced at it.

"Who is she?"

"Laura Barksdale."

"Your old flame? Where'd you get it?"

"It was in the glove compartment of the Bentley."

"What do you think it was doing there?"

"I don't know. But there has to be a reason it was there."

"Do you think it's connected to what's been going on?" asked Reel.

"Again, I don't know. But we need to find out."

"Sherman's dead."

"But Pete's not."

"And he might have been driving the Range Rover. But you don't think he killed Sara Chisum?"

"I didn't. Now I'm not so sure. But I want to ask him about this picture."

"Did you ever find out what happened to the Barksdales?"

"Just that they apparently left Cantrell without a trace," replied Robie.

"How does a family leave a small town and no one know?"

"Well, apparently it happened."

"Your dad should know, shouldn't he? I mean he was here all that time. And he knew them."

"He says he doesn't know what happened to them."

"And you believe him?" asked Reel.

"Maybe I'm getting cynical in my old age, Jess, but I'm starting not to believe anybody."

"Good, I haven't believed anyone in years. Sometimes, not even myself."

They drove on.

Doc Holloway was waiting for them, dressed in a white shirt, a tie, and a white lab coat.

His nurse was not in attendance.

She didn't get in until nine, Holloway told them, and it was not yet seven in the morning.

He examined Reel first, cleaning up her gashes, slashes, and cuts from where bits of material blown off by the fired rounds had punctured her skin.

"You hurt anywhere else?" asked Holloway as he finished stitching up a gash on her neck.

"Nothing that won't keep," she said.

"How'd you come by all these?" he asked.

"Fast living."

Robie was up next and the prognosis wasn't as good.

"You've completely torn the scar tissue, which in turn has torn some ligaments and done more internal damage," said Holloway. "I can patch up the other areas, but that one's going to require surgery." He slowly lifted Robie's arm up and back, and Robie winced with each movement.

"I'm goin' to put you in a sling for now. You'll need to keep it as immobile as possible. But you need to have that surgery done, Mr. Robie, or the damage really could be permanent."

"Understood, Doc. Thanks."

After Holloway cleaned up his other wounds, he helped Robie put his shirt back on. Then he fixed up the sling for Robie's damaged arm.

Holloway glanced at him as he put his instruments and equipment away. "You and your friend have certainly been busy in our small town."

"Wouldn't be here if we didn't have to be," said Robie.

"No, I understand about your father. I hear he's out of jail."

"On bail."

"When will the trial be?"

"Maybe there won't be a trial."

"Oh really, why is that?" asked Holloway suspiciously.

"If we find who really killed Sherman Clancy."

"I understood the evidence was fairly damnin' to Dan Robie."

"Evidence is a funny thing. It all depends on perspective."

"Are you yourself in law enforcement?"

"You could say that."

"Clancy and the two Chisum girls, three murders

in a relatively short period of time. We're not used to that here."

"I hope most places wouldn't be used to that."

"Do you think it's one person doin' all of this?"

"I don't know," replied Robie, watching him closely. "What do you think?"

"I'm just a doctor, not a detective."

"But doctors have to be sort of like a detective. Investigating symptoms and arriving at the truth of a person's condition."

"That's actually a large part of what we do."

"Speaking of a person's true condition, have you been by to see Billy lately?"

"Billy Faulconer, you mean?"

"Yes."

"I have, as a matter of fact."

"And how is he doing?"

"He's dyin', Mr. Robie. And there's nothin' any of us can do about that."

"Well, that seems to be the case for a lot of folks in Cantrell," Robie shot back.

63

"Okay, you officially look like death warmed over," said Reel as they walked out of Holloway's office.

He examined the sutures on her neck, gauze on her face, and bandages on both arms.

"Well, then we make quite a pair because you look like shit," Robie retorted.

They drove back to the Willows.

Dan Robie met them on the porch.

"My God," he said as he saw them fully. "I've seen infantry comin' out of a firefight in Nam look better than you two."

"It wasn't too pretty," conceded Robie.

"Taggert called me," Dan said. "And filled me in a little." He looked at his son's arm in a sling. "Is it bad?"

"I'll get it fixed up at some point."

"Some point soon," added Reel. "Or the damage could be permanent."

He glanced at her.

"I was standing on the other side of a partially open door when Holloway told you that. I'm just naturally curious."

Dan led them inside and insisted on making them breakfast.

Priscilla had taken Tyler to get a haircut, he said, and Victoria was still in bed with a migraine.

Eggs, bacon, grits, biscuits, and fresh coffee were served up and they all sat down to eat.

"So tell me what happened," Dan said.

Robie and Reel took turns filling him in.

Dan shook his head. "So it was Clancy's Range Rover that was used when Sara Chisum was killed. I thought it must be somethin' like that when you two ran out of here after I made that comment."

"It did make me start thinking," said Robie. "And we nearly got killed in the process. But the bullet hole was there."

Dan said, "And the Wendells? Who would've thought they'd be mixed up with such criminals?"

"Bad stuff happens in all kinds of families," said Reel.

"I know, but I would have thought that Bobby Wendell would've been smarter about it. Hirin' thugs to make this problem go away? Well, you play with snakes, you're gonna get bit."

"And he was officially bitten." Robie put his cup of coffee down, pulled out the photo of Laura, and slid it across to his father.

Dan took it up and stared at it. "Where'd you get this?"

"In Sherman Clancy's Bentley."

"I wonder what it was doing there."

"I wonder, too."

The tone of his voice made his father glance up.

He said sternly, "Why don't you just say what you're thinkin', son, instead of beatin' around the bush like you always do?"

"What happened to the Barksdales?"

"I told you I didn't know."

"And not to beat around the bush, I don't believe you."

"So you're sayin' I'm lyin'?"

"Whatever you want to call it," said Robie evenly.

Dan rose and said menacingly, "You want to take this outside, boy?"

"I'm not a boy."

"And he's a little beat up for hand-to-hand combat, Dan," pointed out Reel. "And the fact that he's been nearly killed a few times trying to help you should count a little in his favor, don't you think?"

Dan blinked at her, his face changed color, and he abruptly sat back down and stared at the tabletop.

"The Barksdales?" prompted Robie.

His father growled, "That was over twenty years ago. What does it matter?"

"Because it might be connected to what's going on now."

Dan shot him a glance. "How do you figure that?"

"The photo was in Clancy's possession. Clancy was a blackmailer. I can't think of another reason why he

would have that photo. As far as I knew he didn't even know the Barksdales. They were from far different classes of people."

"That's true. And those classes generally don't mix in Mississippi."

"But they might have mixed. We were told that Nelson Wendell used a shack on Sherman Clancy's farm to have his little get-togethers with the kids. It was how Clancy got on to what Wendell was really doing and then started his blackmailing."

Dan looked disgusted. "What scum. He should have gone to the cops."

"He was after dollars, not doing the right thing," commented Reel.

Robie added, "Pete said his father thought the shack was being used by Wendell for liaisons with women. He probably would have blackmailed him either way. But the kid thing was far worse than having mistresses. But let's get back to the Barksdales."

Dan said, "So you think he was blackmailin' them, too?"

"Did he have a way to?"

"How would I know that? I was a humble Cantrell lawyer back then. Just like Clancy, I didn't rub elbows with the likes of the Barksdales. I told you that!"

"But I dated Laura. In fact I wanted to run off with Laura."

Father and son stared across the table at each other while Reel glanced between them.

"So that was what happened," said Dan accusingly. "Thanks for finally gettin' around to tellin' me."

"No, it didn't happen, because Laura decided to stay. So I went alone."

Dan eyed him fiercely. "And why did you do that? You had a damn college scholarship to play football at Ole Miss. Sure you were a little undersized for quarterback but you had grit. And you would've gotten an education, made something of yourself."

"I *did* make something of myself."

"But not here," said his father. "You had to run off to do it. Cut me and your mother right out."

"She was already gone, Dad. Long gone by then. You saw to that."

Reel rose. They both glanced at her.

"I think what's about to come should be between you two men only. I'll be waiting outside, Robie, when you're done." She paused and looked in turn at each of them. "Do I have to check for weapons?"

She wasn't entirely joking.

"We'll be fine," said Robie.

She walked out after giving him a meaningful glance.

Robie turned back to his father.

"I had to get out of Cantrell."

"Why?"

"You damn well know why. Because *you* were here."

"Is that right?" snapped his father. "Just up and left without a word."

"You left home. So did I. Why was it okay for you and not me?"

Dan erupted, "Because my old man was a—"

"A what?" interrupted Robie. "An asshole that made his son's life a living hell? Who made things so bad that his own wife couldn't live with him and finally up and left, leaving the son alone with him?"

"You just blurred two lives, Will, mine and yours," said his father.

"Apparently, they were identical," shot back Robie.

"You can't understand. You don't know anythin' about—"

"Then why don't you explain it to me, *Dad*? Because I'm here *now*. And I'm listening."

"You don't want to hear anythin' I have to say," his father scoffed.

"Actually, that's the reason I came back here."

"Bullshit."

Robie continued on, his tone level and calm. It was as though he had rehearsed his entire adult life to say what he was about to.

"I have a job, Dad. A complex one that requires me to be absolutely perfect at what I do. But on my last two missions I wasn't perfect. I was far from it, in fact." Here Robie paused, and when he continued his voice had grown strained. "I killed someone I shouldn't have. And the next go-round I saw something that wasn't

even there. A little boy and his old man. But they weren't there. They were just in my head." He tried to say something else but the words were all muddled in his head. He had thought through what he would say to his father many times. Now that he had the chance, he just couldn't manage it.

The case clock in the foyer ticked out the time as the men stared at each other. It felt nearly an eternity, perhaps longer to both of them.

Finally, his father spoke. "I told Laura you'd gone off without her."

Robie felt like someone had fired a bullet right into his brain.

"What?" he said quietly, trying to keep what he was feeling restrained inside him, because he wasn't sure what would happen if he didn't.

"I told her you wanted to start life fresh away from here."

"When?"

"She came by a few days after you left. She wanted to know where you were. I saw your stuff was gone. And that old clunker, too. I knew what'd happened. Even if you hadn't bothered to leave me a damn note. Anythin' could'a happened to you. Anythin'!" Dan slammed his fist on the table.

"You had no right to tell her anything."

"I had every right! You were my son. Even if you had run off. And you didn't take her with you, so I

figured you just . . . just didn't want her. So I told her that flat-out."

"And what did she do?"

"She ran off cryin'." Dan lowered his head, his angry expression gone. But Robie felt it all building inside of him. For one split second he imagined himself pulling his gun . . .

"You didn't need her," continued Dan.

"Stop talking, Dad," Robie said, his voice barely a whisper.

"She just would'a weighed you down. You wanted out of Cantrell? Well, you needed to make a clean break of it. And that father of hers—"

Robie stood. "Shut up, Dad."

Dan looked up at him, anger flashing across his features, until he saw the look on his son's face. And, perhaps for the first time in his life at least since Vietnam, Dan Robie seemed afraid for his life.

Before he did something he might regret, Robie turned and walked out.

64

"How'd it go?" asked Reel.

She and Robie were out on the rear porch of the Willows.

"I'm not talking about it," snapped Robie. His heart was racing, his blood pressure had spiked, and he thought he might be sick to his stomach. He was the exact opposite of cold zero, a physiological level he might never experience again.

Robie slowly pulled out the photo of Laura Barksdale.

"So, was he able to enlighten you on that?" asked Reel.

Robie nodded. "In a way I never imagined."

"What does that mean?"

But Robie shook his head. "Not now, Jess."

Reel took the photo and studied it. "She was very beautiful."

"Yeah, she was."

"I could see how a young man would fall head over heels for her."

"Yeah," said Robie as he took the photo back.

"So you must have come to this house a lot back then?"

"Not that often, actually."

"Why?"

"Her parents wouldn't have approved."

"What, you weren't blue blood enough?"

"They loved it that I was the starting quarterback on the state championship team. But other than that, no, I wasn't blue blood enough."

"When we were talking to Pete you mentioned she had a brother?"

"Yeah, he was a couple years older. Emmitt Barksdale."

Reel looked around the property. "So a prominent family just disappears and no one in Cantrell knows anything about it?"

Robie said, "Apparently."

"Well, they sold the house, right?"

"Right. But not to my father. There was apparently an owner in between."

"Then why not ask the Realtor who did the deal? Or check the real estate records. You sell a property, there has to be a record of it, right?"

Robie looked at her. "That's right."

"And while you're doing that, I have something to take care of."

"What's that?"

"Talking to our buddy Pete Clancy, and asking him about a certain bullet hole in his Range Rover."

They drove off in separate cars.

In the window overlooking the front of the house stood Victoria, watching them leave.

Dan Robie came up behind her and wrapped his arms around his wife as they watched both cars disappear under the canopy of long-leaf pines.

Pete Clancy sat at the table clenching and unclenching his hands as Taggert and Reel sat across from him.

They were in the visitor's room at the jail. Pete was dressed in his own clothes, since he was not technically under arrest.

Taggert had reminded him that this status could change.

"Let's go through it one more time," said Reel patiently. "Where were you on the night Sara Chisum was killed?"

"And I told you, I don't remember. Probably drunk somewhere. I was on the run. Scared shitless."

"So you're scared shitless and you get drunk and aren't able to defend yourself or think straight because . . . ?" countered Reel.

"Because I'm stupid, I guess," said Pete. He tacked on to this statement what he doubtless thought was an ingratiating smile that had probably worked with most women he'd encountered, the majority of whom were probably drunk.

Yet it fell like a punctured balloon when confronted by the stern faces of these two.

"Not good enough, Pete," said Taggert. "Your vehicle has a bullet hole in it."

"That's not my *vehicle*, okay? It was my daddy's. I never even drove the damn thing. I have my Porsche."

"Where were the keys kept?"

"I don't know. In the house somewhere, I guess. Anybody could'a taken 'em. I never locked the damn doors."

"So you've got no alibi for the time Sara was murdered?" said Taggert matter-of-factly.

"If I did I would'a told you, but I don't. Can I go back to my cell now? I got some sleep to catch up on. And, hey, can I get a beer in here? And maybe some barbeque?"

He started to get up, but Reel reached across and pushed him back down.

"You can't leave yet because we're not done."

"I want a lawyer."

"You're not entitled to one," replied Taggert.

Pete pointed a finger at her. "You can't screw with me. I watch TV. When you say you want a lawyer you guys have to back the hell off and can't ask me no more damn questions."

"You're not entitled to one," said Reel, "because you're not under arrest."

Taggert nodded. "That's exactly right."

"What kind'a shit is this?" bellowed Pete. "Then I want the hell outta here."

Reel said, "Fine. The guys who almost killed you

I'm sure are still out there watching this place. Tell them I said hello."

"This is fuckin' unbelievable," yelled Pete.

"Well, the world's not perfect, is it," said Reel calmly. "So why don't you take a deep breath, compose yourself, think back, and tell us where you were on the night Sara was killed."

"I already told you—"

Reel reached over and gripped his wrist. "Take a deep breath, compose yourself, and try to remember, then you can go back to your cell. That's the carrot, Pete, so go get the carrot. Or else you are the prime suspect for Sara's murder."

She removed her hand and Pete slumped back, rubbing a hand through his unkempt hair. He drew a long breath and his features calmed. "Okay, when was she killed again?"

Reel told him.

"Right." Pete bent over, his brows nearly touching as he concentrated. Then he smiled. "Hell, I know. I was in New Orleans. At the OK Corral Bar on Bourbon Street. Got my ass thrown off the mechanical bull like five times."

"When did you get there and when did you leave?" asked Taggert.

"Got there around eleven that night. And left around four in the morning."

"Anybody verify that?"

"My buddy is one of the bartenders there. And

there was a girl I met there. She left with me." He smiled. "If you know what I mean."

"Names and numbers, please," said Taggert.

"My buddy's name is Kyle. You call the bar they'll find him. He served me my last drink so's I remember."

"And the girl?"

Pete fished around in his pockets until he found a square patch of what looked to be foil. He slid it across the table. In black Magic Marker was a phone number and a name: LuAnne.

Both women looked at the square without touching it.

"That's a condom wrapper," said Taggert with disgust.

"I know it is. Only thing I could find for her to write on."

Reel said, "Well, at least you're practicing safe sex. Count me among the astonished."

"I don't want to be no daddy. You know what kids cost? It's a damn disgrace."

Taggert sighed and left to make the calls while Pete went back to his cell.

She came back into the room about thirty minutes later and sat down next to Reel.

"Okay, Kyle from the bar remembers Pete clearly. He said he got there about half past eleven. He remembered because he was expectin' him at eleven and he had just checked the clock and was goin' to

text him when Pete walked in. And he didn't leave the bar until nearly four, so that corroborates Pete's account. And not that we needed to know, but I talked to LuAnne, and she said Pete and her were together until about eight in the mornin' when he went to get coffee and beignets and never came back. Since I'm a lady and don't use that kind of language, I won't tell you what she called him, but it rhymes with 'other pucker.'"

"So there's no way he shot Sara or was driving the Range Rover?"

"No way," agreed Taggert. "Not even if he had a private jet."

"So somebody else took the Range Rover and killed Sara."

"Looks that way."

"Which means we're just going around in circles," said Reel with a sigh.

65

Robie closed the heavy book. He was in the court-house's real estate section. Not all records were digit-ized yet, he'd been told by the clerk, so he had done his research the old-fashioned way: by flipping through pages of dusty deed books she had gathered for him.

The documents had the signatures of the parties on them, and Robie had studied the signatures of Henry and Ellen Barksdale. He couldn't swear they were their authentic signatures, but these documents had been recorded and thus notarized, and ID would have had to be produced, he'd assumed. Though everyone here-abouts would have known the Barksdales by sight.

Then there was the transaction where his father and Victoria had purchased the home from the family that had bought it from the Barksdales. He looked at his dad's precise signature, as ramrod straight as he was. And next to his was Victoria's signature, loose and flowing.

He stopped by the clerk's office on his way out.

The clerk was a heavyset woman in her sixties with

thinning hair dyed a muted burgundy. Robie didn't know if this was intentional or an experiment gone wrong, but the woman was cheerful and helpful.

She told him that the Willows had been sold by the Barksdales a little over twenty years ago. The buyer had been a businessman and his wife from Baton Rouge. They had lived in the property for years, and they had sold it to the Robies because they were getting on in years and were downsizing. She believed they had moved over to Alabama.

"I remember the sale because it was the largest in the county up to that time."

"I knew Laura Barksdale," said Robie.

"I know you did. My son went to Cantrell with you. He wasn't on the football team, but the year you boys won the championship I think the whole school thought they were part of the team."

"It *was* special," said Robie.

"And weren't you and Laura Homecomin' King and Queen that year?"

"Yes, we were." Robie hadn't thought about this in a long time, but the image of a young man in a dirty and sweat-stained football uniform and Laura in her tight dress and tiara instantly came into his mind. The ceremony had been conducted during halftime of a game.

Laura had made him promise not to get her dirty while they walked across the field. Although she did

let him kiss her when they snuck under the bleachers right before the half was over.

He felt himself smiling. When he came out of this memory he saw the clerk staring at him, a grin on her face.

"Nice memory?" she asked.

"Pretty nice," said Robie. "So the Barksdales sold out and what? Did they move away?"

"They must have. If they had bought here I would've known about it. I've been here over thirty years."

"But you don't know where they went?"

She shook her head. "It always seemed peculiar to me that they sold that place. I always thought it would be kept in the family. You know, handed down to the kids and all. I mean it had been in the Barksdale family for the better part of two centuries."

"And you've never seen any of them since?"

"Well, I've seen Emmitt Barksdale."

Robie gaped. "Really? When?"

"Just a few days ago."

Robie started. "A few days ago? Here?"

"Yes. I was goin' up the steps of the courthouse and he was comin' down 'em."

"You're sure it was him?"

"Well, I don't know if you remember Emmitt. But he was tall and good-lookin' and had the bluest eyes I've ever seen. I know it'd been twenty years, and his hair was a lot thinner, but I could swear it was him."

"But you didn't talk to him?"

"I started to say hello, but then I was interrupted by somebody I worked with here. She had a question about somethin'. When I was done with her, Emmitt was gone."

"But he was coming out of the courthouse?"

"That's right."

"Any idea what he did in there?"

"Well, I could ask. I'm not the only clerk here."

"Would you?"

The lady rose and came back a few minutes later.

"Seems he was doin' what you were doin'. Lookin' at land records."

"Any in particular?"

"He had the exact same deed books you did."

"For the Willows?"

"That's right."

"Thanks."

"Any time. Go Panthers!" she said, referring to the mascot of Cantrell High.

Robie walked out of the courthouse and saw Reel leaning against her car, waiting for him.

"Saw your car. Figured you were in the courthouse checking records."

"Any luck with Pete?"

"If he killed Sara Chisum he had to hire someone to do it. He was drunk and having sex in New Orleans at the time."

"Lotta sex going on here," he commented.

453

"Wishful thinking?" replied Reel.

He glared at her.

"Okay, okay," she said. "Just trying to lighten the mood. But what about you?" she asked. "Anything at the courthouse?"

"The clerk doesn't know what happened to the Barksdales. They sold the property to the folks that sold it to my dad and Victoria. This was a couple years after I left Cantrell."

"Okay."

"But she told me that she had seen Emmitt Barksdale, Laura's brother, coming out of the courthouse a few days ago. He was checking out the land records for his old home."

Reel looked blankly at him. "Why would he be doing that? Thinking of buying it back?"

"No idea. But why would he want the place?"

"Nostalgia?"

"After all this time? Why not buy it when the other owners wanted to sell?"

"Maybe he didn't know about it back then. Or maybe he didn't have the money."

"The guy I saw sneaking around outside the Willows my first night there? I thought it might've been Pete. But now I think it could've been Emmitt. The person I saw was taller than Pete. And probably older, now that I think about it. And Emmitt is a couple years older than me."

"Why would he be sneaking around the place?"

"I don't know."

"Robie, there aren't bodies buried at the Willows, are there? I mean, the Barksdales sell the place and nobody ever sees them again?"

"You kill people and bury them and hope the new owners don't notice the freshly turned earth? How likely is that?"

"I don't know how likely it is. I've never been to Mississippi."

"That can't be it," he said.

"So what's your explanation?" she asked irritably.

"I don't have one."

"Then don't just discount mine out of hand. But if something about the Barksdales is connected to what's going on now, how does that work exactly?"

"We come back to what we talked about before. What if Clancy was blackmailing one of the Barksdales?"

"That would be a motive for his murder."

Robie sighed. "But all these years later?"

"Maybe the blackmailing didn't start until recently?"

"That presumes Clancy knew where the Barksdales moved to."

"Maybe he did."

"This is getting way too complicated, Jessica."

"Maybe that's because we're making it too complicated. But if Emmitt Barksdale is hanging around here, then he might know all about it."

"Right, but we don't know where he is."

"You said he was sneaking around the Willows. But the woman at the courthouse said she saw him coming out. So it's not like he's in complete hiding. He might surface again."

Robie said nothing for a few moments, and then his brow cleared as an idea obviously hit him. He pulled out the photo of Wendell and the children.

"Wendell was in his midsixties when he died."

"Okay."

"And Henry Barksdale was roughly the same age. Same generation as my dad."

"Wait a minute, are you saying . . . ?"

Robie held up the photo. "What if Henry Barksdale was the one taking the picture?"

66

Reel stared over at him, her brows elevated. "That's a leap of logic, isn't it?"

"Not so much."

"So do you mean Sherman Clancy cut a deal with Barksdale? Give me enough stuff I can blackmail Nelson Wendell with, and I'll let you alone?"

"Well, Wendell probably had a lot more money."

"But Barksdale would be a fool to trust Clancy."

"Maybe he didn't have much choice. And Pete said his dad let Wendell use his shack. He thought at first for women. Maybe they never intended for Clancy to know what they were really doing. But he found out."

"Now that makes more sense."

"And I always wondered about the connection between Nelson Wendell and Clancy. They didn't move in the same circles. Hell, Wendell didn't even live in Cantrell. But Wendell and Barksdale, now they moved in the same circles. So maybe Barksdale arranged all of this after he found out he and Wendell shared a thing for kids. That could be how Wendell and Clancy hooked up. Through Barksdale."

"Or maybe Clancy was never supposed to know Wendell was even involved."

"Right. That's more likely. But Clancy was enterprising, saw his chance and took it."

"But you found out that Barksdale didn't leave Cantrell until a couple years after you did."

"Maybe that's when Clancy started to put the squeeze on him. He had pictures. It would be the blueblood Barksdale's ruin. Hell, maybe he sold the house in order to pay off Clancy."

"This is something we need to find out for sure."

Robie pulled out his phone. "Well, we know a place that's good at gathering information."

Blue Man answered his phone on the second ring.

Robie patiently explained the situation and asked for what he needed.

Robie could hear the man jotting down no-doubt-meticulous notes. When he was finished Blue Man said, "Interesting theory."

"I hope you can confirm it as more than a theory."

"I'll get right on it."

"And thanks for sending Jessica down here. I wouldn't be talking to you if she hadn't been around to save my butt."

"I like to plan for all contingencies. And Robie?"

"Yes?"

"I can understand why you're doing this, even if I don't agree with it."

"Thank you for that," replied a surprised Robie.

"My relationship with my father was something less than ideal, too."

He clicked off.

Robie looked at Reel as he put his phone away. "He's on the case, but we can't rely just on that. We need to work the angles we can, too."

"Starting with?"

"Sherman Clancy's first wife. She was in court when my father was arraigned."

"Do you know where she lives?" Reel asked.

"No, but I'm sure we can find out."

"Even if she knows something do you really expect her to admit it to us?"

"Like you said before, it's all in how you ask, Jess."

Cassandra Clancy had never remarried. She lived about twenty miles from Cantrell.

As Robie and Reel drove up the cobblestone drive and pulled to a stop in front of the large, well-appointed two-story home with a BMW sedan parked out front, Reel said, "Looks like she got her pound of flesh from her husband in the divorce."

"Hopefully, she managed her cash better than her ex did."

They got out and went up to the door.

Robie knocked, and they heard footsteps heading their way.

The door opened, and Cassandra stood there. Robie had not gotten a good look at her in the courtroom,

but now he could see that she had aged poorly. Her skin sagged and was mottled with sun damage. Her hair had been permed to such an extent that it was thin and wispy, and her scalp showed through in various places. Her clothes were costly, though, and fit her stout body well, hiding the depth of the belly and width of the hips.

"Can I help you?" she said cautiously.

"I'm Will Robie. This is my friend, Jessica Reel."

Cassandra looked from one to the other before settling her gaze back on him. "Damn, Will, you've changed, honey. Didn't recognize you. Not that we knew each other all that well way back when."

"No, I guess we didn't. But I went to school with a couple of your children."

"I remember now I saw you in the courtroom. Didn't put two and two together."

"It's been a long time."

"Well, if your daddy killed Sherm I owe him my thanks."

"I take it you didn't get on with your ex-husband."

"I hated his guts. He dumped me for a floozy."

"I'm sorry to hear that."

"So was I," she said sharply.

"I saw you sitting with the floozy in the courtroom."

Cassandra took a pack of cigarettes from her pocket, tapped one out, struck a match, and lighted up. "Time heals wounds. You two want to come in?"

They followed her inside, and Robie noted the luxurious appointments throughout the rooms they passed. She led them out onto the back patio, accessed through French doors. The grounds were fenced in, and there was a large, tiered fountain, professional landscaping, and wrought iron benches parked in various places.

Robie looked around. "Well, I'm glad to see you did okay financially."

She grimaced. "I should have gotten more, but old Sherm, while a total shit, was cunnin' as a gator on the hunt. He hid assets. He was worth ten times what he said he was when he filed the divorce papers. But I did okay. And I managed my money well. I'll never have to work again. And who knows, since the son of a bitch died without a will, I might get a few more bucks from his estate."

She pointed to a full pitcher and some glasses set on a wooden console. "Y'all want some sweet tea?"

Knowing that it might put him into a diabetic coma, Robie declined. So did Reel. Cassandra rose, poured herself a glass with plenty of ice, and sat back down. She took a long sip, smacking her lips.

"Nothin' better on earth."

"I'm sure," said Robie. "So the money had come from the sale of the mineral rights on the farm you both owned?"

She tapped ash into an ashtray and eyed him suspiciously. "Look, what the hell is all this about?"

"Just following up leads with my dad's case."

"I see. I didn't know your daddy all that well. But I never heard anyone say a word against him. Good man. I was sorry to hear about all the trouble he's in now."

"Do you think he could have killed your ex?"

"I don't know. I can tell you I wanted to kill Sherm many times. Just never had the guts to do it." She paused. "He was proud of you, I know that."

"Who? Your husband?"

"No. Your daddy."

"How do you know that?"

"Many's the time I sat on the bleachers next to him at the games, that's how. This was before I got divorced, of course. Two of my boys played for Cantrell. They were ahead of you in school by a few years, but I still went to all the home games even after they graduated. Anyway, your daddy would cheer like mad. Tellin' everybody around him what a tough son of a gun you were. Thought the man would pop with pride."

"He never said anything to me."

"Well, some men are like that. I don't think Sherm ever complimented his boys either. Probably afraid it would make 'em soft if they thought they'd get praised for everythin'. So the idiot never said a kind word to 'em."

"I guess some men are wired that way," said Robie quietly, drawing a sharp glance from Reel.

Cassandra smiled and pointed a finger at him.

"Now, you quarterbacked the Panthers to the state championship. Only good thin' that ever happened in Cantrell, far as I'm concerned."

"Thanks." He paused and pondered how best to say it. "I remember your farm. It was a big one."

"I remember that farm, too," she replied. "And none of those memories are fond ones. We never made a dime growin' crops. Worked our asses off for peanuts."

"But then the mineral rights were sold. And Sherm parlayed that into business ties with the casino folks. And then the cash flow picked up nicely. And then you divorced. All pretty fast, actually. Just over a few years."

She looked at him suspiciously again. "You seem to know a whole lot about our business."

"I like to know things. Like, for instance, what sort of dealings your husband had with *Henry Barksdale* and *Nelson Wendell*."

Robie emphasized the names to see the woman's reaction.

Her complexion changed. "Nelson Wendell? The oilman? How would we know him?"

The lie was not very good, thought Robie.

"What energy company bought the mineral rights to your property, Ms. Clancy?" asked Reel.

The woman turned to face her. "Why does that matter?"

"It would matter if it was Coastal Energy."

Cassandra stood and said darkly, "I want you two outta my house. Right now."

Neither Robie nor Reel moved.

Robie said, "People have died, Ms. Clancy. Murdered. Including your husband. We know why he was murdered. Do you? And do you want to be next?"

Her lips were trembling but Cassandra still stood there looking defiant.

"I think you should sit down," said Reel. "And let's talk about this before things get even worse."

Cassandra abruptly sat, smoked down her cigarette, and hastily lit another.

"There's a shack on the back part of your farm, you remember that?" asked Robie.

Cassandra said nothing.

He took out the photo and slid it across to her. "This was taken inside that shack, wasn't it?"

Cassandra glanced at the photo and then just as quickly looked away.

"And that man is the late, if unlamented, Nelson Wendell," added Reel.

Robie tapped the photo. "The thing is, Cassandra, where did the little kids come from?"

The woman's face turned red and she started to breathe more heavily. She grabbed her chest. "I think I might be having a heart attack," she gasped.

"I think you're having a *panic* attack. We can call an ambulance if you want. But my question will still be

out there. And maybe the police will be the ones to come and ask you next time."

Her chest stopped heaving and she glared at him venomously. "It's not legally actionable anymore. They have to file criminal charges before they turn twenty-one. And the statute of limitations has run on the civil side, too."

"You checked the law, so you must have known all about it, then," said Robie.

Cassandra was trembling. "If my ex did somethin' bad, that's on him, not me."

"So where did the kids come from?"

"I have no idea what you're even talkin' about."

"But like you said, you're home free, Ms. Clancy. The law can't touch you now."

She tapped her ash and said nothing.

"Your kids doing okay?"

She said warily, "Yes. And the grandkiddies, too. Got six of 'em. All just fine."

"Unlike the kids in the shack. Did you and your husband befriend folks saying you'd take care of their kids for them while they were working, maybe? And instead you let two pedophiles loose on them?"

She barked, "You two get the hell outta my house. Now! Before I call the cops."

"The cops know we're here," said Robie. "We're working with Sheriff Monda on this."

Cassandra nearly dropped her cigarette. "He . . . he knows you're here?"

Robie nodded.

"He knows a lot," said Reel. "Pretty much every-thing we do."

She sputtered, "I-it's not actionable. I-I'm tellin' you that. It's n-not."

"But that's not the same as the truth coming out. They may not be able to take you to court, but I wonder how your kids will take the news. And your grandkids."

"I'll sue you. That would be slander. I'll sue you!" screamed Cassandra.

"Well, one absolute defense to slander is the truth." He pulled out his phone and held it up. "I recorded everything you said."

"That's . . . that's illegal."

"Is it? Maybe, maybe not. I don't think it'll matter to your family."

"I . . . I . . ."

"You might want to think about moving to an-other country and assuming a new identity," said Reel. "Because your life, as you know it, is over. I don't think folks around here would like a pedophile's helper." Reel looked around at the fine property. "I hope it was worth it," she added.

Cassandra slumped back in her chair. "Look, can we come to some sort'a understandin'?"

"Like what?" asked Robie.

"I tell you what I know and you forget I'm part of this at all."

"Let's hear what you have to say."

"But—"

"Let's hear what you have to say," said Robie more firmly.

Cassandra finally nodded and sat forward, stubbing out her cigarette. She drew a few long breaths and began.

"See, the thing was we had seasonal workers comin' through," she said, her voice trembling a bit. "They came through every year, usually from Mexico or Central America. And some of them were black folks, itinerant workers, tryin' to get by."

"But no white kids then?" said Robie.

"No, none that I can remember. They worked the fields all day when we were harvestin'. Most had kids, little kids. Me and my daughter would watch 'em and even do a little schoolin' with 'em. That was all. I swear to God."

"Okay, when did things start to change?" asked Robie.

"Sherm came to me one day and said he'd had a visitor. Apparently, Henry Barksdale got wind of the little kids we kept in the shack on the edge of our property. He had a friend, he said, who would pay well if we . . ."

"If you left him alone with the kids for a while each day?" said Reel.

She nodded.

"When was this?" asked Robie.

"Hell, I can't recall exactly. Probably twenty-five years ago."

"Did your daughter know?"

"Absolutely not!" snapped Cassandra. "She's a good person. She never would have"—she drew another long breath—"she never would have been part of that. So, I just had her head up to the house when the man was comin' by."

"But you obviously had no problem with it?" said Robie quietly.

Tears started to spill out of the woman's eyes. "I *did* have a problem with it. But I talked myself into believin' it was really doin' no harm. And those kids were so little and most of 'em didn't even speak English. And the money, my God, the money was—"

"—just too good? It made you forget about what was happening to the kids?" said Robie.

"You can judge me," said Cassandra spitefully. She added in a more resigned tone, "And Lord knows God will one day, but I didn't know those kids. They were just part of these families comin' through. And they didn't take good care'a their kids neither, let me tell you. But when they were with me they were fed and clean and taught some—"

"—and molested," Reel finished for her.

Cassandra wiped her eyes on the sleeve of her blouse.

"Did you see both Henry Barksdale and Nelson Wendell at the shack?" asked Robie.

"Once. As a rule they didn't come till I was gone. Sherm and them had it all worked out. Fewer people knew about it the better. And to tell the truth, I didn't want to know. But I left late one day and they got there a bit early. They didn't see me, but I saw them."

"And the kids?" asked Reel.

Cassandra looked at her. "I swear to God they didn't seem no worse for it. They were so young and all. Whatever they did to 'em, I don't think it messed 'em up. Probably didn't even know what was happenin'. And their parents never said anythin', so I guess the kids never even told 'em. So, I think they're okay, right?"

Reel said fiercely, "No child walks away from being molested without being damaged."

"No, I . . . I guess not," admitted Cassandra, sniffling a bit while Reel looked at her in unconcealed disgust.

"Okay, Sherm was getting well paid for his 'services.' So when did he start blackmailing Wendell?" asked Robie quietly.

"That came later, a few years or so after this whole thing started. He didn't tell me he was going to do it, but I called him out on it after he told me who was buyin' our farm."

"Coastal Energy?" said Robie.

"Yes. Hell, we never had oil or gas on our land. I knew that. And nobody had come out there to check for it, so why was some big oil company writin' us a

huge check for our farm? I mean millions and millions of dollars. Well, I knew why. Nelson Wendell."

"So you were rich now, too?"

"Yes. And Sherm had big plans. About twenty years
ago we moved into a nice house outside of Cantrell.
Then he got in on the ground floor with the casino
folks at the Rebel Yell. He made a lot more money
there. I was surprised at how smart he was at business,
to tell the truth. Things were going good." Her voice
rose. "Till the son of a bitch came home one night
less than a year later and basically told me I was being
replaced by a floozy he'd been shackin' up with
behind my back and who was pregnant with that pissant Pete. I got my money, though he screwed me on
that, and bought this place. He built that monstrosity
over near Cantrell and he and the floozy had Pete.
Then the floozy got the boot and it was just him and
Pete. And Pete only stayed because he's a lazy ass livin'
off Sherm's money. He's barely nineteen and probably
can't even wipe himself."

"The house burned down," said Robie.

"So I heard," said Cassandra, not hiding her glee. "I
guess what Sherm did came back to bite him in the
ass."

"And the Barksdales?" said Robie. "They sold the
Willows and slunk out of town. Why?"

"I don't know why. I just know that Henry was the
go-between with Sherm and Wendell."

"And he was a pedophile too, of course, and Sherm knew that," noted Robie.

"No, he wasn't."

"What?" asked Robie sharply.

"I know he sometimes came to the shack where the kids were, but from what Sherm told me, he wasn't into the kids. Never touched 'em. That was just Wendell."

"But why be part of it at all then?" asked Reel. "If he wasn't into kids?"

"That's easy. It was for the money too. Sherm told me Barksdale had bet on somethin' big and it went south. He was broke. Goin' to lose the Willows and everythin' else. He needed the cash bad, and Wendell had more than enough for everybody."

"So Wendell was paying him to arrange things with the kids?"

"Yes."

"Do you think Sherm might have been blackmailing Henry Barksdale as well?" asked Robie. "And maybe that's why he left Cantrell so abruptly?"

She shook her head. "Sherm was an asshole, but as crazy as it sounds, he was a man of his word. Sherm would've gotten zip if not for Henry Barksdale bringin' him in on this. Sherm never forgot that. He told me that mor'n once. He wouldn't have done nothin' to hurt Barksdale."

"So if they were getting paid, why start blackmailing

Nelson Wendell and make him buy the farm for an exorbitant price?" asked Reel.

"Hell, that's an easy one. Sherm was greedy as they come. And, yeah, we were gettin' paid, but Sherm wanted more. A lot more. He had plans and he needed big money. So he got pictures of Wendell and the kids and that was his way of takin' the guy to the cleaners. Sherm called Wendell his golden goose."

"I bet," said Reel. "And it seems that Henry Barksdale might have supplied the pictures to Sherm just to make sure the guy never turned his sights on him."

Robie looked confused. "Okay, but if Wendell refused to pay, what leverage did Sherm have? If the truth came out, so would his role in the whole thing. They could have all gone to jail."

"Hell, Sherm was a nobody. Nelson Wendell was rich, from a well-known family, and everyone looked up to him. Sherm had nothin' to lose if the truth came out. Wendell had *everythin'* to lose. And Sherm might have been a blackmailer. But Wendell sexually abused little kids. Which do you think folks would find worse?"

"I guess that makes sense," said Reel.

Cassandra said weakly, "So, can we just keep this between the three of us?"

Robie and Reel rose together.

Staring down at her, Robie said, "I guess only time will tell on that."

Her face fell. "So that's all the assurance you can give me? I'll worry myself sick."

"Then consider yourself lucky," retorted Robie. "Because everybody else has ended up dead."

67

"Damn, what a piece of work," said Reel as they got back into their car.

"I guess people can rationalize anything," commented Robie, staring up at the big house. "For the right price."

Reel put the car in gear at the same time Robie's phone buzzed. It wasn't a call. It was an e-mail.

"It's from Blue Man."

He read through it, twice. "Well, this has taken an unexpected turn."

"What? Did he find anything out about the Barksdales?"

"A man named Ted Bunson is the guardian of a patient at a state mental institution. It's about an hour's drive north of here."

"Who's Ted Bunson?"

"His real name, apparently, is Emmitt Barksdale."

"Laura's brother?"

"Yes."

"How did Blue Man score that?"

"One of the things I asked him to do was track

down the Barksdales. Well, Emmitt Barksdale had an arrest record, DUI, from when he lived in Cantrell. His fingerprints were taken and recorded. Apparently, they got uploaded to some database. Blue Man had a search done and a pair of prints belonging to one Ted Bunson came back as a match. Mr. Bunson had been fingerprinted for another DUI a number of years ago."

"And he's the guardian of a mental patient?"

"Jane Smith."

"Jane Smith? Think it's an alias?"

"Well, 'Ted Bunson' is. So her name might be as well. Not very imaginative though, *Jane Smith*?"

"Does he have an address for Bunson?"

"An old one. He no longer lives there. They're still checking on other possible ones. But if Emmitt is the guardian, he may visit the person. We could get on to him from that angle."

"Worth an hour's drive," said Reel, and they sped out of the driveway.

The facility was old and foreboding in appearance. The brick façade was water stained, the cracked driveway was badly patched, and even the surrounding trees and grass lawns looked worn out.

As they parked and got out of the car, Reel said, "Well, if I was mental I don't think this place would make me feel any better."

They headed to the front entrance. After speaking

to the receptionist they were handed off to the assistant administrator, a heavyset man in his forties wearing a short-sleeved dress shirt, wide tie, thick glasses, and a bad attitude. He sat at his desk in his tiny office with the air of a king on his golden throne.

The name tag clipped on his shirt read DUGAN.

In answer to their query he said, "You can't visit Ms. Smith without the requisite permission."

"And we could get that from her guardian, Ted Bunson?" said Robie.

Dugan looked at him without answering. He held a clipboard like he was about to fling it at their heads.

"Or from one of her doctors?" suggested Robie.

"Do you have that permission?" asked a scowling Dugan.

"No."

"Then I don't know why we're havin' this conversation. Now if you'll excuse me, I have a lot of work to do."

"Is there any other way to see her?" asked Reel.

"Oh sure. A court order. You got one of those in your pocket?" he added snidely.

"Well, we can arrange that," said Robie, pulling out his phone and heading over to a corner of the room where he could talk in private.

Dugan looked startled by this and gazed up accusingly at Reel. "Are you cops? You didn't show ID. You're supposed to."

"Actually, we're *more* than cops," said Reel.

"What does that mean?" said Dugan warily.

Reel took out the perfectly valid credentials she used in the States, which showed her to be a member of an instantly recognizable federal agency.

Dugan dropped the clipboard.

"You're . . . you're . . ."

"Right," she said in a clipped tone.

"But what are you doin' here?"

"What's your first name?"

"Doug."

"Okay, *Doug*. We're here running down a lead. That led us to Jane Smith. She might be connected to some very grisly murders that have been going on in your fine state and that might point to a foreign element being present."

"Foreign element?" said Dugan confusedly. "What's that mean exactly?"

"Another name for them would be *terrorists*."

Dugan's jaw went slack. "What? In Mississippi? Are you shittin' me?"

She shook her head. "No shit, Doug."

He dropped his voice to a conspiratorial level. "Look, are we talkin' A-rabs or what? If so I can get me some boys together loaded for bear to go after them desert suckers."

"I don't know if they are Muslims. We were hoping Ms. Smith could enlighten us."

He waved this off. "If you're countin' on that, you're outta luck."

"Why?"

"Because she's nuts, that's why."

"So she can't communicate?"

"No, I mean she can talk. But it's like talkin' to a damn four-year-old."

"Or maybe she's actually speaking in code."

"Give me a break. Do you get what I'm sayin'? She ... a ... wacko bird. What terrorist would involve someone like that? She could give it all away."

"Are you sure she's really wacko?"

"I think the docs would know if she's fakin'."

"But if she's, let's say, autistic, or has Asperger's, she may be able to remember long streams of data that could be used to communicate plans and orders to various cells. And use the cover of being here to avert suspicion."

"That sounds mighty unlikely to me. A-rabs and Jane Smith? Besides, there haven't been any A-rabs come to visit her. They'd stick out here, don't you think? This is Mississippi. We're a God-fearin' people. Our God, not theirs," he added forcefully.

"Well, think about it, not all terrorists are Muslim. Some are homegrown, like Timothy McVeigh."

"Still—" said Dugan, looking highly skeptical. "Ted Bunson is the only one who does visit her."

"And we have not ruled out Mr. Bunson as a possible suspect in this, considering that the name Ted Bunson is an alias."

Dugan paled. "Oh, okay. I didn't know nothin' about that. But I still don't see what I can do."

"Look, Doug, our investigations led us here. But if you won't let us in to see her without a court order and something happens in the interim?" She took out a pen and a small pad of paper. "Is your full first name Douglas?"

"Why?" he said suspiciously.

"I have to get it right for my report. If heads roll on this I don't want anyone pointing their fingers at me. See what I mean? They'll have to point 'em elsewhere. Like at you."

"But I got rules to go by. And the administrator's out this week. It's just me runnin' the show."

"Hey, Doug, it's your call. But I have to tell you, that excuse will not cut it if a building blows up or a plane goes down. What are you going to say when *60 Minutes* sticks a camera in your face? 'Sorry, I had petty rules to go by'? Good luck with that."

Dugan looked like he might faint. "But what the hell can I do?"

"You can let us see Jane Smith."

"But I could get in trouble."

"Anybody comes down on you, we will take care of it. Way I see it you're being a patriot. Putting your duty as a citizen above a stupid rule."

"I . . . don't know about this."

"Fine, Doug, I hope the other shoe doesn't drop on

this because about a dozen people have died so far and I don't see it getting any better."

"A dozen people! In Mississippi?"

"Have you been reading about the goings-on in Cantrell?"

Doug nodded. "I remember readin' about a couple of murders down there, yeah."

"Well, the body count has gone way up but they're keeping it under wraps. Don't want to panic the public."

"Shit, you think this is connected to all that?"

"Only reason we're here, Doug. Don't know about you, but I don't have that much time to waste. We are trying to keep America safe from its enemies."

"Sure, of course. I get that."

"So can we count on you to help us on this? I don't want to have to make a phone call and bring in more firepower on this. You won't be a happy camper if I do."

Dugan set his clipboard down and wiped a bead of sweat off his forehead. "No, look, that won't be necessary."

She clapped him on the shoulder. "I knew you'd come through for us. I can always tell a straight-up guy."

Dugan smiled. "Hey, if this turns out to be part of some plot, will I get like a medal or somethin'?"

"I don't see why not."

He beamed. "Hot damn. Wait till I tell my girl-friend."

"So what do we need to get this going?"

He handed her two visitor's badges. "These. And I'll take you down there myself."

Robie came back over. "What's going on?"

"Doug has seen the light. He's helping us prevent a potential terrorist situation."

"Right, good, thanks, Doug."

"No problem, sir." Doug gave him a little salute.

As they walked down the hall Robie said, "How often does Bunson come by?"

"At least weekly, sometimes more often."

"How old is Jane Smith?" asked Reel.

"File says forty."

"How long has she been here?"

"Two years."

He stopped in front of a door and took out a key from his pocket.

"What's wrong with her?" asked Robie.

"Like I told your partner, she's just a wacko."

"But is there a technical term in her file?" he said.

"Oh, right. She's a schizophrenic, if memory serves. But I'll check her file."

"Do you have an address for Bunson?"

"I can check on that, too. How long do you think you'll be in there?"

Robie put his hand on the doorknob.

"As long as it takes."

68

The walls were a pale gray; the floor, not overly clean linoleum, was peeling up. A window looked out onto the back of the property.

The bed was against one wall.

A nightstand was next to the bed.

A chair was next to it.

There was a door leading off the bedroom, presumably to a bathroom.

A small, freestanding cabinet acted as a closet.

That was it.

The entire space was about twelve feet square, Robie figured. Not much bigger than a prison cell.

And that was really what she was here, a prisoner.

Jane Smith was sitting in the chair. She had on a dull yellow hospital gown, her feet encased in grungy white slippers. Her hair was dark and cut quite short, which accentuated the sharp angles of her face.

Robie closed the door behind them and they drew closer to the woman, who had yet to even acknowledge their presence.

Robie studied her face and then suddenly put one hand against the wall.

Reel said, "Are you okay?"

Robie shook his head. "I don't know. There's something about—"

He drew closer still to the woman.

She finally looked up and saw him. Her eyes widened and then shrank. She looked back down at her hands, which were twisting and turning in her lap, like she was attempting to solve a Rubik's Cube, without the cube. She started giggling and then chirping and clucking, then stopping abruptly before starting up again.

Robie squatted down in front of her.

"Ms. Smith?"

She didn't acknowledge him, just kept moving her hands and making noises.

He ran his gaze over her again.

"Laura?"

She glanced up at him when he said the name.

Robie heard Reel behind him catch a quick breath. He turned and looked at her.

"Laura Barksdale?" Reel said. "Is that really her?"

Robie turned back. "I don't know. She . . . looks like her."

Reel drew closer. "You can't lock somebody up in here, Robie, under a false name."

"Really, so you think Jane Smith is her real name?" he said impatiently.

"Do you have the picture?"

Robie took it from his pocket and handed it to her. Reel looked at it and then compared the image to the woman in front of her.

"There is a definite resemblance," she conceded. "The jaw, eyes, hair. But something is off. It's like somebody took Laura's picture, smeared it, and got this person."

"She looks shorter than Laura," Robie estimated, though the woman hadn't stood. "Laura was about five-six, though she might have shrunk some in here. And she's a lot thinner. She's all hunched over. Probably sits like that all day."

"That would make anyone look smaller. And she probably gets no exercise in here."

Clearly frustrated, Robie said, "But it's been over twenty years. I can't be sure if it's her or not."

"But how does Laura Barksdale end up in here under a false name with her brother as her guardian and who's also using an alias?"

"I have no idea."

"Were there problems in the family?"

Robie stood and faced her.

"Laura was usually positive, always putting on a brave face."

"Meaning there *was* trouble at home?"

"She never talked about it, but it always seemed to me that she really wasn't happy. Living up to the Barksdale name was not easy. But now that we know

what her dad was involved in, maybe the answer lies there, at least partly."

"Maybe she found out and that's why she wanted to run away with you?"

"If so, why didn't she?" Robie shot back.

"Maybe she couldn't, Robie."

"I saw her at the house that night. She looked fine. She wasn't a prisoner. And I wrote her, too. Left phone messages. Never got an answer."

"You're a boy."

They turned to see "Jane" looking at them. She pointed at Robie, smiled shyly, and said, "You're a boy." She pointed at Reel. "And you're a girl."

Jane looked very pleased with herself for this observation.

"That's right," said Robie, squatting down in front of her again. "I'm Will. Will Robie." He waited to see if either his name or his face sparked any hint of recognition from her.

"Will?"

"That's right."

"Who's the girl, Will?"

"I'm Jessica," said Reel. "Can you tell me your name? I bet it's a pretty one."

"Jane. Is it a pretty name?"

"Yes it is. And your last name?"

Jane looked confused by this question. "It's Jane. What's your name?"

Robie and Reel looked at each other.

He said, "Jane, does Ted come to see you?"

She nodded. "He brings me things to eat. I like to eat, but not the things they have here." She lowered her voice to a near whisper. "They have stinky things here."

"Will he visit you today?"

She nodded. "He comes to see me. He brings me things to eat, not stinky things."

"But he hasn't been in today?" asked Robie.

She nodded. "Ted comes to see me."

Robie sighed and stood. "What things do you like to eat, Jane?"

She said immediately, "Hamburgers and French fries. They're not stinky. Ted brings me hamburgers and French fries because they're not stinky."

"Anybody else come to visit? Your mother or father maybe?"

"Hamburgers and French fries. They're my favorite."

She rose and shuffled like an old woman over to the window and looked out. There was a solitary tree visible, and flitting around it were some birds.

Jane pointed at them. "What are they? Those things?"

Robie walked over and stood next to her. "They're called birds."

"How do they do that?" She began to hop off the floor. "That?" She looked at Robie questioningly.

"They have wings, so they can fly."

By her expression she clearly had no idea what this meant.

She sat back down, hunched over, and started twisting her hands around again. Then the chirps, giggles, and clucks started up. She sounded like a small child at imaginative play.

"I saw a McDonalds on the way over," said Reel. "Maybe some nonstinky food will jog her memory."

"I don't think she has a memory. I think she is what she is. I wonder what sorts of meds she's on."

"Maybe Dougie can enlighten us."

Dugan read off the names of three different drugs from Jane's file when they asked him a few minutes later.

"Those are all antipsychotics," said Reel.

"That's right, how'd you know?"

"What's her condition?" asked Robie.

"I was right—the file said schizophrenia and bipolar."

"She talked to us. She was obviously not all there, but she seemed relatively calm."

"Then this is a good day for her. And you haven't seen her off her meds. That happened a couple of times because of screw-ups here. I thought she was goin' to kill herself. Screamin' and bangin' her head against the wall, sayin' people were tryin' to eat her. Scared the crap out of everybody. So she is definitely not normal. Even on her meds she can't take care of

herself. She'd burn the house down thinkin' she was roasting a marshmallow."

"Was she committed here or was it voluntary?"

"Committed."

"Who initiated the proceedings?"

"I don't have that information. You'll have to talk to somebody else if you want anythin' more."

"Has Bunson been in to see her today?" asked Robie.

"Nope."

"You get his address?"

Dugan handed him a slip of paper. "It's about thirty minutes west of here."

"What can you tell us about him?"

"Nice guy. He brings Jane food and stuff. We chit-chat a bit. Nothin' important."

"He ever talk about his family? About Jane? What happened to her?"

"No, nothin' like that."

"So what's the connection between the two of them? Family?"

"Don't know. None of my business. He's her guardian, that's all that matters to us. We have the papers. All in order."

"Does Jane like Big Macs?" asked Reel.

"Couple miles away. You passed it on the way here. That's where Bunson goes," Dugan added.

"Thanks."

"Don't forget my medal," Dugan called after them.

They drove to the McDonalds and bought a Big Mac, large fries, and a Coke, and brought them back to Jane. She carefully unwrapped the burger and ate very slowly and delicately, taking the time to lick all the special sauce off her fingers. She ate her fries one by one, looking at each fry for a few seconds as though wondering what it was before popping it into her mouth and chewing slowly and methodically. She drank her Coke in short, hesitant sips.

When she let out a loud burp she looked very embarrassed.

"That was bad," she said pitifully. "I'm not supposed to do that."

"It happens," said Reel.

"Who are you?" Jane asked, looking at her curiously. "Do you want some of my hamburger? You're a girl."

They later walked to their car.

Reel said, "You really think that might be your *Juliet*?"

"I don't know. And even if we run her prints, I doubt she's in a database."

"Schizophrenia can happen to anyone at any time. It happens to teenagers. In fact, a lot of cases are diagnosed between eighteen and twenty-one."

"But if that is Laura and she's forty and she was committed only two years ago, that means she was diagnosed in her late thirties."

"No, she *came* here two years ago. She could have

been in another facility before this. Or she could have been in someone's home and she became too much to handle, so they committed her. We have no way of knowing how long she's been like this without taking a deep dive into her personal and medical history."

"Damn, could she change that much, though?" asked Robie.

"Like you said, it's been twenty-two years. You've been away from her longer than you knew her. People can become unrecognizable, Robie. Especially someone with her condition."

"I guess."

"But let's look at this logically. If she was committed, there had to be a court hearing. So how could they commit Laura Barksdale as Jane Smith? It's inconceivable."

"Unless she was brought to the court as Jane Smith with accompanying documentation," noted Robie.

"But with what purpose? To cut her out of the will? It doesn't seem like Henry Barksdale was exactly rolling in dough. And she obviously isn't all there. She *should* be in a place like this under a doctor's care and with medications. She clearly can't be on her own."

"But it doesn't explain what happened to her. Unless, like you said, she became schizophrenic."

"The thing is, when that happens, and depending on the severity, the person can sometimes manage it with meds. And lead a relatively normal life. Every situation is different, of course, but if Jane's on three

very powerful antipsychotic meds and she still has the mental capacity of a four-year-old, something else is going on."

"Like maybe she suffered irreversible brain damage?" asked Robie.

"Yes."

"But how? An injury?"

They got in the car and Reel started it up.

"Well, maybe Ted-slash-Emmitt can provide some much needed answers," she said.

69

"Well, the guy's not rich," said Robie as they pulled into the neighborhood where Emmitt Barksdale lived under the name Ted Bunson. The homes and yards were in good condition, but the houses were modest and old.

"So there goes any theory of skullduggery and a will."

They pulled into the driveway of Barksdale's house. There was a Toyota Camry parked there that was a good ten years old. The yard was small but well maintained, and a few potted plants were on the front porch, though the flowers in them drooped in the heat.

They got out of the car and approached the house. Robie looked to his left and saw a woman out watering some flowers in a planting bed. To his right a man worked on his car in the driveway.

Neither paid much attention to Robie and Reel.

Robie knocked on the front door.

And waited.

They heard nothing from inside.

He knocked again.

Once more, nothing.

"Think he has more than one car?" asked Reel.

"I don't know. The carport's a single."

"Are you looking for Ted?"

They glanced over to see the woman watering her flowers staring at them, the hose still in her hand.

"We are," said Reel. "Do you know if he's home?"

"Well, he should be. He only has the one car."

"Have you seen him recently?"

The woman paused to think. "Maybe two or three days ago. My memory's not as good as it was."

"Maybe he went somewhere with his family?" suggested Reel.

"Oh, he has no family. No wife, no kids."

"You know him well?" said Robie.

The woman frowned. "Not that well, no. He's nice enough, but keeps to himself mostly."

"Do you know what he does for a living?"

"Who exactly are you?"

"We're trying to find Ted to ask him about Jane Smith?"

The woman looked at him blankly.

"He's her guardian. She's a patient at a mental institution. We have some information that needs to be conveyed to Mr. Bunson about her."

"Have you tried to phone or e-mail him?"

"It's information that needs to be communicated in person," said Robie. "Fairly serious."

"Oh, dear, I see. Well, I don't know what to tell you. I didn't even know he was someone's guardian."

"I think he might be home."

This came from the man who'd been working on his car.

He wiped his hands on a rag as he walked over to them.

"Are you cops? Is Ted in some kind of trouble?"

"I really can't say. We just need to speak with him. You said you think he's home? Why?"

"The car's in the exact same position it was two days ago. Ted usually pulls it into the carport. Keeps the sun from beatin' down on it. And I would've heard it start up. I'm a light sleeper."

"How about when you weren't here?"

"Thing is, I've been here the last three days. Got laid off from my job, so I've been workin' here fixin' a bunch of stuff up. Haven't left once."

"So you saw Ted come in?" said Reel.

"Yeah. Two days ago. And that car hasn't moved from that spot."

"How can you be so sure about that?" said Robie, glancing at the car's positioning.

"I'm a mechanic. I notice stuff about cars. You see the left rear tire? It's a retread. Has those yellow marks on the sidewall? Well, you see that yellow arrow? It's pointin' straight down. It was pointin' straight down when he drove in and stopped. I noticed because I asked him what had happened to his tire. He said he'd

run over a nail and had to get that one. I went over and looked at the retread to make sure it was okay. Sometimes they screw you on that, but it looked fine. That's how I got a real good look at that arrow. So how likely is it he'd park a second time with that arrow in the exact same position?"

"Not likely," said Robie. "Good eye."

He glanced up at the front door and then at Reel.

"What do you think?" he asked her.

"I think we need to find out if the man is home or not."

"Do you think somethin' might have happened to him?" said the woman.

In answer Robie and Reel drew their weapons.

Both the man and the woman took steps back.

Robie said, "If we're not back out in five minutes, call the cops, okay?"

The woman looked like she might faint, but the man said, "Right, got it. Five minutes." He looked at his watch as Robie went to the front door and Reel headed around back.

Robie picked the front door lock.

Reel put her elbow through a glass pane of the back door, reached through, and turned the knob.

They met in the middle of the first floor, having each cleared their half of the main level.

They both eyed the stairs going up.

"Mr. Bunson?" called out Robie. "We need to speak with you. Are you okay?"

There was only silence as a response.

"Okay, this is getting weirder by the second," commented Reel.

They headed up the steps, their guns still out and pointing ahead.

They cleared one bedroom, then a second.

And then came the bathroom in the hall and their search was over.

The man was lying in the bathtub. There was no water in the tub but he was naked. His eyes were open. He was not breathing and had not been for a while.

There was dried blood between his legs.

They took a closer look.

"Damn," said Robie.

The man's privates had been cut off.

"Emmitt Barksdale?" asked Reel.

"Sure looks like him. It also looks like the guy I saw in the bushes at the Willows."

"I don't see any obvious wounds. Other than someone turning him into a eunuch. I doubt he bled out from that."

Robie drew closer and touched the dead man's arm.

"He's not in rigor."

"If it came and went we're talking at least twenty-four hours."

Reel pulled out her phone and punched in 911.

With a resigned sigh she said, "The Mississippi cops are really getting to know us."

70

Reel had also called Taggert, and she showed up an hour after the local police did.

It had taken Robie and Reel a long time to explain things to the locals, but when Taggert arrived she pitched in, and it seemed unlikely that either Robie or Reel would be arrested for breaking into the place.

The local detective, Clyde Driscoll, was young and obviously nervous. He had mentioned to Taggert, in a voice loud enough for Robie and Reel to overhear, that this was his very first homicide after five years as a beat cop.

Taggert suggested that she could assist and then recommended that Robie and Reel could as well. The result was that, while the coroner was examining the body, the four of them made a very thorough search of the crime scene and the house.

Barksdale's bed had been slept in, and his pajamas were on the floor next to the bed.

"So maybe the killer disrobed him here," Driscoll had suggested. "There's no blood on the pajamas."

They had found financial records in the name of

Ted Bunson that indicated Barksdale made his living through investments. He wasn't wealthy, but he did make enough to live modestly. There were bills for the care of a Jane Smith, and they were fairly substantial.

"Maybe that's why he lives so modestly," said Reel.

"I remember Emmitt from his time in Cantrell," said Taggert. "And though it's been a long time, I could pretty much swear that was him."

Robie nodded. "Though he hasn't aged well."

"Well, being dead doesn't help one's looks," retorted Taggert.

They had told Taggert about meeting Jane Smith at the institution.

"You really think she could be Laura Barksdale?"

"Let's put it this way: I can't say for sure that's she not."

They found only one item from Emmitt's past life in Cantrell as a member of the prestigious Barksdale clan.

The photo was on a table in the bedroom. It presumably would have shown the four Barksdale family members. Only Laura and Henry Barksdale's images had been cut out.

"Okay," said Robie. "Two members deleted and two members left. Father and daughter gone. Mother and son left."

"And that symbolizes what?" asked Taggert, who was staring closely at the photo and the two dark holes where the images had once been.

"Maybe Laura in a state mental institution and father Henry . . . out there somewhere?" said Robie.

"You think Henry came here and killed his only son?" said Taggert in disbelief.

Robie said, "I don't know. It's one possibility. But to cut off his penis?"

There were also numerous Bibles in the house and writings associated with religious studies, which showed Emmitt Barksdale to be a very devout man. They also discovered he was a youth minister at the local Baptist church.

"I don't remember Emmitt being that religious," said Robie.

"Neither do I," said Taggert. "He was mostly a party animal who did what he wanted and to whoever he wanted. He even tried it with me once when he was drunk."

Robie looked at her surprised. "What happened?"

"His nose took a long time to heal."

"Well, sometimes people find religion later in life," said Reel. "To atone for a past misdeed."

Driscoll had one of his techs dust the frame for prints, and then the tech took the photo out of the frame and did the same.

The tech said, "What's this?"

He had turned the photo around. There was writing on the back. It looked relatively recent.

Taggert read out each word and number.

"L 18, Calvin, R-O-H."

The tech looked at the others, bewildered. "What the hell does that mean?"

"A code maybe," said Reel uncertainly.

Driscoll nodded. "We have a guy who's good with that. I'll get this to him." He put the photo in an evidence bag and sealed it.

"What we *didn't* find was interesting," said Reel.

"What we didn't find?" asked Driscoll curiously.

Taggert answered. "No smartphone and no computer. Most people have both. Everyone has one or the other."

"The killer could have taken them," suggested Reel.

"You folks explained about the possible connection to the events down in Cantrell," said Driscoll. "But who would want to murder this Barksdale person?"

"Sherman Clancy, Janet and Sara Chisum, and now Emmitt Barksdale, if he was indeed murdered. They could all be connected," said Reel. "We just have no idea how."

The coroner, a petite woman in her forties with short auburn hair, came into the room.

"Okay, I'm goin' to need to take the body back and open him up, but my prelim is that the cause of death was poisonin'."

"Poisoned?" said Taggert. "With what?"

"I won't know until I do the tox screens, but there are no fatal wounds on his body, at least that I can find now. However, I found some bloodstained froth inside

his mouth. I hit the top of his trachea with my light and found some more froth. That would point to a poison like cyanide."

"If it's cyanide, how long would it take for him to die?" asked Taggert.

"If it was pure acid, ten minutes or so. Potassium or sodium cyanide, a half hour. It's nasty stuff. Fatal in small doses and it doesn't take long." The coroner smiled grimly. "Someone is an Agatha Christie fan, because that was one of her favorite ways of doin' someone in. The screens will take a while to get back, but I'll let you know as soon as I've finished the autopsy. Cyanide leaves telltale signs in the body. I'm goin' to start the autopsy as soon as I get him back. I'll have preliminary results in a few hours."

"And what about what was cut off him?" asked Driscoll uncomfortably.

The coroner pursed her lips. "More likely *chopped* off. There was a small indentation in the tub where whatever was used, maybe a hatchet, struck the tub's surface. Now I'm not a psychiatrist, but that one definitely smacks of symbolism."

After she left, the others looked at each other.

Taggert said, "Okay, the killer slips him the poison some way."

"Which suggests he knew the person," said Driscoll. As soon as he said this the young man looked both pleased and surprised that he had thought of it.

Reel gave a small smile and said, "Excellent point.

Except he was in his pajamas and his bed had been slept in."

"So it was more likely he was asleep when the person came in and somehow got the poison into him," added Taggert.

"Right," said Driscoll, looking crestfallen.

Taggert continued, "The poison kills him. Then the person takes off his pajamas and puts him in the bathtub. It would have to be a pretty strong person. Barksdale is a big guy."

"It could have been two people," pointed out Driscoll.

Reel said, "That's true. But someone should have seen this person or persons come or go. The guy next door noticed that Barksdale's car hadn't moved."

"Then I better go talk to him," said Driscoll hurriedly.

"I'll go with you," said Taggert.

After the two left Robie and Reel sat in chairs and stared at the floor.

Reel said, "But for the penis being cut off, I'd think he was killed because he was a loose end."

"Right. But why kill him at all? Because of his connection to this Jane Smith? Who is she? Laura Barksdale? And if so, why is that important enough to kill all these people? If they are connected?"

"It has to tie in to what happened all those years ago. The kids in the shack. Henry Barksdale. Clancy."

"And maybe this Jane Smith," said Robie.

"It would be great if we could either positively ID her as Laura or eliminate her as being Laura."

"And find out why Emmitt was her guardian and living under an alias."

"Do you think Henry Barksdale is still alive?"

"He certainly could be. He's my dad's age."

"Unless someone killed him, too."

"Or he's the one who's been killing people."

"What would be his motive?"

"He had a deal with Clancy that if it came out could mean the ruin of maybe the only thing he had left: his good name. So he killed Clancy. He found out Clancy might have told the Chisum girls. Or they found out about him and approached him to black-mail him. Remember Emma said Jane knew a big secret. And that she was going to meet someone about important people in town. She might have been referring to the Barksdales, though they didn't live in Cantrell anymore. She could have told Sara. So he killed them."

"And his son, Emmitt?"

"He knew what his father had done and had to die."

Reel said, "I guess it's possible but there are a lot of holes in that theory, including the cutoff penis. And it's not like we're trained detectives, Robie. We're about as amateur as Driscoll when it comes down to it."

"But we're trained to obsess about the details and see what others don't."

"Well, all I see right now is a whole lot of fog."

"And we have a killer out there who has nothing but a clear sight line."

Reel looked at him and said, "So I wonder, who's going to die next?"

71

Robie and Reel returned to the Willows, where they found Little Bill Faulconer waiting for them on the porch.

Robie said, "Everything okay?"

Little Bill shook his head and Robie could see his reddened eyes and puffy face.

"Is it your dad?"

Little Bill nodded and wiped his eyes. "He passed on this mornin'. Momma found him out in the Airstream."

"I'm really sorry, Little Bill," said Robie.

Reel put a hand on the young man's shoulder. "It's hard, I know."

Little Bill said, "He was only forty-one years old. Damn young to die."

"Too young," agreed Robie.

"Funeral's goin' to be on Thursday if y'all want'a come."

"We'll be there," said Robie. "Do you and your mom need anything?"

Little Bill shook his head. "We doin' okay. I mean, we knew it was comin', but still."

"Yeah," said Robie quietly.

Little Bill got in his old, battered car and drove off.

Robie watched him, the anger building.

Reel looked at him. "You okay?"

"I got somewhere to go."

"You want me to come?"

"No, I've got this one."

Thirty minutes later Robie pulled in front of Dr. Holloway's office.

He marched right past the nurse/receptionist, who scrambled after him, protesting his intrusion.

Holloway was in his office going over some paperwork when Robie barged in.

He looked up at Robie and his nurse behind him.

She said, "He doesn't have an appointment, Doctor. I tried to stop him from comin' in here."

Holloway said, "It's all right, Gladys, I'll see him."

Robie closed the door behind him and stood in front of the doctor.

Holloway eyed the sling. "How's the arm?"

"You heard?" asked Robie.

"About what?"

"About Billy Faulconer! He's dead."

"Yes, I did hear. Angie Faulconer phoned me."

Robie looked a bit taken aback by this. "Angie called you?"

"Yes, she did. I was his doctor after all. Would you like to have a seat?"

"No, I'll stand," Robie said angrily.

"All right. Now, you seem to have an issue with my treatment of Mr. Faulconer. Is that right?"

"Yes, I do."

Holloway nodded. "That's why I asked for Mrs. Faulconer's permission to share with you details of her husband's diagnosis and treatment. HIPPA regulations do not allow me, without that permission, to discuss these types of things with outside parties."

"I know that," said Robie curtly. "But she said it was okay to talk to me about Billy's condition and treatment?"

"Yes, she did. Please sit down, Mr. Robie. This might take a few minutes."

Robie drew up a chair and sat.

Holloway said, "I know you're from Cantrell and thus you understand well the history of our state, which has certainly had more than its share of, shall we say, misfortune."

Robie said nothing.

Holloway steepled his hands. "My father, Mr. Robie, was also a doctor. And a good one. He was competent and professional and his bedside manner was very reassurin'." He paused. "If you were white, that is. Now if you were black, he was none of those things, principally because he refused to provide medical care

to those folks. And he would refer to them in the most repugnant terms you could imagine."

"So he was a racist?"

"Absolutely. To the extreme. Not so uncommon in men of his generation from the Deep South. He would have been ninety-four this year if he had lived. I was the youngest of seven children. And the only one to follow in my father's footsteps and become a doctor. Half my siblings took after my father's views on race, and the other half marched resolutely into the twentieth and twenty-first century. I would count myself among the latter."

"Okay," said Robie impatiently. "But what about Billy?"

"When Mr. Faulconer came to me I did a thorough examination, which included X-rays, sophisticated blood testing, and other analyses as part of my diagnostic protocols. I may be a small-town doctor who does a little bit of everythin', but I received an excellent medical education and was even an organ transplant surgeon early on in my career. I had dealt with many cancer cases, some hopeless, others treatable, over the course of my practice.

"But out of an abundance of caution I sent my findings on Mr. Faulconer to a good friend and professional colleague of mine who's the chair of the Radiation Oncology Department at Ole Miss Medical Center. He's a world-renowned authority in the field. He confirmed my diagnosis of stage IV non-small

cell lung cancer that had metastasized irreversibly into other major organs, including Mr. Faulconer's brain and liver, and also his bones. At that stage there are some treatment options, but no realistic possibility of a cure. This particular cancer was virulently aggressive and options were limited.

"Nevertheless, we explored the various options, includin' radiation, chemotherapy cocktails, and a combination of both. I even looked into some experimental trials that were goin' on in different states, but unfortunately, Mr. Faulconer, for various reasons, did not meet the test criteria. In any event treatment would have been physically arduous and, at best, would have bought him only a few more months of life, and hardly at a high quality. I discussed this at length with the Faulconers, and they ultimately made the decision to forgo any type of treatment. The decision was made to make him as comfortable and pain free as possible until the end came."

"But Billy told me all he was taking was oxygen!"

"Billy did not understand many of the things that I explained to him. He was not educated in medical matters, and his brain had already been impacted by the cancer. His short-term memory was very poor and his grasp of details lackin'."

"He remembered our championship football game in great detail," interjected Robie.

"I'm not surprised by that. I said his short-term memory was impacted. But memories from long ago

might very well be crystal clear. When the end draws near the mind reaches out for ... some comfort. Some happiness. I suppose it makes it bearable."

Robie nodded. "I guess it does," he said quietly.

"But Angie Faulconer is very capable and was very aware of all that we were doin'. He received morphine and other painkillin' medications daily through a port I had placed on his forearm. He received every medication and treatment that was possible under the circumstances to ensure that his sufferin' was as limited as it could possibly be. Either I would travel there to administer them and also check on his condition, or she would. I instructed her precisely on how to do so. Billy's condition was constantly monitored by a portable sensor system that he wore under his clothing, and that was read every two hours. And I would vary his pain medications based on that."

"I didn't know any of this."

"Mr. Robie, he never suffered unduly. Everythin' that could be done for him *was* done for him."

"I guess just seeing him in that trailer with the oxygen tank. It just seemed that he was all alone."

"Angie and I implored Billy to go into hospice. He either could have done it in a facility nearby, which I had located and made arrangements for, or else home hospice would have been provided by a local agency that I knew to be very good. I had filled out all the forms, and there was government money available. It

wouldn't have cost them anythin', really. It was all ready to go."

"Only Billy didn't want to leave the Airstream?" said Robie quietly.

"Only Billy didn't want to leave the Airstream," Holloway repeated. "And who was I to question the wishes of a dyin' man?"

Robie looked at the other man, contriteness in his features. "I'm sorry, Dr. Holloway. I obviously got this completely wrong and made a complete ass out of myself."

"No, you were just lookin' out for an old friend."

"That's very kind of you," said Robie. "I'm not sure I deserve it, though."

"I watched my father's bigotry and hatred eventually destroy not only his marriage and his family but ultimately himself. From a very early age, I told myself I would never be like him. And I'm not."

"Billy was lucky to have you as a doctor. And he's in a better place now."

"I truly believe that he is. My father went to church every Sunday and *pretended* to understand a God who had made it his life's work to love and welcome all people. I too attend church every Sunday. I read my Bible every day. I worship a God that is truly color blind, as we all should be. But I don't blame you for thinkin' what you did. Lord knows there are racists aplenty, not just in Mississippi but everywhere. Fortunately, I am not one of them."

The two men shook hands.

"Thank you," said Robie.

Holloway pointed at the sling. "Have you attended to that?"

"Not yet. I have some unfinished business."

Holloway nodded. "I'll be at the funeral."

"So will I," said Robie. "So will I."

72

When Robie returned to the Willows, he found Reel on the rear porch with his father and Victoria.

Dan Robie said, "Your partner here has been fillin' us in. So Emmitt Barksdale's dead?"

Robie took a seat, glancing momentarily at Victoria, before nodding at his father.

"We're waiting on a positive ID, but it looks that way."

Victoria said, "But why? Who would have wanted to kill him?"

"Don't know. He was the guardian of a woman named Jane Smith. It might be connected to her."

Dan said, "Guardian? What was the connection with Emmitt and this Smith person?"

"Again, we don't know. It all just happened. We went to see her. She's at the state mental institution in Lancet."

"What's wrong with her?" asked Victoria.

"Schizophrenia," replied Reel. "And even with all the meds she's on, she's not really there. Like talking to a young child."

Victoria looked at Dan and said, "I guess we should consider ourselves lucky. Even if Ty can't talk, we know his mind is fine."

Dan nodded and gripped her hand. "That's right, hon. Ty is goin' to be just fine."

"So who will care for her now?" asked Victoria.

"That's up in the air. Unless she has relatives, I guess she'll become a ward of the state. She certainly can't live on her own."

"But do you think this is connected to what's been happening in Cantrell?" asked Dan.

"Yes, I think it is," answered Robie. "Only I can't tell you how."

"Yet," amended Reel. "We're working on it."

"Where is Ty?" asked Robie.

"With Priscilla," said Victoria.

Robie's phone buzzed. It was Taggert.

He listened to what she said, clicked off, and rose. Then he looked at Reel. "We need to go."

She stood, leaving Dan and Victoria staring up at them.

"Is someone else dead?" said Victoria fearfully.

"No, just a development."

As they were walking through the foyer toward the front door Priscilla came down the hall carrying Tyler. The boy looked like he'd just gotten up.

"Nap time?" said Reel.

Priscilla nodded. "He likes his sleep, this one. He climbs in my bed here, and sometimes when we're

515

traveling with Ms. Victoria. I think he just wants warmth like a little bear cub, and I got me lots of that." She laughed and smacked her broad hip with her free hand. "Like a Crock-Pot. Keep you stewin' all night long."

Tyler smiled and hugged her neck.

"Well, it certainly gives Victoria a break," said Reel. "Little kids are a handful."

"It *does* give me a break."

They all turned to see Victoria standing there. "I really don't know what I'd do without Priscilla."

"You got kids, ma'am?" a smiling Priscilla asked Reel.

She hesitated. "I did. But not anymore."

"I can understand that, honey," said Priscilla, her smile gone.

Outside, Robie and Reel got in their car.

"So what's up?" she asked.

"The coroner found a mark on the back of Barksdale's neck commensurate with a needle stick. She thinks that's how the poison was administered."

"What else?"

"While the tox screens aren't back yet, when she cut him open she found evidence of cyanide-type poisoning in the organs. That would tie in with the bloody froth she found in his mouth and upper trachea."

Reel nodded. "So he was murdered, placed naked in a bathtub, and his penis was cut off."

"With a cryptic message left on the back of a photo with two family members ripped out."

"Father and daughter."

Robie said, "Right. Henry and Laura Barksdale."

"And the latter might be sitting in a mental institution thinking about a Big Mac and fries."

"And the former?" said Robie.

"Who the hell knows? What about Henry Barksdale's wife? It might have been a man and a woman who did this to Emmitt. His own parents maybe?"

"I don't know. Maybe. If she's even still alive. Or if he is."

"And the connection to Sherman Clancy could come from what they did with those little kids. And the Chisum girls maybe found out from Clancy, like you said. And they had to die, too. I guess that all makes sense. Preserving the Barksdale honor."

Robie nodded. "But if it is him, how do we find him? Or them? And stop another murder?"

They met with Taggert and Sheriff Monda at the police station. Taggert looked worn and depressed. Monda just looked angry, probably that something like this was happening in his town and he was pretty much powerless to stop it.

"Another one dead. Well, at least it wasn't in Cantrell," he said, with some relief in his voice.

"So, injection in the neck?" said Reel.

Taggert nodded. "The condition of the internal

517

organs showed that it was a really powerful com-
pound. She said the person would have been dead in
minutes."

"Without ever waking up?" said Robie. "Even
when he felt the sting of the syringe?"

"Doc said it was possible the poison would have
incapacitated him right from the get-go. He might
have thrashed around a bit when the needle stuck
him but he probably wouldn't have been able to
defend himself."

"Have we found out anything else about this Jane
Smith person?" asked Reel.

"Workin' on it," said Taggert. "It's not easy, though.
Patient confidentiality. We had to apply for a court
order. It'll take some time."

"I'm not sure how much time we have left," said
Robie.

"Meanin' you think this person will kill again?"
said Monda.

"Well, he's killed four people already, and if the FBI
is right and our murderer and his serial killer are one
and the same, then the body count is actually a lot
higher."

"But how can that really be the case, Robie?" said
Taggert. "That would be a helluva coincidence."

"Coincidences are often in the eye of the beholder,"
retorted Robie.

Taggert looked at him as though she had no idea
what *that* meant.

He said, "The other murders were an older man and a younger woman. There was a pattern. And here we have Clancy and two younger women being killed."

"But there were probably other reasons to kill Clancy," said Reel. "And the Chisum girls as well. They might have been attempting to blackmail the killer."

"They could well have served two purposes," said Robie. "Fulfilling the patterns but having other motivations to kill them."

"Whoever is doing this is seriously screwed in the head," interjected Monda.

"Did you find anything else in Emmitt Barksdale's house that could be helpful?" asked Robie.

"Not really. The killer presumably took his phone and/or his laptop because there might have been incriminating items on there."

"Did you dig up any family or friends who'd had contact with him?"

"Not yet. He really didn't seem to have anyone like that. And the neighbors saw and heard exactly nothin'. Whoever did this was pretty stealthy. And it might've been quite late at night, since Barksdale was already in bed."

"Anything on where his parents might be?"

"No," said Taggert. "We're makin' inquiries. But they've been gone from Cantrell for over twenty years. No tellin' where they are, if they're even still alive."

"Do you remember when they left?" asked Robie.

"Not the exact day, no. It was like they were here one minute and gone the next. I remember not seein' Laura or Emmitt for a long time. It was like they just stopped comin' into town."

"I know Laura wanted to leave Cantrell and do something with her life."

"You mean leave with you?" asked Taggert, eyeing him closely.

"Why do you say that?" asked Robie suspiciously.

"Small town, Robie. Hard to keep things secret. You and Laura were in love, everybody knew that. And then you up and leave and she's still here. Somethin' was off."

"Maybe things just didn't work out," he said tersely.

"So she didn't go with you and now maybe she's sittin' in a mental institution. I think she might have made the wrong choice."

"That wasn't Robie's fault," said Reel.

"Not sayin' it was," replied Taggert. "Everybody needs to take responsibility for their own life and live with the choices they make."

"You sound like you speak from experience," said Reel.

"Hon, you live long enough, we all damn well speak from experience."

73

The day of Billy Faulconer's funeral was so hot that the flowers drooped precipitously, right along with the people. Many turned out for the graveside service, both blacks and whites.

As Robie surveyed the crowd, he wasn't sure why this was, until he saw that many of the whites were young people. And then he saw Little Bill Faulconer smack in their midst accepting their collective condolences.

Maybe there *was* hope, Robie thought.

Toni Moses came up to him before the service.

"Sad thing when someone dies this young," she said.

"Nobody is guaranteed a tomorrow," said Robie.

And don't I know that, he thought.

"I don't see the esteemed county prosecutor," he observed.

"He's probably home lickin' his wounds. He sees the case against your daddy evaporatin' right before his eyes. And that means he can kiss his political career good-bye. And the winners on that score are everybody 'cept Aubrey Davis."

Robie had volunteered to be one of the pallbearers, and it was depressingly easy—even with his bad arm—to lift the coffin containing the remains of his old friend, who had once loomed so large on the gridiron.

He glanced at Reel as he walked past bearing the coffin. They exchanged a telling look that might have been interpreted as:

When our time comes, will we even get a funeral?

A black minister spoke, and then Angie and Little Bill said a few words.

The coffin was lowered into the dirt and folks started drifting away.

That was the way it was, the burial ritual. You set them in the earth and walked away to keep living, until it was your turn to be left behind.

Dr. Holloway was waiting for Robie at the line of cars parked along the quiet interior street of the cemetery.

"It was a nice service," said Holloway.

"Yeah," said Robie. "As nice as it can be, considering the purpose."

"Will you be stayin' on much longer here?"

"Unfinished business."

"Clancy and the Chisum girls?"

Robie nodded as Reel joined them.

"Anythin' I can do to help?" asked Holloway.

Robie was surprised by this but said, "Not unless you have a miracle or two up your sleeve."

Holloway smiled weakly. "I don't think that I do, sorry."

Robie stared at him for a few moments and then decided it was worth a shot. Holloway was an educated man. "Does 'L 18' or 'Calvin' or 'ROH' mean anything to you?"

Holloway frowned. "Not 'Calvin' or 'ROH.' But 'L 18'? In what context?"

"That's the problem. We don't know," said Reel.

Holloway thought about it for a few moments. "Well, it's not normally referred to in such a shorthand way, but if the context, for instance, is religious it might mean Leviticus chapter eighteen."

Both Robie and Reel tensed. He said, "Leviticus— you mean from the Bible?"

"The Hebrew Bible, yes."

"Do you know what it refers to?" asked Reel. "My biblical knowledge is a little rusty."

"To the commands given to Moses on Mount Sinai."

"Regarding what, exactly?"

"Well, the Holiness Code. It lists certain sexual activities that are considered unclean and therefore prohibited. Verse twenty-two of the chapter has caused all the controversy regardin' homosexuality, you know, that man shall not lie with mankind as with womankind."

"You don't happen to have a Bible with you, do you?" asked Robie.

"I have one in my car. You're welcome to it."

They went to Holloway's car, and he gave them the copy of his Bible.

"I'll bring it back to you," promised Robie.

"No, keep it. I try to give them out to people as often as I can. I consider it a way of payin' it forward. I don't agree with everythin' in there. I mean we must all come into the twenty-first century. But just the golden rule and its progeny would certainly make the world a better place if more widely followed."

"Thanks," said Robie.

"And don't forget about your arm, I was serious. You don't want permanent damage."

Holloway drove off while Robie flipped to Leviticus chapter eighteen. He read down the passages.

"Anything strike you?" asked Reel.

"It deals with homosexuality, like he said. But it also talks about something else."

"What?"

"Incest."

"Incest? What kind?"

Robie read a bit more, then looked up at her. "Between brother and sister for one."

Reel gazed at him. "So do you think . . . ?"

"Emmitt and Laura?" Robie grimaced.

Reel said, "He was older, she was younger. Her own brother having sex with her might make her depressed and confused and want to get the hell out of town."

"But I never would have thought that Emmitt—"

"Robie, you said people can justify anything they do, whether it's incest"—she paused for a moment—"or killing people."

He looked at her for a long moment. "Are you talking about us with that last part?" he said quietly.

"Maybe I am."

He looked back at Billy Faulconer's grave and all the air seemed to go out of Robie. He turned back to Reel. "Then let's go get a drink and get out of this damn heat before we wade too deeply into the crap inside our heads. We might never get back out."

They drove to a local bar, ordered beers, and sat at the back table where a wall AC unit was blasting away.

People were staring at them from all corners of the place.

"I love being in a place where I'm so popular," Reel said dourly.

"Cantrell is just that kind of place."

"What kind of place?"

"One you don't visit. But if you do people will stare at you until you get the hell out."

They each had another beer and the afternoon slowly gave way to evening.

Reel pulled out her phone and started tapping keys.

"What are you doing?" asked Robie.

She held up a finger and then finished typing.

"I just Googled *incest* and *ROH*, the term from the back of the photo we found."

"Did you get a hit?"

She stared at the screen. "This one looks promising." She read over the article. "Okay, *ROH* stands for 'runs of homozygosity.'"

"That explains a lot," said Robie sarcastically. "What the hell is homozygosity?"

Reel read some more. "It's related to genetics. Inbreeding results in big upswings in homozygosity. The article says that means that identical chromosomal segments by descents are basically paired off together. That's a bad thing, obviously. It leads to lots of undesirable things happening to any offspring of an incestuous relationship."

"That's what happened with the royals, right? Bluebloods and 'mad kings' syndrome? They kept marrying close relatives to keep their bloodlines pure, but they were really screwing them up. It's why doing that's now outlawed."

"Yes. And that ties in with Leviticus eighteen, which deals with those sorts of incestuous situations."

"And Jane Smith?"

"Could be the result of that," answered Reel. "Not that she was the product of an incestuous relationship, of course, which is what *ROH* refers to. But if Jane is Laura, twenty-plus years of shame and loathing and emotional scarring could change anyone, Robie.

Anyone. Even damage their minds. I'm surprised she's not even more screwed up."

Robie looked confused. "Okay, But *ROH* comes from the product of an incestuous relationship, like you just said. The offspring. So why would someone have written *ROH* on the back of a family photo if it didn't have some relevance?"

Reel said, "You're right. But Jane Smith is forty. She can't be Laura and her brother's child. She has to be Laura."

Robie nodded. "That's right. And someone killed Emmitt."

"Well, we know it wasn't Jane Smith–slash–Laura Barksdale. She was locked up."

"So that brings us back to Henry Barksdale."

"Unless you have a better guess, I'd put my money there," said Reel.

"Why kill his son all these years later?"

"Maybe he just located him. Emmitt was living under a different name. Blue Man did it relatively quickly, but he has a lot of horsepower behind him."

"We have to find out for sure if Jane Smith *is* Laura," said Robie.

"Can't they take DNA samples from Emmitt and Jane and compare them? That will show if they're related or not."

Robie pulled out his phone.

"Who are you calling?" asked Reel.

"Our friendly neighborhood FBI special agent Wurtzburger."

"You think he'll help us on this?"

"If there's even a chance his serial killer is mixed up in this, then yes, I think he will."

74

Wurtzburger agreed to arrange for the DNA testing after Robie filled him in on the latest developments, and their theory that Henry Barksdale very well might be their killer.

After that Reel and Robie drove back to the Willows as the dusk gave way to darkness.

Halfway there the car's AC simply quit and they had to roll down their windows.

"My God, is it always this humid down here?" asked Reel.

"Well, I remember it not being so bad in January and February."

"Is that why you left? You thought you were in Hell and wanted to get out?"

"That wasn't the only reason."

She glanced at him, her brow furrowed. "You never really told me what you and your dad talked about."

"We didn't talk about anything. I said stuff that he ignored. Like always."

"So no progress?"

"No, I did learn something I didn't know before."

"What?"

"Laura came by the house after I'd left and wanted to know where I was. And my father told her, basically, that I'd gotten the hell out and left her and him behind to start a new life for myself. Can you believe that?"

"If he were angry at you for leaving, then, yeah, I can believe it."

He shot her a glance. "Don't take his side on this."

"I'm not taking anyone's side, Robie. I'm just trying to understand a really complicated situation."

"But it's not complicated. My dad is an asshole and does whatever he can to screw up my life."

"Well, if that's your attitude, I don't see you ever working this out and getting back in the field. And that's what you want, right? To get back in the field?"

They sat in silence for some minutes.

"I don't know," Robie finally said.

"Well, you may have to answer that question before you can answer any of the others."

"But what makes no sense to me is that I wrote and called Laura after I left. And got no reply. Ever. But she shows up at my house a couple days after I left and wonders where I am?"

"Well, maybe your letters and phone messages never reached her."

"Shit. All these years and . . ."

The silence lasted another several minutes.

Finally Reel said, "Let's move on to something a little more tangible. Henry Barksdale?"

"Yes. But how do we find him?" asked Robie.

"Well, if he's killing people in Cantrell, he has to be somewhere close by."

"I wonder how he lured Janet and Sara Chisum? He wouldn't have even known them. They came here only recently."

"Was he a good-looking guy?"

"Over two decades ago, yeah he was. Tall, very handsome, distinguished. He's probably still all of those things. Different rules for guys versus girls as they age."

"Well maybe it's as simple as that. Older guy tells them he has money. We know they have sex for money."

"But Emma Chisum seemed to think that Janet knew something about someone important. And that was going to be the source of the money."

"Maybe she was wrong. Or lying. She seems really good at lying."

"Maybe," said Robie doubtfully.

"Whatever the case, we need to find Henry Barksdale."

"I wonder if he ever visits Jane Smith."

"Dugan said only Emmitt did."

"He couldn't be sure about that. And now with Emmitt gone—"

"You think he might go to visit her?" Reel asked.

"It seems to be our only low-hanging fruit on this one."

He took out his phone and called Dugan. The man told him that no one had visited Jane Smith since they'd been there. Robie told him to call immediately if anyone came to see the woman.

"Stakeout?" said Reel.

"Stakeout," said Robie.

She turned the car around, and they headed off in an entirely new direction.

An hour later Reel steered through the last curve and the mental institution came into view. Against the backdrop of darkness, its lighted interior looked like a multi-eyed beast waiting to devour unsuspecting prey.

They parked in front and climbed out of the car.

The next moment they heard the siren.

They both instinctively looked at each other.

The sounds grew louder.

"Sounds like it's coming this way," said Reel.

The facility was really the only thing out this way. The strip mall where the McDonalds was located was a couple miles distant.

Robie and Reel sprinted toward the entrance.

Doug Dugan and a passel of upset people were crowded in the lobby. When Dugan saw them he rushed over. "Oh my God!"

"What happened?" barked Robie.

"It's Jane Smith. I called the cops."

Robie and Reel were already running down the hall toward her room.

The door was open.

The light was blazing.

A tray with untouched food on it sat on a table next to the bed.

Robie's gaze darted around the room and then came back over to the window. He stepped slowly into the room.

The window glass was cracked. Its epicenter was a small hole, and the cracks radiated out from that like a spider's web.

Right below the window Jane Smith was lying on the floor.

Robie could see the entry wound. It was a bullet hole dead center of her forehead.

Blood had pooled under her. The woman's eyes were open and unseeing. She would chirp and cluck no more.

Reel stepped to the window and looked out.

"Nothing." She looked down at Smith. "The blood's already started to coagulate. This didn't just happen. Whoever shot her is long gone."

Dugan appeared in the doorway.

Robie strode over to him.

"What the hell happened?" he demanded.

"One of the staff came to take her dinner tray away, and . . . found her."

"And then you called the cops?"

"Yes."

"When was she found?"

"Maybe ten minutes ago. As soon as I was alerted I called the police." He listened to the sirens, which seemed to be right on top of them.

"The shot came through the window," said Reel. "Did anyone see someone back there?"

"Not that I know of. But I haven't really asked, either."

"Did anyone visit Jane Smith since I called you?"

"No! No one's been since you two were here."

"Any unusual visitors here today to see anyone else?"

"What do you mean by unusual?"

"Anyone who hadn't been here before," snapped Robie.

"No, I mean I don't think so, no."

"That's not good enough," said Reel. "We need to be sure."

"I'll . . . I'll have to check."

Robie thought of something. "Did anyone call today to ask about Jane Smith? Maybe what room she was in?"

Dugan looked at him puzzled. "Why?"

"They had to know which room she was in to shoot her from outside," replied Robie impatiently. "Can you please check?"

Dugan ran out of the room and then was back in less than two minutes.

"No one called. And there were no unusual visitors."

"You're sure."

"Yes."

Robie looked at Reel. "Then how the hell did the shooter know she was in this room? The room numbers aren't posted on the outside of the building, only on the inside."

They heard cars screeching to a halt outside and the sirens ceased.

Dugan said, "Shit, they're here. I've gotta go."

He raced out of the room.

Robie looked around, saw the door of the bathroom, opened it, and spotted a box of Q-Tips in a box on a shelf. He pulled out a Q-Tip, stepped back out, and raced over to Jane Smith.

He swabbed the inside of her mouth with the Q-Tip and then looked at the dead woman's face.

Reel said, "Robie, we've got to go. They're coming."

Robie said quietly to the dead woman. "I'm sorry."

The next moment they were racing down the hall in the opposite direction from the entrance.

They exited the building at a side door and flitted back to the front. When the area was clear, they slipped to their car and drove off.

Once they hit the surface road, Reel punched the gas and the car flew down the asphalt.

Robie held up the Q-Tip.

"We need to get that to Wurtzburger," said Reel.

Robie nodded but said nothing.

Reel shot him a glance and saw his frozen features.

"Robie, I'm really sorry."

"We don't know that it was Laura," he said immediately.

"I know, and I hope it wasn't."

"But whoever it is, she's dead. And someone murdered her."

"And we'll find out who it was."

"Yes, we will," said Robie.

75

Robie had called Wurtzburger, and they met up with the FBI agent back in Cantrell and gave him the swab sample.

"We got a sample from Emmitt Barksdale's body," Wurtzburger said. "I've asked for the highest priority on this. We have a lab in Jackson that can get this done ASAP."

After leaving him, Robie and Reel drove back to the Willows.

It was late now and they didn't expect anyone to be up when they got there.

But they didn't expect the house to be completely dark.

"Hello?" said Robie as they walked in the partially open front door.

They both pulled their weapons.

"Hello?" Robie said again.

They went through the first floor until they got to the wing where Priscilla lived. The door of her bedroom was slightly cracked.

"Priscilla?" said Robie. "It's Will Robie."

There was no reply.

Robie eased the door open and looked around.

Reel was right next to him.

She saw it first.

Or rather, her.

"There," said Reel.

Priscilla was lying on the floor next to her bed.

Robie raced over to her and knelt down.

"Damn it!" he said.

She was on her side. The knife was still sticking out of her back.

Reel looked over her shoulder.

"She's dead," said Robie. "Looks like the blade went right through her heart."

He touched her skin. "She's still warm. It wasn't long ago."

He looked back toward the door.

"There are still three people who are supposed to be here."

They ran out of the room and up the stairs, and reached Dan and Victoria's bedroom first.

It was empty. But there were signs of a struggle. A table was knocked over and a lamp had been broken.

Ty's room was empty and had not been slept in.

"What was that?" asked Reel.

It had come from somewhere on the second floor.

They ran out of the room and looked in either direction.

"That room," said Reel as the sound came again. "What is it?"

"I don't know," said Robie. "I've never been in there."

The sound came again. It was a groan.

Robie pushed the door open and looked around.

It was set up as a study, with a desk, bookshelves, and comfortable chairs.

"Dad!" cried out Robie.

His father was lying on the floor next to his desk. His head had a bloody gash in the back and Dan Robie was struggling to get up.

Robie and Reel rushed over to him.

"Dad, just stay where you are. What happened?"

"Some . . . somebody hit me. From behind."

"Are you hurt anywhere else?"

"N-no. Just m-my head."

"Did you see who hit you?"

His father shook his head and then slumped back down.

Reel was already calling 911. She ordered an ambulance and then phoned the police.

"They're on their way," she said.

Robie was holding his father's head.

"Get me a wet towel."

Reel ran out to do this.

Robie said, "Just take it easy, Dad. You're going to be okay."

"Vic-Victoria. T-Ty?"

"It's okay, just keep still. The ambulance is on its way."

While Robie was waiting for Reel he glanced around the office looking for any clues that might lead them to whoever had done this.

One shelf was devoted to sports memorabilia. As he saw this, he gaped.

When Reel came back in with the wet towel, Robie had her apply it to his father's head wound, then he bolted out of the room and down the stairs.

He hurtled onto the front porch, hung a left, and rushed around to the rear of the house. He reached the garage and went inside.

The Volvo was gone.

The Range Rover was there.

Robie raced over to it and stared for a moment at the New Orleans sticker on the back of the SUV. He used his knife to peel it off.

Underneath was what he thought he'd find.

A bullet hole.

The bullet hole caused by my gun when I fired it at the vehicle driving away from Sara Chisum's murder.

The bullet hole in the Range Rover in Sherman Clancy's garage had been created later. So it would be found and concluded that that vehicle was involved and not this one.

The ambulance arrived at the same time the police did. Taggert had phoned and let Robie know that she and Sheriff Monda were on their way. A BOLO had

been put out on the Volvo and Victoria and Tyler Robie.

Robie led Reel back to the garage and showed her the bullet hole.

"How'd you find that?" she asked.

"The shelf full of Dallas Cowboy memorabilia in my dad's study. Why would a Cowboys fan have a Saints sticker?"

"But who put it there?"

"Whoever shot Sara Chisum. The same person who took Victoria and Ty."

"But why the hell kill Priscilla?"

"I don't know."

They raced back around to the front of the house.

"Where do you think they've taken Victoria and Ty?" asked Reel.

"I don't know."

"Why even kidnap them?"

"I don't know, okay?" barked Robie.

"Okay," said Reel calmly. "Okay. It could be Henry Barksdale."

"Why would he come here and do this?"

"It's his old homestead. If he's crazy enough to kill all these people, then he might have come here and attacked your father, killed Priscilla, and then taken Victoria and Ty. Maybe he saw them as interlopers."

"If it was Barksdale he could be anywhere," noted Robie.

"Not anywhere. Like you said, Priscilla's body was

still warm. This did not happen that long ago. He couldn't have gone far."

Robie's expression cleared and he said, "Maybe he went to—"

At that moment his father came out on a gurney and Robie and Reel helped load his father into the ambulance.

"How is he?" Robie asked one of the paramedics.

"Concussion and a nasty gash, but he seems okay otherwise. Vitals are strong. He's a tough guy."

Robie said, "Give me a minute." He climbed up into the ambulance and sat next to his father.

"You're going to be okay," said Robie. "Lucky they hit you in the head. It's unbreakable."

His father stared at him grimly. "Where are they? They told me Victoria and Tyler are missin'."

"We don't know. We believe Henry Barksdale is behind this."

"Barksdale! Why the hell would he take Victoria and my son, damn it?"

Robie put a calming hand on the older man's shoulder. "We'll find them. I have an idea of where they might have gone. Somewhere on the old Clancy farm. And Dad, whoever killed Sara Chisum was driving your Range Rover."

"What?"

Robie explained about the New Orleans Saints sticker covering the bullet hole.

His father had partly risen in his anxiety. Then he slowly lowered himself back down.

"You okay?" asked Robie anxiously.

"I'm . . . I'm just very tired." He gripped his son's hand. "Please find them."

"I will, Dad. I promise. I will."

Robie climbed out of the ambulance, the paramedics closed the doors, and the vehicle drove off. Then he sprinted toward the car with Reel right behind him.

"Where are we going?" she called out.

"To where all this really started."

It took them nearly an hour to get there. They drove as close as they could to the old shack on Sherman Clancy's farm, then continued on foot from there.

There was little moonlight, and twice they stumbled as they made their way quickly over the uneven ground.

Even at this late hour the air was so humid that Robie's clothes were plastered to him. They heard rustlings and the occasional rattle from the woods, but trudged on.

They slowed as they drew closer to the old wooden structure. It was dark. They could hear nothing from inside. They circled the building and then came back around to the front.

Then they pulled their weapons and approached the door slowly.

"I didn't see the Volvo anywhere," whispered Reel.

Robie nodded, his gaze tight on the shack. In his mind he imagined little kids trooping in there, no doubt believing they would be fed and looked after only to have something else, something horrible, happen to them.

They reached the small porch. The wood creaked under their feet.

Robie's hand tightened on his gun. He slipped off the sling so he could make use of his other arm.

Reel flitted over to the other side of the door. She leaned against the wall and looked at him. In barely a whisper she said, "No back door. This is the only way in or out."

He nodded, pointed at Reel, held up three fingers, and then slowly dropped them one at a time.

When the last finger went down, Reel kicked open the door and sprang inside.

Robie was right behind her. They started to do their sweeps and then stopped.

In the middle of the room was Tyler, sitting in a chair.

Robie froze for an instant when he saw the little boy. In his mind flashed the child he'd seen reaching for his father. It just came from nowhere, like the thrust of a knife into his belly.

"Robie!"

It was Reel. He jerked out of his paralysis. But not in time.

The shot rang out.

There was a grunt, then a gasp, and a body dropped to the floor.

A light came on, blinding Robie.

He looked down to see Reel on the floor unconscious and bleeding.

Then the voice called out from the periphery of darkness.

"Hello, Will, it's been a long time."

76

The light was shifted, and Robie could see it was coming from a battery-operated camping lantern.

Now he could see the person standing in one corner of the room.

It was not Henry Barksdale holding a gun pointed at Robie.

Victoria looked back at him, the tightest of smiles playing over her lips.

Robie stared back at her, his mind unable to process what was happening.

She took two steps forward.

"Please put your weapon on the floor and kick it toward me," she said. "And I know you keep another one in the waistband at the small of your back. I saw that before. Do the same with that one."

When Robie didn't move, Victoria pointed her gun at Reel. "The next one is the kill shot."

Robie placed his gun on the floor, then took out his backup and kicked them both toward Victoria.

"Please do the same with your partner's."

Robie did so, and Victoria, without ever taking her

gaze off Robie, used her foot to move the four guns to the far back wall and behind her.

"Who are you?" asked Robie.

"I'm very surprised by that question, Will. I thought by now you would know."

He looked at Reel. "She needs medical help. Now!"

"That won't be happening."

Robie bent down to check Reel. The shot had hit her in the oblique and gone completely through. Still, the bleeding was bad. Robie used his sling to staunch the flow.

"Get away from her, Will."

"She's going to die if I don't stop the bleeding."

"You're *both* going to die, so it doesn't really matter. Now stand up."

He glanced at her to see that her pistol was now pointed at Tyler. The little boy looked up at his mother with an expression of horror.

"You'd . . . you'd shoot your own son?" said Robie slowly.

"Stand up," she said once more, the absolute calm in her voice more unnerving than if she had been screaming at him.

Robie slowly rose.

"Who are you?" he asked again.

"How was your trip to the east coast, Will? Was it fun going solo? Did you not miss me the least little bit when you left Cantrell?"

Robie stiffened like he'd received an electric shock.

"You can't be . . ." He couldn't finish the thought.

"I can be. And I am."

"Laura Barksdale is dead. Back at the mental facility."

"Well, in a great many ways, you're right, Laura is dead. But in one important facet she's not." She ran a hand over herself. "The proof is literally standing in front of you, Will."

Robie swayed a bit on his feet. Then he shook his head stubbornly. "You don't look anything like her. You're taller. You're blonde. Your face. Your voice. You're *not* her."

"I grew two inches when I was nineteen. Barksdale trait, apparently. Really changed my body. The face? Plastic surgery. The hair? Dyed. The voice? You don't sound anything like you used to, either. You leave Mississippi you start pronouncing your *g*'s again. And my brown eyes turned to baby blues by the miracle of laser surgery."

"I don't believe this."

"How many people do you think recognize their high school classmates at their twenty-fifth reunion, Will? Between eighteen and their forties, people change. They get fat or thin, bald or bottle blond. We remember them as taller or shorter." She paused. "But I must admit, I changed more than most."

"Why? Why do all that?"

"Because I didn't want anything left of the old Laura. I really didn't like her very much, Will. Or

rather I didn't like what had happened to her. What others had done to her."

"This is not possible," said Robie. "You can't be Laura."

"The last thing you said to me twenty-two years ago? Do you want me to tell you? I remember it like you said it twenty-two seconds ago. Do you want to hear it, Will?"

When Robie said nothing she continued. "You told me, 'I will always be there for you, Laura.' That's what you said to me by the rock wall next to my dear mother's fabulous Barksdale garden."

Now Robie took a step back, his glistening eyes widening in shock as the truth swept over him.

"But you weren't always there for me, Will. In fact, you were *never* there for me, were you? Not when I really needed you."

When Reel moaned, Robie looked down at her and then back to Victoria. "Please let me get her help. Then you can do what you want with me."

Victoria shook her head. "Doesn't work that way. This plays out on my terms, not yours."

Robie knelt next to Reel and put a comforting hand on her shoulder while he tightened the sling around her wound, trying to stop the bleeding.

"I told you not to do that. I won't say it again."

Robie rose. "Why did you kill all those people?"

"It wasn't madness, if that's what you're thinking. Not all people who kill are mad, Will. You've killed,

right? You've killed people here. And Dan told me that you serve your country somehow which also involves killing people. So are you deranged? Are you mad? I doubt you *think* you are."

Robie said nothing, but his breathing accelerated and he felt as if a giant hand were smashing down on his chest.

Victoria leaned against the wall but kept the gun pointed at him. "If you want explanations, here they are. Janet Chisum was a slut. She sold herself to Sherman Clancy. So did her sister. For money. I befriended both of them. And then killed them."

"Emma Chisum said Janet was going to make money off some secrets of important people in town."

Victoria snorted. "Janet Chisum was a liar. But she told her kid sister a little of the truth. I was the important person who was going to give Janet money. After Janet was dead I told Sara that maybe her father was the killer. That maybe all that religion had made him nuts. I told her she needed to get out of town. That I would help her. That I felt sorry for her. Wanted her to have a better life." She added in a scoffing tone, "As if. Old horny men and stupid, greedy young women, just doesn't work out. I didn't like it. So I stopped it. But I have to admit, I didn't know you two would be there when I killed Sara. That was a bit of a complication. It was lucky I saw her in town that day and told her to meet just off the road instead of in

the clearing. Otherwise, we might have had this confrontation earlier."

"I put a round in the Rover. You covered the hole with a New Orleans Saints sticker. And then you fired a round into the Rover in Clancy's garage to make it seem as though that Rover was used. Only you apparently didn't remember that Dad is a Cowboys fan."

She shrugged. "We all make mistakes. And it wasn't like I had a whole lot of time. I barely had time to wash the damn truck before you two showed up. But then I distracted you by having Ty run under the hose. I mean why would I suddenly be washing both cars? The Rover supposedly hadn't been driven since your father was arrested."

Robie slowly shook his head, silently berating himself for missing that.

"And Sherman Clancy?" he asked. "I found a photo of you as a teenager in his car. Did he know you were Laura?"

She laughed. "He was clueless about that. I drove over to the Clancys' and put the photo in there the night I killed Sara. That's when I put the bullet into his Range Rover."

"Why?"

"Why not? I had already slit the man's throat a while back. He thought he was going to have slam-bang sex with me because I told him that's what I wanted. Instead, he got sent to an early grave. So I left a little reminder of who had really killed him behind.

The police had already searched the car. I doubted they would go back again."

"But why did you need Clancy? You told me he was blackmailing you about your drug addiction problem."

"No, that was a lie. But I needed Clancy. You see, while people thought I was Sherm's alibi that got him off for killing Janet, he was actually *my* alibi for when I killed her. I had arranged to meet with Janet that night. I went to Biloxi and left Ty with Priscilla in her room. Then I came back to Cantrell and went to Clancy's house by prearrangement. I knew that Pete was away. Sherm wanted us to be all alone. We started drinking. Only he drank and I poured mine down the sink. And I was real flirty and let him grope me just to keep him focused. And then I slipped a sleeping pill into his drink. When he finally passed out, I went and killed Janet. Then I came back to Clancy's."

"But then he started remembering things?" said Robie.

"Exactly. Like the fact that I wasn't there when he woke up from what he thought was his drunken stupor. And then when he found out Janet had been killed that night he put two and two together. It was ironic that he was arrested for her murder when I had actually killed her. And then I had to swoop in to save poor Sherm by giving him an alibi, when he was actually providing me with one. But once he was out of jail he secretly met with me. And told me what

he'd figured out. And then he really tried to blackmail me. Well, I knew he was experienced in that endeavor, but it wouldn't work with me. He was going to die. In fact, I had already planned to kill him regardless."

"Why?"

"How else could I get your dear old dad arrested for murder? The unfaithful wife? The angry husband? The dead lover? The arrest? The noble life ruined? It was a nice story. And it fit together so damn well. You see, he was the object of my revenge because I didn't know where you were. And I looked, Will, but I could never find you. And then you just walked right back into Cantrell. I couldn't believe my luck when I saw you at the Willows."

"So you planted all that evidence against my father?"

"Of course I did. I'm nothing if not thorough."

"Why do that to my father? He never did anything to you."

Her smile disappeared and her voice hardened. "Oh really? When I came by your house to find out what had happened to you, he told me you had gone off without me. By choice. You'd abandoned us both. And your father told me it was best. He made it seem like we were from two very different walks of life. But I knew what he meant. I wasn't good enough for you. I would hold you back. I was so furious I wanted to kill him right then, only I didn't have the guts."

"But you married him. You had a child with him."

"That's right. I did. My *second* child."

Robie drew back another step, nearly stumbling over an old pile of wood stacked on the floor. "Who was your first?"

"You met her. Jane Smith?"

"But she's your age."

"No, she just *looks* my age. She's actually twenty. Or *was* twenty."

"So Emmitt was the father?"

She chortled. "Emmitt? My God, no, not Emmitt. He was too scared to try to rape his little sister, though he probably wanted to. That compulsion evidently runs deeply in the Barksdale male line. Perhaps from inbreeding." She paused. "No, it wasn't Emmitt." She paused once more. "My father is the dad."

"Your father impregnated you?"

Robie put a hand out and steadied himself against the wall. He could barely process what she was saying. He had figured Henry Barksdale for some messed-up pervert, but he had never imagined he had committed incest with his own daughter.

"He raped me. Many times, Will. Remember when we were teenagers and you would ask me what was wrong? Well, now you have your answer." She smiled. "But I got over it, for the most part. By killing those who had hurt me. Like Emmitt. You see, my dear brother held me down in a bathtub while that ... thing came out from between my legs. It was so bloody, that bathtub. And the pain. I thought I was

going to die. I think you saw him in his bathtub. There wasn't nearly as much blood, but it was the best I could do under the circumstances. The poison I injected into him was something I learned about when I was a pharmaceutical rep. Nasty stuff. Paralytic first and then the kill dose. I took his phone and laptop because it might have had something on it I didn't want others to know."

"But why cut off his . . . ?"

"Because he didn't have the balls to stand up to my father. And since he never used his balls anyway, I decided to take them."

"So it was Emmitt at the Willows?"

"And you're right, he did search my car. And he left me a note, wanting to meet with me. Luckily, I found it before you did. And we did meet."

"How did he know you were Laura?"

"He told me he had his suspicions when he heard someone had married Judge Robie and moved into the Willows. He said he watched me one day, recognized certain things about me that I guess even I didn't know and thus couldn't change. And then he went down to the courthouse and checked my signature on the paperwork for when Dan and I bought the Willows. It matched Laura's handwriting, which he knew very well. I would have hardly given him the credit for having the brains," she added wistfully.

"Why did he want to meet?"

"To reconcile, I think. I wasn't really paying attention to that part, because I was preoccupied with pondering how I was going to murder him. Like you, I had no idea where he was. And then he just walked back into my life. But he also wanted me to assume care for Jane. He had a terminal illness of some kind, he told me. I'm sure his autopsy will show it."

"Why was he caring for Jane?"

"Because I suppose my brother had some guilt. I didn't. That's why I left. I had no idea where she was until Emmitt told me."

"You abandoned your daughter?"

"She wasn't my daughter!" snarled Victoria. She continued more calmly, "She was my father's daughter. I was just the violated vessel that got her here. That's why we left Cantrell so quickly. I was pregnant. Dear old Daddy didn't want the shame. But he wouldn't let me abort either because, well, he was such a God-fearing man. It was immediately apparent that Jane would never be right in the head. Her blood was blue, you see, not red. That's why they have laws against such things. But Daddy was a Barksdale and thus above it all. I wasn't going to live with that, take care of *that*. But I'm sure you noticed the resemblance when you met her."

"I thought it was you. But how can she look so much older if she's your child?"

"Nasty genetics when father beds daughter. You just never know what you're going to get."

"ROH," said Robie.

"Very good, Will. So you looked at the back of the photo?"

"And Leviticus eighteen?"

"Ironic that it doesn't expressly prohibit father-daughter sex. Did you note the omission?"

Robie shook his head.

She smiled. "Most believe it's because that particular act is so obviously heinous, so why even bother banning it?"

"And who is Calvin?"

"John Calvin. French philosopher. You see, I read up on the subject. He didn't believe that Leviticus eighteen prohibited fathers from screwing their daughters. But he also believed it was immoral to do so. What an insight! Too bad my father wasn't as enlightened."

"But you killed Jane?"

"Emmitt told me what room she was in. I had convinced him that I really cared about her, wanted to assume responsibility for her. I killed him and then I killed her. That's my idea of assuming responsibility."

"Emmitt I can maybe understand. But why kill her?"

"What sort of life did she really have? She was permanently four years old. I tapped on her window. She came over to it, her little face all full of wonder and surprise. And I put a bullet right between her eyes."

Robie just shook his head at this cruel comment. "She didn't deserve to die. None of this was her fault."

"And you think it was my fault, Will? Trust me, I had different plans for my life. Do you think I really wanted all this? I think I've handled it rather well, actually."

"And Priscilla? What the hell did she ever do to you?"

"She told you that Ty slept with her a lot. At the Willows. *And* when we traveled. You saw me hear her tell you this, though you didn't make the connection. But it was only a matter of time before you wondered enough to ask her if Ty was sleeping with her when we were in Biloxi. Because that was my only alibi for when Sherm was killed. And later that day I saw Priscilla looking at me suspiciously. It was clear that this thought had now occurred to *her*. Because she knew that Ty had slept with her that night in Biloxi. Which left me free to kill Sherm. Priscilla was sharp. It was only a matter of time before she went to the police." She snapped her fingers. "So, poof, there goes Priscilla."

Robie said slowly, "You need help. You're sick."

She smiled patronizingly. "Well, then you wanted this 'sick' lady really badly, Will. When we were sitting in my bedroom. I could feel the heat coming off you. You just wanted to take me."

"I never felt that way," said Robie. "Never. You just imagined it."

But Victoria clearly wasn't listening. "You wanted me because you'd already had me all those years ago

when we were two horny teenagers. And you knew how *awesome* it was. Think about it. I had both father *and* son. And when I let your daddy screw my brains out after getting out of jail, the whole time I had my eyes closed and was imagining it was you, Will." She looked at him coyly. "And given time I would have gotten you into my bed again, you know I would. Because you, like all men, are weak. Guided primarily by your prick."

"Were you the source of the credible threats against my dad?"

"Of course. With him in prison I was free to move about and do what I needed to do."

"And your father?"

"Dear old Daddy." She tapped the floor with her foot. "He's resting comfortably under the little shack where he brought all those poor kids to get screwed by Nelson Wendell."

"So you knew about that?"

"After the fact, yes. Daddy was too refined to work for a living. So he made his money the old-fashioned way, by profiting off the misery of others."

Robie glanced down. "He's really buried here?"

"This seemed to be the proper place to put him for all of eternity, don't you agree? A native Mississippian laid to rest in Mississippi soil. I hope all the manure laid in the surrounding fields leached down here. Shit should be with shit, after all."

"Why did you want to live at the Willows? With all that happened to you there?"

"It's about taking control of your life. I loved the Willows. I just didn't love any of the people who lived there with me. Mother died from cancer. Lucky for her, because if she hadn't, she would have died by my hand."

"So she knew?"

"And as a proper Barksdale lady, she kept quiet. It would have ruined her reputation. She couldn't have that. My welfare was a distant second on her priority list."

"You didn't kill my father, though. You just knocked him out."

"It wasn't for sentimental reasons, Will. I'm long past that. If he were dead he wouldn't have to suffer through the loss of *both* his sons."

"How did you know I'd even come to the shack?"

"How could you not? It was very helpful of you and your partner to keep me in the loop on the investigation. And I asked discreet questions here and there, if you recall. So I knew you suspected my father. And I also knew that you had found out about this place. And if you didn't show up here, I'd have reappeared all beaten up and disheveled with a perfectly believable story of kidnap and assault with little Ty in my arms. And he can't talk, so he couldn't dispute one word. And then I would have killed you another time. But you *did* show up. Like I knew you would."

"And did you kill all those other people? The ones the FBI is here about?"

"Well, practice makes perfect, Will. I've always believed that. And old horny men and young, stupid, and greedy women? Well, I already told you how I feel about that. So relieving the world of a few? I consider it time well spent. The gap in between the last killings in Arkansas and here? I met your father, got married, got pregnant, and had Ty. That all takes time."

"You committed murder," he said. "You can't explain that away."

She pointed her gun at his head. "What about you? You told me you loved me? And yet you never came for me. Explain that!"

"You didn't show up. I went to your house. I saw you in your room."

"My *locked* room. My father found out what I was planning. He beat me, and raped me, and locked me in that room. I escaped long enough to go see what had happened to you. And that's when your father said what he said."

"Laura, if I had known what he was doing to you I would have broken into the house and taken you with me."

"Bullshit! You should have known I would have been there for you if I could. You should have rescued me. But, no, you just left. Because you wanted to."

"I thought you had changed your mind."

"People in love don't just change their mind. You

wanted a life without me, like your father said. That meant you didn't really love me. That meant you lied to me."

"Damn it, that's not true. I . . . wrote. And, and phoned. I left messa—"

She sent a round ripping past his ear so close he could feel the wake of the bullet. He ducked down.

She looked at him stonily. "Letters? You wrote me letters? And left phone messages? And you really thought that was good enough? My father made sure I received none of them. You should have known that."

Robie straightened. "I tried, Victoria. I really did."

"Well, you didn't try hard enough."

Robie calmed. "So how does this end?"

She looked over at Ty. "Jane Smith was a genetic freak, thanks to Daddy. Ty, now Ty was mine. And he doesn't even talk." She shook her head. "It must be me, Will. I had always blamed things on my father, but maybe I was the problem."

"You can kill me, but don't hurt him, Victoria. He's just a little boy."

"I can't say that I don't have feelings for Ty. I actually do. I don't want to hurt him. He's nice enough. But he's a freak, Will. Just like Jane. Just like dear old Dad. Hell, just like me." She pointed her gun directly at Ty's head.

"Laura, don't do this," Robie said quickly.

"*Don't* call me that," she screamed.

"Okay, okay, I'm sorry. *Victoria*. Please, please, don't."

"Begging? So weak. So ... unattractive, Will. I would have expected so much better from you. But then my taste in men? Not so good."

She swiveled her gun around and took aim at his head.

"When you see him in the world of shit, tell Daddy I said hello."

The scream destroyed the silence of the night so completely, so jarringly, that Robie nearly collapsed and Victoria almost dropped her weapon.

It was Ty.

His mouth was open and he was screaming so loudly it was as though he had been saving all of this up during his nearly three years of life to unleash it now.

Quick as a flash Robie grabbed one of the pieces of wood and hurled it at Victoria. She fell back against the lantern, knocking it over and throwing them all into darkness. But she struggled back up, rubbing the blood off her face where the wood had hit her.

By the time she had regained her footing, however, Robie had snatched up Ty and raced through the doorway. The next moment his feet hit dirt, and he was sprinting toward the woods.

77

A hundred yards from the shack Robie hit a tree root and sprawled on the dirt, cutting his face on a bush with leaves sharp as knives as he went down. Then his shoulder hit something hard and he felt a pop. Tyler flew out of his grasp and rolled along the ground. Robie clutched his arm, which was bleeding where the scar tissue had reopened. He could barely raise the limb now. It might be broken, too.

He picked up Tyler again and, holding him in one arm, ran on.

Cradling Tyler against his chest, he managed to pull out his phone and dialed 911. The call did not go through. He glanced at the upper screen.

No service.

He heard movement behind him.

She was coming.

And as he looked back Robie could see that she had a flashlight.

He ran to his left, knifed between two trees, and then ran a zigzag route toward where he knew the Pearl River was.

As a boy and then a teenager, he had sought out the serenity of the water when his father had driven him to near tears.

Now though, there would be no peace at the Pearl.

But there might be escape.

He redoubled his efforts. He had listened for but had not heard a gunshot. He prayed with all his heart that Reel was still alive. He didn't really have a plan for going back to get her, but he knew that that was the ultimate goal. Yet he and Tyler had to survive first.

The terrain here had changed over the course of two decades, and he found himself stumbling and nearly falling time and again.

And then the clouds parted, allowing the full moon to illuminate his surroundings better.

That was good. And bad.

Good that he could see.

Bad that it would be easier for Victoria to find him and Tyler.

He had not even had time to think about the astonishing fact that his high school sweetheart was now his stepmother. Or that she had been the killer they'd been searching for this whole time.

Ordinarily, Robie would have simply attacked and killed his opponent.

But he had no weapon, a useless limb, and a two-year-old in his one good arm.

And a partner who desperately needed medical attention.

And an armed serial killer right behind him.

He cleared the last line of trees and reached the mossy, wet bank of the Pearl.

He looked left, then right, and then straight ahead. The river here was barely a hundred yards across. But as he stepped closer Robie could make out a pair of eyes just above the surface of the water glinting in the moonlight. As a native Mississippian he knew what that was.

A gator. Gators could hunt pretty much anytime, but night was when they did their real damage.

He looked behind him. The steps were growing closer. He could see shafts of her flashlight cutting through the trees.

When Victoria reached them she was going to just shoot them. He didn't know which one of them she would kill first, him or Tyler.

He looked down at the little boy, who was shaking so badly it was like he had been plunged into Arctic waters. Robie had no idea how much emotional trauma all this had caused the two-year-old, but he knew it had to be a lot.

He took another step toward the water, drawing within a few feet of the bank. The pair of eyes slowly slid out of sight. As they did so he was able to see part of the body, including the tail. The thing was just waiting, and praying—if gators did so—that Robie would step into the water. That battle wouldn't take long. Even with two good arms and no little boy in

tow, Robie would be hard put to fight off what looked to be a full-sized gator on the blood hunt. In his current situation, it would be hopeless.

The steps behind him were growing closer.

Her voice called out. "Will, this is just delaying the inevitable. I always sized you up as being brave. Come out now and I'll kill you first. That way you won't have to see Ty die. That's the best deal you're going to get."

Tyler now started shaking so badly that it was all Robie could do to keep hold of him.

He backed to the edge of the water. There was nowhere else to go, except into the Pearl.

So how did he want to die?

By Victoria's bullet?

Or a gator's bite?

He shifted Tyler to his bad arm. The pain was so awful that Robie had to clench his teeth and fight the waves of nausea that swept over him. He squatted down and picked up a fist-sized rock. Not a terribly potent weapon, but better than nothing. He hefted it in his hand. He had been an accurate passer as a high school quarterback. And though this was more shot-put than pigskin he was not going to have to heave it as far.

He listened to the sounds coming from in front of him.

And also to the lapping of water behind him.

The gator apparently had no patience. If Robie

would not come into the water, the gator would come onto the land to earn his dinner.

Tyler squirmed more.

Robie whispered, "Ty, please hold still. We've got one chance with this. Just one."

His bad arm was crumpling under the weight of the boy.

"I need to set you down, Ty, okay?"

The boy immediately gripped Robie with all his strength. The shock wave of pain hit Robie like a bolt of lightning. He felt a huge swath of scar tissue tear completely away. His shirt became wet as the blood started to flow from where the tear had reached the healthier part of his flesh.

"Ty, just for a second, son. This is our only chance. Please. Please do this. Trust me. Will you? Trust me."

Tyler slowly nodded his head.

Robie bent down until Ty could reach his feet down and touch the ground.

"Now get behind me," said Robie. He looked back. The gator's eyes were visible again, but he was at least fifty feet from their side of the bank.

Robie gazed back toward the front. The footsteps were almost there.

The flash of light broke through the trees.

The next second there she was.

Victoria illuminated them with her flashlight.

"Very disappointing, Will. Very."

Robie had hidden the rock behind him. His grip tightened around it.

He figured they were separated by fifteen yards. Too far.

She had to come closer.

"There's a gator in the water," he said.

She took a few steps toward him and smiled.

"So, your choice. Gator bait now, or he gets you after I shoot you. If I were you I'd take the bullet first."

"I've told Tyler to run as soon as you fire. You're too far away to shoot him from that distance. He's too small."

"Well, that's easily remedied."

She took another step forward. And then another.

Robie figured ten yards now, maybe less. Thirty feet. He had thrown footballs through tire rings at a greater distance than that.

"Why are you doing this, Laura?"

"I told you not to call me that!"

"But that's your name. It's not Victoria. It's Laura. A woman I loved. A woman I wanted to share my life with."

"You're lying. You left me."

"I thought you didn't want me, Laura. If your dreams were shattered, so were mine. I thought we'd be together. I really did."

"But your father told me—"

"He was wrong. He didn't know what he was

saying. He was pissed at me for leaving him. He just took it out on you. He shouldn't have said what he did."

She glared at him, her eyes suddenly glistening with tears, the grip on the gun now shaky.

"You can kill me if you want, but don't hurt Tyler. None of this is his fault."

"It's your fault!" she blurted out.

"That's right. It is. This is not about him." He reached out to her and inched forward. "Just give me the gun, Laura. You don't have to kill anybody else. We'll get you the help you need."

She smiled, and the look on her face was truly paralyzing. "You asked back at the shack how this was going to end, Will. Well, not by my giving you my gun. It's going to end like this."

She drew closer still and her finger went to the trigger guard. This was it.

Tyler screamed.

Robie whirled.

He saw the armored head coming out of the water, barely two feet from them. He had lost track of the gator that could swim faster than any Olympian.

Yet as Robie eyed the gruesome creature, everything seemed to slow down for him. His heartbeat eased, his blood pressure dropped a few points. His breathing calmed.

Cold zero.

His little brother was not going to die in the jaws of a gator.

Robie took aim, with his naked eye instead of through optics, and threw the stone, not at Victoria but at the gator. His aim was as good as it had been back when he was flinging touchdowns for Cantrell High. The stone hit the gator directly in the eye with great force. Blood spurted out of the socket. The creature's jaws snapped open but it backed away, and the now-half-blinded reptile slid into the water once more.

Robie turned to Victoria. She was within six feet of him now, covering the distance in one long stride.

Two-year-old Tyler could have pulled the trigger and killed him at that range.

And Robie was out of weapons. And ideas.

The muzzle was right in his face now.

He looked at the woman and her smug, triumphant expression.

"I hope it was worth it," he said quietly.

"You'll never know how much. Who loves you, Will? Surely not me."

The shot rang out.

Robie braced for the impact. He imagined himself falling to the dirt, nothing but blackness for a future.

He opened his eyes in time to see Victoria still staring at him.

But the smug expression was gone, replaced with surprise.

And blood was flowing down the side of her face, reaching her lips and then passing to her chin, like a river following its banks.

Robie felt something warm on his face. He touched the spot and then pulled his hand back to reveal the blood there.

Her blood.

The next instant Victoria toppled sideways and hit the dirt, the gun falling from her dead hand.

Robie staggered back as Tyler started screaming. He reached the boy and lifted him up, his injured arm surprisingly numb.

He looked to his left.

And saw the person.

The gun was still pointed at where Victoria had been standing a few moments ago.

Then it slowly lowered.

"Dad?" said Robie in disbelief. He had thought that it would be Reel, with some Herculean effort, standing there.

For one long moment Dan and Will Robie stared at each other over the distance of a fatal shot fired. Then Dan dropped his pistol, hurried over, and hugged his sons with the little strength he had left.

78

"Wake up, sleepy boy."

Robie slowly opened his eyes, the effects of the anesthesia fading as he did so. He hadn't slept this well in years.

As his vision focused Sheila Taggert came into view. She was not in uniform.

"Doc said you came through it just fine," said Taggert.

Robie slowly nodded. A lot had happened since his father had appeared at the river's edge and fired that shot. Part of it was blurry and part of it was crystal clear.

They had gone back to the shack, gotten Reel, and driven off in the same ambulance that Robie's father had been loaded into back at the Willows.

While his father drove with Tyler buckled in the seat next to him, Robie had called Taggert and triaged Reel on the way to the hospital. She had been immediately taken into surgery.

It was only when Reel was safely away that Robie had collapsed from his own blood loss and what

was later determined to be a broken clavicle and a perforated artery in his arm that had come close to rupturing.

He had been stabilized and then taken by medevac chopper to Jackson for the surgery that had permanently fixed his injuries.

Robie focused more fully on Taggert. In a croaky voice he said, "Jessica?"

"She's going to be fine. She came out of surgery fine, Will."

He closed his eyes and let out a long breath. When he reopened them he said, "My dad showed up in an ambulance? How?"

Taggert drew up a chair and sat down next to him.

"Well, the way my colleague laid it out to me, your daddy sat up in that ambulance, took the deputy's weapon, and made everyone get out, and then he drove off in the damn thing."

"But how did he know where we were?"

"I have not been made privy to that information."

"Where is he now?"

"At home. With Ty."

Robie slowly nodded again. Though the anesthesia was receding he still felt in a fog. It was disconcerting. He didn't like it. "Is Ty okay?"

"Physically, yes. Emotionally? It might take a while. I got briefed a little, but you're really the one who knows everythin' that happened. We're goin' to need a statement from you when you feel up to it."

"I know," said Robie groggily. "Don't worry. I won't be forgetting a single detail. Ever."

"So, Laura Barksdale, huh? Who would have ever thought?"

"Yeah," said Robie. "Who would've thought?"

A week later Robie was brought back to Cantrell and spent several hours with Sheriff Monda and Agent Wurtzburger. Evidence linking the crimes across the various states was compared with forensic evidence taken from Victoria's body. The results matched, and the case was closed on each of them.

The woman had indeed been busy.

He was reunited with Reel the next day.

She was in a wheelchair, looking pale and tired. The shot fired by Victoria had done more internal damage than was first thought. A full recovery was expected to take at least a few more weeks. Clearly not fast enough for her.

After Robie filled her in on everything they sat together in a room at the Cantrell police station.

"Mississippi did not turn out to be so good for us," said Reel, wincing slightly as she adjusted herself in the wheelchair.

"No, it didn't." Robie fell silent and studied the floor. His arm was back in a sling and would be for a while.

"What?" she finally asked.

"I left you behind, Jess. I . . ."

"You had no choice, Robie. You were between a rock and a hard place. You took Ty. You saved him from that . . . monster."

"I was going to come back for you."

"I had no doubt. I only wished I could have been the one to shoot her."

"When I saw my dad I'd never been more stunned in my life."

He fell silent again, his features troubled and brooding.

Reel noted this and said, "She wasn't Laura anymore; you realize that, right? She wasn't your . . . Juliet anymore."

"Maybe she never was."

"Like you said, people can rationalize anything."

"But I keep thinking that none of this would have happened if I had just walked into the house that night and taken her with me out of Cantrell. But I just drove off to a new life and left her behind. I abandoned her. Or at least she saw it that way. And maybe she was right."

Reel considered this for a few moments. "You can't put that burden on your shoulders, Robie. You can't live someone else's life for them. Hell, it's hard enough living your own."

"I guess," he said, not sounding convinced.

Reel looked down at her hands. "But what happened to her, well, it *was* terrible."

He looked at her in surprise. "So now you're defending her?"

"No. I would never do that. But I guess I can understand how all this happened. We're not all created the same. Some are more fragile than others. And you never know which one you're going to get. Or which among us is going to crack."

The door opened and Taggert poked her head in.

"You guys ready?"

"Ready?" said Robie. "For what?"

"To go see your dad."

79

They were driven over in a transport vehicle to accommodate Reel's wheelchair. As soon as they entered the foyer of the Willows, Robie received a shock nearly equal to that of seeing his father standing under the moonlight holding the gun he'd just used to shoot his wife.

Blue Man was emerging from the front room with Dan Robie.

As always, Blue Man was dressed in a suit and tie, but apparently in deference to his current location, and taking in the heat and humidity, he was wearing, of all things, seersucker.

"What are you doing here?" asked Robie.

Reel just looked on in amazement from her wheelchair.

"Briefing your father and getting debriefed in return. Enlightening. Quite enlightening. I think I'll leave you to it. I'll be at the airport. You two are riding back with me. Until then, I have one more person to visit."

"Who?" demanded Reel.

"Little Bill Faulconer, I believe he's called. We can always use talented hackers. Even more so now that the NSA's actions have been uncovered. One agency's loss is another agency's gain."

And then Blue Man was gone as quickly as he had appeared.

Robie looked at his father. Dan Robie looked like he had aged ten years. The posture wasn't as straight, the shoulders sagged, the hair seemed less thick, the man's energy level was not as robust.

And who could blame him?

"How are you two doing?" Dan said quietly.

Reel said, "I'll be doing better when I can ditch the wheels."

Dan looked at his son. "And you?"

"I'm okay."

"Let's go in here."

Dan led them back into the front room. Robie rolled Reel into the room and then sat in a chair next to her and across from his father.

"Your colleague filled me in on some things," said Dan.

"That is stunning. And possibly illegal," noted Robie.

"Nothin' classified, he assured me," said Dan. "But enough to let me know what you've been up to gen-erally, Will." He looked at Reel. "Both of you."

Robie could only gape at his father while Reel

looked just as surprised but found her voice. "Were you surprised at what your son is doing?"

"I guess I am surprised that I ever found out anythin' about it." He looked over at Robie. "Seein' as how I never thought I'd see you again."

"How's Ty?"

"He's with some friends right now. People he knows. People he feels safe with."

"But he's coming back, right?" said Robie.

"I'm not abandonin' my son," replied Dan firmly.

As he said the words it was clear to Robie that the man was not simply talking about Tyler.

Robie said, "He saved my life, you know. If he hadn't screamed when he did I wouldn't be sitting here."

He reached into his pocket and pulled out the drawing that Ty had done of him and Robie. Stick figures with a heart in between. "I've never had anything personal where I live. No photos, no mementos." He held up the drawing. "But this one I'm framing."

Dan smiled and nodded. "Ty spoke a few words to me and I almost fell over. But now he's quiet again. The doctors said not to push it. He's been through, well, through hell and back. He saw me . . . he saw what I did to his mother. Even though I had to . . . she was goin' to . . . I'm not sure he'll . . ."

Dan looked away, shaking his head and rubbing at his eyes.

Robie could imagine what his father was thinking right now. Having to choose between his wife and sons. Under the circumstances it hadn't been much of a choice, he knew. But that didn't make it any easier. He hoped to God he was never faced with such a dilemma.

"How did you know where we were?" asked Robie.

His father's head dropped. But with an effort he lifted it and gazed at his son. "There had been rumors about that shack on Clancy's property. I mean from many years ago. One of the clients I represented on the oil platform case had been a migrant worker for several years. He told me some things that his child had said about that old shack. It wasn't enough for an investigation, and I wasn't a judge back then. But I never forgot about it. And somehow Henry Barksdale's name came up as well. And in the ambulance you told me you suspected Barksdale was involved in this and you thought he might be at a location on Clancy's old farm. I thought if Barksdale had taken Victoria and Ty somewhere, it might be to the old shack."

Robie looked at him closely. "So you never suspected Victoria?"

Dan wouldn't look at him now. "If you mean did I know that my wife was Laura Barksdale, no, I didn't." He hesitated. "But if you mean did I suspect that somethin' was amiss, then, yes I did."

"Why?" asked Reel.

"The Range Rover that night. You kept askin' me if I was drivin' it. I wasn't. But . . ."

"But you thought she might have been? Even though she was supposed to be in Biloxi?"

"I know that sometimes Ty sleeps with Priscilla when they're travelin'. If Ty did when they were in Biloxi, then Victoria had no alibi for Sherman Clancy's murder. She could have easily driven back here, killed him, and gotten back to Biloxi before mornin'."

"Victoria believed that Priscilla had concluded that same thing. It's why she killed her. But why would you suspect her of killing Clancy in the first place?" asked Robie.

"I didn't. I thought she might have been . . . cheatin' on me with someone closer to her own age."

"Did you believe she had been sleeping with Clancy? He's hardly her own age."

"I didn't want to, but I couldn't be sure. It's why I threatened him. Things looked so fishy. And her story made no sense. She was drinkin' with him? Why? But I never thought that she killed the man."

"She planted the evidence against you at the crime scene. She wanted you to be arrested and convicted of the murder."

"I know that now," said Dan. "It's just hard to process that the woman I had a child with . . ."

"But the Range Rover *was* seen near where Clancy

was killed," Robie pointed out. "They thought it was you driving but it was actually Victoria."

"At first I thought the witnesses had to be mistaken. Or else they had seen Clancy's Rover and not mine. I must've been asleep when she came back and took the truck. But I never put that together, principally because I did not know the woman I had married was . . . what she turned out to be."

"But you showed up in time to save us. How?"

"I got there just as she was runnin' into the woods. I followed her. I saw that she had a gun. Somethin' was off, way off."

"And when you saw her on the banks of the Pearl?"

"I heard the exchange between you two. I knew then what she had done. And what she was about to do."

"You saved my life. There was nothing I could have done. Without you there, both Ty and I would be dead." A long silence ensued until Dan slipped his glasses from his shirt pocket, put them on, pulled out his wallet, and extracted a picture. He looked down at it for a few moments and then slid it across to Robie.

Robie gazed down at it and saw a young man with a granite jaw and a flinty expression wearing the uniform of a United States Marine.

Dan said, "That was my father. Your grandfather, Adam Robie. I know you two never met and he's been dead for years now, but that was him. In that

picture he was just back from the Pacific. Fought the Japanese all the way across the biggest ocean in the world: Guadalcanal, Kwajalein, Guam, Iwo Jima, Okinawa. All hellish. All beyond human comprehension. His company suffered a seventy percent mortality rate. He was awarded pretty much every medal they gave out to a fightin' man. Probably killed more men than he could remember, and saw more of his buddies die than he would ever care to recall. He came home, threw all the medals in a box, and never talked about the war. I only learned later from other people what'd he done. He was a braver soldier than I ever thought of bein'."

Robie lifted his gaze from the photo. "Okay?" he said questioningly. "But what's the point, Dad?"

"Look, son, he didn't just throw his medals in that box. He threw *himself.* Or who he used to be, which was a simple farm boy from Arkansas who wanted to play baseball for the St. Louis Cardinals and marry his childhood sweetheart. He did neither. He just killed Japanese soldiers and then he came home, got married to another woman he didn't love, because his sweetheart had married someone else, and they had me."

"So what are you saying happened to him?" asked Robie.

"They didn't even have the term *PTSD* back then. But what those boys saw and did? Nothin' prepared them for it. It changed them forever, and not in a

good way. The soldiers who fought in World War Two never talked about that. They were expected to just get back to their civilian lives and carry on like the last four years of Hell had never even happened. Like they were supposed to hit some big reset button. And they did. With varying degrees of success. Or failure." He reached over and tapped the photo. "Like your grandfather."

"So he had PTSD?"

His father nodded. "That's what they would call it now. He seemed to think I was the enemy, Will, that he had to attack. Relentlessly. With his fists and with his tongue. The mind games he played with me were just . . . cruel. One time he even called me by a Japanese name." Dan took off his glasses and wicked the moisture from his eyes. "Damnedest thing," he said hoarsely. "Like he was livin' it all over again. The whole nightmare. A big, strong, brave man, reduced to . . . reduced to that."

Reel and Robie continued to watch him, both of their faces tightly drawn, as though they could feel the older man's pain.

"So when I turned seventeen, you're right, I left. No, I *retreated*. He couldn't touch me then. I had my life to lead and I led it. Without him. Because with him, I was done."

"But you joined the Marines, too. Right in the middle of Vietnam. You knew you were going to be in combat."

"I know."

"So why? After all that?"

Dan didn't speak for nearly a minute.

"As crazy as it sounds when I say it, I guess I wanted to show my old man that you *could* fight a war and not come home the way he did."

"They really didn't understand PTSD after Vietnam, either," said Reel slowly.

"No, they didn't. And we didn't come home to tickertape parades like the World War Two boys did. We came home to hatred and disgust and . . . maybe even worse, indifference. After gettin' your ass shot up for years in jungles you couldn't find on a map, it was a little . . . disheartenin'."

"So what you did to me?" said Robie slowly.

Dan leaned back in his chair. "I guess what I showed, son, is that it's impossible to fight a war and not come home changed. At least speakin' for Adam and Dan Robie." He cleared his throat. "Funny how the mind works. When I was yellin' at you or roughin' you up I could see in my head my father doin' the same to me. And I'm not tryin' to make light of what I did to you, but what he did to me was even worse. And part of me was tellin' myself I would never do that to my own boy, while the other part of me was doin' just that."

As his father sat forward and put his hands on the table, Robie could see that they were trembling.

Dan said, "But most vets don't do what we did to

their children. And I thank God for that. I thought I was strong, but I actually turned out to be one weak son of a bitch."

He rubbed his nose and then took out a handkerchief and blew into it.

"And you were a popular kid here, Will. Sports star, all the girls were after you, but you were a good kid, you helped people. All you had goin' for you, you never once thought you were better than anybody else when you sure could have." Dan paused. "I had every reason to be proud of you. And a part of me was. You were my boy. But another part of me, at least the one that won out, wasn't proud. Maybe I was jealous. Because you had the life I'd wanted and never had. So . . . so I guess I had to ruin it for you. Make it more like mine. I don't know, son. I'm not a shrink. I can't analyze it any more than that. You had every right to hate me. The years we . . . we could've been . . . a family. Wasted. All gone."

Several moments of silence passed before Robie said, "Why are you telling me all this now?"

Dan glanced at his son's arm and then up at his face. "Talk is cheap, but actions . . . actions, son, are the real deal. You came back to help me. Nearly got killed doin' it." He paused. He held up one finger. "And when you came back here you asked me for one thing. You asked me for the truth. So I guess it was time." He took out his wallet again, slid out another picture, and handed it to Robie.

"I have two regrets in life, son. That was the first."

Robie looked down at the photo of his mother.

"And the second?" asked Robie as he stared at his mother's image.

"That would be losing you."

Robie lifted his gaze to meet his father's.

The older man's eyes were filled with tears.

And then Robie's eyes filled, too.

Another first.

Robie said, "You don't have to look back anymore. Just look forward."

His father shook his head. "What do I have left?"

"Well, you have Ty." Robie drew a breath and added, with an encouraging glance from Reel, "And you have me."

His father gripped his hand even as the tears trickled onto his cheeks. "I'm sorry, son. I'm so damn sorry."

"We're all sorry for something. But we need to move on, both of us. And we'll do it together."

Robie put his good arm more tightly around his dad's broad shoulders and the two men just held on to each other.

Jessica Reel put a hand up to her eyes, rubbed the moistness away, and then looked away, giving the two men a respectful privacy.

80

Hours later the small jet lifted off into a clear sky over southern Mississippi.

Robie, Reel, and Blue Man were the only passengers on board.

Robie looked out the window as the rugged terrain of the Magnolia State fell away.

He silently said good-bye to the forests, the abundance of chickens, and the Pearl River. And the gators lying in wait therein.

And to the ghosts of his past that had haunted him so, but a bit less now.

As the plane leveled out Blue Man rose and poured out three drinks from the small bar. He handed glasses to Robie and Reel before retaking his seat.

Robie said, "You never did say why you came down here."

"Didn't I? Well, perhaps I didn't."

"And?" said Reel expectantly.

"It's all about asset management," said Blue Man, taking a sip of his drink. "You are my assets and it's my job to manage you properly. That involves me

inserting myself in situations that, at first blush, seem of a personal nature but may impact the professional side."

"Well, that's an answer that says nothing," replied Reel. Then she lifted her glass in silent praise.

"What did you tell my father about me?" asked Robie.

"I told him that he had a son who had served his country faithfully and well under the most extreme conditions imaginable and at the constant risk of his life."

"And what did he say to that?"

"Why, is that important to you?"

"It might be."

Blue Man appraised them both. "After your assorted injuries heal, will you be returning to the field?"

"Do we have a choice?" asked Robie.

"Well, of course you do." He glanced between them before his gaze resettled on Robie. "It's just that in your case it may be a more complicated one."

"What if I told you I can't answer that question yet?"

"I would say that was perfectly reasonable and that we should adjourn this discussion until a later time. For both of you."

A little over two hours later the jet glided to a landing at a private airstrip, and they deplaned.

Robie helped wheel Reel toward some waiting vehicles while Blue Man walked next to him.

"He said he would have expected nothing less," said Blue Man.

"Who?"

"Your father, when I told him what you did for us."

"Why do I think you're lying?"

"I may be very good at prevaricating. But I also know when it is time to tell the truth. And I just did. Let me just see to our transportation arrangements."

He left them and walked ahead to the vehicles.

Reel reached up and gripped Robie's hand.

"You know you're going to be okay, right?" she said.

"And how exactly do you know that?" he asked.

"Just two reasons, but they're compelling ones."

"What are they?"

"You've got me, Robie. And I've got you. And while we might fall sometimes, together, well, together we are unbeatable."

Five minutes later they were driven off. Back to what, neither of them was exactly sure.

But they were returning to their world so secure in the knowledge that they would, at least, not have to face whatever it was alone.

And for Will Robie and Jessica Reel, where each new day could easily be the last one they would ever have, that was all that really mattered.

ACKNOWLEDGMENTS

To Michelle, for rolling right along with me.

To Mitch Hoffman, for a stellar editing job.

To Michael Pietsch, for captaining the mother ship with a steady hand.

To Jamie Raab, Lindsey Rose, Karen Torres, Anthony Goff, Bob Castillo, Michele McGonigle, Andrew Duncan, Christopher Murphy, Dave Epstein, Tracy Dowd, Rick Cobban, Brian McLendon, Matthew Ballast, Lukas Fauset, and everyone at Grand Central Publishing, for always having my back.

To Aaron and Arleen Priest, Lucy Childs Baker, Lisa Erbach Vance, Frances Jalet-Miller, John Richmond, and Melissa Edwards, for being my champions in so many ways.

To Anthony Forbes Watson, Jeremy Trevathan, Maria Rejt, Trisha Jackson, Katie James, Natasha Harding, Sara Lloyd, Lee Dibble, Stuart Dwyer, Geoff Duffield, Jonathan Atkins, Stacey Hamilton, James Long, Anna Bond, Sarah Willcox, Leanne Williams, Sarah McLean, Charlotte Williams, and Neil Lang at Pan Macmillan, for all your incredibly hard work.

The Guilty

To Praveen Naidoo and his team at Pan Macmillan in Australia, for leading me to the top of the mountain.

To Sandy Violette and Caspian Dennis, for being my champions across the pond.

To Kyf Brewer and Orlagh Cassidy, for your superb audio performances.

To Steven Maat and the entire Bruna team, for continuing to build my career in Holland.

To Bob Schule, for making me look good yet again.

To Mark Steven Long, for a great copyediting job.

To auction winners Keith Monda and Jon Wurtzburger, I hope that you enjoyed your characters. Thank you for supporting two terrific organizations.

To Kristen and Natasha, for keeping Columbus Rose running straight and true even in rocky seas.

And a very special thank-you to my dear friend Ron McLarty, for bringing my stories to life with your incredible talent.

Want to find out about the latest BALDACCI NOVEL before anyone else?

Want to meet David at an event or book signing?

For all the latest news, signings, events, extracts and competitions, sign up to the

DAVID BALDACCI
MONTHLY NEWSLETTER

Visit panmacmillan.com/author/davidbaldacci

 /writer.david.baldacci /davidbaldacci

Memory Man
DAVID BALDACCI

Amos Decker would forever remember all three of their violent deaths in the most paralyzing shade of blue. It would cut into him at unpredictable moments, like a gutting knife made of colored light. He would never be free from it.

When Amos Decker returned home eighteen months ago to find the bodies of his wife and only daughter, he didn't think he could carry on living. Overwhelmed with grief, he saw his life spiral out of control, losing his job as a detective, his house and his self-respect. But when his former partner in the police, Mary Lancaster, visits to tell him that someone has confessed to the murder of his family, he knows he owes it to his wife and child to seek justice for them.

As Decker comes to terms with the news, tragedy strikes at the local school. Thirteen teenagers are gunned down, and the killer is at large. Following the serious brain injury Amos suffered as a professional footballer, he gained a remarkable gift - and the police believe that this unusual skill will assist in the hunt for the killer.

Amos must endure the memories he would rather forget, and when new evidence links the murders, he is left with only one option.

The Last Mile
DAVID BALDACCI

Melvin Mars awaits his fate on Death Row. He was one of America's most promising football stars until, aged twenty, he was arrested and convicted for the murder of his parents just as he was due to begin a very lucrative contract with the NFL.

When Amos Decker, newly appointed special agent with the FBI, hears the news that Melvin was saved in the final seconds before his execution – because someone else confessed to the killings – he persuades his boss to allow him to carry out an investigation into the murders.

There are facts about the case that don't add up and, as the investigation deepens, Decker and his team uncover layer upon layer of lies and deception rooted in a period of American history most would rather forget, but which some seem keen to remember.

There is someone out there with a lot to hide, and a secret that everyone is looking for. A race against time ensues when information is revealed that threatens to tear apart the corridors of power at the very highest level.

The case proves to be life-changing for both Mars and Decker in ways that neither could ever have imagined.

The Last Mile brings more non-stop, thrilling action from one of the world's most popular storytellers.

D0182185